THE DRAGON'S STONE

BOOK ONE OF THE DARK HEART CHRONICLES

THE DRAGON'S STONE

Edited by Ben Wolf
www.benwolf.com

Thank you for your support and for taking the time to read my work! Please leave a review wherever you bought the book or on a book list website and tell your friends or blog readers about the book to help spread the word.

Published by Drezhn Publishing LLC
PO BOX 67458
Albuquerque, NM 87193-7458

Print Edition - October 2019
First Edition

Previously published as *Dark Lament* in 2018

Cover design by Kirk DouPonce, DogEared Design
www.dogeareddesign.com

ISBN 978-1-947328-22-8

READ *SCOURGE* FOR FREE

Curious about Eshtak's tattoos?

danielkuhnley.com/become-a-conqueror

Sign up and read *Scourge*, A World Of Centauria Novella, and also get **EXCLUSIVE** access to additional *The Dark Heart Chronicles* series content. Be the **FIRST** to get sneak peeks at my upcoming novels and the chance to win **FREE** stuff, like signed books.

Thank you for reading!

To save her son she must destroy a civilization.

Emorith used her persuasion magic on the wrong man, and he's controlled her ever since. Now, she must find a test subject for his spell, Scourge. She knows Magus, the powerful wizard who rules the southern realm, will use the spell to obliterate anyone without magic. But she can't live without her son, and Magus will kill him if she fails...

To defeat Magus's ominous plot, Emorith must betray him and trust a friend with her young son. However, her smooth talking and determination may not be enough to prevent an apocalypse.

Scourge takes place in the World of Centauria 1200 years prior to the events in *The Dark Heart Chronicles* epic fantasy series. If you like thrilling adventures and heroic characters, then you'll love Daniel Kuhnley's dark and creative novella.

BOOKS BY DANIEL KUHNLEY

FANTASY

<u>The Dark Heart Chronicles</u>
The Dragon's Stone
(previously released as Dark Lament)
Reborn
Rended Souls

Scourge (novella)

MYSTERY THRILLER

<u>Alice Bergman Novels</u>
Birth Of A Killer (novella)
The Braille Killer

Visit Daniel's website to find these books and more!
danielkuhnley.com

This book is dedicated to Marsha, my wife and my best friend. You helped me with every aspect of this endeavor, save the actual writing. You believed in me even when I couldn't, pushed me when it felt pointless, and supported me without end through the process. I love you more than words could ever express!

Amber, Ben, and Kirk – thank you for your hard work. This book wouldn't exist without you all.

Tim and Ben, your feedback on the story was immeasurably valuable. Thank you so much for your time.

THE DARK HEART CHRONICLES

THE DRAGON'S STONE

DANIEL KUHNLEY

CHAPTER ONE

The shallow, fall sun warmed Nardus as he sat on the long wooden seat of the wagon, bouncing along with it as he and his family made their way down the dirt road. He turned his head to the right and eyed his wife, Vitara.

She sat atop their maple-brown steed, Rydar, keeping pace alongside the wagon. In her arms, their one-year-old daughter, Savannah, lay fast asleep against her breast. He beamed at them, only as a proud father and husband could.

Beauty, perfected.

He turned toward the back of the wagon and verified Shardan and Shanara, his three-year-old twins, were still fast asleep.

Whoosh!

Nardus knew the unmistakable sound of a flying arrow. He rose to his feet, still grasping the reins, his senses heightened.

Shick!

The familiar bite of an arrow ripped into his left bicep, twisted him around, and left him unbalanced. A burst of energy dulled his sense of pain, and the wound fleeted from his mind like a leaf in the wind.

Whoosh! Whoosh!

Two more arrows loosed. By the time he twisted back toward Vitara, it was too late. Words of warning caught in his throat, infused with bile. They burned with acid as he coughed and choked them back down.

Thunk!

He watched in horror as an arrow buried itself in the back of Savannah's skull. Her head bounced off Vitara's right breast for a brief moment, and then pushed against it, the arrow pinning her to Vitara's chest like a brooch.

Vitara screamed, but the ear-piercing sound quickly morphed into a low gurgle as the third arrow burrowed itself into the center of her throat and pushed its way through the back of her neck, silencing her.

Ɛäţūr, my God, don't do this!

Tick.

Everything moved in slow motion. Vitara fell backward from her horse, still clutching Savannah in her arms.

Tick.

Nardus's heart thundered in his ears. He leapt from atop the wagon, hoping to catch Vitara and Savannah before they collided with the ground.

Tick.

He stretched his arms out and willed himself to reach them in time, but he didn't. Vitara landed firmly on her back. Savannah's frail body flailed in her loosened arms like a rag doll. Vitara's head snapped backward and slammed into the ground with a *thud*.

Tick.

Nardus grunted as he belly-flopped against the ground and scrambled to his feet. He raced to Vitara's side, knelt beside her, and gently lifted her head in his hands. Savannah lie still against her chest; in his heart, he knew his precious little angel had died, but the thought of never hearing her sweet laughter again lingered beyond his comprehension.

No! No! NO!

The chaos of the moment rushed back into full motion around him. Behind him, the twins cried. Vitara, her head still cradled in his hands, coughed. Blood oozed from the corners of her mouth.

A few paces south, Rydar squealed and reared. Several arrows protruded from his massive chest and neck. He fell on his side with a *thump*, whimpered, and then lay still.

Nardus lay Vitara's head on the ground and rose to his feet, exposed. His heart jumped in his chest like a wild bird trapped in a cage. Every muscle in his body bulged against his skin, full of adrenaline and begging to fulfill his need for vengeance.

At the edge of the forest stood three figures of average height, all dressed in dark leathers and furs. Black scarves covered their heads, leaving only their eyes exposed. Each had an arrow nocked and ready for flight, but they didn't loose them.

What are they waiting for?

Whoosh!

Nardus bolted toward the wagon and dove for cover behind it just as an arrow sailed past his right leg. He rolled to a crouch behind the wagon. He gazed up at the wet faces of his twins. Terror filled their eyes as they trembled. He desperately wanted to comfort them and let them know everything would be okay, but the threat on their lives left him without time for it.

"Stay in the wagon, and stay down." He did his best to produce a smile for them.

Nardus peered over the top of the wagon's bed, toward the forest's edge. The three figures stood like statues, unmoving. Their strange behavior made his skin crawl.

Nardus knew what must be done, but the idea of leaving the twins behind tore at his soul. He looked at them again and smiled. "Shardan, take care of your sister. Stay hidden and stay quiet. Papa will be right back."

The twins protested, but Nardus put his finger to his lips, quieting them. "I'll be right back, I promise."

Nardus kissed each of them on the forehead and then reached over them and grabbed his bow and quiver. He quickly lifted the quiver over his head and pulled his left arm through the strap.

He forced air through his nostrils. Anger boiled his blood.

You've taken my wife and child without cause. I'll destroy you all.

He looked at Shardan and Shanara one last time. The fear in their eyes left his heart aching with guilt, but he'd made his decision. No other choice existed.

"I love you both."

"Papa—" Shanara sniffled.

He wiped the tears from her cheeks with his thumbs. "Just think of sandcastles, and I'll be back before you know it."

Nardus strung the bow, pulled an arrow from the quiver, and nocked it. He moved toward the edge of the wagon and poked his head around its side. The three figures hadn't moved. He looked over at Vitara and Savannah and his stomach roiled with grief.

A deep, dark fury welled up within him. It consumed him, changed him. He flew around the side of the wagon like a demon and charged the three figures, firing arrows as quickly as he could nock them. He opened his mouth and let out a guttural, bone-chilling howl.

His manic cry and the flurry of arrows sent the three attackers retreating into the cover of the forest. A white-hot, blinding rage separated him from his humanity, and drove him into the forest after them.

The shadows of the forest moved around him like spirits, driven by the wind. His pulse raced as he picked up on their trail. The three of them moved as one.

Easier to kill.

He raced through the brush like a lion after its prey, giving little care to the ruckus he stirred up. Ten paces ahead he saw a flash of movement and turned to the side just as an arrow whooshed by his shoulder. He loosed an arrow of his own and boldly pushed forward.

The *thud* of a body dropping to the ground registered in his mind just moments before he stepped over it.

One down. Two to go.

A twig snapped behind him. His beating heart echoed in his ears like a thunderous drum, banging out the final moments before his untimely death.

Thump-thump.

Nardus twisted on his left heel, and brought himself around to face his attacker as he fell back toward the ground.

Thump-thump.

The glint of a steel blade flashed as it arced just over his head. Had he not been falling to the ground, he would've been headless.

Thump-thump.

He loosed his last arrow just as he hit the ground and watched it bury itself into his attacker's chest. The attacker twisted and fell to the side.

Thump-thump.

The air rushed from his lungs and past his lips as the third attacker jumped on top of him.

Thump-thump.

Cold, hard hands wrapped around his throat and squeezed. Nardus fought against his attacker's grip, but their strength seemed inhuman. He kicked his legs in the air to try and disrupt their leverage, but it did no good.

Thump-thump.

Nardus fought against the fire in his lungs and forced himself to stay alert despite his mind urging him to give up. He reached down and felt the hilt of the knife on his belt.

Thump-thump.

Nardus worked his fingers around the hilt of the knife and then down to the snap holding it in its sheath. The attacker let go of Nardus's neck with one hand and backhanded him square in the jaw.

Thump-thump.

The attacker grabbed for Nardus's arm, but Nardus freed the knife and plunged it into the attacker's side. Nardus twisted the knife and the attacker grunted.

Thump-thump.

Nardus thrust the knife into the attacker's side repeatedly. Their hand moved from Nardus's throat and grabbed at their side. Nardus pushed them off himself and scrambled backward. He wheezed as he drew air into his lungs.

The sensation of wind rushing through an open canyon brought the world around him back to speed. He coughed as he stood to his feet and spat on the ground. A few feet away, the attacker huddled on the ground, moaning and clutching their side.

Nardus walked over to the attacker and kicked the side of their head with his boot. The attacker screamed as their head snapped to the right. Even in the shadows, Nardus could tell the attacker neared death.

Nardus reached down and pulled the black scarf from around the attacker's head. He staggered backward a few paces and fell to his knees, stunned by what he'd uncovered.

"Bradwr?"

Bradwr choked on his own blood as he spoke. "I'm so sorry, Nardus."

Vomit swelled in Nardus's throat, making it difficult to breathe or talk. "Why would you do this? You're my best friend."

Blood oozed from the man's graying lips. "I swear I had no choice. They took Izzy."

Nardus could barely contain his rage. "And so you slaughter my family? Who put you up to this? Who told you to do this?"

Bradwr coughed and then grew still.

Nardus crawled over to Bradwr and shook him. "Answer me! Who put you up to this?"

Nardus pounded Bradwr's chest with his fists. "Answer me!"

The dead man held no more answers and Nardus snapped. He roared at the sky and gave in to his madness.

He tore the three men apart, limb by limb, with his bare hands. With his serrated blade, he removed their eyes so they couldn't find their way to Ҽäҭūr and salvation in the next life.

He ripped their hearts from their chests and squished them in his hands like fists full of mud, and watched them ooze between the cracks of his fingers. He castrated them and cursed their children, signifying the death of their lineage. He set a blazing fire and burned every remnant of their existence within it.

With the deed done, Nardus shed the rage from his heart like a snake sheds its skin. Beneath the rage, only emptiness and sorrow remained. He hadn't known two of the men, but Bradwr? The betrayal crushed him.

Nardus stumbled through the trees until he came upon a small brook. He bent down and scooped the fresh water into his mouth with his hands. The water tasted of iron—of *blood*—and he spat it out.

Beams of light shone through the canopy of trees and fell on his face. He looked down and saw that his clothes were covered in blood. His hands were stained crimson. He dropped to his knees and plunged his hands into the cold water and scrubbed them with fervor. He cupped the water in his hands and bathed his face in it, desperate to cleanse himself of the blood.

He pulled himself to his feet and stumbled back into the shadows, drunk with the guilt of failing to protect his family. Three losses in a single day. It sickened him. He purged the contents of his stomach and then spat the rancid taste from his mouth.

How do I move on from this? I've lost the love of my life, my precious Savannah, and my best friend.

The fledgling protruding from the back of Savannah's head flashed in his mind and knocked the wind from him like a punch to the gut. His knees buckled, and he grabbed the nearest tree to keep himself upright.

My precious little angel.

Nardus closed his eyes and relived the past few hours in his mind, scouring his memories for anything that could've altered the events. Everything had happened so fast. He'd reacted to the attack like a seasoned man of war, not as a father.

Something felt amiss. The precision of the three attackers' shots were right on their mark, except the first shot that'd sunk into his bicep. Had they missed a kill-shot on purpose? In fact, every shot they'd taken at him had been off-mark, as though intentional.

Was I drawn away on purpose?

A grapefruit-sized lump rose in his throat.

"The twins!"

He wiped his tear-filled eyes and then rushed through the maze of trees, desperate to get back to the wagon and his twins.

"Shardan! Shanara! It's Papa." He pushed his way through the last few trees.

No answer.

He burst into the clearing and his pulse quickened.

Vitara, Savannah, and Rydar lay on the ground—undisturbed.

Where's the wagon?

Tracks led toward the east, along the road, but there were more than just the ones from the wagon and horses. Tracks like wolves—but significantly larger—littered the ground.

My God!

Fear slithered across his skin and seeped into his bones, and he shivered. He swallowed hard to stifle the vomit rising in his throat.

He sprinted down the road, but the feeling in his gut told him he'd be too late.

Don't do this to me, Ɂäṭūr. You've already taken two from me. Don't take them all.

A mile down the road he spotted the wagon, turned on its side and propped against a tree. His muscles tightened with anticipation, and he charged toward it.

Please, Ɂäṭūr, let them be alive.

"Shardan! Shanara!" he yelled, nearly upon the wagon.

No answer again.

He rounded the side of the wagon and dropped to his knees, unable to stand or breathe. He grabbed at his chest. His heart slammed against his ribcage, trying desperately to separate itself from the searing pain racing through his bloodstream. He wrenched over and vomited.

Blood. So much blood.

Blood splattered across everything. Too much blood for two small children, wasn't it? The sight of its crimson hue brought back memories of war—memories he'd fought to forget for more than two decades. Some of the things he'd seen and done during the war were horrific, but the scene before him would forever haunt him.

He crawled over to what remained of his precious twins, Shardan and Shanara. Their limbs were torn from their bodies and strewn along the forest line. Their torsos and faces were shredded with claw and teeth marks— mauled beyond recognition. He turned his head dry-heaved.

His head spun with emotions.

My fault. This is all my fault. How could I let this happen?

He sat there and wept for hours, unable to think or move as the last remnants of daylight gave way to nightfall.

I'm sorry, my children. I should've listened to your mother. I've let you down again. I've let you all down.

The night passed into day and back into night. The incomprehensible violence spread before him left him immobilized. He wanted to end his life right there and rid himself of the pain, but the idea of leaving them that way—exposed—was unthinkable, unacceptable, and intolerable.

I must bury them. I know just the place, my loves.

He righted the wagon and unhitched bloodied yokes. Virtually nothing remained of the two horses that'd pulled the wagon but bones and hooves. He carefully loaded the remains of his twins into the back of the wagon and then pulled the wagon back onto the road.

He took one of the breast collars, slipped it over his head, and attached it to the wagon shaft. The weight of the wagon fought against him, and it took every ounce of his strength to pull it down the road to where Vitara and Savannah lay.

Nardus pulled the breast collar over his head and dropped to the ground next to Vitara, exhausted. In the moonlight, her once beautiful, violet eyes were glazed over, their exquisite sparkle extinguished for eternity. He lifted her head in his hands, smoothed back her matted, blood-soaked hair, and kissed her soft, beautiful lips—only they were cold, dry, and cracked.

The pungent smell of her dead body lingered in his nostrils, but he didn't care. He'd suffer anything just to be close to her.

He fought back a swarm of emotions. "My anchor, my heart, and my everything. This wasn't how it was supposed to be with us. We were supposed to grow old together."

He held her corpse through the night and sang her favorite song to her repeatedly. His heart felt trapped in a tangled mess of pain, but he didn't allow a single tear to fall from his eyes.

You'll always be my everything.

With the first light, Nardus rose to his feet and scooped Vitara and Savannah into his arms. He placed their bodies in the back of the wagon, alongside the remains of the twins. He swallowed hard as he fought to stay in control of his emotions. The four of them lying in the back of the wagon— dead to the world—tortured his soul.

I'll find you again, my loves.

Three days he hauled the wagon—through the valley, across the river, and deep into the forest—until he reached a secluded grove of giant, sacred-heart trees.

He and Vitara had spent many a day there, enjoying the cool summer air and relaxing in the shade of the trees. They'd oft spoken of the day they'd build a house there and live out their lives, free of care.

In a way, he'd kept his promise to her. He placed the four of them in a single grave beneath the blossoming branches of their favorite tree. He took special care to wrap his children safely in Vitara's arms.

She'll take care of you now, as I've failed.

Each shovel-full of dirt he placed over them brought more tears with it until he could no longer see their bodies through his blurred vision. He buried his heart with them.

His hands trembled, and tears streaked down his cheeks as he carved each of their names into the tree's trunk. "I do this to honor your lives and memories forever."

†††

After burying his family, Nardus spent two weeks trying to track the beasts that'd killed his twins. The prints surrounding the wagon resembled those of wolves—only much larger. The tracks went in nearly every direction, and all of them ended in disappointment. His hope of closure withered into a deep despair, and he wanted to be done.

A week later, his failure extinguished his last thread of hope. He sat in the woods on a log, covered in dried blood, sweat, and urine. He cared for nothing and deprived his body of sleep, food, and water for days, hoping death would come for him.

At the frayed ends of his sanity, he wanted to carve out the darkness from within. His heart threatened to punch a hole through his chest just to escape the grasp of his marred and twisted soul.

Kill me, Ɛäţūr. Strike me dead. I no longer have purpose. My life means nothing now. You've taken everything from me. Just let me die.

Desperate to end his life, Nardus held a blade to his throat. He could endure a lifetime of physical pain, but the mental pain tortured his soul relentlessly.

One deep slice. That's all it takes.

The notion of never seeing his family again paralyzed him. No more hope existed for him, did it? If not, why did he allow the task to remain unfinished?

His whole body trembled, but his hand stayed firm. "Bah! Just do it."

He knew what he'd done to those filthy animals. Seeking justice would've served him well, but he'd gone far beyond that. To complicate matters, he felt little remorse.

They deserved what they got.

Vengeance drove his thoughts that day, and with it had come his downfall. Because of his hotheaded, swift justice, he now carried with him not only the loss of his entire family, but also the mark of a lost man. It weighed on his heart like an anvil. Nothing—not even Ɛäţūr—could bring back what he'd lost. He only regretted not dying with his family.

You've separated me from my family and damned my soul. You've left me with no choice. I now damn You, Ɛ̄ţūr!

† † †

One year later

Nardus staggered along the rutted, frozen road that split the small town of Diabolus Pes down its middle. Haggard, wooden structures lined the narrow road like lumps of rotted flesh, and people moved through and around them like maggots.

Just ahead on Nardus's right, a large iron sign hung out over the road. The sign donned no words, but its emblem of a large, wolf-like head couldn't be mistaken: *Ferzh's Head Inn.* He trekked there daily and drank until Ferdi, the owner, kicked him out, or he ran out of coins.

Nardus stepped into the shallow alcove underneath the sign and grunted as he pushed his way through the heavy, wooden door. The door's rusted hinges screeched. Every head in the room turned toward him, shook with recognition, and turned away.

Ferdi glared at him from across the room. "Shut the door, ya clakker." Her thick accent harshened her words further. "Feel the cold creeping upon me skin already."

More blubber hung on Ferdi's bones than what one might find in a pod of whales. *Her being cold is an impossibility.* Nardus scowled at her and gestured with his middle and third finger.

Ferdi's large lips parted and curled upward into a crooked-toothed smile and she winked at Nardus. "Save it for later."

A bitter-cold blast of air rushed through the open door and sent a flash of gooseflesh up Nardus's neck. He shrugged it away, but the cold bit. *A few swigs of ale will warm me right up. And dull my mind.*

He shoved the door closed with his shoulder, then he scanned the large room. Men and women laughed, shouted, and flirted at nearly every table. The only unoccupied table in the inn sat in the far corner, away from the crowd. *Perfect.*

Nardus wove his way through the gauntlet of tables and people and sat down on one of the two long benches that flanked the table, his back to the room. He reached into his coin purse, withdrew three silver coins, and stacked them on the end of the table.

Moments later, Ferdi arrived with four frothy mugs of ale. "How long ya gonna keep this up?"

Nardus set his jaw. "Until it kills me."

Ferdi frowned, and her cheeks drooped like a hound's. "Listening tis me gift."

Nardus scowled. "Is it now? You've yet to use it for what—a year now? Use your gift on someone who gives a care. Leave the ale, and leave me be."

She snorted like a bull. "So be it." She shoved the mugs in front of Nardus, scooped up the pile of coins, and stomped off.

Nardus closed his eyes and dove into the darkness of his mind. Every minute he continued to exist tortured him, and he only found solace in maintaining a constant state of drunkenness. Often, he couldn't remember where he was, but no amount of spirits took away his memories.

He grabbed the first mug and downed its contents without pause. He slammed the mug down, grabbed the second one, and drained it too. The third met its fate as quickly as the first two, but with the fourth he took his time. The alcohol settled in his empty stomach and left him numb.

Is this all that's left of me? My love, how will I ever find you again?

Hot tears wet his cheeks and he swatted at them like flies. "Damn you, Bradwr!" He picked up one of the empty mugs and slammed it down on the table. "Damn you." He leaned over the table as his vision rocked him like a boat at sea.

A tall man sat down on the bench on the opposite side of the table from him. Nardus straightened and eyed the man for a moment. The well-dressed man—more so than any other in the inn—looked out of place.

The man's top hat sat back on his forehead and touched his rounded ears, but it didn't sit on top of them. His dark-purple overcoat—likely made of silk—gleamed in the candlelight, and the look in his golden-brown eyes hinted at an air of superiority, but his demeanor spoke against it.

Nardus spat on the floor and slurred, "Table's taken. Find someone else to pester."

The man leaned forward, his brow creased, and his jaw tensed. "I don't believe you understand. I've traveled a great distance to see you, Nardus."

"I don't—" The sound of his own name registered in Nardus's mind. His nostrils flared as he eyed the man further. "Do I know you? No, I think not. How is it you know my name? No one in these parts knows me. Who are you and what do you want?"

The man leaned back. "The name's Pravus, but I'm certain that's of no significance to you. The only item of pertinence is the business we must discuss."

Nardus squinted as Pravus doubled in his vision. "We've no business. Leave me to my ale." He blinked several times, but the two Pravuses lingered. He shook his head, but it only distorted his vision further. "On second thought, it doesn't matter. I'm leaving."

Nardus started to stand, but Pravus put his hand over Nardus's. Nardus glared at him.

You have the audacity to touch me?

Nardus gritted his teeth. "Remove your hand before I remove your face."

Pravus smiled and made no attempt to comply.

Nardus's hand started tingling. He tried pulling it out from under Pravus's hand, but found he couldn't move it. In fact, he couldn't move anything below his neck.

Nardus's eyes widened, and his pulse raced. "What've you done to me? Release me at once."

The man's thin lips curled at the corners. "Take a deep breath, friend. I'm here to offer you my help."

Nardus snarled, "I don't know who you think you are, but I don't need help from *your* kind."

"My kind?" Pravus leaned across the table and gazed intently at Nardus. "Even without mezhik, I see the lack of hope and purpose in your eyes. I'm here to offer you both and more."

Nardus scowled. "I want no part of whatever you're peddling, wizard. Leave me before I cause a scene."

"You would've caused a scene long ago if you really wanted to. Besides, I doubt any of the peasants in this sordid establishment would rush to your aid."

"Maybe not, but are you willing to find out? Ferdi's quite fond of me."

Pravus's smile widened and his eyes narrowed. "Oh, she is, is she? So you're unaware of what she and the others say about you behind your back then?"

Nardus glanced over his shoulder. "I'm not deaf, but none of their empty talk matters. They know nothing about me and neither do you."

"The alcohol speaks for you, but I know what's in your heart."

Murder. Let me loose, and I'll tear you apart.

Nardus forced air out his nose. "And what might that be?"

"First, let's take care of business." Pravus swept his free hand across the table, and six stacks of golden coins appeared.

Nardus eyed the coins. *Are those all there, or is it just my eyes?* He glared at Pravus. "You think you can entice me with your blood money?"

Pravus tapped the table with another coin. "There are thirty gold coins in total. You know as well as I that this amount of money in the Ancient Realm is hard to come by. You could add up a year's worth of income for every person in this town, and it wouldn't match a quarter of what's on the table. All I'm asking is that you listen to my offer. Take it, and these coins are yours."

Pravus lifted his hand from Nardus's. The tingling sensation faded, and Nardus slumped over the table. *Damned mezhik.*

Nardus flexed his stiff hand. "What is it you're playing at, wizard? What do you want from me?"

The man smoothed out the wrinkles in his dark-purple sleeves. "There's something I need you to do."

Nardus leaned back from the table. "And what makes you think I'd be willing to do anything for you?"

"You're still sitting there." Pravus's perfect teeth gleamed in the candlelight as he smiled.

Why am I still here? Because I have nowhere else to be? A simple truth shone bright in the dimly lit inn, and he salivated. *I could drink myself to death with those coins.*

Nardus rubbed his left bicep. *Does anything matter? Have I not lost you already, my love? Children? I'm damned to this world without you.*

Nardus looked around. "I guess I am. So what is it that you want?"

Pravus rapped his knuckles against the table. "Complete one task for me, and I'll give you back what you thought to be lost."

Nardus frowned. "And what might that be?"

"Why, your family, Nardus." A thin smile parted Pravus's lips. He cracked his knuckles.

Nardus's pulse quickened, and his palms moistened. "What do you know of my family?"

Pravus removed his top hat and sat it on the table. His raven locks caressed the table as he leaned over it. He stared at Nardus for a long moment.

"I've been watching you for several months. A lot can be surmised about a man just by observance. You wear a ring on your middle finger, but return to an empty house every night. No man wears a ring like that for show.

"I also see the pain in your eyes, and it reminds me of the pain I once knew. The excessive drinking you do brings you no closer to what you want, does it? I'm no stranger to loss myself and have traveled the treacherous and lonely road you're going down now.

"With mezhik, there are ways to accomplish the impossible. Trust me when I say that I can help you."

Nardus slammed his fist on the table. "You think me a fool? They're all dead. My whole family's dead. How do you expect to help me with that? Do you believe yourself to be some sort of god?"

"A god—" Pravus's eyes sparkled with energy. "—perhaps not, but what makes you believe only a god can raise the dead?"

Nardus's heart stuttered and his breath caught in his throat. His mind spun with madness.

What he says is impossible. He's more delusional than I am, or a liar.

In his mind, Nardus rose from the bench and walked out of the inn, but reality rooted him to the bench and to that moment. More than reality, something deep within himself rendered him motionless and speechless. A dormant feeling he'd forgotten existed. A power stronger than mezhik itself: *hope.*

Could it be true? Is there really a way to get my family back? Does it matter? If there's even a slim chance of bringing them back, how could I possibly turn the man down?

Nardus blinked. His thoughts flowed freely, clearly. The haze in his mind dissipated and he felt more sober than he could remember.

How's this possible?

Pravus leaned back and folded his arms across his chest. "Is that what you believe? I'm incapable of such a feat?"

Nardus rubbed his left bicep again. The scars, a reminder even through his shirt, remained. Nothing could ever change the past, but the future felt more malleable than he remembered.

Nardus raised his hands. "Okay. As impossible as it is, let's say you've found a way to raise the dead. Why do you need me? What's in it for you?"

"My motives are of no concern to you. Focus on your family and what it would mean for you to reunite with them. And do not forget about the thirty pieces of gold."

"You've garnered my attention. What's the task? I'd do anything for my family."

Pravus's right eyebrow rose. "Even risk death to bring them back?"

"Given the choice, I'd switch places with them. Nothing matters to me, except them."

Pravus tented his fingers. "Good. No one's ever returned from where I'm sending you. I hope you'll be the first."

Nardus stood. "Look at me. I've traveled through many cesspools throughout the Ancient Realm and met some of the foulest brutes and beasts around. I've been cursed by Ɂäṭūr to survive everything I've ever faced. Death eludes me."

Pravus waved his hand. "Yes, I'm sure you have. However, I'm sending you to the lower world—*Ef Demd Dhä.*"

"Ha!" Nardus slapped his knee. "You're sending me to the land of the dead? Do you think I'm mad? As though raising the dead weren't impossible enough! Are you going to kill me to get me there?"

Pravus sighed heavily and pointed at the bench. "Sit down, and listen."

Nardus shook his head, but sat down. *Forgive my madness, my love. I stay for you.*

Pravus leaned in. "There's an ancient gateway that leads into *Ef Demd Dhä,* and I know its location. The gateway—*Zhäíṭfäí Fäíṭᴈ*—will transform you, but you must get past the gatekeeper to enter. Once you've gone through the gateway, you'll face seven trials created by some of the most powerful wizards who ever lived."

Nardus took one of the empty mugs and looked inside of it. "And why is it that I'm going there?"

"Inside *Ţämbəll Dhef Däd Dhä*, you'll need to find *Ƹţōn Dhef Dädh*—a stone so powerful that it can raise the dead. *Ƹţōn Dhef Dädh*—the stone of death—is the reason *Ef Demd Dhä* exists. Do you understand now? The stone will change everything—your past and mine."

Nardus turned the mug upside down and sat it in the middle of the table. "So why don't you retrieve it yourself? After all, you've got mezhik."

Pravus folded his hands together. "Even if I could get past the trials, I wouldn't be able to take the stone. It's protected by ancient mezhik. I intend on using the stone, and that fact would prevent me from taking it, and I'd be trapped there forever. However, you have no such desire to use the stone yourself, so you're the perfect choice. The *only* choice."

Nardus shook his head and wrinkled his brow. "But why me? Of the millions of people in the Ancient Realm, why choose me?"

Pravus opened his hands. "Isn't it obvious? You've nothing to lose and everything to gain."

Nardus rubbed his left bicep. "You're right, but how can I guarantee you won't go back on your word as soon as I return and hand over the stone?"

"Relationships are based on trust. I'm giving you my word and my gold. What more would you have me do?"

Nardus eyed the coin stacks. "Double the price, and I'm your man."

Candle flames danced in Pravus's eyes like demons, and the ends of his lips curled upward. "Greed is a dangerous trait, friend, but this night it benefits you."

Pravus reached inside his overcoat, pulled out a large coin purse, and sat it on the table. The stacks of coins vibrated, then coins from each stack flipped into the air and into the open coin purse. The coin purse bulged by the time the last coin dropped into it.

Nardus reached for the coin purse, but Pravus grabbed his wrist. "There's no turning back from this, Nardus. Once you open *Zhäíțfäí Fäíţƹ*, you'll either succeed in retrieving *Ƹţōn Dhef Dädh*, or you'll be lost in *Ef Demd Dhä* forever. Can you live with that?"

Nardus shrugged. "I've got nothing left to live for."

Pravus smiled, released Nardus's wrist, and cracked his knuckles. "Then let's get started."

CHAPTER TWO

N ardus navigated through the dark, narrow passage quickly, dragging his hands along its rough rock walls for guidance and balance. The skin of his palms had long since snagged and torn against the sharp rocks, wearing through decades of calluses. They'd morphed into seeping wounds.

His hands sucked up bits of rock and dust from the walls, trapping them like bugs in spider webs within the congealing blood oozing from his open wounds. He trudged on with little thought of it. He preferred the superficial flesh wounds to the excruciating, drawn-out death he'd face were he to fail. The wounds kept his mind sharp and focused and would keep him alive.

His mind fixed on one task: finding the Ƨʈōn Dhef Dädh. It was the key that would give him back his family. He had no idea how, but nothing else in his abject life gave him hope. Everything hinged on this suicide quest.

He imagined the walls moving back and forth ever so slightly, fluctuating from the intense heat radiating from them. The heat permeated the air with sulfuric fumes that burned his nostrils and clogged his lungs. His eyes stung with dryness; his body couldn't produce the moisture they so desperately needed.

The heat pulled moisture from his pores, drenching him in sweat from head to toe and leaving him parched. His sandpaper lips, cracked and bleeding, chafed his tongue with every lick. He desperately needed water. His haste to begin the quest left him without a waterskin and now threatened to take his life.

Dust particles swarmed around him like furious little gnats, drawn from their sleep by the incessant pounding of his leather boots against the hard rock surface. Dirt caked in the crevices of his weathered skin, bonding with the beads of sweat running down his brow and hardening like clay.

Amidst the repulsive smell of sulfur and dust, a faint, nearly undetectable odor of blood and urine—*of death*—lingered, evidence leftover from a time long passed. His imagination painted pictures in his twisted mind with ideas of what purpose this place had once served and the reason behind its construction.

One thing he knew: based on the low ceilings and narrow passages, there could be no other responsible party than the derros—the only race small enough and capable of working in such tight quarters. The only ones crazy enough to have done it, too.

How much time had passed since he'd found his way into the passage, he didn't know, but he gauged at least six hours had elapsed. His back ached from hunching over for so long, and his shoulders burned with fatigue.

He wanted to stop and rest for a bit, but if he did so, he might not get back up. He'd begged for death to take him many times over the past year, but the suffocating darkness surrounding him left him wanting to live just a little longer.

The ground dropped from beneath his feet. His arms lashed out, and he clung to the rock walls even as they dug into his flesh. His whole body quivered with pain, and it took every bit of his waning strength to steady his arms.

He wedged his feet against the walls and relieved some of the pressure on his arms, but his fatigued legs would soon give out—nearly as quickly as his arms.

Despite the darkness, he closed his eyes and steadied his breathing until he calmed enough to focus on the situation. Carefully, with slow and precise movements, he reversed direction until he found solid ground again. Caution gave way to relief as he released his grip on the walls and sat down on the ground.

He scooched over to the edge of the drop-off and hung his legs over it. His toes settled on a solid surface about a foot-and-a-half below. Relief flowed through his body and he fell backward without thinking.

His head cracked against the hard rock surface. He grunted, and a slew of profanities floated through his head. Even though he sat alone in the dark, he didn't give them voice.

He sat up and leaned against the scorching wall. His head throbbed. With every passing minute, his lungs worked against him, burning with every inhalation. A puff of dust filled the air each time he coughed, or so he imagined. He wanted so much to give up.

In his head, the quest had seemed unpretentious, but the reality of it ate away at his sanity. Nothing ever turned out as simple as it appeared. The plot always twisted, and the situations always intensified. He wanted easy, just once in his life.

Is it too much to ask for?

He picked and tore at the loosened flesh on his palms, biting and chewing off the pieces he couldn't grasp with his fingers. He stalled, and for no good reason. He gathered his strength and pulled himself to his feet.

Upon further investigation, he found himself at the top of a set of steep stairs. The stone steps were slick as ice beneath him, worn smooth by thousands of years of use. They tested him with every move, checking his balance and stamina, and drained him of what little energy he'd regained while resting.

This task is madness. I guess that makes me a lunatic.

He laughed aloud, adding fuel to his mania. He continued down the spiraling stairway, burying himself farther and farther beneath the ruins of Mortuus Terra.

Because of his nature, he counted each step, and, with every step, he forced himself to recite each detail of the quest. Ultimately, nothing mattered except acquiring the stone, but there were so many steps between him and it. He had a good idea of his heading and what he must do once he arrived, but the details were fuzzy at best. Uncertainty twisted his stomach in knots.

"Seven trials," he muttered.

But what would they be? Pravus hadn't given him specifics as to their nature—only a warning that they'd be brutal.

Congratulations, Nardus. You've earned yourself a one-way trip into the bowels of Ef Demd Dhä. Hope you packed lightly.

The reality of the thought hampered its intended comedy and brought him another notch closer to giving up.

397, the number of steps he counted before finally reaching the bottom of the stairway. The number soured in his stomach like rancid meat. He couldn't believe it. He wished he'd miscounted the steps, but he knew he hadn't. He leaned against the wall and retched violently.

His face burned with anger as he screamed, "Why must You torture me? Answer me, Ɛätūr! If You truly are my God and Savior, answer me!"

Silence answered him.

He beat his fists against the sharp rock wall, indifferent to the pain and of the blood that seeped from freshly opened wounds. Like everyone else in his life, Ɛätūr had abandoned him as well.

A phantom arrow whooshed through his memories and ripped into his left bicep—he massaged the scars. "I hate You," he whimpered. "You're no God of mine."

A dim light flickered through an archway about thirty paces ahead and to his right. He shielded his eyes with his forearm and walked toward the archway. He ducked under it and stepped into a small, circular chamber.

The walls within the chamber were comprised of smooth, grey stones— each an exact duplicate of its kin—and directly contrasted the walls of the passage and stairway he'd just navigated. Everything outside of the chamber appeared to be nothing more than an afterthought.

Something about the chamber felt special—*wondrous*. His physical pain and fatigue blurred in his mind like a distant, fading memory.

Within the confines of the chamber, a single sconce adorned the far wall—its torch burned bright and cast demon shadows across the walls. He watched the shadows in silence, completely rapt by their ceaseless, flowing dance. He swore he heard drums beating in the distance, keeping rhythm for the tireless shadow dancers.

The chamber—and time itself—melted before his eyes as memories from a life he'd once lived flooded his mind and filled his vision.

Vitara. Children.

A loud pop from the torch startled Nardus and pulled him from within his mind and back into the present. The chamber materialized once again.

He found himself sitting on the ground, slumped against the wall. Tears streaked his clothes and his cheeks. Snot and dirt hung from his nostrils. He wiped it all away with the sleeves of his tattered shirt.

It'd been 397 days since the *massacre*. He'd never forget that day, and he'd never forgive Ƨäțūr for letting it happen.

"Vitara!" A thousand voices echoed through the chamber and matched the agony in his cry. "My love, don't give up on me. I'm coming for you!"

His knees cracked and nearly gave out as he stood. He steadied himself with the assistance of the smooth wall—cold as ice against his torn, swollen skin. The room swam around him, and his head threatened to explode. Darkness swirled at the corners of his vision.

He closed his eyes and focused on memories of his sweet Vitara. Her name ran through his mind continually, and the image of her beautiful smile warmed his heart.

My rock and my anchor. My love, keep me grounded.

Tranquility slowly settled the invisible sea and his legs stabilized under him. He opened his eyes and watched the darkness recede from the corners of his vision. The chamber eased into focus once again.

Before him, the circular chamber—approximately twenty feet in diameter—sat empty, save a lone pedestal standing in front of the far wall. From the brief—but detailed—description given to him by Pravus, he recognized it immediately.

"*Zhäíțfäí Fäíțƨ*," he said.

Fate's Gateway.

The pedestal, a hand-crafted work of art, shined with such beauty—more so than any image he'd conjured in his head. Its glistening surface defied time, looking freshly polished but an hour before. Carved from a single piece of the darkest green obsidian he'd ever seen, it measured roughly four feet in height from its circular base to its triangular top.

He cautiously stepped toward the pedestal, his eyes trained on the large, black serpent coiled around its base and up its central column. Three black heads swayed in the flickering light as the serpent peered out from under its top.

The serpent's six sapphire-blue eyes glowed in the shadows, and hissing filled his ears as its tongues probed the air. Three pairs of pearly fangs glistened in the light, and drops of venom hung from them in anticipation of striking flesh.

Less than a foot away, Nardus knelt before the pedestal, bringing himself

face-to-face with the serpent's leftmost head. He gazed deep into its eyes—
into the haunting reflections of himself.

His pulse raced.

Without fear, he slowly reached out and touched the serpent's muscular
body. He ran his fingers along its dorsal and ventral scales—they felt cold and
clammy against his broken skin.

In his mind's eye, he saw a flash of the serpent's fangs strike his face
repeatedly. The image brought with it an unexpected, morbid desire to feel
those fangs pierce his skin and sink deep into his flesh. He wanted to feel the
sting of its venom as it poured into his veins and paralyzed every inch of his
body, working its way through his nervous system. He wanted to feel death.

"You're magnificent," he whispered.

The serpent's body became rigid under his fingers. He slowly pulled his
hand back, never breaking eye contact.

Steady.

He realized the hissing had ceased. He rolled back on his heels and stared
in disbelief. In all its horrific beauty and elegance, the serpent became part
of the pedestal—its body carved from the same stone. He reached out and
touched it again and felt the smooth obsidian underneath his fingertips.

He had more than thirty-five name days to his credit, but he still felt the
fool at times. Throughout his life, he'd heard tales of mezhik, but he'd never
given much thought to them.

His knees popped as he pulled himself to his feet. He'd always thought
only those weak of mind could fall victim to the effects of mezhik. Either he'd
been wrong, or his mind wasn't as strong as he'd hoped.

"With age comes wisdom. Bah! With age comes foolery. Mezhik indeed."
He spat at the ground.

He glided his hand across the top of the pedestal—smooth as silk under
his skin. Its icy surface soothed his tattered flesh. An outline of an eye,
detailed in white gold, marked the center of the pedestal. Three words,
etched in the stone in Ancient Centaurian, circled the eye and glowed like
red-hot coals. He read them aloud, "*Í Dhef Fäíṭ.*"

His skin turned to gooseflesh as the meaning registered in his mind.

The Eye of Fate.

He knew the power that the eye held and the price he'd have to pay to use it, but the knowledge brought him little comfort. No other way existed for him to accomplish his quest. Even if there were another way, he had no time to figure it out.

He traced the eye with his finger and gathered his nerves. He harbored no doubts as to his strength and ability to endure its gaze, but that didn't lift his spirits. He closed his eyes, breathed deeply, and resolved himself to give into the hands of fate.

For Vitara. For my family.

Nothing else mattered.

He placed the palm of his right hand over the eye and spread his fingers wide.

So cold.

Gooseflesh raced up his arm. He took another deep breath and slowly exhaled.

With his eyes closed and without thought, he allowed the ancient words to flow like water from his parted lips. *"Ɂä Í dhrū zíū, Meɀtär. Ɂzhō mä bedh dhä."*

I see through you, Master. Show me the path.

Nothing happened.

Did I say the words wrong? Should I say them again?

Another moment later, he had his answer. The stone eye rotated beneath his palm, twisting his stomach with dread. Its fiery gaze ignited his flesh and tore open his wounds anew. Nardus screamed. Blood dripped from his palm into the stone eye and hissed as it boiled upon contact. The smell of burning flesh and blood filled his nostrils and the taste of it settled on his lips.

Nausea twisted his stomach, but he didn't give in. Pain flowed up his arm and into his chest, spreading out and attacking every inch of his body. He wanted to pull his hand away—to free himself from the excruciating pain— but it'd kill him if he did.

He battled with every breath to fill his lungs with air as they slowly caved in, but he lost ground with each exhale. A screamed bubbled up from his gut, but the sound never reached his lips.

Let me die.

With each passing moment, his body shut down further: his lungs ceased filling with air and his heart stopped pumping blood. His flesh shriveled and burned and fell away into nothing.

Please, Ɂäṭūr, just let me die.

His blood boiled and then evaporated from his veins, shriveling every muscle in his body and ripping the tendons from his bones.

Let... me... die!

He opened his eyes and stared into the mirror hanging on the wall. A ghost of himself stared back. He didn't recall the mirror being there before, but its presence was undeniable.

He watched himself in the mirror as his eyes melted in their sockets, leaving nothing but gaping holes.

Yet I can see?

His brain gelled and oozed from his eye sockets, nostrils, and ears, and slithered down his vertebrae like a slug. Nothing of himself remained but hollowed-out, brittle bone, yet he'd stayed conscious.

Somehow—without flesh or nerves—he still felt. His pain subsided, and elation swelled in his chest.

I'm still alive.

He laughed. Never had he felt so alive and aware in his life.

I'm alive!

Everything around him seemed more vibrant and full of energy. Colors were brighter, textures more distinct. The crackle of the lone torch echoed in the chamber, and he smelled and tasted the smoke it gave off.

"This is too good to be true." He beamed.

As though triggered by his words, coldness crept into his bones, and his giddy mood crashed down around him. His phantom heart pounded in the hollows of his chest, and the floor shook beneath his bony feet. Though lacking eyes, he watched darkness spread across the wall next to the pedestal, forming what looked like a doorway.

After what seemed an eternity, the eyelid under his palm rotated again. He removed his bony hand from the pedestal and stared at the darkness. The light from the torch failed to penetrate the confines of the doorway.

He stepped back.

I can't do this. I can't succumb to the darkness again. I'm finally alive for the first time in ages.

But beyond the doorway lay the only chance he had of resurrecting his family. He had no choice. He'd do anything for them.

He stepped forward. Beyond the doorway awaited certain death.

Vitara. Her beautiful violet eyes filled his mind.

Beyond the doorway, he knew in his heart, lie Ef Demd Dhä. *Of the Damned.* Perhaps not literally Ef Demd Dhä, but how could one be so sure? He believed the place of eternal damnation existed in many forms, his life taking on one of them.

"Diзäfär." Despite whispering, the Deceiver's name echoed in the chamber and left a bitter taste on his transparent tongue. He yelled, "Give me back my family, you soulless bastard!"

He stepped forward and the darkness pulled at him. A faint, ghostly voice echoed his name, calling to him from within. Her song of sorrow drifted through the air and awakened a deep, carnal desire he'd thought long extinct. Without remembering taking any further steps, he found himself just inches from the doorway—from the darkness.

"I need you, Nardus," called a voice from the darkness, drenched in anguish.

"Vitara!" he screamed.

The darkness swallowed him.

CHAPTER THREE

The darkness, thick as tar, crawled onto his bones and wrapped itself around him like a swaddling blanket. It pulled at his feet and made each step harder than the previous. Its backbreaking weight crushed him, but he didn't stop. Each step carried him closer to his family and their presence grew stronger within his heart.

My beautiful Vitara and Shanara. My brave Shardan. My precious Savannah. I'm coming for you.

Memories of them flooded his mind, excited him, and drove him forward.

But where am I going? No idea. Damn this darkness.

Stopping, even for a moment, wasn't an option. Fear of sinking into the darkness and being lost forever ate away at his mind like moths on wool blankets.

Every direction looked the same: sightless, endless darkness.

Now would be a great time to have a torch.

Nothing in particular drove him down his current path—no feeling or sight he could latch onto.

Madness. Madness and darkness. My only friends.

Doubt rose in his mind like dough, expanding with each passing moment. In the beginning, his dedication to the quest didn't waver, and he kept his focus razor-sharp, but now he struggled to remember what'd brought him to this wretched place.

I should just give in to the darkness. No one would ever know. No one will miss me or care that I'm gone anyway. And there's no end to this madness!

He knew he'd never give up, but the thought of doing so eased his tension a bit.

He felt trapped inside a vortex of swirling darkness, devoid of most of his five senses, but he continued to pump his legs and fight against the darkness. The sensation of actual movement, of making progress, eluded him.

I might be walking in circles.

Every passing moment multiplied his level of frustration and pushed his sanity to its very edge. He screamed as loud as he could, sensed the strain on vocal cords he no longer possessed, but produced not even a whisper of sound.

This darkness is maddening!

How long had he been trudging through the darkness? Hours? Days? Weeks? Years? Never had he felt so utterly alone. Had he the means, he surely would've vomited.

Is this what it's like to be separated from You, Ɛ̌ǎţūr? Is this my fate? My damnation? To be trapped in this darkness forever?

Madness!

Emotions of every kind bombarded him from every direction. He felt amiss. His mind swirled with incoherency.

"Give in to me," a voice hissed in his ear.

Had he any skin, he would've jumped from it. He turned toward the voice, but found only darkness.

"Where are you?" Had he actually spoken the words, or had they only echoed in his mind?

"Everywhere," said the voice. "You needn't be afraid. Just let yourself go."

He grabbed at the darkness and, for a brief moment, swore something slick and wet had slid through his fingers. An image of the pedestal and its three-headed snake slithered up from his memory, and he shuddered.

Did I really hear a voice, or am I truly going mad?

Confusion sickened him.

Nothing here makes sense.

His thoughts outpaced his thumping phantom heart.

Voices. Snakes. Darkness. Family. Death.

Madness!

"No!" He grabbed his head with his hands, hoping it would stop his spinning mind.

I need to focus.

He continued tramping through the heavy, hopeless darkness in the same general direction, and refused to ponder where he headed. He concentrated his energy on clearing his mind. He visualized every thought as it passed, categorized it, and filed it away.

Slowly, the thoughts twisted and wrapped around each other, melding together until they formed a singular and coherent one. In his mind's eye, the picture clarified, and he couldn't deny its significance or power.

Vitara, my light. Show me the path. Lead me to you. Be my reasoning in this cesspool of madness.

Birthed by his thoughts, or so he imagined, a single, faint beam of light pushed through the darkness and caught his eye.

This can't be coincidence. Thank you, my love.

Its origin looked to be miles away, yet its penetrating warmth caressed his face like a ray of sunlight. It fixated him and drew him toward it like a moth to flame. His legs carried him toward it without need of thought.

The light. A beacon of hope. A lighthouse for ships on stormy seas. It called him. Beckoned him. Pulled him. Its intensity increased as he drew nearer, and his desire to know its source pushed every other thought aside.

The darkness relinquished its hold on him, and he ran as fast as his legs would carry him toward the light.

Sanctuary.

Farther and farther he ran, yet the light kept its distance from him. How far must he travel?

Stay still so I can reach you. I need you.

"Let me come to you," it whispered.

His body jerked to a halt. He froze in the darkness—both in body and mind. Every inch of him ached with desire to be in the light.

Please don't keep me waiting!

The light rushed toward him like a shooting star. As it neared, he realized it seeped around a door that stood slightly ajar in its frame. He blinked, and the door stood before him. Nothing existed beyond the boundaries of the frame as the darkness firmly held its ground.

Nardus traced the lettering on the wooden door with his eyes, remembering every cut he'd so painstakingly made into its beautiful loral pine surface. Tears drifted down his cheeks with every beautiful image conjured in his mind.

Vitara. Shardan. Shanara. Savannah.

He'd walked through that very same door countless times, and never once had he stopped to ponder its significance. His heart threatened to burst from his chest at any moment.

"Home," he whispered. "I'm finally home."

His hands trembled with anticipation as he imagined what he'd find on the other side of the door. He reached to push it open farther.

Light fell on his hand and stopped his motion and his heart. Fresh new skin covered his hand where the light caressed it. He pulled his hand away from the light and back into darkness. He wiped his cheek, felt the moisture of tears on his fingers, and could barely contain his joy at its wonderfully wet sensation.

He pushed the door open as far as it would go, letting the warm light bathe him from head to toe. Its warmth on his skin overwhelmed him. New skin covered his naked body. He touched his left bicep—soft and free of scars. But why would it have been scarred?

Like a small child discovering something new in the world, a loud giggle escaped from his parted lips. His cheeks flushed with the pure sound of his laughter—literally music to his ears compared with the vacuum-silence of the darkness he'd waded through.

He stepped through the doorway and onto the cool, hard, dirt floor. He welcomed the roughness of it against his bare feet. He swore a lifetime had passed since he'd experienced anything as real, and he never wanted to lose the feeling of it again.

A lump caught in his throat, and his eyes welled with tears as he drank in the woman across the room. For the second time in as many minutes, his heart failed to beat. She sat in front of a large fireplace with her back to him. Her auburn hair twisted and curled down to the small of her back. The light from the fire shone through her sheer white robe and silhouetted her beautiful body.

My angel.

His head spun like a top and his vision wobbled. He grabbed the edge of the door for support. His lungs burned with fire, and the sensation made no sense until he realized he'd stopped breathing.

You've always left me breathless.

With a broad smile that he hoped would never fade, he breathed deeply.

"Vitara," he whispered, barely forcing her name from his trembling lips.

"I've been waiting for you." She rose from the bearskin pelt and turned toward him. Even cloaked in shadow, her violet eyes sizzled with energy.

Her beauty surpassed that of his memories of her. The burden he'd carried over her loss vaporized. He'd lived in his unbalanced world for so long and his journey had seemed endless, yet here he faced it. Everything fell back into place.

I'm really home.

He ran to her, wrapped his arms around her, pulled her tight, and lifted her off her feet. He buried his head in her hair and breathed in the wonderful scents of cedar and lilies. He lowered her back to the floor and then cupped her face in his hands. She looked up at him. Her thin cheekbones raised along with the corners of her mouth.

He leaned down and lightly pressed his lips against hers—so warm and moist. She gently parted his lips with her tongue and he quivered with desire. She tasted of freshly ground mint.

Reluctantly, he pulled back and looked deep into her eyes. He fought desperately to hold back his tears. "I've been so lost without you."

She stroked his head with her hand. "I'm here now, my love."

"I thought I'd never see you again." He lost the fight and the tears streamed down his face.

"It's okay." She gently wiped his tears away with her thumbs. "We'll never have to part again."

"Never," he agreed. "I would've ripped the sun from the sky and destroyed the world just to hold you in my arms again."

Her eyes spoke volumes of seduction, consuming his every thought and twisting them into unbridled desire. He ached for her—to be with her.

"Lie with me," she whispered. She pulled him toward the bedding laid out in the corner of the room. He offered her no resistance.

She pushed his naked body down onto the bedding and stood over him. Lightly, playfully, she tugged at the ends of the lace fabric binding her robe.

He swallowed hard. She smiled as the last bit of lace loosened from its bow. She untwisted the two ends of the lace and let them fall to her sides.

Her body glistened with perspiration between the ends of the parting fabric. The robe slid from her soft shoulders and fell on the floor, leaving her fully exposed before him. She embodied perfection.

He couldn't have kept from smiling if he'd tried. "What did I ever do to deserve you?"

"It is I who doesn't deserve you." She knelt beside him and tenderly kissed his lips.

He wanted to ravish her, and the thought of it made him feel like an animal. She softly nipped at his neck and pulled his skin with her teeth. Chills marched across his skin like a microscopic army. He grabbed fistfuls of bedding to restrain himself from taking hold of her and pulling her onto himself.

As if reading his thoughts, she swung her right leg over him and straddled his waist. Her hot, moist flesh felt like a smoldering inferno against his.

"I'd do anything for you, Nardus—" She licked her lips and smiled wickedly. "—anything."

He smiled up at her and then pulled her over to his side.

Why am I resisting her? She's my wife.

Her brow wrinkled. "Is something wrong?"

He couldn't think of a single logical reason to fight the urge. "No. I just want to savor this moment. It's been so long since we've been together." He gave her his best smile, but he knew she saw right through him.

She lightly stroked his chest with her soft, delicate fingers. "It's okay, my love. You just need to relax."

The notion that something felt out of place nipped at his nerves. He shook it off as best he could and stared into her eyes again. "I could lose myself in your beautiful violet eyes."

She leaned over him and kissed his forehead, the tip of his nose, and then his lips. "There's nothing I'd like more than that. Now make love to me before you drive me mad with desire."

He wanted to give in and just live in the moment, but something kept him from doing so. Even though his body urged him to take her, his conscience nagged him to be cautious.

He sighed and stared up at the wood ceiling. "I can't."

I must be mad.

Something was definitely out of place, but he couldn't put his finger on its source.

"Please don't do this to me, Nardus." The hurt in her voice stabbed his heart like a hot poker. "I can't survive without you. It's been so long, my love. I *need* you."

He looked at her again and—for a fleeting moment—thought he saw hatred in her eyes.

What's wrong with me?

"Am I not pleasing to you?" Tears pooled in the corners of her eyes.

"I'm sorry Vitara, but I just can't do this right now." He pushed her away.

"I'm your wife. It's your duty as my husband. When we were joined together, we swore to be one flesh!"

Anger burned in her eyes, and he felt ashamed for denying her. Tears fell from her eyes. She sat up and turned her back to him.

He sat up, pulled her close, and wrapped her in his arms. "You're right, my love. Please forgive me. I'm just not thinking clearly."

Pull yourself together, Nardus.

She turned over in his arms and stared into his eyes. "I've been without you for so long, my love. Please don't deny me this pleasure."

He ran his fingers through her thick, luscious hair and stroked her back and neck. Her soft, radiant skin glowed like a woman with child.

"My angel." He kissed her soft lips.

She turned his head, ran her tongue along the inside of his ear, and then sucked on the lobe. Chills danced across his body and he trembled.

"I need you, Nardus," she murmured in his ear.

The warmth of her breath brought him back to the edge.

How can I keep denying her? She only wants what I've been dreaming of for so long.

He heard himself say, "I'm yours," though his lips never moved. He fell from the edge of reason and found himself completely under her spell.

The smell of her drove his desire. He grabbed the back of her head and smashed her mouth against his. Their teeth clicked together as he rammed his tongue deep into her mouth. They rolled around on the bedding and came to a rest with him on top of her.

He pinned her arms over her head with one of his hands and held himself up with the other. She giggled as he kissed her all over. He loved the sound of her laughter. She wrapped her legs around his waist and pulled him to her.

She closed her eyes and bit the edge of her lower lip. A drop of blood streaked the side of her porcelain cheek. "Take me now," she moaned softly.

He needed no further prompting and obliged. They moved together as one, synchronized to perfection.

He loved her so much. This is where he wanted to spend the rest of his life. With her. Making love to her. Forever.

My everything.

He looked down at her just as she opened her eyes. She licked the blood from the side of her mouth and smiled.

In that moment, behind the exterior of her vibrant eyes, he caught a glimpse of the real her, of her true nature. He saw what she really was, what she was capable of, and it sickened him. He gagged on his own spit and nearly vomited.

She's not Vitara.

CHAPTER FOUR

Nardus threw himself backward and crawled across the floor, putting as much distance between himself and the false Vitara as he possibly could. He held his hand up. "Stay away from me! I know what you are!"

She crawled toward him, pleading with him, "Don't do this to me, Nardus! I love you!"

"I see you now. There's no love in you. She's dead, and you're not her!" He kicked at her as she tried pulling herself onto him again. "Get off me! You're not my wife!"

"If I'm not your wife, as you say, then be done with me. Run me through with the fireplace poker. End my life." She sat up and raised her arms in submission. Tears streaked down her face and pooled in little mud pits on the dirt floor. "I've nothing to live for if I don't have you."

"I've seen what lies beneath your porcelain skin." He pointed at her. "You're the darkness that fills this wretched place. You distort the truth with your mezhik derk. Find another soul to feed on. Mine's not for the taking!"

"Does it matter what or who you think I am? I'm begging you, Nardus, stay with me. I'm her, even if you can't see it. Your mind is so twisted with madness that you can't see the truth sitting right in front of you." Her tears turned crimson as they fell from her eyes. "Lie with me, Nardus. We'll be together forever."

"I'd rather be damned to *Ef Demd Dhä* than spend another moment with you!" He pulled himself up from the floor.

She jumped to her feet and stepped in front of him, blocking his path. He shied away from her gaze. "There are only two paths, Nardus. Either take my life, or be with me—your wife. The choice is yours, but I promise you'll never regret the second one."

He shoved her aside and walked through the door only to find that he'd walked right back into the same room.

"What kind of madness is this?" He looked back through the doorway and into the same room again. He spat on the floor. "Damn your mezhik."

A wicked smile curled her lips as she crossed her arms. "You cannot walk away from here. As I said, there are only two paths. You must choose one."

How could I be so foolish?

He'd been warned of the temptations he might face, but still his emotions bettered him. She looked and sounded so much like Vitara, but a void filled the space where her heart should've been.

A black hole of hatred.

"Two paths..." he muttered, turning away.

"Choose me and you'll never regret it," she said.

"I can't allow myself to be with you. You're only a shadow of who she is—a flawed image conjured by my twisted mind."

He ran his fingers through his hair and massaged his temples. "This isn't my destiny. I don't belong here." He closed his eyes. "You'll never be her. You can't be."

"So you've made your choice then. Kill me. I won't resist."

He opened his eyes and turned back to her. "I will not kill you while you wear her skin!"

"Wearing her skin," she mused.

He felt the veins in his forehead and neck bulge and his whole body shuddered violently. He shook his fist at her, "Show me your true form, demon, and I'll gladly take your life!"

She laughed at him. "Listen to yourself, Nardus. You sound like a raving lunatic, my love. I *am* your wife." She raised her arms above her head and turned in a circle. "This is my true form. I cannot shed my skin as I did the robe. I'm no serpent." She moved toward the fireplace and plopped down on the bearskin pelt.

She was right about one thing: the circumstances were complete and utter madness, and his hotheadedness furthered the despair of the situation. He slowed his breathing and focused on reining in his temper. Spent of energy and mentally depleted, no other solutions arose to free himself of the situation. His legs trembled. How would he deal with the likes of her?

"It appears we're at an impasse." His head pulsed.

"So it seems." She lay back on the pelt and closed her eyes. "I can wait here for all eternity, Nardus. How long do you really think you can resist me?"

"Forever." He walked over to the corner of the room and sat down on the bedding. "Now leave me to my thoughts."

What've I done?

Never in his life had he hated himself as much as he did right then. His recklessness seemed to know no bounds. He drew his knees to his chest and rested his arms and head on them.

Foolish to the end.

"Wallow in your madness all you want, *husband*. Just remember that I had no hand in bringing you here. You accomplished that all on your own."

On my own? Bah! If she only knew the half of it.

He rolled onto his side, stared at the wall for a few moments, and closed his eyes.

I'll find a solution. I have no choice.

Nardus retreated further in his mind, seeking refuge from the false Vitara. The very thought of her naked body left him cold and disgusted. She tainted the memories of his beloved Vitara, and he couldn't just sit there and bear witness to it further.

Something must be done with her.

Somehow, he'd find a way to rectify the situation and restore the damage she'd caused. But where would he start? The situation left him devoid of solutions. He couldn't walk away, and, despite his certainty of her falsehood, her physical likeness to Vitara overwhelmed him. He'd never lay a hand on her while she maintained that form. Even if he were to, he estimated it wouldn't end well for him. Instinct told him that both choices she gave him would garner the same result for him.

Rest assured, I'll find your poison, demon!

Very few times in his life had he encountered a problem that held no solution. He set his jaw. This wouldn't be another. If he concentrated fully on the problem—looked at it from another perspective—a solution would present itself. One always did—without fail—and his true quest depended on finding it.

His thoughts drifted to Vitara and the moment their paths had first crossed.

It'd been a breezy spring day, not a cloud in the sky. He swam in the lake that lay just outside the village. She walked along the shore with some of her friends.

Even from a distance, as his eyes slowly caressed her flawless, porcelain skin, he knew they were made for each other and he wouldn't rest until he had her. He'd never been with a woman before, and he knew at that moment that she'd be the only one he'd ever be with. She'd be his one and only, for eternity. They completed each other.

Her memories filled him with joy. Her warm, naked body rested against his. Her soft arm draped around his waist and her warm breath caressed the back of his neck. The touch of her lips on his skin sent his heart racing.

Nardus's eyes shot open as his mind raced from the past and forced him back into the room.

I'm not alone.

CHAPTER FIVE

F alse Vitara's relentless pursuit—and the sight of her naked body—gnawed on his nerves. Nothing Nardus said or did deterred her. Her lust for his soul filled her every breath, and he knew she wouldn't be satisfied until he gave in to her.

Her magnetic scent saturated his every breath. It took every ounce of willpower to keep his animalistic lust for her at bay.

He'd lost track of the days, and his hope of freedom dwindled. Only his dreams kept him from giving up.

Nightly, or at least what he imagined as such, he traipsed through an enormous library. Honey-gold dorus pine shelves lined the walls and stretched from the polished white marble floors to the thirty-foot ceilings above.

Rows of marble pillars, swirled in hues of brilliant blue and grey, ran parallel to the northern and southern walls. Massive chandeliers hung from the great arched ceiling, each loaded with hundreds of crystal shards. The soft, natural light from the high windows refracted through the crystals, casting miniature rainbows across the surface of everything.

Drawings, maps, and books filled every inch of space on the shelves, most of which were written in languages he'd never seen before. He'd had no idea there were so many languages in the world until he thumbed through a few of them. The thought of any one person being able to read them all perplexed him.

He figured most of them were dead languages, their scribblings forever lost to interpretation. The items followed no logical organization, and he found no evident markings or signs on the shelves to the contrary.

Every detail of the dream was clear in his mind—the texture of how each book felt in his hands, the smell of the shelves, the resounding *clicks* of his boot heels on the white marble floors. Everything felt so real. Each time he dreamt of the library, he experienced an inner peace so distinct and fulfilling that he abhorred the thought of waking again. It was his sanctuary amidst the relentless pursuit of his captor.

Nardus sat in the corner of the room, his legs drawn to his chest and his arms wrapped around them, pondering the meaning of the dream. Before his family had been slaughtered, he was a man bent on the belief in the natural order of things. Even still, in a world full of chaos, he believed a thread of order could be found if one were to look hard enough.

He knew the dream held some great significance, but he couldn't put his finger on its source. Parts of the picture were missing or hidden from him.

Maybe I'm looking at this dream the wrong way.

A crazy thought forced its way into his mind and worked its way to his lips. "What if it's real?" He laughed hollowly, but the sound of the words rang true.

"This *is* real, my love. I'm real, and I'm all you need." Every word dripped from her mouth with lust. "Why must you keep insisting on making us both suffer? We *need* each other, Nardus. We *belong* together."

Every time she spoke, he prayed for deafness. Her words were a seductive poison, and, the longer he endured them, the closer he came to conceding.

Stay out of my head, demon. I'll not give in to you.

"Ignore me all you want," she said. "But sooner or later you'll cave. No one's ever succeeded in resisting my charm. You won't be the first."

Nardus looked over at her. "Then you admit you're not her?"

"Twisting my words won't free you, my love." She squeezed her breasts with her hands. "I'm as much her as you've ever known."

Nardus turned away from her, unwilling to look at her nakedness and twisted smile. He blocked her from his mind as best he could and turned his thoughts back to his dream.

How can I test if it's real?

Sitting in his corner, trapped in a world between worlds, he was naked.

In his dream, amongst the books and freedom, he was fully clothed. He'd never woken up from his dream to find himself clothed and therefore it seemed logical that he couldn't take something physical in or out of the dream world.

Am I aware of this wretched place while I'm dreaming?

He couldn't remember any thoughts from his dream and concluded that it was unlikely.

Do I need to be asleep to go there?

Now that was a question he could test, and so he set to work willing himself into the grand library. He closed his eyes, visualized the white marble floors, and strained to hear the *click* of his boot heels against the stones as he walked across them.

It's not just in my head. I know this place exists.

His eyes clamped shut, his cheeks puffed out, his brow furrowed, and his nose wrinkled as he willed himself into the dream world. He strained with every ounce of his energy, bent on achieving the impossible. No matter how hard he tried, the room refused to materialize.

You're a fool, Nardus. This whole idea's madness.

Another thought struck him like a bolt of lightning, filling him with a renewed energy: *purpose.*

Maybe I just need a specific reason to summon the room.

Trapped with the false Vitara, every bone in his body ached to be rid of her. He needed to escape.

Maybe I can find a solution in one of the books.

He wanted to kick himself for not thinking of it before. He could've saved a lot of time if he'd thought of it long ago. Then again, he'd had no recollection of his current state inside the dream. The smile on his face morphed into a frown and his brow furrowed.

Hopefully I can find a book written in a language I can read.

The sensation of crisp paper between his fingers registered in his mind. He jerked his eyes open. A smile spread across his face as he stared at the large, leather-bound book sitting on his lap. He held the book propped open against the edge of a honey-colored oak table. Two large piles of books sat atop the table. Excitement fluttered in his stomach.

He remembered everything.

The false Vitara. The darkness. The quest to get my family back!

His hands trembled as he leafed through a few pages of the book in his lap, but his mood quickly soured as he found himself unable to decipher the cryptic symbols it held.

"How's this going to work when I can't read a single word of this book? Cyrus, *Ef ʒäfn Dhä*. Bah! Try writing in an understandable language, you fool!" He slammed the book shut and tossed it on the table with the others.

"Oh, my!" exclaimed a male voice from across the table.

Nardus gasped as a small man, no taller than two-and-a-half feet, grunted as he climbed from his chair onto the table.

The man clicked his tongue repeatedly with reprimand. "That's no way to treat a book."

The little man pushed his glasses up the length of his elongated nose and pulled a swatch of beige cloth from his pocket. He picked up the discarded book and carefully wiped its surface with the cloth, muttering under his breath and clicking his tongue now and again during the lengthy process.

Seemingly satisfied with his work, the little man placed the cloth back in his pocket and then gently laid the book back down. The orange irises of his eyes reflected his foul mood as he glared at Nardus through thick, wire-rimmed glasses. "Respect the books, or I'll show you out."

The books are nearly as big as him!

Nardus chortled to himself.

"You think I'm incapable of removing you?" questioned the little man. He snorted and crossed his arms at his chest, and the scowl on his face made his thin grey lips pucker like a gulpfish.

Nardus coughed as he struggled to choke down another fit of laughter. "I'd never make an assumption like that. That kind of thinking can get a man killed before he even knows he's in danger."

The little man continued glaring at him, but his features softened some. "As well you shouldn't."

Nardus chewed on his lower lip, carefully weighing his next words before speaking. "To be honest, I've never seen the likes of someone such as you."

"Oh, my. Never seen a gordak?" His bushy, white eyebrows bobbed up and down as he chuckled, his warm smile vanquishing the last remnants of his disapproval. "Not hard to believe, I suppose." He smoothed the wrinkles in his turquoise shirt with his three-fingered hands. "I'm fairly certain I'm the last of my kind. It's sad, to be sure."

"I'm Nardus." He stuck his hand out toward the gordak.

"Nardus, you say? Well, I suppose you must be." The little man grabbed Nardus's finger between his small hands and shook it vigorously. "I am Gnaudius, of House L'Dorak, Librarian of Nasduron." His firm grip surprised Nardus. "You can call me Gnaud if you'd like." His face beamed.

"Gnaud it is, then." Nardus leaned back in the chair and crossed his legs at his ankles. It'd been a long time since he'd had a conversation with another individual, outside of the painful ones with the false Vitara. The prospect of a newfound source of interaction elated him.

Nardus twisted in his chair and craned his neck. "What is this place?"

Gnaud's voice went up an octave. "This is the Great Library of Nasduron."

Nardus turned back to Gnaud, his brow furrowed. "Nasduron? I've never heard of it."

Gnaud gasped. "ȥätūr's mercy. Never? The City Beneath the Sea? Ring a bell?"

Nardus sighed loudly. "Nope."

Gnaud plopped down on the table. "I suppose the legend of this place may have died before your time."

"Suppose so." Nardus leaned toward the table and rested his arms on it. "Why was it called the City Beneath the Sea?"

Gnaud chortled. "Oh, my. That is a story for another time, but let's suffice to say we're sitting at the bottom of the Gelu Ocean."

Nardus twisted his finger in his ear. "Say again? I swear I heard you say we're at the bottom of the ocean."

"You heard it correctly." Gnaud hopped off the table, settled back into his chair, and disappeared behind the pile of books.

Under the ocean? How's that possible? Then again, how did I even get here?

Nardus cleared his throat and leaned over the table. "So... how did I get here, Gnaud? Did I walk in here? Was I just suddenly here? Or have I been here awhile?"

Gnaud peered up at Nardus, his eyes enlarged by his glasses. "What do you think happened?"

"It was sudden… I think." Nardus scratched his head and sat back down. "You don't seem at all surprised that I'm here. Why is that?"

The edge of the table muffled Gnaud's voice, and Nardus had to strain to make out his words. "I've been expecting you."

Nardus jumped up from the chair, and it fell over with a loud *thwack*. The ruckus echoed through the room. "Expecting me?" Leaning over the table, Nardus could just make out the mischievous grin spread across Gnaud's furry little face.

"Surprised?" Gnaud thumbed through a book.

Nardus stuttered, "What did… how the…" His brow crumpled as he tried to find the right words. None of his thoughts seemed to form a sentence—or anything coherent for that matter.

"Ah." Gnaud smiled again. He looked up at Nardus with a sparkle in his eyes. "It was through prophecy, my friend." A hint of certainty laced his words.

Nardus had heard the word prophecy before, but had no direct knowledge of any of them. His life was pathetic at best, and the notion of one being written about him exceeded his comprehension.

Why would anyone have written about me? I'm no one.

"Oh, my. I can see the confusion written all over your face." Gnaud jumped back onto the table, waddled over to its center, and plopped down. "Sit down, my friend, and I'll fill you in on a few of the details."

Nardus righted his fallen chair and sat back down. "I thought prophecies involved significant people and events. Why would there be one about me? I'm nothing. No one. Less than that, even."

"ʿäṭūr's mercy! Surely you must know there's no such thing as an insignificant person." He pushed his glasses back up his nose. "Every breath, every choice, every life makes a ripple in the pond. Not acting upon something creates a ripple just as big as if you'd acted. No choice is still a choice you make.

"Every action creates a chain of reactions. Those actions create their own reactions, and the cycle continues forever. A ripple created thousands of years ago still blurs the waters of tomorrow with its continual chain of reactions."

Nardus stared at his folded hands in his lap. "I'm sure that in some twisted way that makes sense to you, but I'm not so sure I follow or even believe your words."

"Your non-belief in my words makes no difference. They're true without question. Let me give you a brief example."

Gnaud cleared his throat. "Say you're hunting in the woods and come across a rabbit. You kill this rabbit five minutes before a starving fox has a chance to, and then the fox dies because you've taken its food.

"When this fox, who happened to be a mother of three, dies, her pups go out looking for her and are killed by a wolf. Because of this, the population of foxes has been put in jeopardy, and an overpopulation of rabbits may have been sparked. One simple, small act ripples through nature. I could go on and on, but it would just be more examples of the same."

"So, you're saying I shouldn't kill the rabbit then?"

"Oh, my." Gnaud gasped. "That really doesn't matter. It's not the point. What's important is knowing that every decision you make has consequences, whether good or bad. You do what you must, but be cognizant of the ripples you create in doing so."

"I guess I can follow what you're saying. Not sure I ever think about the consequences of my actions though. At least not until after the fact."

"I cannot tell you what to do, but I pray that ʔäʈūr guides your mind, your heart, and your tongue. There's a darkness out there that preys on ignorance and innocence. It skillfully weaves small seeds of truth into its fervent lies to a point where they seem valid and ring true on the surface. If you look no deeper than that, you'll be led astray."

Darkness. I certainly know of it.

Nardus sat back up in his chair. "So, what does this prophecy say about me, Gnaud? What kind of a ripple will I create? Or have created?"

Gnaud pulled at the grey hairs on his furry chin. "There are always three forks to a prophecy. Two by choice, and one by the lack of choosing."

"Which path is the right path, Gnaud?"

"ʔäʈūr's mercy! That's a question without an answer. Sometimes there are three right paths, and sometimes there are none. The only thing you can do is trust in the wisdom and guidance of ʔäʈūr and let Him lead you down the right path. Whatever you do, never let yourself be led by or trust what's in your heart, for within the heart lies deceit."

"But that seems so backward. My life's always been a straight path, led solely by my heart. It's what drives me, the only thing that keeps me alive. Daily, my mind tells me to give up, but the love of my family fills my heart and pushes me forward."

"Love is indeed a wonderful, powerful thing, but it can also cause you to do terrible things."

"Fine. Agreed. Now, let's get back to the subject at hand, this prophecy you mentioned I'm in." Gnaud just stared at him with a blank expression. "You're not going to tell me about this prophecy, are you?"

"If it were that simple, Nardus, I'd be glad to. The fact of the matter is that there isn't just one prophecy about you."

"More than one?" Nardus sank back in the chair. "How many are we talking?"

"There are numerous volumes surrounding the life of you and your family."

Nardus leaned forward again, placing his arms on the table. "Numerous volumes?" He eyed Gnaud. "Why? What's so special about my life? My family's dead. What am I missing here?" He leaned back in his chair again, his mind unable to wrap itself around the idea of his life being significant.

"How—"

Gnaud put his hand out, and a look of sadness replaced the smile he'd been wearing. His round shoulders slouched as though under tremendous pressure, and his head lowered toward the table. He seemed to have aged a hundred years within a few seconds. His sullen demeanor left Nardus deflated.

Nardus wasn't sure he wanted to hear about the prophecies anymore. He was unsure about everything.

Gnaud drew in a deep breath, held it for a few moments, and then let it out. He looked up from the table with resolve in his eyes. The sparkle that had been there before was gone.

"You're the key to many branches of prophecy, Nardus. Every decision you make will impact the future of the Ancient Realm. Be wary of the path you choose. You may wind up being the hero, the villain, a victim, or a combination of the three. For your sake, and the sake of all those in the Ancient Realm, I pray you're the former."

"Why me?" was all Nardus could think to say.

He was ready to go back and let the false Vitara take his soul away, freeing himself of any unrequested responsibility.

I don't want any part of this. I just want my family back.

But he'd lose his family forever if he gave up, and he couldn't allow that to happen.

Gnaud sighed and shrugged. "One may never know the reasons he is chosen for his destiny. One can only trust in the wisdom of Ɂäʈūr and follow Him and His plan as best as possible."

"Bah." Nardus chuffed. "If Ɂäʈūr were a wise and all-knowing God, He sure wouldn't've chosen me. He sat back and watched as my family was slaughtered, and now He looks to me to save this *pathetic* world? Maybe He should've thought that one through a bit more. Perhaps I would've been more willing to do His bidding if my family were still alive!" His face burned with anger.

"Sometimes the least likely person makes for the best choice." Gnaud removed his glasses, fogged them with his breath, and wiped them with a cloth he pulled from his pocket. "I've never been one to question the wisdom of Ɂäʈūr. He placed me here knowing I would've been just as happy spending the rest of my life with my family. I felt His calling, but the choice was mine. I don't regret my decision."

"It makes no difference what I believe," said Nardus with a note of finality. "Right now, I have a problem to solve, and I need your help." He pushed his hands through his tangled hair. "Are you willing to help me, or not?"

Gnaud put his glasses back on and stood. He carefully straightened his shirt, and then looked Nardus in the eye. "I'm the librarian." His voice oozed with authority. "If there's a book that can possibly help solve your problem, I'll know of it."

"Well…" Nardus scratched the back of his head. "I went through *Zhäíʈfäí Fäíʈe.*"

Gnaud gasped.

"And now I'm being held captive by some sort of demon."

"Oh, my. The guardian of the gateway." Gnaud's tone made Nardus squirm in his chair. "This is a grave matter, indeed. What sort of madness would cause you to enter the gateway?" Gnaud's eyes narrowed. "And don't even think of lying to me."

Nardus stared Gnaud straight in the eyes. "My family. There's nothing I wouldn't do for them."

"Those are dangerous words, my friend."

"That they may be, but they're true to my heart. I've already made my choice, and there's no going back for me. Now make yours."

Gnaud plopped back down on the table with a sigh. "I'll help you, my friend, and I pray to Ɂäṭūr that I don't live to regret it."

"So do I," said Nardus. "So do I."

Gnaud repeatedly uttered "Oh, my" to himself as he stroked the fur on his chin with his left hand, completely consumed in thought. His right hand shot into the air, led by a pointed finger, only to be withdrawn a moment later.

Thankful that Gnaud kept his muttering to himself, Nardus's thoughts drifted to Vitara and the children. In his mind's eye, their cold, dead bodies lie in an open grave beneath the sacred heart tree. His gaze is met by mauled faces, hollow eyes, and blank stares. Suffocated by their pain, he gasped for air, but it did little good. He tightened his stomach and clenched his fists and willed the tears to recede.

I'm coming for you.

"I have it!" Gnaud snapped his fingers. He shot straight up, and some youth returned to his face as well. He vaulted from the table in a forward somersault, landed on his feet, and then quickly disappeared within the labyrinth of shelves.

A few minutes later, a large book floated toward the table where Nardus sat. The book halted beside his chair.

"A little help?" squeaked Gnaud from under the book.

Nardus reached down and grabbed the book. He grunted as he lifted it up to the table. The book must've weighed three or four times as much as Gnaud. He couldn't believe the little gordak had managed to carry it from one of the shelves all the way over to the table. He felt a tad bit guilty for not offering to help.

Gnaud jumped into his chair and then onto the table. Small beads of sweat glistened as they hung from the hairs on his furry forehead. Gnaud gave Nardus a tight-lipped glance, but made no mention of being put out.

The book looked thousands of years old, much older than any of the others Nardus had seen in the library. Its soft leather cover, faded and worn, donned intricate rune patterns pressed into it. Nardus imagined the pockmarks in the corners of its cover once contained gemstones, but all of them were now lost or looted. A tear sprawled halfway down the length of its spine.

"Oh, my." Gnaud inspected the book and clicked his tongue. "Maybe we should rethink opening this old girl."

"You said the fate of the world lies in my hands, Gnaud." A lump caught in Nardus's throat as he thought about the weight of his words. "If my fate lies within the pages of this book then I need to know. We have no choice, my furry friend. Let's ease her open."

Gnaud solemnly nodded, punctuating it with an exaggerated sigh. "Be careful with her, then. She's one of my favorites."

Nardus held his breath and carefully pulled open the cover. The binding held.

So far, so good.

The veins in his neck bulged and pulsed as he stared at its yellowed pages. Hundreds of years of use had worn the paper thin and made the pages nearly transparent. His hand trembled as he reached for the corner of the first page.

Steady, Nardus.

"Ʒätūr's mercy," said Gnaud, adding to Nardus's anxious state. "Careful now."

Sweat poured down Nardus's face and the back of his neck. He felt as if he'd ran for days; every muscle in his body ached with fatigue. He looked over at Gnaud, who appeared to be just as anxious as him, his whole fist shoved in his mouth. On another occasion the sight would've inspired a chuckle, but in the current situation it only frayed his nerves further.

Nardus closed his eyes as his fingers met the edge of the page, fearing it might turn to ash if he were to watch. He delicately slid his finger under the page and then closed his thumb on top of it, making sure he put as little pressure on the page as he could while still being able to turn it.

He swallowed hard.

As lightly as he could, Nardus lifted the page. The sound of ripping paper met his ears and his eyes shot open. He looked at the page between his fingers, but found no tear. However, he did find a worthless, two-faced gordak gasping for air as he rolled around on the table laughing. He clutched a torn piece of paper in his furry little hands.

Nardus wanted to take the book and squash the life out of Gnaud. Instead, he sank back in the chair, seeking relief from his near heart attack. "I ought to kill you," he said, out of breath.

"Oh, my!" Gnaud jumped up and retreated to the end of the table. "Harmless joke!"

"*Harmless*? Nearly caused my death is what you did," hissed Nardus.

He forced himself to push away the anger. He had no idea how long Gnaud had been left alone there, and he couldn't even imagine being the last of his kind.

Gnaud smoothed his shirt and then pushed his glasses back up his nose. "She may look a bit fragile, but you can't tear her pages. She was bound by a wizard." He smiled at Nardus and then winked. "Should've seen the look on your face, though!"

Nardus strained to produce a smile and pushed as much kindness into his voice as he could muster. "Now that you've had your fun, shall we move on?"

"Have at it." Gnaud plopped back down on the table.

With the tension of tearing the pages lifted from his shoulders, he rifled through the book like a lunatic. Page after page flew by, and none of its scribbling made sense. His heart sank lower with every page turn, and his frustration peaked. "What a waste!"

"You ever think that maybe I could read it?" Gnaud smiled from ear to ear—his pink mouse-ears poked out of his grey fur.

Wouldn't be surprised to find a tail stuffed into those trousers.

Nardus pictured Gnaud scurrying through the tunnels under Mortuus Terra like an oversized rat and broke out in a hearty laughter. "I suppose it hadn't crossed my mind."

"I have a knack for languages." Gnaud winked. "I believe that's why Ʒäṭūr chose me for the job."

"Well, then—" Nardus slapped his hand down on the open book. "Let's stop wasting time and find me the answer I'm looking for!"

† † †

Hours later, Nardus found the left side of his face soaked in his own drool. Sticky tendrils of saliva slowly pulled apart as he lifted his head from the puddle on the floor.

The scent of *her* turned his skin into gooseflesh. He had no doubt where he lay. His head throbbed, and his left arm burned with fire.

"I was beginning to think you were dead," she said with a laugh.

A torrent of images rushed through his mind and filled the space behind his eyes.

Books. So many books. And fire.

The fire seared his flesh. The fire seared his flesh with a word from one of the books. He had the answer he needed. It was part of him now—a reminder of temptation and the despair it can bring.

He opened his eyes and stared at the five letters burned into the flesh of his left forearm. Five fresh wounds upon his skin. Fresh wounds to set him free. Each one burned badly, yet nothing had felt so good in a long time.

He stood, kept his seared arm from her prying eyes, and walked over to where she sat. She looked up at him, and he smiled. "Get up."

With his right hand, he reached down and helped her to her feet. Her hand in his sickened him, but he didn't pull away.

"I told you the time would come when you could resist me no more," she said.

I really wish you were her.

He bent down, kissed her lips, and then her forehead. He let his cheek brush against hers as he placed his mouth next to her ear. She squeezed his hand with hers.

He whispered in her ear, "Goodbye," and then pulled away from her.

Her eyes narrowed as she looked up at him. "What do you mean goodbye? We've only just begun. You know you'll never leave here alive."

He smiled at her again. His lips parted, and her name fell from them as quietly as an autumn leaf falls from a tree: "*Akuji.*"

The force of the word—of her name—struck her like a thousand swords, piercing and slicing her flesh. Blood seeped from her wounds and rage and agony filled her eyes. Nardus watched, mesmerized, as finger-like shapes clawed underneath her skin. One by one, ghostly vapors in hues of green and blue burst from under her skin like festering boils.

Trapped souls? I could've been one of them.

The ground trembled with their deafening shrieks. Nardus closed his eyes and covered his ears with his hands as best he could, but the sticky warmth of blood ran from his ears, through his fingers, and down the sides of his neck.

Even with his eyes squeezed tight, the light from Akuji's exploding body blinded him. Its force sent him flying into the wall like a rag doll. When he opened his eyes again, the room spun around him and twisted and smashed into itself like a wad of paper.

Then the room vanished altogether, taking him with it.

CHAPTER SIX

It began with a symphony of bone-chilling howls: deep, dark, and close. Aria sat up in bed, covers clutched in her fists. Shadows stalked her from every direction as they lurked about and crept up the walls and across the wooden floors. Bloodcurdling screams joined the howls and prickled her skin.

ʔäṭūr, what's happening?

Under the door, a shadow slowly approached.

Papa? Or something else?

Aria released the covers and slid off the side of the bed and onto the floor. Thunder rumbled and quaked the cottage and sent her pulse racing. She reached under the bed and grabbed her bow. Her hands trembled, and she futzed with the string too long.

Hurry up, Aria!

Someone stood at the door. Had they knocked, or had it been her heart beating against her ribcage? She couldn't be certain.

Papa?

The flimsy knob rattled.

Finally, she strung the bow. She reached over and grabbed an arrow from the quiver that hung on the bedpost.

The knob turned.

She eased back up on the bed, rose on her knees, nocked the arrow, and aimed at the door. Sweat gathered at the nape of her neck and droplets ran down her spine.

The dry hinges creaked and moaned as the door slowly swung into the room.

She breathed softly and drew the string back; the tension shook her arm.

A long shadow stretched across the floor and crawled onto the foot of her bed. The silhouetted man stood in the doorframe for a few moments, a long blade clutched in his right fist and a deadly hook in his left.

Fear unhinged her, but her voice didn't quiver. "Move, and you're dead."

The string slid on her damp fingers. A few moments more, and the arrow would fire, her will or not.

"Easy, Aria. It's only me." Red entered the room.

Whoosh!

Aria jerked the bow to the left just as the arrow loosed. She screamed. Red cried out and ducked to his left, but not before the arrow tore a hole through his billowed shirtsleeve and thudded into the doorframe.

Aria dropped the bow and leapt off the bed. "Papa! Are you okay?" Hot tears blurred her vision.

Red turned toward the light, checked his sleeve, and whistled. "No blood, no harm."

Aria sobbed. "I'm so sorry, Papa. I didn't mean to shoot the arrow. The string slipped from my fingers."

Red set the long eaves knife and eaves hook on the floor and wrapped his strong arms around her. "It's okay, my princess warrior. You did the right thing. I'd rather you be ready and nervous than unprepared."

Aria nuzzled Red's broad chest. The rhythm of his slow-beating heart calmed her. "What's happening out there, Papa?"

Red kissed the top of her head. "That's what I'm about to go find out." He pulled away and knelt to grab his tools.

Aria went back over to the bed and grabbed her bow. She lifted the quiver off the post and over her head. "I'm coming with you."

Red's brow wrinkled, and he set his jaw. "You'll do no such thing. No matter what happens, stay inside and don't open the door for anyone."

"You know how strong I am. I could help—"

"No!" Red's glare rooted her to the floor. "Promise me, Aria. I can't go out there and do what must be done if I'm worrying about you."

Fear and anger drove her forward. "We've already lost Mama. I can't bear losing you, too."

Red's shoulders slumped a little. "There are so many things you don't know or understand. Once this is over, I will tell you everything, but for now you must trust me on this, Aria. No matter what you see and no matter what happens, stay inside. You're safe in here."

Red turned and left the room. Aria followed him into the living room. No candles burned, but light filtered through the sheer curtain over the lone window next to the front door. Red yanked the front door open, glanced back at her with a grimace, and then walked out into the screaming night and slammed the door behind himself.

Smoke reached her nostrils and she coughed. She ran over to the window and pulled the curtain back. Breath caught in her lungs, choked her like a half-swallowed apple, and brought her to her knees.

Dear 2ätūr!

A few hundred yards from their doorstep, the village burned. Mournful screams echoed in the night, several cutoff midstream. Red raced toward the village, but a massive beast blocked his path. The beast swung a double-edged axe wide, barely missing Red.

Red caught the beast under its elongated jaw with his eaves hook, and then lopped off its head with his long eaves knife. Several more of the beasts surrounded him. Aria rose to her feet and screamed. One of the beasts drove a dagger into Red's back and he dropped to his knees. Red's hook and knife tumbled to the ground.

Aria forgot everything Red had told her and threw the front door open. She nocked and loosed an arrow and it flew right through the back of the beast's head that'd stabbed Red.

Aria nocked another arrow and stood at the threshold. "Papa!" She loosed the arrow and bolted out of the house. The arrow met its mark and only two beasts remained. She fumbled for another arrow.

Another beast she hadn't seen broadsided her and drove her into the ground. She grunted under the beast's weight and couldn't draw a breath. Sharp claws ripped into the back of her hand and she released the bow. She screamed, but the beast clamped its giant, paw-like hand over her mouth and yanked her head backward. Pain shot down her spine and into her extremities, and a hot, white light blinded her for a few moments.

Papa!

The beast rose and pulled her up with him. He held her by her neck and her feet dangled several feet from the ground. The world rocked in her distorted vision.

Red knelt, his body and head held up by one of the beasts. They'd turned him around so he faced Aria. Sorrow filled his eyes and his lips moved, but he produced no words.

The beast that stood next to Red spoke, his voice thick and harsh. "This is all on your hands, Redante. All you had to do was follow through with your commitment and this could've been avoided."

"Papa!" Aria struggled against the beast's grip, but she had no leverage. In her hand, she held the head and shaft of a broken arrow. She'd find a way to use it to her advantage.

The beast continued, "Every living thing in this village will be slaughtered and every structure burned. All of this for one girl. How can she mean so much to you? Or the rest of them so little?"

Red coughed, but couldn't speak.

The beast took a double-edged battle axe from his back and stepped back.

"No!" screamed Aria.

The beast chopped off Red's head and Red's body fell forward and slumped on the ground. Lightning blitzed across the sky and lit everything like daylight. Blood dripped from Red's severed neck.

Every one of you will die!

Aria positioned the broken shaft in her hand so she could stab the beast that held her.

In front of them, a cloaked figure materialized out of the darkness. Aria froze. The figure lowered their brown hood, and their silver-eyed gaze burrowed through Aria's eyes and into her skull.

Pain erupted behind her forehead as a presence entered her mind and dug deep into her memories.

"She's the one," growled the cloaked man.

"Finish the others," said the beast.

The cloaked man pulled a large silver ring from within his cloak and looked up at the beast that held Aria. "Set her down so I can put this on her."

Aria's feet touched the ground and the beast loosened his hold on her neck. The cloaked man moved forward and shoved the solid ring against her neck. Aria leaned forward and thrust the arrow shaft upward, through the cloaked man's ribs and into his heart.

The cloaked man's eyes grew wide, he gasped, and dropped to his knees. Aria grabbed the silver ring, but somehow the back of it had gone right through her neck and now she wore it.

A flash in her peripheral vision. A clubbed fist to her head and the violent screams, howls, roar of fire, and thunder faded until nothing remained but perfect silence.

CHAPTER SEVEN

The late summer breeze felt nice on Alderan's face as he walked into the small meadow. A chest-high sea of yellow buffalo grass swayed back and forth, singing a sweet lullaby as its stocks gently rubbed together.

The meadow topped his list of favorite places to visit. He'd spent countless hours there, drinking in the scenery, yet its serene and simplistic beauty continued to send chills down his spine with every visit.

Butterflies fluttered in his stomach as his gaze floated past the far side of the meadow, above and beyond the towering sentries of mountain ash and pines, and locked onto the looming, white peaks of the great Procerus Mountains. "The Giants of the West."

From his vantage point, still a great distance away, they ascended high into the heavens.

The top of the world.

Deep within their valleys roamed giant, fire-breathing lizards—or so he'd been told. No one had claimed to have seen them for centuries, and the passes between the peaks were so high and treacherous that no one had ever traversed them and lived to tell of it.

"One day we'll meet, you and I." The notion excited and scared him simultaneously.

Another fact he'd prove—along with the existence of the fire-breathing lizards—were the Darrow Dwarves, a brutal and fierce race known for their battle skills. Rumors circled about their ancient city, Tectus, claiming it to be buried deep within the belly of the mountain—thousands of feet below the surface.

The sun descended below the forest line, casting finger shadows across the landscape. Alderan pushed through the thick grass and made his way to the small spring hidden at its center. He knelt beside the spring and splashed water on his face. Its icy touch refreshed him after the long day. He untied the waterskin from his belt, emptied what water remained in it, and refilled it with fresh water.

He'd been hunting for a few days, but still had nothing to show for it. Often, he managed to find a grey-tailed deer or a forest rabbit within an hour of home.

Rabbit stew.

His mouth watered. Perfectly tuned with his thoughts, his stomach growled, voicing its annoyance with his lack of hunting prowess. He lay his pack down and retrieved a wadded piece of cloth from within one of its pouches. His last piece of hardened sweetbread lay within its folds.

I've gotta get back home.

Home, a two-day journey north, meant two days without food. He'd suffered far worse before, but never enjoyed it. The sweetbread, on the other hand, put a smile on his face as he bit off a corner with his teeth and sucked on it to soften it up. Just what he needed.

A foul odor wafted in the light breeze, drawing his attention and wrinkling his nose. The muscles tightened in his neck.

Danger.

The thought unsettled his nearly-empty stomach.

He slowly rose from his crouch just enough to peer over the top of the grass and survey the area like a sentry. His pulse quickened, thumping in his ears like a beating drum. Perspiration poured from his pores like a spring.

Calm down. Whatever's out there is gonna smell me before it spots me.

His first pass of the meadow revealed nothing out of the ordinary.

The fading light and distorted shadows fed on his nerves, and he flinched with every perceived movement. He squinted into the deep shadows and tried to differentiate between the trees and what he thought might be lurking about. His second scan of the meadow made his heart skip a beat. At the far edge of the meadow, four nightmarish beasts stepped out of the shadows of the forest.

The blood drained from his face, and the hairs on the back of his neck stiffened as a chill rippled across every inch of his skin. Stiff as a stone gargoyle, he couldn't tear his eyes away from the approaching horror.

The four beasts towered over the grass, their waists hovering just above its stalks. They had to be more than seven feet tall.

Ʒäțūr, what are they?

Each of them wore leather armor, and short, reddish-brown fur covered their bodies. Their piercing, yellow eyes glowed in the fading light as they scanned the clearing like hawks on the hunt. Their wolfish ears twisted and turned as they listened for their prey.

For me!

Terror seized Alderan and squeezed him so tight he thought his lungs would collapse. He told himself to run, but his legs wouldn't cooperate. The utter existence of the terrifying beasts transfixed him and rooted him to the ground like a tree.

Move, Alderan!

All four beasts locked eyes with him and each howled. Time was up. In swift, fluid motion, the beasts dropped on all fours and tore through the tall grass in his direction.

Alderan snapped out of his trance and ran for his life. He trounced through the grass and into the forest as quickly as his legs would carry him, not chancing a backward glance. Tree branches lashed at him like whips and ripped the skin from his arms as he barreled through them. His lungs burned and left a bitter taste of iron in his mouth.

His foot caught on a tree root, and he careened face-first into the pine needles, leaves, and other natural debris scattered on the forest floor. He spat dirt and leaves from his mouth as he rolled onto his back and sat up. He strained to hear over his pounding heart.

No birds chirped. No squirrels chattered. Quiet subdued the forest.

Alderan struggled to see through the darkness, unable to discern between the trees and shadows. In the waning daylight, everything seemed ominous, out of place.

He pulled himself to his knees and then to his feet.

This is my forest. I'm the hunter! I should be the one hunting them down. Quiet.

He stepped backward.

Snap. He nearly flew out of his skin, but it was only a twig under his foot. Even so, he'd just given away his location. The sound must've echoed through the forest like a clap of thunder. He wanted to kick himself for being so clumsy.

Quiet.

He inhaled a deep breath to calm his nerves and clear his aching head. Never in his life had he been so terrified. He'd grown up exploring and hunting in the forest and had never once encountered beasts such as those. He'd never thought anything so terrifying existed.

Quiet.

Alderan's father often told horrific stories around the campfire at night, to scare him and Aria, to be sure, but they'd dismissed them as fables and never as actual accounts. The moment those beasts entered the meadow, his perception of the world had skewed, turned upside down. His life would never be the same again.

If I live through this.

He chided himself for having such a thought.

Quiet.

The notion of being watched—toyed with—crept under his skin and he bolted. Flashes of moonlight sliced through the trees and mixed with the deep shadows, leaving him dizzy as he ran. His eyes blurred like the passing trees, skewing what little vision he had.

Thwack! Pain spread across his chest like lightning and his feet flew out from under him. He landed on his back with a *thud*. The collision forced the air from his lungs and he labored to catch his breath again.

Quiet.

I wish I was home.

He lived a nightmare and wanted to wake from it. Tears streaked his face and he wiped at them with his shirtsleeve.

Stop being a child! Crying won't solve anything.

Quiet.

Alderan tried sitting up, but the pain in his chest stopped him. He put his hand to his chest and felt something protruding from it. He would die.

Better this than being torn apart by those beasts.

His thoughts swirled around his family. He'd give anything to wake up safe in his father's arms. He wished he could see his twin sister, Aria, one last time. She was his best friend, and they shared a unique bond, able to feel each other's presence and mood, and hear each other's thoughts as easily as one would breathe.

Aria!

He realized he couldn't feel her with him. He couldn't remember the last time he'd felt her presence; it must've been days ago. A lump caught in his throat.

Aria.

Tears welled in his eyes again. He wanted to scream out her name. The idea of not being with her scared him more than the four beasts hunting him.

Focus, Alderan. You'll never find Aria if you're dead.

He forced his thoughts of her aside and concentrated on his situation.

Quiet.

Did the pain in his chest hurt that bad? Did it really feel life-threatening?

No.

He wrapped his fingers around the branch and slowly extracted it from his chest. Or had it just been caught on the threads of his shirt? He felt around his chest for the hole and for blood, but found neither. His chest ached, but dully. He sat up, rolled onto his hands and knees, and pulled himself to his feet.

Quiet.

He turned in a circle, trying to make out the shapes in the darkness. Nothing moved, but he needed to. He took a small step forward.

Still, nothing moved. His muscles loosened, and a ray of hope crept into the back of his mind.

You can do this Alderan.

He knew the forest as well as anyone—better than most. He'd make it back home safe. He took another step, but he froze.

Quiet.

That foul, pungent odor filled his nostrils again. A few paces ahead of him, piercing, hateful yellow eyes emerged from the shadows. To his left and right, two more pairs of yellow eyes appeared. If he turned around, he expected he'd find a fourth pair.

Nowhere to run!

His hopes shattered.

The beast in front of Alderan took a step forward, rose onto its hind legs, and towered over him. Its voice deep and guttural, "You'll make for a tasty morsel."

The other three sneered and laughed and rose onto their hind legs as well.

"Y-you—?" It was the only word Alderan could voice.

"What? Surprised I can talk?" A smile parted his thin lips, showing off sharp, yellowed teeth. The others continued to laugh.

"Yes," said Alderan, still stunned with disbelief.

The beast ran his thin, elongated fingers through the coarse red hair on his scalp. "You have a way with words, young one—a true scholar, indeed."

The beast to Alderan's left pulled a double-edged battle axe from his back. Spittle flew from his mouth with each word, "Let's get this over with, Rakzar."

Rakzar lifted his paw-like hand in the air. "Patience, Farqel."

Alderan trembled at the sight of Rakzar's razor-sharp claws.

Rakzar tapped the claws of his thumb and middle finger together and tilted his head slightly to the left. "Don't you find it odd that the four of us were sent to kill one small boy?"

Kill? I don't want to die!

Alderan looked over his shoulder. The beast behind him stood closer than he'd imagined. He had nowhere to run and the chances of him fighting his way out of the situation were zero.

"No. I'll take him down myself." Farqel sliced the air with his axe.

Rakzar glared at Farqel. "Exactly my point. Any one of us could easily kill a man twice this boy's size. So, what makes *him* special?" Rakzar took a step toward Alderan.

"I'm warning you—s-stay back!" shouted Alderan.

A grin spread across Rakzar's furry face. The filtered light added brush strokes to Rakzar's face, twisting his features between it and the shadows. In that moment, Alderan swore the beast to be evil incarnate.

"Enough, Rakzar," said Farqel. "Just finish him. Or I—"

Rakzar turned toward Farqel and silenced him with a look. "The boy dies tonight. Do not speak again, or you'll join him. Now put your axe away."

Contempt seethed from Farqel's eyes, but he returned the axe to his back.

Alderan grabbed a stone from his pouch and freed the sling hanging from his belt.

Rakzar returned his attention to Alderan and growled with laughter. "A sling? That's the best you've got, White Knight?"

Alderan blinked, thrown off by the reference. "White Knight?"

Rakzar laughed, "The blood drained from your face the moment you saw us and has yet to return. You wear the name well."

The other two beasts howled with laughter, but Farqel stood with his arms crossed.

"I don't care what you call me. I won't go down easy!" Alderan took aim at Rakzar and spun the sling above his head.

"You may get one shot off, but it'll be your last," Rakzar mocked.

"Then I'll make it count!" Alderan swung the sling underhand and sent the stone flying.

The stone struck the side of Rakzar's snout, ripped away a chunk of flesh, and he grunted. Blood ran through his fur and dripped from the side of his chin. He licked the wound with his long, grey tongue.

"I admire your nerve, White Knight." He snarled and then took two quick steps toward Alderan, closing the gap between them to little more than a foot. His putrid breath soured Alderan's stomach.

Alderan stepped back as he fumbled with his pouch, trying to pull another stone from it. His fingers met its bottom and terror seized him.

No!

Out of stones, Alderan dove to the ground and Rakzar's claws sliced the space where his throat had just occupied. He squirmed backward, but Rakzar jumped on top of him and drove him into the ground.

He couldn't move, and he could scarcely breathe. Rakzar's weight crushed the life from him, caving his chest in a little farther with each breath. He gagged as blood and saliva dripped on his face. Rakzar raised his massive fist into the air.

Alderan closed his eyes and coughed out each word, "Just make it quick."

Scenes from his short life flashed before him. An image of Aria filled his mind, his world. His everything.

Did I ever tell her how much she means to me?

Ẑäṭūr, he prayed. *Save me now and I'll fight for You. I know I don't deserve another chance, but I swear I'll make a difference if You give me one. If not, I pray You keep my sister safe. She's the better part of me.*

"Even at the gates of death you've shown bravery, White Knight. For your valor, I'll honor your request. Now open your eyes and face your death."

For you, Aria.

Alderan drew a deep breath. Would his father be proud of his bravery? He'd find out soon enough. He slowly opened his eyes, for the last time. He'd never pictured his death before, but he imagined it wouldn't have looked that way.

The other three beasts moved in close, and saliva dripped from their jaws. Every muscle tensed, and his stomach gurgled. Fear seized him, and he struggled to keep his eyes open.

Take me, Ẑäṭūr.

His eyes widened as Rakzar's fist hammered toward his face. Something wrapped around his chest and hips and pulled him down. Rakzar's fist came within an inch of his face and then stopped abruptly with a *crack* as it rolled unnaturally to the side. Rakzar roared as a plume of dust rose in the air.

Rakzar's face twisted with rage, highlighted by the faint light. He pummeled the ground with his fists and spat with each word, "Where... did... he... go?"

The other beasts stood in silence, blank stares painted their faces.

Rakzar dug at the ground with his claws and threw dirt everywhere. Alderan flinched, but Rakzar's claws didn't reach him. Rakzar roared and turned on the others.

"He was there," said one of the other beasts. "You had him. Then he just melted away."

Rakzar trembled, his arms bent and fists balled. "Melted away? Melted away? How does one just *melt away,* Lorrav? Tell me!"

Lorrav shrunk away from Rakzar. "I only know what my eyes saw, Rakzar. I cannot say beyond that."

How's this possible? How do they not see me lying here?

Rakzar rose on his hind legs, turned toward the beast named Farqel, and pointed a finger at him. Through gritted teeth, "You'll not breathe a word of this."

Farqel straightened and stepped toward Rakzar. He growled with laughter, "On the contrary, *mighty* Rakzar. A mere boy slips through your fingers, *literally*. Be sure Dragnus will hear of this. I'll personally deliver the message."

"Over my dead body!" Rakzar launched himself at Farqel, and the two of them tumbled across the forest floor, ripping and tearing at each other with their massive claws and teeth. Lorrav and the other beast retreated into the shadows.

Bewildered, Alderan watched the events unfold above him. Chunks of fur, flesh, and broken branches littered the ground as Rakzar and Farqel tumbled around. Crimson drops splattered the foliage like morning dew and glistened in the pale moonlight.

Alderan's heart hammered. What'd saved him from certain death? He needed to know, but he couldn't turn his eyes from the action above.

Rakzar lay on the ground, face-first, with Farqel hunched over the top of him. Farqel wrapped one of his massive arms around Rakzar's neck and pulled Rakzar's torso off the ground, bending Rakzar's spine backward. Muscles bulged under his matted red fur as Farqel squeezed the life from Rakzar.

"I've got the upper hand," grunted Farqel. "You're finished, Rakzar. I'll be running things from now on."

"Not a chance," growled the fourth beast.

Farqel looked up, and the head of the battle axe sliced clean through his neck. His head fell to the forest floor with a *thud*, and his empty eyes stared directly at Alderan, their haunting, yellow glow extinguished.

 Rakzar rose on his hind legs and shrugged Farqel's flaccid body from his shoulders like a sack of flour. Blood poured from Farqel's headless torso, pooled around it, and seeped into the soil. The warm liquid steamed in the cool evening air.

Rakzar wiped blood from his eyes with the back of his hand, lifted his leather skirt, and then urinated on Farqel's lifeless form. Without another word, he dropped on all fours and fled into the trees and out of sight with the other two beasts behind him.

"Thank you, Ɂät—"

Alderan's body jolted and then the forest raced past him with a blur. The motion turned his stomach and spun his head. His pulse quickened, and fear kept his body rigid.

What's happening to me?

He closed his eyes and prayed, *Ɛäṭūr, You saved me from those beasts. Save me once again so that I can do Your work. Give me strength.*

The sensation of motion ebbed and the pressure around his chest and hips dissipated. He opened his eyes. A dark ceiling of dirt and roots hung above him. He sat up, disoriented. His nausea settled, but his heart still galloped in his chest.

Am I in some sort of cave?

He craned his neck to the left and then the right. Eyes were on him, weren't they? His heart sped to a lope.

His hands trembled at his sides and beads of sweat formed on his brow. He scarcely remembered how to breathe, let alone talk.

No fear, Alderan. Be a man.

His gaze locked onto a small table that protruded from the wall directly in front of him. He focused on the two large roots that kept the table suspended. The tension in his shoulders eased.

His gaze drifted to a lone candle that flickered atop the table. The candle gave off just enough light for him to make out his own features, but not enough for much beyond that.

He stood and reached the table in two steps. He reached out and wrapped his hand around the clay cup that held the candle. He lifted the cup and the flame wavered and nearly extinguished. He cupped his other hand around the flame and slowly turned to face the room.

Let the light shine, Ɛäṭūr. Chase away the darkness. Keep the flame lit.

He lowered his hand, but the darkness held its own against the light. Slowly, he crossed the room. Bedding lay on the floor next to the wall on his left, neatly kept. To the right, a solid wall of roots. In front of him, the room stopped.

Four walls. No door!

A brief flutter of wings caught his attention, but the source eluded him.

His voice trembled, "Hello?" A lump rose in his throat.

No response.

He turned in a circle in the middle of the room. Had he imagined the noise? The room sat in perfect silence. He breathed deeply, and his heart slowed.

He walked back over to the table and set the clay cup and candle back down. The dirt wedged into every layer of his clothing and every crevice on his body rose to the front of his mind. Had he been dragged through the desert? The need to scratch came upon him like a flash of lightning.

He stomped the ground, and pulled at his shirt and trousers, circling as he tried to shake the dirt loose. If someone were watching him at that moment, they'd think him a participant in some sort of stag, tribal ritual, dancing to a beat only he heard.

A giggle erupted behind him. Alderan swung around so quickly that he lost his balance, tripped over a root protruding from the ground, and fell backward. His head knocked against the firm ground.

"You needn't dance for my pleasure," said a soft, high-pitched voice. "It was quite entertaining though!"

His vision blurred as he blinked away the threat of tears. The back of his head throbbed. Surely, a large lump had formed already. He reached back and confirmed its existence. He pulled his hand back and inspected his fingers.

Thankfully it's not bleeding.

He sat up. Two candles sat atop the table and circled each other in a dance only he saw. He blinked several times before the candles merged back into one. He pushed his long blonde hair out of his face and wrapped the strands behind his ears.

"Are you okay?" The voice came from behind him and to his right. A mixture of concern and laughter laced the words.

Alderan coughed and imagined a plume of dirt rose from his lips, but saw none. He turned to his right. The source of the voice sat atop the bedding by the wall.

Maybe he imagined it, but the entire room brightened when the beautiful young girl smiled. Her striking, hazel gaze locked on him and he couldn't look away. Another giggle erupted from her small, curvy lips, and sent the curls of her long, chestnut hair bouncing at the sides of her narrow face. Soft laughter lines stretched from the corners of her eyes and mouth, adding to her natural beauty.

Heat rose in his cheeks as he struggled to his feet. She giggled again and then leapt from the bedding. He gasped and staggered backward as she hovered in the air. Two translucent wings shimmered in the light and fluttered at her back, cycling through a vast rainbow of colors. She was a living, breathing vision pulled straight from the pages of legends.

His heart hammered in his chest harder than he thought possible.

A faerie? They're real?

His legs wobbled underneath him, so he dropped to his knees to keep from collapsing.

With elegance, she floated toward him. "You don't need to bow before me, silly." She giggled and lightly tapped his nose with her finger. "I'm not of royal descent."

A raging wildfire, her laughter engulfed him with its flames, spread into his lungs and chest, and spewed from his mouth without restraint. When had he laughed so hard?

I think I'm gonna like this girl. She's so beautiful. A faerie! I can't wait to tell Aria. Maybe she'll come home with me and meet her. That would be the best!

The laughter vanquished his awkwardness and brought confidence into his voice, "I'm Alderan of Viscus D'Silva. I owe you my thanks and my life." He nodded his head and bowed slightly.

Stupid, stupid, stupid!

"Well, Alderan of Viscus D'Silva—" She giggled and spread her arms as wide as they'd go. "—I'm Rayah, of here." She winked at him.

His cheeks warmed again.

"You're easily discomfited, silly."

The heat in his cheeks increased and he pulled at his shirt, his throat constricted.

"I'll accept your thanks." Then, in a more serious tone, "But I won't take credit for saving your life."

He stared into her eyes. No humor remained.

"Ɂäṭūr, in His vast wisdom, led me across your path. He's the one who saved you and deserves the credit. I'm merely an instrument He used to execute His plan. Only He has the power to give the breath of life and only He can take it away. You'll have to thank Him for that."

Alderan nodded, afraid that if he vocalized anything it'd somehow come out all wrong.

Why am I so nervous? She really jumbles my thoughts.

He turned his attention back to the room, purposely avoiding further eye contact with her. A soft glow of light made the room warm and inviting. In fact, light filled every inch of the room, leaving no place for shadows to form. The light emanated from everywhere and nowhere simultaneously.

That's odd.

"Where's the light coming from?" he blurted and then quickly covered his mouth with his hands. Judging by Rayah's wide-eyed expression, she must've thought him to be the biggest oaf alive. He dug a hole and threw himself into it, or so he wished.

Rayah laughed so hard she fell to the floor, only to laugh even harder. He glared down at her as she rolled around on the floor with tears of laughter streaming down her cheeks. His scrunched-up face seemed to fuel her hysterics, but her joy infected him, and he soon found himself rolling on the floor alongside her.

His sides ached, and he scarcely remembered the last time he'd laughed so hard. A vision of Aria came to him again.

I miss you, sister. You'll like Rayah. She'll really make you laugh.

He knew nothing about Rayah other than her name, yet he believed that she'd forever be his friend. He felt comfortable with her, and her beautiful smile made him feel good.

She's just a girl. No, she's a faerie! I think. Hmm, maybe I should ask her. She probably already thinks I'm an oaf. It can't do much more harm, and I can blame my throbbing head if it does.

He sat up and crossed his legs in front of him—better to stay on the floor and not display any more of his clumsiness. Rayah followed his lead and sat directly across from him, about a foot away.

He breathed in the damp, earthy smell around him, and caught a whiff of sweet wildflowers. He'd been so absorbed by her beauty that he hadn't noticed the small, yellow flowers carefully woven into the curly strands of her hair.

So much of her resembles Aria.

Under different circumstances, he would've been content looking at her all day, but too many questions burned in his mind.

Here goes nothing.

He squeezed his eyes as tight as possible, scrunching his nose and pulling up the corners of his mouth. "What are you? A faerie?" He lifted one eyelid to see her reaction.

She slapped him on the leg, playfully. "No, silly. I'm a dryte. Faeries are a whole lot smaller, and extremely devious. You'll want to avoid them if possible."

Yep, I'm definitely an oaf.

He opened his other eye and pushed his hair behind his ears. "I'm sorry."

She put her hand on his leg, "Don't be. No one can know everything, and you'll never learn anything without asking questions."

"Well," he said, more to himself than to her. "I've got lots of learning to do then."

His head ached. He needed a cup of cygnut tea and a good nap. His thoughts swirled in a storm of lightning, firing randomly in fits of chaos.

Beasts. Dragnus. Rayah. Aria. Home.

"Those… things…" He couldn't finish the sentence.

The blood. The horrific smell. The unfathomable beasts. The experience poisoned his mind. Sweat drenched his dirty clothes. His body trembled. The room pulsed and swayed before him. He closed his eyes and prayed that the contents of his stomach stayed put.

Rayah placed her hand on his, and a calm washed over him. He opened his eyes just as she closed hers. He couldn't remember how to breathe.

She's so beautiful.

Dryte or not, he'd never met another girl like her.

She's so different—in a good way.

Rayah withdrew her hand, wrapped her arms around her waist, and gently rocked herself. "Gnolls. Those beasts are called gnolls."

Gnolls.

Another thing he'd never heard of until today. He would've been just fine if he'd lived his whole life without encountering them.

Rayah continued, "They came up from the south. About a week ago, I came across more than a hundred of them. They tore through the forest like a pack of fevered wolves, fighting amongst themselves and killing any living creature that crossed their path.

"They didn't kill for food, but for sport. With every twisted encounter, they swarmed around and reveled in the carnage, howling with pleasure. Never in my life have I seen such evil. Their presence sickened me."

The pounding of his head faded like a storm moving into the distance as he sat silent, engrossed in her story. Her words painted pictures on the canvas of his mind and pulled him into her memories as though he'd lived them himself.

"My friend Leilana—a dryte like me—they caught her, tortured her, plucked her wings from her back, and then tore her apart when they grew bored with her. I only saw what remained of her. I wish I'd been there to try and save her..."

Rayah's emotions flowed into him. His eyes pooled and burst with streams of salty water. Somehow, they were one, and the loss of her friend broke his heart. "I'm so sorry, Rayah."

She looked up at him and the pain in her eyes left him devastated. He wanted to wrap his arms around her and make her feel better. He gave her a smile, but the effort proved fruitless. His words suffered the same fate, falling flat from his tongue, "But you saved me."

Rayah breathed deeply and wiped her face with her arm. "I was on my way home when I saw you surrounded by the gnolls."

She peered into his eyes. Her lower lip quivered. "I knew they'd kill you as well. If you hadn't dove to the ground, I wouldn't have been able to save you, and you'd be dead like the rest of them."

Did I hear her right?

Tears filled her eyes again. "You were so brave to stand against them. I cowered in the shadows when I had a chance to make a difference. I'm no hero."

"The rest of them?" He immediately regretted asking. He closed his eyes and cringed at the thought of what she'd say.

Rayah sniffed and wiped her eyes. "After finding Leilana I wanted to run away, but something drove me to continue following the gnolls. Traveling through the soil, I followed them for days without being noticed."

Alderan's eyes popped open. "Wait. What do you mean, 'traveling through the soil?'"

The images that flowed from her mind and into his were always looking up at the scene, never directly on or down.

Like when she saved me.

Rayah focused her gaze on him. "As I said before, I'm a dryte. A soil dryte, to be exact. I have a way with dirt." He watched with amazement as she sank waist-deep into the dirt floor.

"Ah!" He raised a finger in the air. "That's why you need no doors!"

"Exactly." She giggled and effortlessly rose back out of the ground.

"Please go on, Rayah. I'll try not to interrupt again."

"Certainly."

The smile faded from her lips as she descended back into the despair of the story. Her eyes rolled back as she closed them. Her emotions seeped back into him as well, and left him with a hollowness he couldn't shake. He closed his eyes and fell back into her world.

"Every sick and vile thing they did pushed me further and further into a pit of sorrow, but nothing prepared me for the third day. That day was worse than any imaginable nightmare. From the shelter of the forest, I watched with horror as they descended upon a small village and laid waste to it.

"Bone-chilling screams filled the air as they burned people alive and ripped others apart. My heart ached to help them, but I felt powerless to do anything but watch. The same force that guided me to follow them held me back…"

Images flashed through his mind so quickly it left him dizzy. Glimpses so brief, he knew, because Rayah couldn't stand watching it all again.

Alderan opened his eyes. Tears ran down Rayah's cheeks and dripped from her chin, and left wet streaks down her dark green top. How much more could he endure?

Rayah continued, "And the children, Alderan—they were all so young and innocent. The gnolls had no reason to kill them, but they did anyway. The worst part was the pleasure they took from it. They laughed as they slaughtered them.

"They burned every structure to the ground, torched the fields, and slaughtered the animals. When they finished, nothing remained." Tears marched down Rayah's cheeks like endless waves of soldiers.

The onslaught of images and emotions left him numb. The room blurred around him. He wanted to comfort her and tell her it would be okay, but he knew it'd be a lie. He'd lived her experience and wanted to throw up. Those monsters' evil deeds coursed through his mind, and he wanted them purged. He felt dirty.

It's not okay.

A single question stuck in his mind and twisted his stomach in knots. He knew its answer, but he had to ask—demanded an answer. Bile rose in his throat and he choked on its sour taste.

Just spit it out.

"Rayah..."

His heart thundered in his chest and echoed in his ears. He recognized the fear in her eyes and knew it stemmed from the rage pouring from his own. He tried looking away from her, but couldn't break the bond between them.

His nails bit into the flesh of his palms as he rolled his hands into balls, drawing blood.

She looked down at his hands as tears fell from her eyes again.

He began again, this time through clenched teeth. "Rayah, where was this village?"

"So much blood," she whispered. Her lower lip quivered. "There was so much blood."

He couldn't hold back the anger in his voice and didn't want to. "Where was it?"

"North of here, in the Veridis Forest."

Hearing her utter the word "North" plunged a dagger into his heart. North or not, the Veridis Forest contained only one village—Viscus D'Silva.

His village.

† † †

Alderan awoke to the smell of fresh bread and soup. His head felt cluttered and dizzy and his entire body ached. He opened his eyes to a blurry world, disoriented. The soft fingers intertwined with his fueled his confusion.

"You're finally awake," said a soft, familiar voice.

The voice—*her* voice—lifted the haze from his mind and bombarded him with images of the evening's events. Anguish filled him anew; he sat straight up and screamed, "Aria!"

Anger rushed back to the forefront of his mind and tore into his heart.

Rayah!

He wanted to lash out at her. He wanted her to pay for failing to save his sister. Everything was *her* fault.

You stood there and did nothing but watch. You could've saved them!

He squeezed Rayah's hand like a vise. She screamed and pulled her hand away from his. On the surface, hurting her felt good, but deep within he hated himself for it.

He hated her for being the bearer of bad news. He couldn't even stomach looking at her. The pain of his loss hurt so much, and she was the source of it.

Rayah sniffed. "Why did you do that? I'm not the one you should be angry with. I can only guess at how much pain you must be feeling, and I'm sorry. But I didn't do it."

Alderan huffed, "But you didn't stop it either."

"That's not fair, Alderan."

Alderan's anger deepened. "And my sister and father being dead is?"

"You know that's not what I mean. If I'd tried to stop them, we'd both be dead."

"Maybe you should've. Death would be less painful than this."

"You don't mean that, Alderan."

"You *know* I do."

"Wait—I just remembered something else, Alderan."

The excitement in her voice forced his attention to her. He glared at her. Tears stained her face, but the smile lighting it up made him want to lash out at her again.

How can you be smiling? My family's dead!

Rayah trembled. "Don't look at me like that."

Through gritted teeth, "What could you possibly remember that makes any difference to me now? I've lost everything."

"From the village, they took one prisoner with them. A girl."

Alderan's mouth dropped open and words failed him.

They took a prisoner?

Pulse racing, he moved to the edge of the bed. "What did she look like?"

"You!" Rayah beamed from ear to ear.

An image of the girl filled his mind.

Aria! You're alive!

He jumped from the bed, grabbed Rayah around her waist, and kissed her forehead. He swore the source of the light in the room came from her smile. He squeezed her tight, released her, and then plopped back down on the bed, exhausted with emotions.

"Thank you," he said.

"I'm just sorry I didn't remember earlier."

"Don't be. It's not your fault. And I'm sorry I got so angry with you. I tend to do that. Always have. You can ask Aria when we find her."

"We?" Her voice squeaked.

Alderan ran his fingers through his hair. "If you're willing to put up with me. Someone needs to save me from myself. Besides, you said you wanted to help before, but something held you back. You can help me rescue my sister."

Rayah reached over and squeezed his hand. "I think I'd like that."

He smiled at her. "Together, then."

"I guess we'd better pack for our journey."

"Think there's a chance of eating some of that wonderful smelling bread and soup first? I think I may starve otherwise." His stomach growled with agreement and they both laughed.

"Fresh bread and rabbit soup coming right up," she said with a smile.

She flew over to the table—her wings sparkled in the candlelight. *She's special.* A bond started to form between them, and his heart fluttered with the idea of having a friend.

† † †

Rayah took Alderan's cold and clammy hands in hers—they trembled. "Relax, silly. This isn't going to hurt."

"What if we lose contact halfway up? I'd be buried alive. I don't want to die like that."

Rayah giggled and dropped his hands. "Put your arms around my waist and I'll put mine around yours."

Alderan's face turned bright red. "I... um... yes, okay I guess."

Rayah grabbed Alderan's hands again and pulled his arms around her waist. She turned her head to the side as she leaned into him. He smelled like a dirty boy, but she liked it. She wrapped her arms around his waist and then extended her wings.

"Wait—"

Rayah sighed. "Now what?"

Alderan cleared his throat. "I'm pretty heavy. Are you certain you can lift the both of us? I don't wanna hurt you."

Rayah leaned back in Alderan's arms just enough to see his face. "We've been over this several times, Alderan. I'm much stronger than I look. I can lift many times my weight."

Alderan grinned sheepishly. "But we just ate a little bit ago."

Rayah snorted. "You're one silly boy, Alderan. Now close your eyes and hold tight."

Alderan rolled his eyes at her and then closed them. "Should I hold my breath too?"

"Only if you don't want to be coughing up dirt."

Alderan took a deep breath and squeezed her tight. "Go."

Rayah locked her fingers behind Alderan's back and fluttered her wings. She'd never actually carried someone before, but it couldn't be that hard, right?

Here goes nothing.

She bent her knees slightly and then pushed off the floor as she beat her wings. They burst into the air, through the dirt ceiling, and into the morning air above ground. Their momentum carried them much farther than she'd anticipated, more than six feet above the surface. She stopped beating her wings a moment too long and they crashed to the ground in a heap.

Rayah rolled away from Alderan and sat up, too embarrassed to face him. "Sorry about that."

Alderan coughed and then laughed. "Can we do it again?"

Rayah turned to Alderan with a deadpan expression. "Sure. And I'll let you go halfway through."

Alderan's eyes widened. "What?"

The look on his face sent her into a fit of laughter. "I'd never do that to you. I promise."

Alderan's brow furrowed. "Not sure I believe you. One of these days you'll get fed up with me and leave me in the middle of nowhere, buried to my neck in the dirt."

"Keep it up, and I might do it now."

She stared into his deep-green eyes. She found him easy to look upon, but his gaze penetrated the walls she'd tediously built around herself, leaving her open and vulnerable.

How does he do that? I feel as though I've known him my whole life.

She shivered as a wave of gooseflesh rippled across her skin.

"I'm gonna go get our things." She didn't wait for a response and quickly sank into the ground and down to her home below.

Their two packs sat on the floor, ready to go. She'd packed her whole life in one tiny bag. Would she ever return? A lone tear crawled its way down her cheek.

Either way, I'm gonna miss this place.

She wiped away the tear when it reached her jaw and then reached for the two bags. She wrapped her fingers around their leather straps and then stopped.

"I'm forgetting something... but what?"

She looked around the small room, but nothing jumped out at her. She lifted the bags into her arms and was about to return to the surface when it hit her: "Savric."

How could I have forgotten?

She set the bags back down, flew over to her bed, and sat on it. She reached over to the far wall and put her hand against it. The wall vibrated and then the earth fell away, revealing a cubbyhole ten inches cubed. The cubbyhole held two items: a small leather-bound book and a silver brooch.

Rayah pulled the book out of the cubbyhole and brushed the dirt from its cover. She traced the lines on its cover with her finger. "*2äall Dhef 2äfn Dhä.*" The symbol and what it stood for filled her mind and left her sober.

"A golden iris—*Í Dhef 2äṭūr.*" She shook her shoulders as a chill ran its course.

"Within the iris... a vibrant-blue heptagram—*Ūrdär Dhef 2äfn Dhä.* And at its center a flashing yellow bolt of lightning—'strike randomly, but with precision.'"

A small, golden clasp without keyhole or release mechanism held the book closed. She closed her eyes and placed her hand over ʕäəll Dhef ʕäfn Dhä. "*In əllíṭ Hiz.*"

In His light.

Click.

The clasp released and Rayah opened her eyes. She opened the book to the first page—a blank one. The inside cover contained a small pouch. She reached into it and pulled out a fountain pen.

She touched the tip of the pen to the blank page and watched words form on it: '*Rayah, the time is at hand. You know what must be done. Separate any feelings you may have from the task. The fate of the Ancient Realm lies in your hands. Keep the boy alive and deliver him as requested. In əllíṭ Hiz. -Savric*'

Deceiving someone, even for the right reasons, felt wrong. Her heart, heavily burdened, cried out. Tears slid down her cheeks.

ʕäṭūr, how can I keep the truth from Alderan?

Rayah touched the page with the pen again and the words faded. She scribbled her response on the page: '*I will do as you wish, Master Savric, but they're already on to us. Four gnolls attacked Alderan last night. I saved him from them, but we might not be so lucky again. I know they won't give up. In əllíṭ Hiz. -Rayah*'

Rayah tapped the page with the tip of the pen and the words faded. She placed the pen back in the pouch and closed the book. She grabbed the brooch from the cubbyhole and placed it and the book inside her pack.

She sniffed and wiped the tears from her cheeks with her sleeves. She picked up the two packs, flew to the ceiling, and then pushed her way up through the ground.

Alderan stood at a distance with crossed arms. "I was beginning to wonder if you were coming back."

She dropped the packs on the ground. "I'm sorry it took so long. I nearly forgot something very important to me."

She bent down, pulled the silver brooch from her pack, and then handed it to Alderan.

Alderan turned the brooch over in his hand and then held it up to the light. "What's this?"

Rayah stared at the butterfly-shaped brooch. "It's the only thing I have left of my mother."

Alderan smiled and handed the brooch back to her. "Seems as though we have many things in common."

Alderan reached inside the neck of his shirt and lifted up a leather necklace. A small brass ring, smooth and without decoration, hung from the necklace. "This was my mother's ring. One day it'll belong to my wife."

Rayah smiled. "She'll be lucky to wear it, whoever she turns out to be."

Rayah stuffed the brooch back in her pack and then slung the pack over her shoulder. She picked up Alderan's pack and handed it to him. "Where shall we begin the search for your sister?"

Alderan's brow furrowed as he ran his fingers through his hair. "Um... show me where they carried her away."

"Back at your village?"

Alderan shook his head vigorously. "No, after that. I don't wanna see the village. I'm not sure I ever wanna see that place again."

Rayah put her hand on his shoulder. "I understand. Not sure I'd want to go back if I were you, either."

Deliver him. The words gnawed at her conscience like a rat with cheese.

To what end? If I do, will he ever forgive me?

Rayah turned and walked a few paces. She sighed.

Forgive me, Alderan, but I trust Savric. This must be for your own good.

She set her mind on the task. She looked back over her shoulder. "Follow me. I'll lead you straight there."

Deliver him.

Alderan walked up next to her. "Thank you, Rayah."

Guilt turned her stomach. She walked off, unable to look him in the eye further. "Don't thank me yet."

The foliage crunched under her shoes. Would that be the fate of their friendship too, trampled and crushed into dust?

Guard my heart and guide us on the right path, Ʒäţūr.

Her pulse quickened as they headed northwest, straight toward *deliverance.*

CHAPTER EIGHT

The wound at the back of Nardus's head throbbed, and he winced as he moved his fingers across it. The gelled and tacky blood around the area left his hair a matted mess. He felt trampled, and a sharp pain stabbed his side. Had he broken a rib?

An odor of burning pitch—mixed with a tinge of blood and sweat—rose into his nostrils. Dried blood crusted his earlobes and the sides of his neck, and his ears rang with a brutal, high-pitched noise.

He forced his eyes open and the light stung them. Through squinted eyes, the world seemed a blurry mess with its smattering of color, light, and shadow gummed together in kaleidoscopic fashion. Had he engaged in an all-night bender, been tossed in an alley somewhere, and left for dead?

The gash on the back of his head likely played a significant role in his unsorted condition, but he couldn't rule out the slim possibility of other contributing factors as well. He rubbed his eyes with the backs of his hands and blinked a few times to try to generate some moisture, but the blurriness persisted.

This ought to be interesting.

The shapes in his vision told him that he'd ended up back in the circular room with the pedestal. This time, however, a dim light flowed into the room from the doorway that had previously been cloaked in darkness.

He carefully pushed his way up the wall and into a standing position, keeping himself braced against it. His legs wobbled a bit, but felt stable enough to walk. He stumbled forward and made a beeline toward the doorway.

Standing in the doorway, with his vision clearing but still not crisp, Nardus stared at the dark and portentous red sky. Nothing tried to pull him through the doorway as it had before, and the thought of turning around and leaving tempted him.

I'll be damned if I have to go back out the way I came in. There'd better be another way out of here.

Far in the distance stood his destination: Ţämbəll Dhef Däd Dhä. *The Temple of the Dead.* Its ramparts rose into the red sky and cast a forlorn shadow across the barren land.

The weight of the world bore down on him. He fell through the doorway, landed on his knees, and stared into the bleakness of his imminent future. The blood drained from his face and left his head floating on his shoulders like a feather. His white-flagged face cast against the blood red sand begged for mercy, but he knew no mercy would be granted in that forsaken world.

He raised his head and roared at the sky. "This isn't what I bargained for!"

He half-expected an answer, but none came.

Pain erupted in his knees and sent him springing to his feet. "Ouch!" He smacked at his trousers, thinking them on fire, but he found no flames or smoke. However, his hands met fresh blood.

Gaping holes littered his trousers and blood ran down his shins. It puzzled him until he looked closer at the sand. The sand moved, not from wind, but as though it were alive, and he slowly sank in it. He turned to retreat into the room, but only found more shifting sands behind him.

This isn't good.

He tore a piece of cloth from his tattered trousers and wiped his legs as best he could. It did nothing to reduce the burning; blisters and pus already covered the area.

He loathed the idea of seeking refuge in the temple, but his current set of options hovered at an all-time low. Being eaten alive topped his list of ways he didn't want to die, and he had no time to find an alternative path. *The temple it is.*

His quest led him to the temple anyway, but he hadn't intended to walk up to the front door, knock on it, and wait to find out who or what might answer.

Guess I have no choice.

Gnaud had warned him that further trials awaited beyond fate's gateway. He'd said that this place had been created more than a thousand years ago by seven of the most powerful wizards and mages to have ever lived: Ūrdär Dhef Ɂäfn Dhä.

The Order of the Seven.

The Order went to great lengths to keep items of unimaginable power out of the hands of those who would use them for evil. They eventually sacrificed their own lives to keep its dark secrets hidden.

And here I am, driven by madness to get inside.

He ran through the sand as fast as his tired, old legs would allow. He managed the pain in his side, but the fire consuming his knees sickened him. A feast of flesh—*his* flesh.

He stumbled with nearly every step, fell a few times, and nearly planted his face in the sand once. The idea of the sand eating away at his face drove him to be more cautious. Every time he fell more holes opened in his clothes, and more festering, bloody sores covered his body.

Man on fire, running through the desert. Madness—pure madness. Despite the pain, he chuckled at the mental picture.

Whether sweat or blood ran down his forehead and into his eyes made little difference as it stung either way. Several meters ahead, the sand gave way to sandstone. *An oasis.* Completely exhausted and saturated from head to toe with one sort of liquid or another, Nardus pressed forward.

His thick leather boots held up against the carnivorous sand, and he thanked the cobbler who'd made them. Had they worn through, he would've certainly perished. Even so, he didn't think he could take much more abuse.

As soon as I'm out of this wretched sand, I've got to get back to Nasduron. Gnaud will know what to do.

He reached the edge of the sand, flung himself onto the sandstone, and then dragged himself a safe distance from the vile sand. His chest heaved, his heart raced, and his body burned. He would've traded just about anything for a cold drink to ease his burning throat.

How did I come so ill prepared? He'd only brought the clothes on his back. No provisions, no weapons—only a desire to be united with his family again.

What was I thinking?

The heavy, hot air soured his dry mouth. He lay on his back for a moment and brooded over the sunless, moonless, cloudless, and starless red sky that loomed over him. *Unnatural and eerie.* The whole place left him uneasy.

Mezhik be damned. This wretched quest can't end soon enough.

His burning flesh outweighed his desire to lie there and nap. *I need to find shelter and get to Gnaud.*

His body pleaded to stay down, but he forced himself to his feet. Blood stained the ground where he'd been lying. Blood loss left him lightheaded, and he grabbed hold of his head to keep it from floating away. He closed his eyes and waited for the feeling to subside.

He opened his eyes, turned his back to the sandy dunes, and gasped. He stood at the edge of a great chasm that spanned a few miles and stretched as far down as he could see before it faded into complete darkness. At its center, suspended in midair a thousand meters above the rim, hovered Ţämbəll Dhef Däd Dhä.

Four massive vines, at least seven meters in diameter, stretched into the air and across the chasm, anchoring the four corners of the temple to the ground. He'd never seen such a vision in his entire existence. The view took his breath and terrified him all at once.

Guess I'll go see Gnaud now.

Without a doubt of purpose in his mind, he stepped out of the bleak and barren world and into the Great Library.

† † †

"Gnaud!" he yelled at the top of his lungs and then collapsed among the rows of bookshelves, pulling books off the shelves and onto the floor with him. The sound of toenails ticking on marble tile preceded Gnaud. A moment later, he flew around the corner and nearly tripped over Nardus.

"Oh, my!" Gnaud grabbed hold of one of the bookshelves to steady himself. He stood there in silence, jaw dropped, obviously trying to process the bloody scene before him.

"I need your help," said Nardus, through gritted teeth.

"Ɂäţūr's mercy." Gnaud bent down on one knee. "What have you done to yourself, my friend?"

"The sand was alive... and it burns so bad..." Nardus shook with chills.

Gnaud pushed his glasses up his nose, pulled a small, glass instrument from his pocket, and used it to examine one of Nardus's wounds.

"Oh, my, this isn't good. Not good at all! These wounds are from wizard's fire. They'll continue burning until there's nothing left if we don't treat them, and soon. Bad news, that stuff is. Oh, my, let me think."

Gnaud's little foot tapped against the stone floor, *tat-tat, tat-tat-tat, tat-tat.* "Oh, my, yes, I think I may have something to reverse this. Wait right here."

"Not going anywhere," said Nardus. Gnaud scurried away.

Bottles clinked against each other at the far end of the library along with "oh, my" a few times. *What would I do without you, Gnaud?* This marked the second time Gnaud saved his life—assuming he did. It wouldn't be the last. A few more times and they'd have to consider it standard practice. One day he'd visit without his life being in jeopardy.

I'll find a way to repay him, even if it's the last thing I ever do.

Gnaud returned with an armful of glass bottles filled with liquids, solids, and a mixture of the two, plus a wooden bowl and two wooden stirring spoons. A few of the bottles were empty as well.

"I was a medic in the Great War, you know. Treated all sorts of horrific wounds. Wonderful things can be accomplished with the use of mezhik, but so can horrific acts of evil. Unfortunately, the latter seems to be the rule rather than the exception. This world is so broken."

"The Great War? Seriously, Gnaud? That was 1200 years ago."

Gnaud mixed ingredients as he spoke, "Oh, my, has it really been that long? It seems like only a century ago."

Nardus squinted at Gnaud. "How old are you?"

Gnaud cleared his throat. "Those were trying times, much the same as the ones I fear are just ahead of us. Sure, many uncertainties must be factored into things, but I have strong feelings rooted deep within my bones. The bones never lie, you know. And, if the past is an indicator of what's to be repeated, I'm unlikely to be wrong."

Nardus cocked his head. "Have you ever been wrong, Gnaud?"

"No," said Gnaud. Nardus scowled at him. "Ʒätūr's mercy! Don't look at me like that. I'm not a prophet, never have been, and never will be."

Nardus scoffed, "So you say."

Gnaud added two drops of a golden liquid to the mixture and turned it from a slimy green sludge to a thick, yellowish paste. "Oh, my, I think this will do the trick."

"The sooner the better. Not sure how much more of this burning I can manage."

Gnaud took a small blade from his trouser pocket and cut away the fabric around all Nardus's wounds; twenty-two places needed treatment. "This will hurt quite a bit… maybe more so than the initial wounds… but I promise the pain won't last too long."

"I'll warn you now—" Nardus smiled through the pain. "—I may try to kill you before this is all over."

Gnaud gasped. "Oh, my! Guess I'll be ready to run then." He handed Nardus one of the wooden stirring spoons.

"Is this to beat you over the head with when the pain's too much?" asked Nardus.

"Ɂäṭūr's mercy, no. Put it between your teeth, and whatever you do, don't let it fall out. I can't help you if you bite your tongue off."

Nardus placed the spoon between his teeth and grunted, "Ready."

Gnaud pulled two wads of cotton from his pocket, smiled, and then stuffed them into his ears. He pushed his glasses back up his nose, rolled up the sleeves of his shirt, and set to work.

From the moment the yellow paste touched his first wound until Gnaud wiped it from his last, Nardus never stopped screaming.

Finished, Gnaud slumped down next to Nardus. "I'm sorry that was so painful. The worst is over now. Just close your eyes and rest a bit."

Nardus had no energy left to form words or nod. He closed his eyes and allowed the darkness to consume him.

† † †

Hours later—still sprawled out on the floor—Nardus spat out the spoon. Sweat covered him like a wet blanket, and his throat felt like he'd swallowed shards of glass—left raw from all his screaming.

"When I can move again—" he whispered. "—you'd best not be in kicking distance."

Gnaud sat next to him, leaning up against one of the bookshelves. His eyes were closed, and his glasses sat on the floor next to him. One of his ears still had a wad of cotton sticking out of it. Sweat covered his face and dampened his clothes.

"Oh, my," he muttered. "You're welcome, my friend."

† † †

Several hours later, Nardus sat in a chair, sipping on a cup of sweetened cygnut tea. His wounds were still red and puffy, but the burning sensation had ceased. "I'm not sure I can go through this again, Gnaud. I didn't know physical pain like that existed."

Gnaud sat on the table, legs crossed. He sipped from a cup sized for him. "Ɂäʈūr's mercy. There are far worse things in the world than wizard's fire. I really hope you never have to find out what they are, though."

"I have no idea what horrors I might face venturing into *Ţämbɘll Dhef Däd Dhä*. Seven wizards and seven trials, you said?" He sighed deeply. "Guess I've got five left."

"Oh, my! That'd be six. You've only faced one, my friend."

"Bah!" Nardus set his cup of tea on the table, rolled up his left sleeve, and placed his arm on the table with his forearm facing up. He pointed at the five letters burned into his skin: *Akuji*. "With this, it makes two."

Gnaud shook his head fervently. "I'm afraid the gatekeeper's not one of the seven trials."

Nardus sunk in his chair. "How am I supposed to face something like that wizard's fire six more times?" He knew the answer, but it didn't ease his mind.

My family. I'll succeed or be damned trying!

"Be sure you're doing the right thing—for the right reasons—and you'll be okay." Gnaud sipped some tea from his cup.

"I've been thinking about everything that's happened to me, and I believe I've gained a clearer understanding of it. When Akuji held me captive, I was lost inside my own head. That's why I wasn't able to take things back and forth from there and here."

Nardus sat up and smacked the table with an open palm; the spoon rattled in his cup. "This world exists, Gnaud. The place where the temple resides exists as well. I came here in the same condition I was in beforehand."

"Ɂäʈūr's mercy. Of course the two worlds exist." Gnaud pulled the grey fur on his chin. "As you've discovered, there are a few rules to coming here."

Nardus's eyebrows arched. "And what are these rules?"

Gnaud took his glasses off, wiped them with a piece of cloth, held them up to the light, and then placed them back on his face. "Oh, my... let me see. Yes, yes. First rule—" His eyes gleamed with mischief. "—you must be moving to come here."

"But—"

Gnaud lifted his hand. "Let me finish and then you may ask questions."

Nardus hunkered over the table. "Fine."

"Second rule—you cannot come here to escape death. As an example, plummeting to a certain death does not count as moving. Coming here would only prolong your death until you returned and continued to fall.

"Third rule—you must have great purpose or need. A casual visit, as welcomed as it'd be, isn't possible.

"And the fourth rule—once inside *Ʈämbəll Dhef Däd Dhä* you cannot leave. This applies to other places conjured by mezhik as well." Gnaud set his cup down and stood on the table.

"So that's it, then?" Nardus forced air through his nose and frowned. "That doesn't explain how I came here the first time. I was trapped by mezhik and not moving. That violates two of the four rules."

Gnaud stretched his arms and legs and then sat back down. "Oh, my. You're correct, my friend." He scratched his head. "Honestly, I'm unsure how you did it. Mezhik can be very crafty. Sometimes the laws of mezhik bend even as they hold fast."

"*Mezhik.*" Nardus leaned over and spat on the floor. "The world would be better off purged of it."

Gnaud's eyes widened behind his glasses. "Ɂäʈūr's mercy. What do you think started the Great War in the first place?"

Nardus leaned back in his chair and grabbed his cup of tea off the table. "I know, I know. It just seems like everything wrong in the world stems from mezhik."

"Many things do, but there are far more things that are good."

Nardus sipped the tea. An idea formed in his head and he sat up straight;

a bit of tea sloshed from his cup and dampened his trousers. He rubbed the spot with his hand. "Come with me, Gnaud."

Gnaud chuckled. "Oh, my. There are so many things wrong with that request that I don't even know where to begin."

"Think about it, Gnaud." He leaned over the table. "How long have you been here? How long has it been since someone other than me has been here? You could come see this place with your own eyes."

Gnaud shook his head and slowly blinked. "ʔäṭūr entrusted this position to me Himself. I cannot and will not be persuaded by your words, no matter how tantalizing they may be."

Nardus stood and then circled the table. "It'd be a great adventure. How could you pass up something like this without even putting some thought into it?"

Gnaud removed his glasses and wiped them with a cloth from his pocket. "ʔäṭūr's mercy. Let's change the subject before I become thoroughly agitated."

Nardus stopped in front of his chair. He closed his eyes and squeezed the bridge of his nose between his fingers.

What am I thinking? I don't want to be there, and I'm asking him to come along? I'm such a fool.

Nardus sat back down. "I shouldn't have asked that of you, Gnaud. It was wrong of me." Gnaud fussed with his shirt and pretended to not pay attention. "Please accept my deepest apology."

Gnaud waved off the apology with his hand. "I understand your desire for companionship, and I'm sorry I cannot fulfill that role for you in this matter. What I can do is help you better prepare for the challenges you might next face."

Nardus downed the rest of his tea and then sat the cup on the table. The spoon rattled and then settled against the side of the cup. "I'd greatly appreciate it, my friend."

Nardus stood and stretched his arms over his head; his side no longer hurt. He felt the back of his head, expecting to find a lump where he'd split it open when he'd hit the wall, but he found nothing there but skin and hair.

"Did you heal my ribs and my head too?" he asked.

"ʔäṭūr's mercy! I'm no wizard, my friend. I did nothing more than extinguish the wizard's fire. Your body's done the rest."

"But how's that even possible?" He ran his fingers through his hair and pulled at its ends. "Akuji's still burned into my forearm."

"Maybe that hasn't healed because you haven't allowed it to. Or maybe it hasn't healed because you purposely created those wounds. Maybe only the wounds sustained in the other world heal themselves. I can come up with many possibilities as to what is happening to you, but they'd all be guesses."

"Well, if my body continues to heal from the wounds I sustain, I may yet have a chance in completing my quest."

A ray of hope filled his heart and mind. *You're my strength, Vitara. I love you. Nothing will stop me from getting back to you and the children.*

Gnaud hopped to his feet and then jumped to the floor. "Speaking of your quest, there are a few ways I can help prepare you for what's to come."

Nardus rose to his feet and walked around the table. "Like what?"

Gnaud looked up at him and winked. "Some new clothes, for a starter. And much more. Follow me!"

Chapter Nine

The first time it happened, Aria had wished she'd died. She couldn't fathom how she'd stayed conscious through the excruciating pain. Lacerations and bruises in hues of red, purple, black, and blue painted her thighs. She'd lost so much blood that night. It still covered the floors, walls, and even parts of the ceiling.

Her lips split open, her nose broken, her cheeks nearly scraped to the bone, her forehead gouged and battered as they repeatedly thrust her face-first against the rough, hand-chiseled stone wall. The impact had knocked two of her teeth loose and broken another in half. The lightest touch of air on the broken tooth sent pain surging through her jawbone and into the nape of her neck, and breathing through her nose made it worse.

She screamed once that night and nearly lost her tongue doing so. They'd forced her jaws shut so brutally that she'd nearly bit the tip of it clean off. More than three weeks passed before she could eat more than a few bites without writhing in agony.

Four men. No, *beasts*. She'd fought them so hard. One of them wouldn't be able to father children again. She'd ripped another's eye from its socket with her jagged fingernails. Somehow, in the midst of all the chaos, she'd managed to take the life of another, slitting his throat with his own blade. He'd grossly underestimated her strength. None of them would again.

But they'd left her broken and on the verge of death. The memories brought her to the verge of tears, but she refused to let them fall. The filthy brutes fed upon weakness; it made them crazed, and in turn, they grew even more brutal.

I hate you all and will see you all dead.

Endless night reigned the dungeons. The relentless darkness skewed her perception, turning days into weeks and weeks into months. Time became a hollow and meaningless construct, even as it whittled away her youth. Over the course of several months, her willingness to fight off the brutes gave way to a numbing indifference.

Or so she led them to believe.

Aria allowed them to do whatever they pleased with her, and in turn, their firmness with her had weakened drastically. Her body was merely flesh and blood, a vessel of her soul, and her most precious cargo resided beyond their reach. They could mutilate and destroy her body, but they'd never break her spirit. A daughter of Ɂäʈūr, her service to Him would never cease, not even in the face of death.

Ice-cold water hit her bare skin.

"Get yourself cleaned up, ya filthy little tramp!" squealed the man. "Master Dragnus is waiting."

I'm as much a tramp as you are a man.

His oversized potbelly flopped over the leather belt at his waist like a sack of flour. His short, stubby arms ended with fat, rounded, sausage fingers, and his porcine nose dripped with snot that he never wiped away. More swine than man, she called him Pigman.

Pigman dropped the bucket of water on the floor, waddled out of her cell, and slammed the large wooden door behind him. The iron bar slid into place with a loud scrape and echoed in the small cell, but no clambering footsteps lead away.

Pigman's beady little eyes poked and gouged her skin like hate filled needles, raping her as he watched through a crack in the door. He always watched her bathe through the cracks, never bold enough to stand in the cell and watch like some of the other guards.

In numbers, the filthy brutes were formidable, but alone, each cowered before her like a mistreated dog: ears pinned back, bellies dragging the floor, and tails quivering between their legs. The picture brought a crooked smile to her broken face.

The nearly empty bucket—most of the water thrown on the floor—left her little to clean with, but she did her best. A rag would've helped scrub away some of the layers of dirt and filth that covered her, but she made do with her hands.

Save the simple square knot bracelet around her wrist, they'd stripped her of all her possessions, including the clothes she'd worn the night they captured her. In place of clothing, they strapped a seamless, steel collar around her neck.

She turned the bracelet on her wrist. Its woven yellow and green cords were faded with age. They'd told her she could keep it just in case she wanted to turn it into a noose and hang herself. They were brutally cruel, but the bracelet brought her peace and a sense of home. They'd never know the strength it gave her.

She'd been naked for so long that she scarcely remembered the feeling of cloth against her skin. Such a luxury seemed more like a fleeting dream she'd once had than an actual experience. The guards had stripped her bare to humiliate her, but instead it emboldened her. Her nakedness freed her from fear's slavery and left them without leverage over her.

Aria likened herself to a soldier in battle, wearing her skin like armor and taking pride in the way she presented herself. Moreover, like a soldier, she'd been caught and imprisoned, but the battle of her life had yet to begin.

Her father taught her that everything came down to timing, and so she bided her time. When the proper moment presented itself, she'd strike with deadly force and take no prisoners of her own.

Over the years, she'd acquired many battle scars, each with its own story. She'd dreamt of the day that she'd be able to share them with her children, but the smutty brutes had damaged her and crushed those dreams. She swore she'd bring each of them to justice before she took her last breath.

Death to you all.

Pigman threw the door open and his eyes immediately fell to her bare breasts. "You've had more then enough time an look worse then before." His words sounded tough, but his beady little eyes betrayed him. "Out with ya. And no funny stuff, neither."

They were alone, and the thought of being reckless nearly consumed her. He clutched a short sword firmly in his sweaty little palm, but she could take it from him. He'd be no match for her. But then what? She had nowhere to go. She forced her anger through her nostrils.

Your time will come soon.

The dank, musty dungeon passageways made for a welcomed change to her rancid cell. She walked through the doorway and pushed past him. He grabbed her by the back of the collar and pulled her to her knees. She struggled against the urge to fight back.

Patience.

Pigman pressed something sharp into the small of her back. She winced, but didn't cry out. A warm liquid dribbled down her lower back. "Don't ya move, or I'll run this sword clean through ya."

She wanted to say something, to put him in his place, but her vow of silence kept her quiet. Besides, their ears were unworthy of hearing the elegance and grace of her words, or of the soft and subtly seductive quality in her voice. They'd never have the pleasure. They assumed her a mute and mocked her for it relentlessly, calling her things such as 'the barkless bitch' and 'the voiceless whore.'

Hateful words fell freely from their lips and she gathered them like twigs for kindling. She forced them into her memory where she could recall every detail. In time, they'd answer for their actions, and their words fed the fire of her concealed wrath.

With a grunt, Pigman heaved the door shut and slammed the bar into place. He took a six-foot length of heavy, two-inch linked chain from a hook on the wall. He grabbed her collar and yanked her head back. The cold metal sank into her soft skin, squeezing her windpipes. She gasped for air and Pigman grunted.

He took one end of the chain and pressed the last link against the collar. The link slid through the collar as though it were nothing but vapor and latched itself to the collar, leaving no seam. He took the other end of the chain and attached it to a metal bracelet around his wrist.

Pigman kicked her in the back and forced her down on her hands and knees. "Now crawl to ya master," he snorted.

The damp, bitter cold floor made the palms of her hands ache within minutes. Her knees pulsed as if on the verge of bursting, swollen from abuse. Three needs arose in her mind: to stand up and stretch her muscles, to go home, and—most of all—to kill Pigman.

Before day's end, you'll be dead, Pigman.

With each block of cells came another passageway that faded into the darkness and added to the seemingly endless maze. She mentally mapped her escape route, but the enormity of the dungeons alarmed her and dampened her hope of escape.

Cell after cell passed by, and she wondered how many others were held captive there. *Are they all treated the same way I am? For their sakes, I hope not.*

Pigman jerked the chain to the right as hard as he could. The sudden change in direction buckled her arms. She fell sideways and smashed her right shoulder into the wall. She winced as pain shot down her arm and numbed her fingers. Pigman snorted with laughter.

Laugh all you want. I'm gonna hang you from your own chain.

"Ya like it when I pull on ya chain, don't ya, dog?" he grunted. "I'd choke the life right out of ya if I didn't think ya'd enjoy it." He snorted with laughter again.

A thin line of blood ran down her shoulder from the fresh wound. She turned her head and locked eyes with Pigman. His laughter abruptly twisted into labored breathing. Without taking her gaze away from him, she gently licked the blood from her arm. His pink flesh paled.

She smiled at him with her freshly bloodied teeth. Pigman swallowed hard. Satisfied with her result, she turned and moved on and dragged him behind.

At the next turn, Pigman squeaked out a "Left," and then farther down the passageway squealed, "Right," instead of yanking the chain again. She smiled to herself, knowing that she'd gained the upper hand.

Killing you will be a simple matter. Her mouth watered at the thought.

A large, burly man leaned against the wall next to the door at the end of the passageway with his oxen arms folded under his massive chest. Veins bulged beneath his skin, and he filled most of the hallway with his mass.

The man raised his head and then stood tall as they approached his post. Aria's triumph over Pigman faded into bleakness as she met the man's one-eyed gaze. She quickly averted her eyes, choosing to stare at the cracks in the stone floor.

"Come back for more, did ya?" boomed the one-eyed man. He stepped in front of the door and blocked their path.

They came to an abrupt halt in front of the one-eyed man. The chain links rattled in Pigman's trembling hand.

"Step aside," said Pigman. His voice trembled like the chain. "M-master Dragnus has summoned this f-filthy d-d-dog." His voice cracked like an adolescent boy's.

The one-eyed man bent down, grabbed a fistful of Aria's hair, and yanked her head up. His lips lingered only inches from hers and their noses nearly touched.

"And what does Master Dragnus want with this barkless bitch?" The stench of ale and garlic on his breath turned her stomach. "She's only got one useful quality, and it ain't breeding."

He leaned back and smiled at her. His crooked, yellowed teeth glistened in the torch light, and bits of food lodged between them. She wanted to reach up and rip out his other eye.

"Leave her with me. I'm sure Master Dragnus can find another whore."

She spat in his face and immediately regretted it. *That was stupid, Aria.* She'd pay for it later.

"The d-doings of M-master Dragnus ain't ya concern," said Pigman.

The one-eyed man ignored Pigman and calmly wiped the saliva from his nose and cheeks. Even though he only had one eye, she knew he winked at her as he licked her saliva from his fingers. She wanted to spit in his face again, but her mouth wouldn't cooperate. She hated him and everything he stood for, and she hated looking at his ugly face.

She glared at him. *After I'm done with Pigman, I'm coming after you.*

An air of confidence returned to Pigman's voice. "We ain't got no time fer this. Now step aside."

The one-eyed man released her hair, but he kept his eye on her. "As you wish."

He stood and then kicked the side of Aria's head with his massive boot, knocking her into the wall. The taste of blood filled her mouth, and she spat it on his boots.

"Save it for later, dog. I'll be waiting for you."

And I'll take your other eye, too. And then your life.

The one-eyed man pulled the heavy iron door open without an inkling of effort and held it open. A cold draft swept through the doorway and left Aria frigid. Through the doorway, a narrow set of stone steps led upward and into the night. Happy to distance herself from the one-eyed brute, Aria quickened her pace and started up the slick steps.

She and Pigman were halfway up the narrow steps when the door slammed behind them. The vibration of the stones matched her ringing ears. Louder still, Pigman wheezed and coughed as he tried to catch his breath. It brought a brief smile to her face.

Moonlight bathed the last few stairs with its soft glow, casting shadows all around the small courtyard. The sound of the sea crashing against the sheer rock cliffs filled the crisp night air. The sweet smell of frilac mixed with the salty smell of the sea and created an irresistibly wonderful aroma. The smell livened the air and tickled her nostrils, sending chills down her spine and into her legs.

Captive in the dungeons for so long, she'd forgotten what it was like to breathe fresh air. Her chest heaved as she gulped in as much of it as her lungs would hold.

Thank You for this, ɛ̄ṭūr.

A four-foot high limestone wall lined the northern and western ends of the courtyard. Beyond the wall, a 200-meter drop met the sharp rocks below, and then the Discidium Sea. The southern and eastern ends of the wall nestled up against the towering greenish-grey walls of the fortress.

At the center of the courtyard towered an eight-foot frilac bush. Pink and purple puffs, like cotton, covered every square inch of the bush's surface. Rounded grey cobblestones circled the bush and separated it from the dead, greyish hamid grass.

They headed toward the arched entrance at the southern end of the courtyard. The rough, short grass tickled her hands and feet. She wanted to lie in it and gaze into the darkened sky just as she had when she was a little girl.

The stars fascinated her. She wondered if life existed beyond them, waiting for discovery. She also wondered if her father looked down on her with his kind and loving smile as he always had. Tears filled her eyes as she remembered the soft, loving features of his face.

I miss you, Papa.

She closed her eyes and remembered riding her horse, Peppa, through lush meadows of grass, and feeling the warm wind rush over her skin and through her long, blonde hair. She loved the feeling of freedom it gave her.

She also remembered the first time Peppa threw her to the ground when a lone wolf's howl spooked him. She'd been afraid to get back on him, but her father comforted her and coaxed her into doing so again.

The wisdom of his words conveyed love and courage and filled her mind as though he stood by her side again: *"No matter what life throws at you, or throws you from, face it head-on and without fear. Ƨätür has a plan for each of us, and our destinies are only a moment away. So get back up on that horse and ride like the wind!"*

Determination drove her to make him proud.

A tug on the chain pulled her thoughts back to the small courtyard.

"Keep it moving." Pigman snorted.

"Throw him over the edge," said a voice.

She nearly jumped out of her skin. She twisted around, trying to locate its source. Pigman stood behind her, glaring holes through her. He'd obviously not heard the voice.

They were alone.

Just let go.

His sheathed sword hung at his side.

Let him have it.

Her heart hammered.

What are you waiting for?

Recklessness swelled inside her, and she didn't want to control it.

She wanted to be free again.

She wanted Pigman to pay for the horrible things he'd done to her.

Release me!

She gave in to the raging storm within, letting it fill her mind and soul. Rage washed away all of her aches and pains and freed her, if only for a moment.

Now!

Aria spun around, grabbed the chain tying her to Pigman, and yanked as hard as she could. Pigman stumbled forward, grunted, and pulled back on the chain. She vaulted through the air at Pigman, using his momentum to her advantage. His beady little eyes swelled as he fumbled with the sword at his side.

The smell of fear and sweat filled her nostrils as she tore into his throat with her ragged teeth. Pigman staggered backward, moving them closer and closer to the western wall of the courtyard. He pushed against her chin and forehead with his hands as he struggled to get her off him.

Aria pulled back, ripping a mouthful of flesh from Pigman's neck. He squealed and covered the wound with his hand. She gagged and spit out the chunk of flesh. All traces of fear and humanity left his eyes, replaced by a wild, seething hatred.

Sha-shing!

The sound of a sword being freed from its scabbard rang in the air, drowning out every other sound. Steel flashed in the moonlight as it arced over Pigman's head.

The world around her advanced in slow motion, and every movement lasted an eternity. The *thump-thump* of her heart pounded in her head. Her thoughts raced a million miles an hour. She stood little chance of avoiding the downward-arcing blade.

I'm dead.

She wanted to look away from his beady little eyes; his ugly, porcine face was the last thing she wanted to see before dying. She lunged forward again and threw her weight into Pigman's gut. He staggered backward, but the blade continued its course toward her face.

Pigman's eyes went wide as he slammed against the wall, its rough edge catching the middle of his back. His arms flailed, and the blade *clanged* flatly against Aria's steel collar.

Pigman lost his grip on the sword and dropped it over the side of the wall. The blade fell down the side of the cliff and out of sight, and it clanged against the rocks.

Pigman's eyes rolled to the back of his head and he grabbed his bleeding neck. Aria stepped back until the chain was taut and then ran and kicked Pigman square in the chest with both feet. The blow toppled Pigman over the wall, his arms flailing.

Aria landed on her back, but Pigman's momentum pulled the chain and her with it, crushed her against the side of the wall, and her collar nearly tore her head from her shoulders. The limestone wall ripped into her flesh as she slid up and on top of it. She grabbed at the wall, trying to stop herself from going over its edge.

Her vision blurred with pain, but she didn't give in to its fury. She held on to the wall with every ounce of her strength, afraid to look down, but she did anyway.

At the other end of the chain, cuffed to his wrist, Pigman dangled like a rag doll. His arm twisted behind him in an unnatural position, nearly torn from its socket. He groped at his mangled arm with his other, but it'd be the least of his pain. The sea raged below and drowned out his bloodied screams. The sight of him both sickened her and gave her pleasure at the same time.

At least I've kept one promise.

"ʔäʈūr," she cried. "If this is my time then make it quick."

She peered into the dark sea below. She had nowhere to go but down. Peace washed over her body.

I'm coming, Papa.

She let go of the wall. In a blur, Pigman's weight carried her over the edge.

Pain infused every muscle as she slammed against the face of the cliff. Every bone in her body felt as though they'd shattered. She couldn't feel her legs. Had they been ripped from her torso? Darkness rushed in around her and swallowed everything in its path.

Then it swallowed her.

CHAPTER TEN

R ayah lay in the snow next to Alderan, staring up at the cold, grey sky. The clouds, as dark and ominous as their moods, soldiered north across the Reis Duron Grasslands.

Many months had passed without a sign of Aria and Alderan's fear of never finding her had begun pushing a wedge between them. They'd followed every lead they could find, but each one eventually proved to be a dead end.

Last night she'd received a message from Savric. She must deliver Alderan. But how would she accomplish it? They were at such odds.

You've made a promise, Rayah. You need to keep it.

But could she deceive Alderan? *You've come this far already.* Besides, the fate of the Ancient Realm rested in her hands, right?

Rayah sighed. "We've followed leads that have taken us from the Procerus Mountains to the Quietus Forest, and we still have nothing to go on. I know you don't want to hear it, Alderan, but I think it's time we stop."

Alderan huffed. "What do you mean?"

She knew he understood her statement. He was in another one of his "moods," but she didn't care. "You haven't felt the bond with Aria since the day you were attacked."

"You think I don't know that? I live with that knowledge every day. I don't need you constantly reminding me of something I'll never forget."

His stubbornness made her blood boil at times. He needed a dose of reality, and she gave it to him. "How long are you planning on looking for her before you're ready to accept the fact that she's probably dead?"

The moment the words left her lips she regretted every one of them. She wished she could pull them back into her mouth and swallow them whole. Too late.

"Just shut up!" he yelled. "You don't have a clue as to how the bond works."

Rayah sat up. She really wanted to keep her mouth shut, but in the heat of the moment it seemed beyond her control. "Neither do you. You said you'd been able to feel her presence your entire life and now you feel nothing. What else could it possibly mean, Alderan? Huh?"

"I don't know, but I'm *not* giving up on her."

Why can't he see the truth?

She wished she could just slap some sense into him. "I don't wanna see you waste your whole life searching for someone who can't be found."

"She's my sister!" he screamed. "I'll never stop looking for her." The anger in his voice scared her. "Go home, Rayah. Go back to your precious little life you had before you met me. I don't need your help."

She sat in the snow next to him, shivering with cold. Her teeth chattered. "You know I can't do that."

"Yes, you can," he said. "There's no reason for you to be here. You owe me nothing."

She rubbed her arms with her hands to try and warm the blood in her ice-cold veins. "You know why I'm here, Alderan. I'm just as guilty as you are. I stood by and did nothing while those people in your village were slaughtered. I can't go back home, and I won't leave you. You're my friend."

Besides, you're all I have.

Alderan sat up and glared daggers through her skull. "My friend? Really? You sit there and stab me in the back, twist the knife for additional pain, and then have the nerve to call yourself my friend?"

He shivered too, but she knew it wasn't from the cold.

He jumped up and stormed away, yelling over his shoulder, "Go home, and leave me alone! I don't need you or your help."

I need you though.

Tears slid down her frozen cheeks and hardened into small shards of ice as they fell to her lap. She knew his words were hollow, but they still stung nonetheless.

She'd grown fond of him over the last several months as they traveled around, searching for Aria. She hoped one day he'd be more than just a friend. She'd never been in love before, wasn't sure she'd know if she were, but she couldn't imagine her life without him in it.

I'll let this go for now.

She wiped her cheeks with her chilled hands and pulled her pink scarf tight around her neck. She wanted to jump up, chase after him, and tell him she was sorry, but his mood was so foul she feared it would only deepen the rift between them.

She didn't want that, so she'd let him brood awhile before following after him. She lay back in the snow like a fallen angel.

The last few days of their travel proved brutal, ending with another dead-end in the middle of nowhere. Several days had passed since they'd seen another person and many more since they'd slept in a warm bed. They'd been getting little sleep on the road, and Rayah found her eyelids impossibly heavy.

Tomorrow I'll find a way to deliver you, Alderan. And I pray that you'll forgive me for doing so.

She yawned and wrapped her arms around herself. *I'll just close my eyes for a few minutes and then I'll go after him.*

She went out like a blown candle a moment later.

† † †

Alderan only made it a hundred yards before plopping down in the snow. His eyes blurred with tears, and the thought of Aria being dead terrified him.

She can't be dead. I won't let her be dead. I'll never give up looking for her.

The audacity of Rayah's words ate at his mind like maggots. "Where does she get off telling me to quit looking for my sister?"

Deep down, he knew she was right, but he still couldn't admit it to himself, and admitting it to her seemed impossible. To her credit, she'd stuck with him for months, serving as a shoulder to cry on when he needed it and a verbal punching bag on the toughest of days.

She's been a friend since the beginning. Why do I always treat her so badly?

Ugh! Why does she even put up with me? All I ever do is bring her down into my sorrow and then scold her when she tries to pull me up from it.

What have I ever done for her? What kind of a friend am I? Aria's slipping from my grasp and I'm pushing Rayah away with all my strength.

This can't be the end. I can't imagine my life without Rayah. I need to find her and apologize before I lose her too.

† † †

A loud noise brought Rayah out of her slumber and into the middle of a raging storm.

The wind picked up speed and howled as it raced across the open grasslands. The clouds joined in, sending flurries of snow as they crossed overhead, blanketing everything with frozen mischief.

Not to be outdone by the wind and snow, lightning lit the grey sky in a bright, fantastic display, splitting the air with glorious force. Thunder followed closely behind, rumbling in the sky and shaking the ground with its mighty fist.

Every muscle in her body ached and her bones cracked as she sat up and pushed away the piling snow. Her body fought back hard as she forced herself to stand. She thought she might pass out from the pain, but its brutal punches softened after a few minutes.

She turned in circles looking for Alderan in the blowing white haze. She screamed his name, but the frenzy of the storm vanquished the sound after it left her lips. She looked everywhere for his tracks, but the windblown snow left no evidence of his passing. He'd vanished, and she was lost.

Where are you Alderan? I really need you.

She dug her nails into her palms. She knew it would do more harm than good to cry, and she struggled to keep the tears from forming.

The wind cut through her layers of clothing and stung her skin. Her fingers grew so stiff that she could no longer bend them. She tucked her hands inside her coat, but it made little difference. In the middle of nowhere with no shelter to be found, she sat back down and curled into a ball to try and block as much of the wind from her face as possible.

What hope did she have of survival? The storm showed no signs of letting up, and the likelihood of someone finding her teetered on the impossible. She wanted to believe she'd survive, but the snow continued to cake on her body again.

It's so cold. Where are you Alderan?

She'd pretty much lost all feeling in her extremities. Her lungs froze from the inside out, each breath a forced labor. Certain they were frozen shut, she struggled to open her eyes. Would her eyelids rip apart if she were to force them open? She didn't know, and fear kept her from finding out.

She didn't want to die. She should've begged Ɂäṭūr to spare her life, but her thoughts kept drifting to Alderan. His life mattered to her more than hers.

I hope you're still alive, and I pray Ɂäṭūr watches over you and keeps you safe. I'm so sorry for hurting you. I only said it because I love you, Alderan.

The thought startled her.

Do I? Do I love him?

The thought of him, of being in love with him, warmed her inside even though she knew she teetered on the brink of death. *I think I must.* Had her face not been a frozen sculpture, she would've smiled.

Ɂäṭūr, please save him. And, if I survive, allow him to love me back.

She couldn't explain why, but she knew she'd never tell him how she felt were she to see him again. She'd be content just being his friend—unless he wanted more. She'd leave that decision to him.

She didn't care that they came from different races—different worlds. No one would ever need to know. She hid her wings just as easily as she melted into the ground. *I wish I could melt into the ground now!* The ground beneath her felt hard as rock and may as well have been just that.

Even if Alderan did harbor feelings for her, he might not tell her unless Aria approved, and her being dead would make that even more difficult. His whole world revolved around Aria. She understood why, but it didn't make it any easier on her. *I really do want to like her.*

Mixed in with the sounds of the howling wind, she swore she heard her name. Her heart began beating a bit faster.

Please let it be Alderan.

She strained to block the noise of the wind from her mind and concentrated on the sounds within it. She would've sat up if she'd been able to move.

Again, closer this time, she definitely heard her name. *Alderan!* She tried to make a sound, even move a muscle, but her body wouldn't cooperate.

No! Ɀäṭūr, please let him find me. I don't wanna die. Not when I have so much to live for.

† † †

"Rayah!" screamed Alderan. He stumbled over the frozen ground.

Guide me, Ɀäṭūr.

"Rayah!"

White blanketed everything. He barely saw a few inches in front of his face.

I can't give up on her too.

"Rayah!"

† † †

Rayah knew Alderan stood close. His voice rumbled above the wind. "Rayah!"

Please, Ɀäṭūr! I'm begging You, let him find me!

"Rayah!"

Her blanket of snow burdened her with its weight, and her breathing grew more and more shallow. Before long she'd stop breathing.

Please, Alderan, don't give up on me!

† † †

"Rayah!" screamed Alderan.

Crimson droplets splattered across the pure white snow when he coughed. His lungs and throat were raw from the frigid air. His voice would give out soon.

I'm so sorry, Rayah. Forgive me.

His feet were non-existent as they pushed through the deep snow. His hands blistered with frostbite. He couldn't feel his face. Small icicles of snot hung from his nostrils like fangs and broke off when he placed his hand above his mouth.

"Rayah!" he screamed.

He couldn't even hear his own voice anymore. He shouldn't have left her alone. She'd be dead when he found her, and if so, he knew he'd never forgive himself. He dropped to his knees, overtaken with exhaustion.

"Rayah," he pleaded. "Where are you?"

† † †

Buried in a snowy coffin and unable to move, Rayah knew her time had come.

I'm here, she thought.

She took one last breath and then her world stopped.

CHAPTER ELEVEN

Two torches crackled and popped in their triangular, black-iron sconces, throwing both light and shadow across the cell floor. A young woman who wore nothing but a silver collar and lots of blood slumped against chains that bound her arms and legs to the southern wall.

Amicus leaned against the western wall, transfixed by her. Across the cell, one-eyed Jess sat in a wooden chair and leaned back against the wall. A yellow straw hat rested over the top of his face. His barrel-chest rose and fell slowly, but Amicus didn't think Jess slept.

The young woman moaned softly.

"I think she's waking up," said Amicus. He looked over at Jess.

"Well throw some water on her and help her along then." Jess didn't bother looking up from under his hat.

Amicus sighed. "I don't think it'll be necessary."

"Don't matter what you think," said Jess. "She stinks like a pig. Go get the water or you'll join her in chains."

With a curt nod and a scowl, he hurried from the cell and down the dungeon passageway. At the end of the passageway stood Brently—a lanky fellow. Amicus met his brown-eyed gaze with a smile.

"How's yer family?" asked Brently.

"Great, as always. Vonah never stops talking about her giant friend, Brently. She adores you, you know."

Brently's ghostly cheeks reddened. "She's uh special girl, fer sure."

Jorg, a younger guardsman, walked up to Amicus and Brently. "Ya guys up to something good?" His green eyes sparkled with mischief.

"Funny you should ask," said Amicus. "Run fetch me a pail of water."

Jorg stood there with raised eyebrows and blinked.

Brently scowled at the boy. "Full bucket. Direct order. Why ain't yeh movin?"

Jorg nodded and then took off through the heavy iron door and up the steep steps. The door creaked as it swung back in and then slammed home, vibrating the air.

Amicus chatted with Brently, but his mind kept focusing on the young girl. He didn't know her, but her dire condition broke his heart.

Ʒäṭūr, what can I do to help her?

The dungeon door swung open and Jorg stepped through with a full bucket of water. Steam rose from his shaved head and perspiration glistened on his forehead. He sat the bucket down at Amicus's feet and wiped his brow with the back of his hand. "Anything else?"

Amicus picked the bucket up by its handle. "Thank you, Jorg. That'll be all for now."

He nodded at Brently and then carried the bucket back down the passageway and to the cell with Jess and the girl. He set the bucket down with a grunt. Water sloshed out of the bucket and across the stone floor and mixed with the blood and urine pooled under the girl.

"Don't just stand there," said Jess. "Pick up the bucket and wake her up."

Amicus panted. "Think maybe you should do it, Jess. I don't think I can lift the bucket high enough right now."

"You're pathetic."

Jess jumped up from his chair with speed and grace unbefitting a man his size. He shoved Amicus out of the way and grabbed the bucket with one hand. With the flick of his wrist, he soaked the young woman in ice-cold water.

The links of chain clinked together and pulled tight as the young woman struggled against them. Her eyes fluttered and then cracked opened—they were swollen and bloodshot. Her green-eyed gaze focused on Jess. She didn't scream, but he swore her eyes did—with hatred.

"Looks like someone's ready to play." Jess smiled at her with his crooked and yellowed teeth. "About time, too. I was starting to get bored, but I didn't wanna start without ya."

Jess hurled the bucket at her, and it struck her square in the jaw with a *thud*. Her neck snapped back, and the back of her head slammed into the wall. The bucket fell to the floor with a hollow *thunk*.

Her head slumped forward, and fresh blood trickled down the wall where her head had smacked it.

Amicus gasped. "What are you doing, Jess?" He edged his way toward the door. "Master Dragnus isn't gonna like this."

Jess turned on him, his voice seething with hate. "Far as Master Dragnus knows, she's swimming with the fish. Ya wanna join her, Amicus?"

Jess basically owned the dungeons and wasn't one to be tested. Amicus eyed the floor. "I don't want any trouble, Jess. You know I have a family."

Jess grabbed him by the throat, lifted him off the ground, and pulled him within inches of his face. Amicus stared into Jess's one eye, and gulped as he watched the madness swirl around in its inky, blackness.

"I'd be more than happy to take care of the ole wife for ya, if ya catch my meaning," said Jess. He blinked. Or had he winked?

Amicus nodded, unable to respond in any other fashion. Jess released him, and he crumpled to the floor. He coughed and massaged his neck. He hated Jess.

How dare you threaten my family. I'll see that you get yours, Jess.

Jess sat back down in his chair and leaned back against the wall. "I saved her life. Grabbed her feet as she plunged over the wall. I told her before I wasn't done with her. I keep my word." He gritted his teeth. "I'll have both her eyes to pay for the one she took from me. And then I'll slit her damn throat."

Amicus stared at the floor. *The only throat that's gonna be slit is yours.*

"Well don't just sit there, you pathetic fool. Get a rag and clean her up." Jess lowered his hat down over his eye.

Amicus got up from the floor, still clutching his throat. *Today's the last day I do your bidding.* He grabbed the bucket off the floor and stormed out of the cell.

Who does he think he is?

He brushed past a man in the hallway and ignored whatever the man said.

"I won't be treated this way," he mumbled. "I take pride in my position, and I don't take advantage of prisoners. I do my job, and then I go home to my family."

Brently stood guard at the door at the end of the passageway. His goofy grin faded, and lines of concern marked his forehead when Amicus stopped at the door. "Ya okay, Amicus?"

He gave Brently a nod, pulled the heavy iron door open, and stepped through the doorway. "Never better, Brently. Never better." He turned back to Brently. "I'll be back with some more water shortly. Can you find me a rag?"

Brently's face brightened. "Certain I could."

"Thank you." Amicus slammed the door behind himself and then took the stone steps two at a time.

He stopped at the top of the steps and breathed deeply. The wind scaled the sheer cliff walls and howled as it whipped through the courtyard. Its cold bite nipped at his exposed face and neck. Small flakes of snow twirled in circles around him as they searched for safe landing. Far below the courtyard, the waves of the Discidium Sea crashed against the rocks like thunder and settled his nerves.

His breath plumed in the cold, early morning air. "Winter's arrived."

A square, stone water well sat in the northeastern corner of the courtyard, nestled between the northern wall of the courtyard and the western wall of the fortress. A pitched roof sat atop four wooden stilts that straddled the well.

A wooden crankshaft spanned the width of the well's opening. 300 meters of rope coiled around the crankshaft and its end looped through two hefty handles of a large wooden bucket and then knotted back to itself.

Amicus sat his bucket down and then lifted the catch on the crankshaft. The crankshaft spun and whirred with ferocity, dispensing meter after meter of rope and hurling the large bucket down the dark well shaft. The crankshaft slowed and then stopped with only a few meters of rope still coiled around it. The faint *splash* of water rose from the shaft.

Ought to take the rope and hang Jess with it.

Amicus pushed the catch back down on the crankshaft and turned the crank. By the time the bucket reached the top of the well wall, all the muscles in his arm burned, especially his forearm. He pulled the large bucket to the side and let it rest on top of the well wall.

He positioned his bucket next to the well wall, just below the larger bucket, and then tipped the large bucket so the water spilled out of it and into his bucket. The ice-cold water splashed him and made his hands ache.

How am I supposed to put this freezing water on that poor girl? He hated the simple answer: either it went on her or him. He shook his head.

He left the large bucket perched on top of the well wall and carried his bucket across the courtyard and back down the steep steps. At the bottom of the steps, he kicked at the large iron door with his boot and then stepped back. A moment later, the door swung open. Brently's smiling face greeted him.

"Thank you, Brently." Amicus stepped through the doorway and then Brently closed the door.

Brently held up a greyish-brown cloth. "This do?"

"Perfect. Just lay it over my shoulder." Brently did so and Amicus beelined down the passageway and to the cell. He set the bucket down and leaned against the wall to catch his breath.

Jess laughed at him. "You're sucking wind as bad as that fat pig swimming in the sea."

Amicus's blood boiled, but he bit his tongue and changed the subject. "This is gonna take a while. You may as well go do your rounds, Jess. I'll have her cleaned up by the time you get back."

"Fine," said Jess. He got up and walked to the door. Turning back, he said, "She'd better be ready by the time I get back. Her and I have business to finish." He grinned.

Amicus's stomach gurgled. "She'll be ready."

And so will I.

"You'd better hope so." He walked out.

Amicus pulled a small cup from his pocket, filled it with water from the bucket, and set it aside. He dipped the rag into the bucket of water. *Wow, that's cold.* He wished he'd had time to warm the water a little before cleaning the young woman up with it. He stepped over to her and put his ear close to her mouth. She breathed shallowly, but steady.

"This is gonna be cold," he said. She didn't move or react to his voice.

Can she even hear me?

He wiped the blood on her forehead as gently as he could. She made no sound, but gooseflesh crawled across her bare skin. "I'm so sorry, Caterpillar."

He slowly worked his way down her body, scrubbing as little as he could to keep her discomfort to a minimum. By the time he made it down to her feet, she'd regained consciousness again. He felt her eyes on him, but she said nothing. He'd heard that she never spoke. Maybe she couldn't?

Amicus stood. Her eyes followed him, but she didn't raise her head.

"Would you like some water?" he asked. He took the blink of her eyes to be a "yes."

He reached down and grabbed the cup of water he'd set aside. He tilted her head up as gently as he could and poured a small amount of water between her parted lips. She struggled to swallow. Her condition twisted his stomach in knots and pained his heart.

How can they be so brutal?

He turned away from her so she couldn't see the tear rolling down his cheek, and then coughed to cover wiping it away. He looked back at her; she'd noticed. He smiled and pulled the strands of dirty, blonde hair away from her face.

Under all those cuts and bruises, I see you're beautiful.

Amicus leaned forward and whispered in her ear, "As long as you're here and I'm still breathing, no further harm will come to you. I swear on my life."

This time, a tear came from her eye. He wiped it away with his thumb just before Jess stepped back into the cell.

"Ya better be done with that barkless bitch," said Jess. He glared at them both with his one eye.

"Just finished," said Amicus. He smiled at Jess. His stomach lurched, knowing his plan.

Jess pushed him out of the way. "Leave us," he growled. "This ain't gonna be pretty."

You've got that right.

Amicus pulled the knife from his belt, grabbed Jess by the back of the head with one hand, and slashed the knife across his throat with the other. Blood spewed from Jess's neck, but the big man didn't go down.

Jess turned on Amicus, his eye wild with rage. He grabbed Amicus by the throat and slammed him against the wall. The jolt knocked the knife from Amicus's hand.

Amicus tried to pry Jess's fingers off his throat, but the beastly man held tight. Repeatedly, Jess slammed him against the wall until his arms fell limp at his sides.

† † †

Jess threw Amicus to the floor. He lay there, slumped against the wall like a sack of potatoes. Jess turned on Aria, clutching his bleeding throat.

"You're next," he gurgled.

CHAPTER TWELVE

The storm passed with the night, and the new day sun peeked just over the horizon. Alderan lay in a fetal position atop the flattened, brown grass, surrounded by a deep wall of snow. Any other day he would've wondered why the snow had melted around him and nowhere else, but on this day, the end of a pink scarf, *her* pink scarf, poked out from the snow wall in front of him and captured his every thought.

He called Rayah's name several times, barely mustering a whisper through his raw throat, but she hadn't responded. He wanted to dig through the snow and find her sleeping, but he knew in his heart she wouldn't be. Fear froze him in place. Guilt festered inside him and poisoned his thoughts.

She's dead because of me. Why am I still alive? Everyone I've ever cared about is gone. Am I the only one left in this world? Is this my punishment for neglecting them? Abandoned by all?

Ɂäṭūr, I beg you, please strike me dead. I don't deserve to live anymore.

Warm tears streaked down his cheeks, but he paid them no attention. "I came back for you," he whispered. "I was right here, next to you... calling for you... but you didn't answer." He screamed at the sky, "Why didn't you answer me?"

His heart—a block of ice in his chest—pumped icy water through his veins and left him cold and alone. The warmth of the sun on his side did nothing to relieve the chill in his bones. Perhaps nothing ever would.

His last words to her looped over and over in his mind: *"Go home, and leave me alone! I don't need you or your help."*

I didn't mean it, Rayah. I did need you. I still need you, and it's too late.

You were more than a friend, Rayah. I hope you knew that even though I was too afraid to tell you.

He'd give anything to erase the previous day. "I've lost you both," he whispered.

A few months ago, he would've never imagined his life turning out the way it had. His perfect life had morphed into a living nightmare he'd never wake from.

He sat up and leaned against one of the walls of snow, across from *her* pink scarf. *Rayah. My winged angel. Forgive me.*

"Yesterday—" his voice cracked. He coughed and cleared his throat. "Yesterday was a hard day, Rayah. Harder than most. I wanted to tell you something yesterday, but I couldn't seem to find the right moment. And then, I was afraid that if I did tell you, you'd feel sorry for me, and that was the last thing I wanted. I was in so much agony and I took it out on you. I didn't mean to hurt you, Rayah."

His lower lip trembled. "I know you can't hear me, but this is something I have to get off my chest... before it eats a hole in me. Yesterday was my name day, and now I'm sixteen..."

Tears poured from his eyes, and he could barely speak through the sobbing. "...and Aria would've been as well. We were born just minutes apart, me just before her. I miss her so much, and now I'm completely lost without you both."

His stomach whirled with nausea. The world around him spun out of control, and he had no idea how to stop it.

"Tell me you're not dead, Rayah. Please don't leave me here all alone. I *do* need your help finding Aria, and I *do* need you." He wiped away the tears, but his eyes blurred again.

He reached out and touched the pink scarf. A tingling sensation flowed into his fingers, through his hand, and then traveled up the length of his arm. He jerked his fingers away from the scarf and the tingling faded away.

That's odd...

He touched the scarf again and the sensation flowed quicker—up his arm and across his shoulder. He pulled his fingers away again, afraid of what might happen if it made its way up his neck and into his head. The tingling faded again, but slower than the first time.

He'd never felt a sensation quite like it—numb like when one of his arms or legs fell asleep, but it didn't prickle. Instead, it warmed him like a fire on a cold winter's day and left him cozy and relaxed.

Just take hold of it.

Despite the comfort of its touch, fear seized his nerve. His heart thumped in his chest.

I've lost everything. What else have I got to lose? Nothing.

He closed his eyes, told his arm to reach out and his hand to grab hold of the scarf, but his body didn't move.

Don't do it for yourself, Alderan. Do it for Rayah.

He opened his eyes and gazed at the pink scarf. The world faded around him until nothing remained but him and the scarf. His trembling arm extended, and his fingers met the soft fabric.

The tingling swept up his arm, across his shoulder, and crawled up the back of his neck like a spider. He grabbed hold of the scarf and balled his hand into a fist, determined not to let it go again. A bright light flashed—not before his eyes, but within his mind.

He blinked. Twice. He no longer lay in a hole clutching the end of a pink scarf sticking out from a wall of snow. Instead, he stared up at a large grey face with a crooked nose, brown eyes the size of chicken eggs, and a mouth filled with crooked teeth. Did it smile at him or snarl?

He stared into its eyes and saw a reflection in them, but not of himself. *Rayah!* He watched—through her eyes—as the creature gently lifted her from the snow with its massive hands and tree-trunk arms. She shivered and Alderan shivered with her.

Rayah's alive! But is this creature her savior or captor?

Blood coursed through his veins as his heart roared back to life. Tears of joy spilled from his eyes. *Zäṭūr, watch over Rayah and keep her safe until I can get to her.*

The tingling faded from his head. His vision blurred and darkened until the world around him became unrecognizable. Then everything morphed into a blurry white background with a splash of pink. His eyes refocused as the tingling faded from his body completely.

The pink scarf drooped in front of him. When had he let it go? He reached out with his left hand, but a tingly feeling surfaced on the inside of his wrist.

He pulled his arm back and turned his hand palm up.

At the center of his wrist, a spot about half an inch wide and an inch long glowed with a grey hue. He rubbed the spot with his thumb, but it lingered. The tingling intensified, and the spot brightened, and then something most peculiar happened: four beams of light—one from each corner of the rectangular spot—rose from his wrist at slightly outward angles.

About six inches above his wrist, the beams halted and formed another rectangular plane—like the one on his wrist—about five inches wide and seven inches long. Then the ends of the plane rolled together and formed what looked like a scroll.

The beams of light shortened, and the scroll shrank and melted into the rectangle on his wrist. The rectangle pulsed and transfigured into a scroll. The light faded until only a grey scroll remained. The tingling ceased and Alderan drew a deep breath.

He rubbed his wrist, the scroll branded into his flesh. "Ɂäțūr, what just happened?"

His pulse raced, and his breath shortened. He eyed the pink scarf.

Rayah? What other powers does she have?

He touched the scarf again, but nothing happened. He twisted his fingers around the silky-smooth fabric and tugged on it. It slid out from the wall a few inches and stopped.

He sat up, pulled on the scarf a little harder, and the wall of snow crashed down on him. He wiped the snow from his eyes and spat it from his mouth. A smaller hole lay on the other side of the fallen wall, but Rayah didn't occupy it.

Elation and horror gripped him. *She was only two feet away from me. Why didn't she answer when I called her?*

He stood and brushed the snow from his trousers. "Rayah!" His voice sounded like a dog's bark, but hoarse. "Where are you?"

No response.

With her scarf in-hand, Alderan climbed his way out of the hole and onto the frozen layers of ice and snow. Deep footprints marred the snow's surface. The flat, six-toed prints dwarfed his own. The tracks came from the south and led west.

He had no idea what he might encounter, but if the size of the prints and length of stride were indicators, the creature would be more than twelve feet tall. His stomach turned with unease.

He tucked the pink scarf in his pack and then followed the tracks west. The thought of never catching up with them sat in the back of his mind, and he did his best to keep it there. At least he had hope again.

Hang on, Rayah. I'm coming for you.

CHAPTER THIRTEEN

N ardus sat at the edge of the great chasm with his feet dangling over its side, trying to gain control over his faltering nerves. He'd been atop many high places and had never suffered from fear, but the void beneath his feet left him with an overwhelming feeling of nausea. He stared into the darkened abyss and swore he heard it laugh at him and taunt him.

"I won't let you keep me from my family!" he screamed.

I'm screaming at a pit as though it were alive. He laughed maniacally, and the abyss echoed his sentiment. *Sanity's definitely not my strong point.*

He rose to his feet and gazed across the expanse to Ţämbəll Dhef Däd Dhä. Nestled between massive walls of brown stone, stairs led up to a gated entrance. The great vines that anchored the temple to the ground swayed back and forth, driven by the wind currents rising from the void.

The blistering air carried with it a pungent odor he could only describe as death. Even in its smoldering wake, he felt cold to his core.

In his mind, he pictured the entrance of the temple and imagined stepping over to it as he had with the Great Library, but nothing happened. *Damn! Why does everything have to be so difficult?* The only viable plan he and Gnaud came up with entailed him climbing up one of the four massive vines.

He stared at the vine in front of him—a massive network of smaller vines, continually twisting and choking each other for position along the outer surface. Small thorns covered nearly every square inch, gleaming in the pale light like razor sharp needles.

The vines were alive—not just physically, but consciously. They stared right back at him and waited for him to make the first move while they continuously plotted his demise.

Nardus shook his head. *They're just vines, Nardus. Get a hold of yourself.*

He couldn't decipher the purpose of the vines; did they hold up the temple or keep it anchored to the ground? Either case made his heart race with anxiety. They twisted and swayed and mesmerized him.

Tiny little voices filled the air, all hissing in unison like a chorus, begging him to grab hold of them and release his blood to them.

"Feed us," they whispered. "Spill your blood..."

Chills ran down his body and curled his toes. He rubbed his worn hands together, trying to bring warmth back into them. *My mind's shot. I know vines can't speak, but I still hear them. Madness.*

Nardus couldn't turn back, but he didn't want to move forward either. If he somehow made it to the temple entrance in one piece, he could scarcely imagine what kind of horrors lurked within the shadows beyond its doors.

Dread pulled at his nerves and soured his queasy stomach. His added weight on the vines, as minimal as it would be, would rip their roots from the ground and send him plunging to his death, wouldn't it? An image of himself falling flashed across his vision like a phantom from the future. He shuddered.

For Vitara. For my children.

He set his jaw with determination and worked the doubt from his thoughts as best he could. With a crack in his voice, he muttered, "It's now or never, Nardus."

He reached into the satchel that Gnaud had put together for him and pulled out some thick, leather gloves. He slid them on. *A perfect fit.* They cooled and soothed his tattered, swollen flesh.

He pulled out a couple of thick leather pieces and some leather straps from the satchel as well, and then lifted the satchel over his shoulder. He used the leather pieces as kneepads and the straps to secure them around his legs.

He put his hand to his hip and verified his newly acquired knife still hung from his belt. He took a swig of water from the waterskin hanging from his neck and stepped up to the vine.

He reached above his head, grabbed hold of the vine, and pulled himself up and onto it. The twisting vines provided plenty of foot and hand holds. He stayed there for what felt like an eternity, waiting for something to happen or go wrong. Nothing did.

Onward and upward.

Within a few minutes, he found himself fifty yards above the ground. From that distance, the swaying of the vines grew more exaggerated, and nausea churned his stomach. He looked at the ground below and swore he saw movement. He strained his eyes to see clearer. Nothing moved again, so he chalked it up to his imagination.

I'm acting like a skittish little girl.

He examined one of his gloves and found multiple tiny impressions and punctures, but no gaping holes. *No blood. Thank Ƨäʈūr—ugh! Thank Him for nothing.* Had there been blood, he would've panicked.

Satisfied with his equipment, he moved on, ascending another 300 yards without issue.

From his current height, he could see a great distance. Beyond the great chasm lay nothing but an endless sea of red sand in every direction—no other vegetation existed beyond the four vines attached to the temple.

I'm an ant in this godforsaken world, and I'm alone.

His heart ached. When had he last embraced Vitara? His Vitara, not the demon Akuji.

What am I even doing here? I should just let go and plummet to my death. Be finished with this wretched life.

I hate You, Ƨäʈūr! And myself even more. Madness.

Bradwr—his best friend—had betrayed him. Bradwr had slaughtered his family. The mental wounds left Nardus numb. Who had forced Bradwr's hand though? The answer had vaporized with Bradwr's last breath.

He rubbed his left bicep—even through gloves the scars felt wet against his fingers. He looked at his arm, but found no blood.

His faith in bringing back his family waned as it hung in the balance by one final thread—all but non-existent. One more setback and he feared that thread would snap, and he'd be lost forever, separated from everything he loved.

Nothing in the world would bring him more joy than to be with his family again, but deep within he knew the impossibility of it. By the very nature of being human, he stood a sinner, but, more than that, an unforgiven one.

He'd never repent and ask for forgiveness, would he? *No.* Instead, he'd placed his faith in himself and in a man he knew very little about: *Pravus.* For certain, the man spoke with charisma unparalleled by anyone Nardus had ever met, and he'd drunk the man's liquid-sugar words with a carnal pleasure. Yet he didn't even know the man's last name.

Why am I okay with that? What kind of person am I to just throw myself into this quest with little to no information? I'm desperate and mad. No other explanation fits.

The vines quaked, and he nearly lost his footing. His hands slipped from the vine and he fell. Panic tore through his mind as he grabbed at everything he could, but he slid around the backside of the vine and couldn't stop himself.

His feet slid, and his footing gave way as they slipped off the vine and into the air. His right arm hooked one of the vines and he grabbed it with every bit of strength he had. The thorns tore into his glove as he hung on for his life.

Momentum jerked him against the vine and his body smacked into the side of the vines like a rag doll. A thousand needles punctured his back and the backs of his legs. Droplets of blood formed within every puncture.

A high-pitched scream filled the air and rattled his eardrums, but he could do nothing to stop it. Panicked, he twisted and turned, trying to find its source. A few moments later he realized the scream came from his own mouth. He tried everything he could think of to cut it off, but he no longer controlled his mouth.

"Blood!" he screamed, but it wasn't his voice. The vines cried and screamed through him.

Something wrapped around his ankles, tightened its grip on him, twisted him around to face the mass of vines, and drew his body against the main mass of vines. Something else slipped around his waist and then his legs and neck and tore at his flesh like little teeth. They smothered him face-first against themselves and nearly entombed him. Only his left arm remained free of their grasp.

He worked his fingers through the vines on his left side. Finally, he touched the hilt of the knife with his fingertips. An inch farther and he'd be able to grasp it.

"No!" he cried. The vines still spoke through him. "You don't want to hurt us!" The vines knew his plan, but how?

More vines worked their way around his left arm as he struggled to free the knife. *Just a little more.*

He grabbed the hilt of the knife and freed it from its sheath. *Finally!*

His arm flailed at his side like a fish out of water as he slashed at the air with the knife. *This isn't working!* He stabbed directly at the vines instead. He thrust the knife into the belly of the vines over and over, twisting the knife as he pulled it out each time.

The screaming subsided. "Let me go!" he cried, this time in his own voice.

The vines loosened around him. He carefully cut the vines from around his neck and head, freeing himself to see again. He cut and worked his way out of the rest of them and slowly worked his way around to the top of the main vine again. Smears of crimson painted the vines where he'd been. He felt extremely woozy. How much blood had he lost?

He clung to the vines and closed his eyes for a few seconds to catch his breath. He breathed heavy and labored with each breath. Every exhale came with a tinge of pain. The fresh wounds all over his body should've hurt, but he felt only numbness.

That's probably a bad thing, but I've got to get off this damn vine before I can worry about anything else.

He opened his eyes and panic set in anew. The vibrant, green vines yellowed. He looked down, and the yellow tint gave into brown, then to black. *The vines are dying!* A burst of energy filled him and gave him new strength.

He clambered toward the temple as fast as he could go. Every once in a while, he checked his progress against the dying vines below him. Death gained on him at an alarming rate, and he still had a good 200 yards left to go.

A thunderclap rocked the air, and he stopped. A lump caught in his throat as he gazed across the chasm. The vine directly across the chasm from him collapsed in on itself and broke away from the ground. He looked up to where it attached to the temple and gasped. Without support, the corner of the temple drooped down.

Guess that tells me they're holding it up and not anchoring it down.

Another thunderclap rocked the air, followed by a third and then a fourth.

"Not good!"

The other two vines collapsed in on themselves and broke away from the ground just as the first had. His stomach leapt into his throat. *Damn! My vine's next!* His vine trembled as the shock of it breaking away from the ground reached him.

He found himself suspended in mid-air, clinging onto the vine as Ţämbəll Dhef Däd Dhä descended toward him at an alarming rate. In a matter of seconds, the temple would careen past him and into the bottomless chasm below.

A ripple in the vine raced toward him as the vine's direction whipped into reverse. He analyzed and rejected the thoughts in his mind as quickly as they came to him. He knew of only one thing he could do and he didn't like the thought of it. What choice did he have though?

He positioned himself on the vine as best he could and waited. One second before his plunge into Ef Demd Dhä, he called, "Ɂäṭūr, if You're still there, let this work!"

The ripple reached him just as the base of the temple flashed by. He tightened the muscles in his stomach and used the momentum of the ripple to launch himself toward the temple. The rush livened him like nothing else he'd ever experienced.

His arms flailed in front of him as he stretched toward the temple. Something tugged at his left ankle. His eyes went wide as he looked back and saw one of the vines—still green—wrapped around his ankle. *No!*

He still clutched the knife in his left hand. He had to reach down and hack it off, even if it cut his momentum short. But would he still be able to cover the distance?

I'm dead for sure if I don't cut it.

He reached down and freed himself from the vine with one slash of the knife just as it pulled him back toward the main artery of vines. His momentum stopped, and he fell straight down.

The base of the temple hovered right in front of him now. He stretched his right arm out and kicked his legs like a swimmer. His fingers buckled as they pressed against the stone of the temple. He noticed a small section of missing mortar between the stones. He tried to jam his finger into it, but it wouldn't fit.

The outer rim of the chasm whizzed by. Everything faded into darkness and the temperature rose quickly. The smell of sulfur suffocated and nearly overwhelmed him.

He reached into the darkness with his left hand and mentally guided it toward the spot where the crack in the mortar had been. A small, brief moment of relief washed over him as he found it and shoved the knife into it, but fear replaced the sensation as a dim, glowing light appeared below him.

The light brightened exponentially and formed into a molten sea of lava. *Damn. Damn, damn, damn.*

With the knife embedded in the cracked mortar, he pulled against the wall and lifted himself up with his left arm. He reached up with his right arm and grabbed the top of the wall.

The bottoms of his feet burned with fire. He wormed his way up the wall and pulled himself on top of it just as the temple made contact with the lava. Columns of lava shot into the air, displaced by the weight of the temple.

The force of the impact threw him forward and onto stone steps. He quickly rolled onto his side, curled into a fetal position, and covered his head with his arms, expecting to be showered by lava at any moment.

He cowered against the hard stone, his muscles wound tight. Sweat drenched him and his pulse raced.

"One... two... three," he counted. Nothing happened.

He drew a deep breath through his nostrils and expected the nauseating smell of sulfur to overwhelm him, but he detected none. Cautiously, he pulled his arms away from his face and looked up. No lava loomed overhead, ready to crash down on him. Only the dark red sky pressed in on him.

He sat up and pulled himself to his feet. He walked over to the edge of the foundation and peered down into a great chasm. Everything had reset itself.

"Did I imagine all of that?"

No answer came, but pain pulsed through every inch of his body and served as a good indicator to the contrary. He spat at the ground, muttered some obscenities mixed in with "hating mezhik," and then made his way up the steps toward the temple gates.

CHAPTER FOURTEEN

Blood ran from the corners of Jess's mouth and down his chin. He stepped toward Aria and collapsed to his knees. His face turned white and his hands fell from his throat. The blood flowed freely from his gaping wound.

Jess slammed face-first into the hard rock floor at her feet and drowned in a pool of his own blood. His body twitched a few times and then he lay silent.

Aria couldn't lift her head, but, from the corner of her eye, she saw Amicus's chest slowly rise and fall. At that particular moment, nothing could've made her happier.

Thank You, ʔäṭūr! Thank You for sending me a savior.

† † †

Hours earlier, the torches had burned themselves out and cast the cell in darkness, save the meager light coming in through the open door. The stench of blood ripened the air, but the sweet taste of victory still clung to Aria's tongue.

Amicus slumped against the wall across from her and rubbed his throat with his hand. "First time," he croaked.

Certain of his meaning, she wanted to let him know, but could only blink. *Thank you.* She'd kick and maim the man lying dead on the floor if she had the strength. She wished she could take his death away from Amicus and make it her own, but knowing she had someone willing to help her brought her more happiness than she could remember.

"He didn't lie," said Amicus. "I was there when he grabbed your feet. At the time, I thought he was saving you. I didn't know he meant to make you suffer further. I helped him carry you down here. I understand if you wish me harm, but I promise I mean you none."

In the dark, gleaming in the pale light, she could see the blade of the knife as it still lay on the floor. Little more than a shadow with his dark, chocolate skin, Amicus disappeared completely when he closed his mouth and eyes. She'd never seen a man as dark as him. In her village, Viscus D'Silva, everyone had been pale-skinned.

Until they'd caught fire. The thought sickened her, but she couldn't stop the barrage of images it pushed into her mind.

Forgive me, Ɛäţūr, for I'm weak in mind and spirit.

Amicus leaned over and pulled the knife with the tips of his fingers until he grasped it. She shuddered as it scraped along the stone floor. With a firm grasp on the knife, he pulled himself up the wall and into a standing position. Her heart trembled as she anticipated his next move.

What is he doing? He said he wouldn't hurt me!

With a slight wobble, he took a few steps toward her and then rolled Jess's body over with his foot. Another step and he stood directly in front of her. With the knife still clutched tightly in his fist he lifted her head up with his other hand and smiled at her. She only knew because his white teeth gleamed.

The whites of his eyes shone, but why did he clutch the knife so firmly?

He gave her a wink and then lowered her head again until it rested on her chest. He bent down over Jess's body and plucked out his other eye. He wiped the blade on the sleeve of Jess's shirt and placed the knife back in its sheath at his side.

He stood back up with the plucked eye in his palm and then placed it in her right hand. "May Ɛäţūr give you the strength to squish the sight from his eye so he can't see to claw his way from the grave, no matter how shallow it might be."

She blinked her thanks to him. *Ɛäţūr, grant me the strength.* She focused all the energy she had into her hand and squeezed as hard as she could. She felt a pop and then liquid drained through her fingers, sticky and warm.

He lifted her head up again. "I'll be back in a few minutes with some help." Fear washed over her. "I give you my word, Caterpillar. No one will hurt you again as long as I'm alive." He smiled at her, gently lowered her head again, and then hurried away.

On the one hand, she was grateful to Amicus for saving her life, but on the other, she had nothing left to live for. They'd taken her from her village as a young, innocent girl, and now only a memory remained of that girl.

Her life had ended that day, along with the death of her twin brother. The separation of his presence from her—no longer feeling his existence— far outweighed the pain of her flesh. She'd take the abuse they gave her a thousand-fold and gladly exchange her life for his if it'd bring him back. But it wouldn't.

I died with you, Alderan.

For the first time in months, she allowed herself to think of Alderan, and she didn't have the strength to keep the tears from falling. *Zäţūr, keep him safe in Your arms and let him know I'll see him soon. Let him know I love him, always.*

The light grew stronger through the doorway, and she heard two muffled voices in conversation. She recognized Amicus's, but not the other man's. She strained to hear their words as they halted just outside the door.

"Before we go into the cell, I need you to swear this conversation and everything you see and do stays between us," said Amicus. "If you can't agree to that then I'll ask you to walk away and forget you ever saw me tonight."

"Always thought you's a friend," said the other man in a loud whisper. "But how's I agreed something I don't know 'bout?"

"Agreed or not?" asked Amicus, the tension in his voice raw.

After a long pause and a deep sigh, she heard the other man say, "Agreed, I s'pose."

"I'll warn you now Brently, the sight in the cell is dreadful."

Brently. She didn't recognize the name.

"Seen me share o'er years. I be fine."

"Don't say I didn't warn you."

The cell brightened as the two men stepped through the door, each carrying a torch. Amicus walked over to one of the sconces and replaced the burned-out torch with his own. Brently stopped just inside the door and hadn't moved since. He cradled the blanket in his arms like an infant.

† † †

Amicus looked at Brently. Fear filled the young man's eyes. "You okay, Brently?"

Brently stared at the body on the floor. "One-eyed Jess. What he do?" he asked in a queasy voice.

"He threatened my family and then attacked me. No one threatens my family."

"Never liked 'im," said Brently. "Never said nice to no one." He looked up at Amicus. "What's da plan?"

"As far as Jess goes, we'll just lock the door behind us and let the rats take care of the rest."

"An her? She hurt real bad like?"

Amicus looked at the young girl, still chained to the wall. His heart ached for her. He had a daughter of his own, Vonah, and the thought of her being treated the same way this girl had been treated made his stomach twinge.

I'll keep my promise to you, Caterpillar.

"Yes, but I think she'll be okay. We need to get her out of here. Master Dragnus summoned for her yesterday, and he's gonna be furious if he finds her like this. I have no doubt that we'll be blamed for her condition if we're caught."

Brently swallowed hard. "How's we gonna get her out uh 'ere an not seen?"

Amicus had a plan. He'd been formulating it from the moment Jess's dead body had hit the floor. In addition to serving as a dungeon guard, he doubled as one of the night watchmen. He'd become intimate with the castle's secrets.

"There are secret passages throughout the castle, and I know for a fact that one of the castle's towers hasn't been used for years. We can utilize the passages to get her there. But first we need to get her past the guard at the dungeon door."

Brently sat the blanket on the chair next to the wall. "What we gonna say 'bout her? She don' look good."

Amicus scratched his head. "Kordal's guarding the door this evening. We'll tell him that we're taking her to the infirmary. There's no way he'll question it, given her condition. We need to get moving before someone else comes by and sees Jess though. Now help me get these chains off her."

Amicus and Brently gently removed the young girl's chains and lifted her to her feet. Amicus blinked back tears of his own as he watched tears pool in the corners of her eyes. She didn't let them fall, and Amicus took strength from it.

Thank You for saving her, Ɛäṭūr. You're always watching out for us, even in the worst of times.

"I don't want to alarm you, my dear," said Amicus. "But I'm going to pick you up and carry you out of here."

She blinked, and Amicus took that as an acknowledgment. He grabbed the blanket from the chair while Brently held her up, wrapped it around her naked body, and then scooped her into his arms. "Lead the way, Brently."

Brently grabbed one of the torches, snubbed out the other, and led them into the passageway. No one lurked about, and Amicus sighed with relief. Brently pulled the heavy door shut behind them and then locked it.

Ɛäṭūr, I pray You light our path.

The girl trembled in Amicus's arms as they made their way through the passageways.

Amicus smoothed back her matted hair. Her forehead burned with fever. *Hold on, Caterpillar. I'll keep you safe and make you better.*

Brently, a few paces ahead, disappeared around the corner.

Amicus rounded the corner and came face-to-face with Master Dragnus.

Chapter Fifteen

Days later, Rayah sat in front of the fire warming her hands, but her heart wouldn't thaw. The thought of Alderan still out there—likely dead—left her without an appetite. Every conversation and thought circled back to him. Living without him would be unacceptable.

Come back to me, Alderan.

Krag sat next to her, poking a stick into the fire. He giggled like a child in his brutish tone each time the red-hot ashes flew into the air, and then he'd gasp as they fizzled into the darkness. *Such a gentle giant.* She wished he'd rescued Alderan too. Had Alderan been there, she would've giggled right along with Krag.

Aria. Rayah didn't even know the girl, but she'd turned her world upside down. Her thoughts of Aria had once been filled with wonder and a sense of friendship through her relationship with Alderan. Now they festered like boils and oozed their pus-filled hate into her conscience.

If I had the choice, she'd be dead, and you'd be here with me, Alderan. She doesn't deserve you, and she doesn't love you like I do.

Tears welled at the corners of her eyes. She turned away from Krag as one slid down her cheek and wiped it away before he noticed. Or so she thought.

"Rayah sad?" Krag leaned over her.

She hugged herself. "It's nothing, Krag. I promise."

"No cry if no sad." He stroked the top of her head with his thumb.

"I was just thinking about Alderan, that's all."

"You no cry!" bellowed Krag. He jumped to his feet and the ground trembled beneath her. "Krag hurt Alderan for Rayah."

"No, Krag!" she cried. "I don't want you to hurt him. He's my friend."

Krag stomped his foot on the ground. "Friend not make Rayah cry."

"I miss him, Krag. I wish he was here. He didn't hurt me."

"Krag miss family. Krag not cry. Alderan leave Rayah dead in snow."

"Please, Krag," she pleaded. "Alderan may already be dead." She swallowed hard and choked back her tears. "If we find him alive, don't hurt him. I'm in love with—" Anger flashed in Krag's eyes.

Ꝫätūr, what have I done?

"Rayah not love Alderan!" The hairs on her head trembled from the bass of his voice. "Rayah love Krag! Krag save Rayah!"

"You don't understand, Krag. I—"

"Krag know! Krag *kill* Alderan." With that, he lumbered into the dark forest.

"Krag, wait!" she yelled. He didn't respond.

She couldn't hold her tears back any longer; they fell freely into her lap and soaked into her worn and tattered dark-green dress. "Why do I keep driving everyone away?" She was such a mess, and not just on the outside.

She'd never known her parents, or any of her kind for that matter, save Leilana. They'd abandoned her in the woods and left her to fend for herself well before any of her first childhood memories formed. If not for the kindness of an old hamadryad named Shalaidah, she surely would've died.

Memories of Shalaidah flooded her mind and brought with them more tears and painful regrets. So many years had passed since they'd last spoken. They'd parted ways on such unfavorable terms. Rayah specialized in driving people away—a mechanism she'd devised to keep from being hurt.

Unfortunately, that mechanism had its flaws. Every relationship she'd ever had ended in shambles. Determination filled her. She'd mend her relationship with Alderan no matter the cost.

Alderan. Just his name sent tingles through her body. She loved everything about him, down to the last freckle on his handsome face. She loved his goofiness and clumsiness; they lent themselves so well to his character. Thinking back to their first encounter brought an uncontrollable laughter from deep within her.

She didn't know why, but an urge to shout her love for him built up within her until it reached a point where she thought she'd burst if she didn't let it out. She shot into the air like a firecracker, spinning round and round, screaming "I love you, Alderan" again and again until her vocal cords went raw. Exhausted, she settled back down on the large log next to the fire.

Krag crashed through the trees and into the clearing. "Rayah quiet! Evil beasts coming!" He stomped out the fire with his large, bare feet. "Krag and Rayah leave now."

"Where are we gonna go?" she whispered.

"Higher." He scooped her into his massive arms and plowed into the forest in the opposite direction he'd come from.

"Krag! I need my things!" She beat on his shoulder with her tiny fists.

"No time," he said. "Krag get later for Rayah."

Looking over Krag's shoulder, she watched the trees come into view and then quickly fade into darkness behind them. Her heart raced in her chest and the lump in her throat made it nearly impossible to breathe, let alone swallow.

"I'm scared, Krag," she said.

"Krag no let evil beasts get Rayah. Krag keep Rayah safe."

If Krag's scared, then there must be something terrifying behind us. But what would scare a giant? The massacre of Alderan's village filled her mind and she shivered.

I beg you, Ƶäṭūr, don't let it be gnolls that are after us.

Time worked against them as they made their way through the thick trees. Soon, they'd be caught, pulled to the ground, and ripped apart by whatever chased them. Leilana's broken body crawled through her mind and soured her stomach.

Please, Ƶäṭūr, don't let that be my fate too.

They'd been on the run for what felt like hours, but Krag never slowed his neck-breaking pace. She couldn't quite tell, but he didn't even seem to be breathing heavy. Then again, her pounding heart drowned out nearly every other sound.

The first quarter moonlight burst onto the scene as they finally cleared the last of the tall conifer trees. The forest shrank farther away as they ascended the steep, rocky, snow-covered hill. The moonlight reflected off the snow and created near-daylight conditions.

A few minutes later the unthinkable became reality. Her heart thumped against her ribcage like a trapped animal as three beasts emerged from the shadows of the forest. Despite the rough terrain and the deep snow, they moved unnaturally fast for their size and quickly gained ground on her and Krag.

Gnolls.

"Krag, we're not alone!" she said, barely able to get the words out of her mouth.

"Almost there," said Krag, never once looking back to check on their pursuers.

Rayah and Krag reached the top of the hill and looked down at the welcoming party only fifty yards below. The stench of death and their haunting howls preceded them.

"What now?" asked Rayah, clinging to Krag's neck like her life depended on it.

"Krag fight. Rayah fly," he said with a grunt.

"That won't work for long. I can't stay in the air for extended periods of time, especially after what the cold and snow's done to my wings."

Krag stomped his foot. "Rayah fly until can't!"

She looked around. *Is there an escape route?* Steep drop-offs onto sharp rocks surrounded them. The only safe path down the hill was back the way they'd come.

"We're trapped, Krag! What were you thinking?" She would've beaten her fists on his chest if she hadn't still clung to his neck.

"Bad things smart," said Krag. "Krag more smart. No attack behind. Only front."

The first of the three gnolls pulled himself onto the top of the hill—the same one who'd attacked Alderan. Rayah's eyes widened.

"Greetings," snarled Rakzar. Spittle flew from his mouth. He rose on his hind legs and faced Krag. "Hand over the *dryte* and I'll kill you quickly."

Lorrav and Zartaq reached the top of the hill and stood behind Rakzar. As tall as they were, Krag still towered over them by nearly five feet.

Ɂäṭūr, save us.

"Evil beasts not hurt Rayah!" Krag's voice didn't betray him, but Rayah felt him tremble.

"A simple transaction is all I'm requesting of you," said Rakzar. "The dryte for your life. You give us your life and we'll take hers."

Lorrav and Zartaq howled with laughter.

"Krag die for Rayah," he said.

"Exactly," said Rakzar. "I'm glad we understand each other."

The three gnolls reached over their shoulders and withdrew double-edged battle axes, each gleamed in the moonlight.

"This doesn't need to happen," she said. "Let Krag go and I'll go with you."

Lorrav turned to Zartaq. "I think the dryte's hard of hearing."

"I agree," said Zartaq. "You are *both* going to die!"

Krag stepped backward and yelled, "Rayah fly!"

Rayah didn't like Krag's plan, but she didn't know what else to do. She let go of Krag's neck and flew into the air to watch what would likely be a bloodbath.

CHAPTER SIXTEEN

As Alderan made his way through the forest, his mind drifted back to the pink scarf. *Was it real? Did I really see through Rayah's eyes?* He looked down at the grey scroll on the inside of his left wrist. *I must've. But how's that possible?* The scarf must've been imbued with Rayah's mezhik. Nothing else made sense. *Did she purposely leave it for me to find so I'd know she still lived?*

The trees gave way to a clearing. The acidic smell of urine hung in the air and burned his nostrils and stung his eyes. He raised his arm over his mouth and nose to keep from gagging. Some sort of animal had marked the area recently.

The coals in the fire pit still glowed red; someone had recently camped there. Scattered around the camp in what seemed to be a frenzy of activity were four distinct sets of prints. One set belonged to the giant he'd been tracking. The other three sets looked to be from large wolves, most likely the ones who'd marked the area. All four sets of tracks led away from the camp in the same direction.

As he moved to follow the tracks, something gleamed in the moonlight next to an old, hollowed-out log. He moved toward the log. A small, leather-bound book leaned up against it. He bent down, picked the book up, and turned it over in his hands.

He traced the strange symbol burned into the book's cover with his finger. A golden iris glowed of its own accord and surrounded a vibrant-blue heptagram. A yellow bolt of lightning flashed at the center of the heptagram, and a small, golden clasp without keyhole or release mechanism held the book closed.

Alive in his hands, the book brimmed with energy; only one other thing had ever given him that kind of sensation: Rayah's pink scarf.

This book must be hers, too. She must've been here.

His heart soared, but then crashed back down with the realization that the three sets of prints were not from large wolves, but gnolls. The four sets of tracks led away from the camp. None of them were Rayah's, but she had to be with them. He wouldn't allow himself to think otherwise.

Please, Ẕäṭūr, keep her safe.

He knew whose tracks they were. His heart hammered. He stuffed the book into his pack and followed the tracks deeper into the forest.

Densely packed trees filled the forest and allowed almost no moonlight to penetrate its canopy and made it much darker than Alderan would've liked. Luckily for him, the stark white snow and the trail of bent and broken branches made tracking them easy even with very little light.

He pushed through the trees as fast as his legs would carry him. Within a dozen minutes, he broke through the tree line and came face-to-face with a quickly ascending hill.

A hundred yards above, at the very top of the hill, he found a scene that drained the blood from his face. Three gnolls, battle-axes drawn and gleaming in the moonlight, cornered a giant. Rayah hovered above and partly behind the giant.

Rayah!

In the heat of the moment, nothing else mattered to him but her. He'd stop at nothing to save her, even if it cost him his life. If he hadn't been so self-centered before, she wouldn't have been in danger now. *If we survive this, I'll never leave your side again. I swear it!*

In one swift, fluid motion he pulled his bow from his left shoulder with his right hand and pulled an arrow from the quiver on his back with his left hand. He strung the bow, nocked the arrow, and aimed at one of the gnolls. He drew the string back, released it, and the arrow shot into the air. A moment later, two more arrows followed the first.

Alderan boldly bounded up the hill, his caution left behind. *Hang on, Rayah!*

† † †

Rayah couldn't decide where to focus her attention. Lorrav and Rakzar stood poised to attack Krag, but Zartaq kept his eyes trained on her.

An arrow burrowed its way into the back of Zartaq's neck and punched a hole through his throat. Zartaq cried out, dropped his axe, fell to his knees, and clutched his throat.

Rayah gasped. She didn't see where the arrow had come from, but she hoped it'd been Alderan's.

Lorrav and Rakzar twisted around as two more arrows wisped by; the arrows barely missed their marks. Rayah's right shoulder burned and she screamed as she fell to the ground, unable to float further. She crawled toward the edge of the hill, but kept her gaze on the action.

Amidst the confusion, Krag landed a blow to the side of Lorrav's head with his mighty fist, and a sickening *crack* sounded from Lorrav's neck. Rayah winced as his head twisted unnaturally. Lorrav stumbled backward and fell over the edge of the hill. *Two down!* Krag's momentum knocked him off-balance and he fell to one knee.

Rakzar's eyes bulged and he roared with fury. "You're dead!"

Rakzar picked up Zartaq's axe and lunged at Krag with an axe in each of his paw-like hands. Krag pushed himself back to his feet but had no time to defend himself. Rakzar's axes met each other with a *thud* at the center of Krag's neck. Rakzar released the axes and dropped his arms with a deep groan.

"No, ʒäṭūr!" Rayah cried.

The two axes fell to the ground and Krag's head tumbled off his thick neck. Krag's headless body teetered and fell forward. Rakzar jumped backwards, narrowly escaping Krag's body as it slammed into the ground. The ground trembled beneath Rayah like an earthquake.

Razors tore into Rayah's ankle and she screamed. She clawed at the ground and kicked with her free leg, but Zartaq held onto her ankle like an iron trap. He reeled her in like a fish, trapped her under his bloody body, and then backhanded her on the side of her head, knocking her out cold.

† † †

Alderan pulled himself onto the hill and stood in shock as he took in the bloody scene. A few paces away stood Rakzar, rubbing his paw-like hands together. Rakzar looked at him with hateful yellow eyes.

"Ah, the White Knight!" Rakzar's spittle peppered the air. "Come to make good on your promise to die?"

Alderan knew better than to take his eyes off Rakzar, but he grew increasingly worried about Rayah. When he'd started his ascent at the bottom of the hill, she floated in the air just above the giant, but now he couldn't locate her.

"Rayah? Rayah! Where are you?" She didn't respond.

Ƶäţūr, don't let her be dead!

"Seems you've arrived at this party a little too late," said Rakzar. "And you're not even dressed for the occasion. Let me help you get into something a little more appropriate, a little more... red!"

Alderan's hands balled into fists at his sides. "You've chosen the wrong day to mess with me."

Rakzar roared with laughter. "Have I now? We'll see about that."

Rakzar lunged at Alderan, his razor-sharp claws poised to rip him apart. Alderan dove under Rakzar's advance, rolled, and came back up on his feet. A moment later he had his bow in hand and an arrow nocked and ready.

Alderan glared at Rakzar. "Make a move and you're dead!" The veins in his hands bulged.

"A few extra months under your belt, and now you're a skilled warrior?" Rakzar scoffed. "Just one problem though, your failure to assess the battlefield has given me the upper hand."

"How so, beast?"

"Look behind you." Rakzar's lips curled into a smile, revealing his sharp yellow teeth. "Seems Zartaq's found your precious dryte!"

Alderan didn't need to turn around to know Rakzar told the truth. His stomach riled with the knowledge. *How could I be so stupid? I thought I'd killed him!*

He kept his arrow trained on Rakzar and side-stepped so he could get a better view of the situation. Zartaq rose to his knees and held Rayah's limp body by her throat. Zartaq's eyes were full of pain and Rayah's body trembled in his weakened arms.

Am I too late? Is she already dead?

Rayah's eyes fluttered and then opened and his heart soared. He smiled at her and knew immediately what must be done. "Me for her. Let her go and you can do whatever you want with me."

Fear and objection filled Rayah's eyes, but he didn't care. Nothing mattered but her safety. "I'm sorry, Rayah. I should've never left you."

"Deal." Rakzar nodded to Zartaq. "Let that filthy *dryte* go."

Zartaq tossed Rayah at Alderan's feet. Alderan looked down at Rayah. Her blood-soaked dress overwhelmed him. *Rayah! What have they done to you?*

Rage filled him with an intensity he'd never experienced before. He felt detached from his body, like something or someone else controlled it and he merely looked on from afar. The whole scene seemed to zoom out as though he flew above.

From his vantage point he saw everything happen, all in slow motion. He watched himself turn the bow on Zartaq and shoot him right between the eyes. Before the arrow even met its mark, he'd tossed the bow aside, bent down, and pulled Rayah's limp body into his arms.

Don't die on me, Rayah!

At the same moment, Rakzar narrowed the gap between them and set himself on a course to collide with them and drive them all over the edge of the cliff.

Just before Rakzar collided with them, a light emanated between him and Rayah and surrounded them like some sort of barrier. Rakzar collided with the barrier of light and repelled backward like a rag doll.

Wind rushed by Alderan as he flew back down and joined his body once more. The light that surrounded him and Rayah dissipated. Alderan exhaled, completely drained of energy like he'd overexerted himself under a hot summer sun.

"Rayah," he said in little more than a whisper. "Don't leave me. I can't live without you." She didn't stir in his arms and she breathed shallowly, but she still lived.

Thank You, 2äţūr!

About six feet away from them, Rakzar sat up and shook his head and blinked several times. Rakzar rose to his feet. Alderan's heart pounded. If

Rakzar attacked again, he wouldn't be able to do anything to stop him.

To Alderan's surprise, Rakzar turned away from them.

From over his shoulder, Rakzar growled, "This isn't over, White Knight!" He slipped over the side of the cliff and disappeared into the night.

Relief washed over Alderan like an ocean wave on the beach. He lay on his back with Rayah still clutched in his arms and let the tears slide from his eyes.

"Thank you for saving us, Rayah." He gently kissed her forehead; she burned with fever.

No, no, no! This can't be happening right now.

"Ɂäṭūr, do something!" He sat up and cradled Rayah in his arms. She lay limp in his arms and didn't stir. He shook her gently to try and bring her around. "Rayah."

He pulled her close; something raggedly sharp bit into his arm. He gently turned Rayah over in his arms to get a look at what poked him.

A broken arrow shaft—*his* arrow—protruded from Rayah's shoulder blade and rent his heart. Tears blurred his vision. *Ɂäṭūr, what have I done?*

CHAPTER SEVENTEEN

N ardus stared through the massive, black gates that stood before him. "Ţämbǝll Dhef Däd Dhä," he muttered. *The Temple of the Dead.* He swallowed hard, but the implication of the temple's name left a lump in his throat.

The gates, millennia old and forged by the great iron workers, stood more than twelve feet tall. Each side of the gate featured intricate patterns weaving in and out of themselves, but the defining and overwhelming feature was the skull, split at its center between the two; its beauty stole the air from his lungs.

The skull was formed from the same iron as the gates, but its ivory-colored coating brought it to life. Nardus reached out to touch the skull, but the gates swung in on their own and his fingers raked the air in their absence.

He walked through the parted gates and into the temple's courtyard and then halted. Eight statues, cut from single pieces of dark-green basalt, lined the walkway leading up to the door of the temple like sentries guarding a palace. Each statue had a uniqueness all its own, but all eight of them depicted the same savage creature, one he'd never seen the likes of before.

Each statue angled slightly toward the temple gates and faced the pathway that led through the courtyard. The sight of them and their ferocity set Nardus on edge. *Wouldn't want to meet any of you in a dark forest.* The gates clanked shut behind him and he flinched.

He closed his eyes and took a deep breath to steady his nerves.

"This is for my family," he said to himself, trying to build up his faltering confidence. "I must get the stone. I've no other choice."

His skin crawled with anxiety like he'd never felt before. His heart knocked against his chest as he opened his eyes and stared up at the beasts again.

They're watching me.

He swore the statues followed him with their malicious eyes. Their eyes bore holes into his mind and poisoned his thoughts.

Time to die, Nardus. You're nothing. Worthless. Less than that even. Was he?

His heart pumped liquid fear through his veins and pounded in his ears.

Damn them! Get a hold of yourself, Nardus. They're just statues.

His eyes focused on the statue to his left, a ghastly form carved to perfection. The seven-foot-tall creature towered over him. Long, matted fur covered its body, four horrific fangs protruded from its stiff-jawed, gaping mouth, a wicked-looking tail wrapped around its side and rested in front of its cloven hooves, and two large, leathery wings folded at its back and spanned from just above its shoulders all the way to its ankles.

Like watching a beheading, he couldn't pull his eyes away from it. *I swear you're staring back at me.*

Crackle.

The noise emanated from the statue like water flowing over ice. He stepped toward it to investigate. The statue vibrated from top to bottom, and thin, hairline cracks formed all along its surface. He stepped backward.

Crack.

The statue split from top to bottom and sent tiny shards of basalt flying in every direction. Nardus quickly covered his face with his arm for protection. A bone-chilling shriek ripped through the air and stopped his heart.

He trembled from head to foot as he lowered his arm. Where the statue had stood moments before now stood the same creature, alive and in the flesh. He confirmed with a quick, sideways glance that the other seven statues had shattered as well. Eight horrific beasts now stared him down.

The first of the beasts spread its wings into a thirteen-foot span, bent its knees, pushed away from the ground with powerful legs, and took to the sky with a whoosh of air that nearly knocked Nardus off his feet. The other seven beasts shrieked in unison and rattled Nardus's eardrums. They took to the sky as well and circled above Nardus with the first beast.

Nardus ran back to the black gates and tried pulling them apart, but they wouldn't budge. Instinct told him to duck and roll to the side and he did so, just an instant before one of the creatures crashed into the gates where he stood.

Nardus groaned. His back seared with fire. The creature's talons had ripped into his flesh.

The creatures moved with unnatural speed. He had no chance of outrunning them. Even if he could, there were eight of them and only one of him. They surrounded him. His mind numb with fear, Nardus ran toward the temple. Death shrieked behind him and drew close.

His heart lodged in his throat. His lungs failed to contract and expand. His mind faltered.

I'm dead.

He tripped. Fell flat on his face. His forward momentum threw him into a somersault and he pushed back to his feet, hardly missing a step.

Beating wings drummed his ears. He dove to the ground just as one of the creatures swooped over his head. Its talons grazed his scalp. The pain cleared his mind and focused him.

He knew what must be done. One chance. He only had one chance.

Gnaud.

† † †

Nardus lay on the floor of the Great Library. He jumped to his feet and raced through the aisles, screaming at the top of his lungs, "Gnaud! Where are you? I'm facing certain death, and I need your help!"

"Ƨätūr's mercy!" Gnaud's head popped around the corner of one of the rows of shelves farther into the library. "What've you gotten yourself into this time?"

Nardus doubled over when he reached Gnaud, breathless. Drops of blood fell from his forehead and splattered on the white marble floor. "Give me a minute."

"Oh, my, of course. Take all the time you need." Gnaud pushed his glasses up his nose. "Your head's bleeding, and you look like you've been wrestling with a thistle."

Nardus stood straight and gathered his composure and thoughts before speaking. "I'm way past the crown of thorns I wore earlier. I've reached the courtyard of *Ţämbäll Dhef Däd Dhä*, and now eight angry beasts are attacking me. I need to know how to deal with them before they turn me into a pile of bloodied flesh with their claws or talons."

Gnaud gestured toward a table in the center aisle of the library. "Come, let's sit down and talk this through."

Nardus pulled a chair out from the table and sat down with a deep, elongated sigh. Gnaud vaulted onto the table in two leaps and sat down in front of him with his legs crossed.

Nardus rubbed his head and winced. *Damned demons.*

Gnaud leaned forward. Concern wrinkled his brow, narrowed his lips, and poured from his orange eyes. "Can I get you something for your head?"

Nardus waved his hand. "I'll be fine. It's just a flesh wound."

"Describe every detail you can remember about them, and I'll help you try and figure out exactly what you're dealing with."

"Well, they're two-footed and must be at least seven feet tall. Their lean, muscular bodies are covered in matted, black fur, and their eyes are orange at their centers and transition into a deep blue at the outer edges, like a circular flame."

Gnaud grabbed a fistful of his shirt and cringed. "Oh, my!"

"They have snouts kind of like a lion's, with large fangs protruding from their upper and lower jaws. Their red, skin-like wings span a good thirteen feet. They also have long, whip-like tails with triangular-shaped, pointed ends."

"Ʒäţūr's mercy!" Gnaud chewed on his nails. "Oh, this isn't good. Not good at all." He grew still, and his eyes glazed over.

Nardus leaned forward and touched Gnaud's bony little knee. "Gnaud? Are you okay?"

Life rushed back into Gnaud's eyes and he gasped. "Oh, my, yes. So sorry. Caught up in my memories." He adjusted his glasses on his head. His hands trembled.

Nardus leaned back and pulled his matted hair from his face. "You know what these things are, don't you?"

"Creatures of dark mezhik, they are. They were conjured during the Great War by a legion of Magus's wizards. Those of us who opposed Magus called the creatures *Dämnz Fallíinzh.* The flying demons." Gnaud shook and snapped his eyes shut for a moment.

"I want to reemphasize that I really loathe mezhik." Nardus spat on the floor. "If I somehow find a way to complete this damned quest without dying, I'll be happy to never see or deal with mezhik again!"

Gnaud clasped his hands together, firmly, and shied away a bit. "Oh, my, it gets worse—"

"*Worse?*" Nardus slammed his fist into the table and rose to his feet so quickly that he knocked his chair over. "How can it possibly get worse, Gnaud?"

Nardus turned and kicked the fallen chair and sent it careening across the marble floor where it slammed into one of the dorus pine bookshelves about twenty feet away. He turned back toward Gnaud.

Nardus grabbed onto the edge of the table with both hands and braced himself as he leaned over it. Frustration tightened every muscle in his face. "Drat!" Spittle peppered the air and fear flashed in Gnaud's eyes.

"Ʒäţūr's mercy!" Gnaud fell backward into a reverse somersault and sprung to his feet.

Nardus breathed deep and reigned in his anger. "Sorry about that, Gnaud. I swear my anger isn't toward you."

Gnaud pulled his glasses off his face and wiped Nardus's spittle from them with his shirt. "It's okay. I know you're frustrated and tired and have already faced and overcome so much. I also know there's much more you'll endure before the end. I'm truly sorry for that, my friend."

Nardus retrieved the discarded chair and sat back down at the table. "Please continue, Gnaud. I'll try and keep my temper under check."

Gnaud returned his glasses to his face and sat back down. "As I was saying, there's more to those creatures, and it gets worse. What you saw isn't matted fur, but an impenetrable armor—"

"Impenetrable armor? Are you *serious?*" Nardus raised his arms in the air and let them fall to the table with a *smack.*

Gnaud sighed. "Not even wizard's fire can damage them."

Wizard's fire. Damned mezhik.

They sat in silence for a few minutes, both deep in thought.

Nardus tried to process the information, but grew more and more agitated the longer he thought about it. "How am I supposed to deal with these creatures when they can't be killed? Is there anything else you can tell me about them?"

"Well, nothing you'd *want* to hear." Gnaud looked down at his lap and drew circles on the table with his fingers. "They're known to have an insatiable lust for human flesh."

"Human flesh..." Nardus leaned back in the chair and massaged his temples. In his head, the creatures tore him limb from limb and kept him alive to watch them feast on his flesh. *Bastards!*

"I just want this to be over." Nardus sat back up. "I never thought I'd make it this far. I was disillusioned in the beginning, driven by an insane idea of seeing my family again. I'm more a fool than I thought possible, Gnaud. A madman."

"Oh, my," said Gnaud. "Don't lose hope now! Ɂätūr has a plan for us all. You're exactly where you're supposed to be. You can never be anywhere else."

"Ɂätūr? He's been the center of my problems for quite some time now. As I said before, I'm done with Him. To me, He's as dead as my family." The words stung as they crossed his lips. *Have I really lost hope in seeing my family again?*

Gnaud crossed his arms in his lap. "It doesn't matter how you feel about Him, Nardus. He is, was, and will always be. He is unchanging, steadfast in His love for you. For us all."

Nardus massaged his left bicep. "There's no escaping Him, is there?"

"Oh, my, no. How can you escape the One who created everything?"

"I feel as though He's been hammered into my mind. Etched into my soul. His existence frustrates me. I loathe the thought of relying on Him when He's let me down so many times, yet I find myself calling out to Him in my darkest hour." Nardus leaned forward and placed his head on the edge of the table. "How mad is that?"

Why must You torture me? Have I not suffered enough for You?

"Ɂätūr's our Creator. A Father of sorts. He's put eternity on our hearts. Denying Him is like denying yourself breath. You can fight it your entire life, but in the end, you'll bow to Him and answer for the sins you've committed."

Sin. He put me on this wretched path. Nardus lifted his head and spat on the floor. "Enough of this worthless talk. I'll speak of Him no more. Now, is there anything I can do about these *Dämnz Fallíinzh*, or shall I go find a nice beam to hang myself from?"

Gnaud clicked his tongue against his teeth and shook his head with disapproval. "Ɂäʈūr's mercy. You're in the foulest of moods today, my friend."

"Apparently being attacked by flying demons puts me in a terrible mood. I'll try to keep my brooding to myself."

"I've searched endlessly for information on *Ʈämbəll Dhef Däd Dhä* while you've been away. Unfortunately, there are very few writings on the subject. On the bright side, I've an intimate knowledge of nearly every book in this place."

Nardus slouched in his chair and peered up at Gnaud, incredulous. "There are thousands of books in here, Gnaud. How can you possibly know what's contained in them all?"

"Oh, my. You can get a lot of reading done in more than a thousand years of solitude." Gnaud chortled. "And there are tens of thousands of books here, not just thousands."

Pointing to his left, Gnaud continued, "This book's the only reference I dug up on the subject. Even in it, there's little knowledge to be found. Let me give you a rundown of the facts I gleaned from it."

"By all means," said Nardus. "A little information is better than none at all."

Gnaud's smile faded. "Once you've breached the threshold of the temple doors there's no turning back. The temple won't allow you to leave. For *any* reason. That includes coming here."

"The damned place is alive? Perfect. On my own and without help." Nardus sunk in the chair farther. "Every word from your mouth makes this day better."

Gnaud glared at Nardus and continued, "Once inside, four more challenges await you. The temple will take you beyond your breaking point. You'll struggle physically and mentally. You must be prepared to face your demons, Nardus. Your resolve mustn't waver, not even a moment. If it does, you'll be swallowed in your own madness and spat into the bowels of *Ef*

Demd Dhä, where there's no coming back."

"No need to worry about surviving." Nardus ran his fingers through his hair, wincing as they slid over the holes made by the demon's talons.

"Despite your faltering belief in Him, I'll be praying that Ɔäṭūr protects you."

"Don't waste your breath, Gnaud. Ɔäṭūr has no time for me."

Gnaud frowned and shook his head. "Ɔäṭūr has time for everyone and everything, including you. He doesn't require a person to believe in or follow Him to perform miracles. His strength and glory are not reflections of our own, but of His steadfast, unfaltering character."

Nardus smacked the table with an open palm. "Even if that were so, this quest's not about Him." He spat on the floor again. "It's about *me*. It's about *my* family. *I'm* the only one *I* can trust to bring *me* through this. The weight of the world rests on *my* shoulders, not His. I'm alone in this quest of madness, and I'm damned no matter the result."

Gnaud shook his head slowly. His features softened, and the corners of his eyes welled with tears. "Oh, my..." His voice trembled and then fell away. He turned away and wiped at his cheek with the back of his fur-covered hand.

Guilt rose in Nardus's throat and he swallowed its bitter taste down. He sat up, took the book from the table, and leafed through it, unsurprised to find it written in a language he couldn't read. *Worthless symbols and words.* Frustrated, he threw the book back down on the table with a *smack*.

Gnaud sprung to his feet with a gasp, his glasses skewed on his face.

"Okay, Gnaud. Let's get back to the *Dämnz Fallíinzh*. How do I get past them if they can't be killed?"

Gnaud straightened his glasses, cleared his throat, and sat up straight. "I never said they couldn't be killed, I merely said wizard's fire couldn't harm them. However, I *do* know how to kill them."

Nardus leaned forward. "Then let's have it."

"During the Great War, legions of *Dämnz Fallíinzh* attacked our forces and slaughtered us like mindless sheep. On the brink of losing the war, *Ūrdär Dhef Ɔäfn Dhä* formulated a plan to regain the ground we'd lost and turn the tide of the war in our favor. Their plan was so simple: they forged a golden sword born of dragon's fire, aptly named *Brinzhär Dädh*, or, in your tongue, Death Bringer."

"Dragon's fire?" Nardus rolled his eyes. "Simple enough. I keep that stuff tucked inside my coin purse for cold days."

Gnaud smiled and continued, "That sword was the key to the success of the war. They selected a great Furdor warrior to wield the sword—Haldur The Conqueror. With *Brinzhär Dädh*, he attacked the *Dämnz Fallíinzh* from behind and severed their wings.

"Once their wings were clipped the *Dämnz Fallíinzh* withered and died like cut flowers. It's the only way to kill those wretched beasts, and Haldur mastered the technique."

Nardus sighed. "That's well and good, Gnaud, but unless you happen to have the sword here in the library, I'm as good as dead."

Gnaud's eyes beamed with excitement, and a giant smile spread across his face. "Turns out I may have come into possession of said item!"

"Excellent!" Nardus jumped to his feet and knocked his chair over again. Then, with less enthusiasm, he asked, "Does the sword happen to come with instructions?"

Gnaud's eyebrows rose above the tops of his glasses. "ʔätür's mercy. I thought you were a soldier in your youth."

"Certainly, but I was a bowman. Skills with the sword were never my thing." He rubbed the back of his neck with his hand, trying to work out a knot.

"You're in luck! Even a child could wield *Brinzhär Dädh*, my friend." Gnaud pushed his glasses back up his nose. "You will not use *Brinzhär Dädh*, but it'll use you."

Nardus sighed again. "I'm not following what you're saying, Gnaud. Speak plainly."

"The combined mezhik of dragon's fire and that of *Ūrdär Dhef ʔäfn Dhä* imbued the sword with energy and life. Haldur was indeed a great warrior, but *Brinzhär Dädh* did most of the work. I cannot explain it further. When the time comes for you to wield the sword, you'll understand."

Nardus groaned. *Swords. Dragons. Flying demons. Mezhik. What have I got myself into?*

"I'll be back in a jiffy!" With that, Gnaud vaulted off the table in a forward flip and sprinted through the library as fast as his little legs would carry him.

Despite his feelings of insanity, a small but noticeable thread of hope weaved its way into Nardus's thoughts and gave him an airy sense of confidence. *I've made it this far. I can do this. I must do this. For my family. I can't give up hope of seeing them again. They're all I have left worth fighting for.*

A few minutes later, Gnaud returned carrying a sword twice as long as he was tall. Nardus took the sword from Gnaud and laid it on the table. He stared at it with awe, and his heart thumped in his chest.

Intricately woven, diamond-shaped patterns adorned the scabbard, and golden buckles adorned the leather straps that would fasten it over the shoulder and around the midsection. The locket and chape of the scabbard were forged with the same metal as the sword itself, and they gleamed in the natural light with a bright, red-gold hue.

Magnificent.

The pommel of the sword matched the locket and chape in color and material and was circular and hollow at its center. Dark leather wrapped around the grip, and golden ferrules secured it at both ends. The guard, half an inch thick and matching the pommel, twisted ninety degrees as it protruded from either side of the sword and each side ended in a cross shape.

The words *"Fiall Bä Ʒfift Dädh Zíūr"* were etched into the sides of the guard. Nardus pointed at them. "What do these words mean, Gnaud?"

Gnaud vaulted onto the chair and then the table. He pushed his glasses up his nose and settled down next to the sword. He smiled. "Your death will be swift."

Death Bringer. Makes sense.

"Gnaud—" Nardus's hand trembled as he ran his fingers along the length of the scabbard. "—I'm lost for words."

"Oh, my." Gnaud looked left and then right, deviously. Then, in a hushed tone, "Wait until you see the blade."

"I'm not sure I can. I'm so unworthy of its magnificence."

"Your unworthiness is what makes it right, Nardus. This sword will humble the greatest of men."

With great reluctance, Nardus lifted the sword and its scabbard into the air. He firmly gripped the hilt with his left hand. The cold leather felt smooth against his skin. With his right hand, he grasped the scabbard just below the locket.

He closed his eyes, drew in the deepest breath he could muster, and let it out slowly. Calmness washed over his entire body and transformed his trembling hands into ones stout and steady. Gently at first, and then with more power, he slid the blade from its scabbard; its sweet song rang through the library. The tingle of mezhik flowed into his hand and up the length of his arm. He loathed and savored the feeling, his mind torn.

He opened his eyes. "Brilliant!" he exclaimed, more to himself than Gnaud.

The golden blade glowed with supernatural power. The double fuller cross-section was forged to perfection and its double-edge looked sharp enough to cut through anything. Nardus lay the scabbard on the table and then rested the blade on his forearm.

He lifted Brinzhär Dädh to eye-level and peered down its unwavering length. *Straight as an arrow.* He found no blemishes of any kind. *A true masterpiece.*

He let the sword rest on a single finger—the pommel balanced it perfectly. He closed his eyes and the weight of the sword evaporated. *How can it be so light?*

Odd. He felt its presence in his hand, almost like a living being, but stranger still, he swore it spoke to him: *"We shall be one, united."* The experience exhilarated and frightened him. He opened his eyes, picked the scabbard up, and slid the blade back into it. *Magnificent.* He set the sword and scabbard down on the table.

"Gnaud, are you certain I should take this sword? What if I don't make it back? How will I return it to you?"

"Oh, my!" Gnaud shook his hands and jumped to his feet. "It's not my sword to be returned, and I'm certain the blade's chosen you. It's yours now."

Nardus wanted to argue with Gnaud, but holding the sword felt like nothing else he'd ever experienced before. He desired to hold it again, his mouth moist with anticipation.

"I understand, Gnaud. The sword spoke to me as I held it. I thought I'd imagined it, but, reflecting on it now, I know it to be true."

Gnaud's eyes widened. "Spoke to you? What did it say?"

Nardus ran his finger along the length of the scabbard. "We shall be one, united."

Gnaud grinned. "Stupendous! It's settled then. Strap that blade on your back and go take down some *Dämnz Fəllíinzh!*"

Nardus chuckled. "You make it sound so simple."

He picked up the sword and scabbard, lifted the shoulder strap over his left arm and around his neck so that its hilt rested over his right shoulder. He pulled the waist straps around his sides and cinched the buckle to a firm position just above his navel.

Gnaud stood on the table, glasses in hand, and wiped tears from his eyes with the sleeve of his shirt. "Oh, my," he said with a sniffle. He returned his glasses to his face.

Nardus reached up and placed his hand on Brinzhär Dädh's hilt for a moment. Its tingle soothed him. *Damned mezhik.* He released his grip on it.

Nardus looked at Gnaud. "You've most likely saved my life again, my furry friend. I'll never forget this."

Nardus reached over to shake Gnaud's hand, but Gnaud leapt forward and wrapped his arms around Nardus's neck instead. Nardus patted Gnaud on the back and then urged him to release his grip. Gnaud pulled back, his cheeks rosy and tears in his eyes again.

Nardus smiled, touched by Gnaud's sentiment. "I'll be back before you know it."

Gnaud nodded, vaulted off the table in a forward flip, and disappeared into the endless rows of books.

I really hope I see you again, my little friend.

Nardus breathed deep and gathered his courage.

Time to face my demons.

† † †

Nardus stepped out of the Great Library and back into the courtyard of Ţämbəll Dhef Däd Dhä. He unsheathed Brinzhär Dädh. The sound of steel against steel rang in the air. The sword shined like a beacon of light against the backdrop of the dark and ominous red sky. Power raced through his hands, up his arms and neck, and into his head.

His scattered thoughts melded into a single, focused one: *kill or be killed.*

Before the shriek even left the curled and deformed grey lips of the

Dämnz Fəllíinzh that swept down at him from behind, he turned to meet the attack. The demon raced toward him with unnatural speed, claws ready, but Nardus moved even faster.

Nardus slid to the ground and rolled underneath the demon as it made its passing attack. And, even before the demon had swept past him, he sprung back on his feet and launched himself into a twisting back flip, his sword at the ready above his head. He slashed the demon twice, severing its wings at the joints. It shrieked and crashed to the ground.

The demon struggled to its feet. Its furry armor sagged and shriveled like skin exposed to too much water. It took a few steps toward Nardus and collapsed. Its body jerked and pulled into a fetal position—less than a quarter its original size—and solidified.

Nardus eyed the sword, satisfied with its result. *Lead on.*

Subsequent attacks came from every direction and all at once in a chaotic flurry of motion. The beasts' shrieking diminished from ear-piercing to a distant hum as the sword filled his head with what he could only describe as the singing of angels. He became one with the sword, more alive and at peace in that moment than in any he could ever remember.

His body twisted and turned like a cyclone of death, driven by the sword. Every slash of the blade met its mark with deadly precision. Moments later, eight Dämnz Fəllíinzh lie on the ground, wings severed, and their bodies shriveled as death set upon them. The fight ended nearly as quickly as it had begun.

Brimming with excitement, Nardus assessed the scene. His breathing remained at a normal level and he hadn't even broken a sweat. *Incredible!* He wiped both sides of the blade on his sleeve and then slid the sword back into its scabbard. His spirits soared and the thought of being one step closer to getting his family back drove his desire to push forward.

He quickly made his way to the temple entrance and came face to face with two large, wooden doors.

"*Dūrz Dhef 2ōəllz Demd,*" he said in awe. *The Doors of Damned Souls.*

Skulls of every shape and size were carved into the double-doors and filled every square inch of their surfaces. Most of the skulls seemed to be crying out in agony, begging to be saved. *Will mine be next?*

An iron plaque hung from the door on his left with the words "*Mäí ənţär* ūall" hammered into its surface. Another iron plaque on the door on his right read "Əlläf äəllíf nō fʊn."

I wish I had Gnaud's understanding of languages.

His heart beat out of control and his mind pleaded with him to turn back, but he placed a hand on each door anyway. The doors sizzled under his hands with energy—no doubt imbued with mezhik like everything else around there.

The thought left a bitter taste in his mouth and knotted his stomach. *Why does everything have to revolve around mezhik? Drat!*

Now or never. He pushed on the doors, but they didn't budge. He put his shoulder into the door on the left and pushed with all his might. His boots skidded on the stones and gave up more ground than the door. His head pulsed, and sweat trickled down his brow. He thought he would pass out from the exertion.

He gathered his strength and gave one final push with everything he had left. The thick door wouldn't budge.

Maybe the sign says to pull. The idea was stupid, but he tried it anyway. The door stood still. *Figures.*

"Think, Nardus." An image of Pravus—the tall man from the tavern— popped into his head and with it the faint recollection of a conversation between the two of them. The memory seemed so distant, just out of his mind's reach. He strained to recall the words, foreign words.

An image of his children torn to pieces burst into the front of his mind. Anger rushed to the surface and exploded in his mind like an erupting volcano. He relived the moment again, and the raw, animalistic rage that had consumed him before threatened to take over again. He fought to channel the rage, and the words came flooding back to him.

He closed his eyes, placed his hands on the doors, and allowed the ancient words to flow freely from his tongue. "Ɂäk dū neṭ Í ɛṭōn dhä fūr míɛäallf, əlläṭ beɛ mä."

The doors swung open, revealing nothing inside but an inkwell of darkness.

He stood at the threshold, afraid to cross into the shadows. He didn't fear the darkness, but the thought of what might lurk within it pricked at his nerves.

Damn this madness! My family's worth everything.

He forced himself to take a step forward and break the threshold. His chest ached, his lungs tight with tension. *Beyond the point of return.* He stepped further inside, and the doors slammed behind him and cast him into total darkness. He didn't need to turn and feel around to know the doors had no handles, but he turned and probed the darkness anyway.

"Four challenges..." he muttered into the infinite darkness.

A thousand voices echoed his words, distorted them, and taunted him. Something about the darkness—within the darkness—violated his mind. The notion that his thoughts weren't the only things inside his head severed what remained of his frayed nerves.

Again, You're not with me, Ӡäţūr. I'm driven mad with paranoia, but You care nothing for me.

Help me, Vitara! I'm all alone now.

"No, you're not," replied a voice inside his head.

It wasn't his own.

CHAPTER EIGHTEEN

A ria stared out the window of the high tower, looking not at the present, but her past. She was two-and-a-half years old, building sandcastles with her twin brother, Alderan. A wave of rushing water, fresh and warm on her ankles and feet, stormed up the beach and attacked their castle. The water decimated the whole structure except for one small tower.

Alderan ran off, upset and crying that their hard work had been destroyed. She, on the other hand, giggled with delight. The next sandcastle would be even better than the first.

Sandcastles. Her body was nothing more than a sandcastle, her walls torn down by filthy, worthless men time and again. They'd breached her castle walls more times than she dared count, and the last time she'd narrowly escaped death. Others would've folded under the abuse, but, given time, she'd build her walls back up again and brim with new life.

Despite all she'd been through, each new day brightened her hope. She anticipated and yearned for the day she'd be able to bask in the unfaltering light of Ɂäʈūr in Kinzhdm ef Häfn. *The Heavenly Kingdom*. The thought of reuniting with her slain family drove her forward and fueled her hope.

Dragnus still held her captive, but her circumstances had improved drastically. No longer relegated to the dark and dank dungeons below the castle, she now resided in the topmost room of the castle's only tower—a princess awaiting rescue by her prince.

Me, a princess? She huffed at the thought. *Who would ever save me?*

The last several months proved her to be more warrior than princess. Most girls would've been dead several times over had they faced the trials she'd endured. *Thank You, Ӡäṯür, for Your relentless love and saving grace. As always, my life is Yours.*

She was all alone in her tower, but she was also safe. Amicus had stayed true to his word, and his actions had earned him a soft place in her heart, forever. Eternally in his debt, she'd never be able to repay him for his kindness. The thought of him warmed her heart. *My true friend.*

A loud rap at the door startled her and drew her away from the window. A key rattled in the door's lock, disengaged it, and then the door swung wide. Amicus stood at the threshold, a wide grin spread across his thin face. His white teeth beamed against his dark skin. Her heart soared at the sight of him.

"Wow!" Amicus whistled through the gap in his front teeth. "You look like an angel in that dress."

Heat rose in Aria's cheeks, and a tinge of embarrassment washed over her. She gave him a smile, closed-lipped—too ashamed to show her mouth of broken teeth. She wanted so badly to speak to him, to offer him her gratitude for saving her life, but the act of producing words, of vocalizing emotions of any kind, lie beyond her grasp.

I'm so sorry, Amicus. I wish I could find my voice again.

Amicus had a way of reading her eyes, and often knew what she felt or wanted to say. "It's okay, Caterpillar. One day you'll emerge from your cocoon as a beautiful and magnificent butterfly. When that time comes, the whole world will envy you."

Only a few days had passed since Amicus rescued her from the dungeons, but it felt more like a lifetime. Aria still wore the silver collar around her neck, but the guards no longer led her around with a chain like a dog. That, and all the other accommodations granted her, save the clothing, increased her thankfulness.

Aria had grown so accustomed to her nakedness that clothing felt too restrictive. She wore clothes while around people, but alone at night in her tower, she'd strip them off, curl up on the floor like a dog, and fall asleep.

"Let's get you down to see Master Dragnus. He's been patient where you're concerned, and that's very unusual for him." Amicus waved Aria toward the door with his hand, and she obliged.

Amicus led Aria down the circular stairway and into the main hallway.

The smell of the sea hung in the air. Moss covered portions of the walls, and calcium stains spotted the floor like a rash. Every inch of the castle fell on hard times; the main floors were a minimal upgrade from the filthy dungeons below. The lack of decoration made a statement unto itself; nothing aside from sconces and their torches adorned a single wall in the entire castle.

So cold and uninviting. How does anyone live this way?

At the end of the hall, wooden double-doors led into Master Dragnus's study. As Amicus and Aria approached, a guard pushed one of the doors open and then stood to the side. They squeezed through the narrow door and into the wide, but shallow room.

The drab study smelled of mildew and wrinkled Aria's nose. A single, high window on the left-hand side of the room faced the sea. A dark-green curtain, moth-eaten and worn, hung to the window's side. Moonlight lit the room slightly, but did little to warm it. The room's cold interior left Aria chilled. She rubbed her arms with her hands.

Rub too hard, and the filth may never wash away.

At the center of the room stood an old oak desk cluttered with scrolls and papers. To the left-hand side of the desk, nearly buried amongst the clutter, sat a lone candle. The candle rose just over the top of its holder and clung to what little remained of its useful life.

As does the man behind the desk.

A portly, squatty man sat on the sole chair behind the desk and read some sort of document. Amicus and Aria approached the desk and Amicus cleared his throat. The man behind the desk peered over the top of the papers, his two beady blue eyes enlarged by the wire-framed glasses he wore.

The man set the document on the desk and rose from the chair, barely taller than he'd appeared while sitting. "Ah, the talk of the castle." He rounded the corner of the desk and Amicus and Aria turned to meet him. The man's thick, unkempt, brown hair bathed his shoulders in what looked to be tiny mop heads—they swished back and forth when he chuckled. The man's rosy cheeks and round face belied his age.

"I am Remy Dragnus, Lord of Castle Portador Tempestade. Welcome, Aria. You may call me Master Dragnus or sire if you so choose." He grabbed Aria's hand and kissed the top of her knuckles. The thick, coarse hairs of his mustache scrub-brushed her skin. She shuddered and nearly pulled her hand away.

"As you may recall, sire, she doesn't speak." Amicus's loathsome tone wasn't lost on Aria, but Dragnus seemed incognizant of it.

Dragnus released Aria's hand and turned his attention to Amicus. "If only I could say the same of my wife. That drab, insufferable woman gaggles on without end. Where she finds the breath to fill her lungs escapes me." He chortled to himself.

Dragnus turned back to Aria. "The last time I saw you, you were asleep in this man's arms. Naked as an infant, I recall." He grabbed Aria's chin and turned her head side-to-side. "You looked worse for wear that night than you do today."

Dragnus slid his hand down the side of Aria's neck and to her left shoulder. He worked his thumb under the edge of her dress, hooked it, and then pulled the sleeve off her shoulder, exposing the top of her left breast.

Aria's cheeks warmed, but not from embarrassment. *Touch me, you bastard. Give me a reason to spill your blood.*

Amicus shifted his weight, clearly uncomfortable, but said nothing to Dragnus. She expected as much, given the fact that Dragnus employed him.

Dragnus's gaze fell to Aria's chest and lingered there. "Have to say I prefer you in the nude."

And I'd prefer you dead.

Dragnus met Aria's hard gaze and he winked at her. She dug her nails into her palms to keep from strangling the man.

"And what do you think, Amicus? Do her perky breasts give you rise as they do me?" Dragnus didn't wait for an answer. "You give youth to these old bones. Were I widowed, I'd certainly give you a go. Perhaps I'll arrange it." He looked Aria over once more. "I know you like it rough, and you've recovered quickly."

Recovered? Aria forced her gaze to remain on the dreadful man. *My family's dead. That was your doing. I'll find a way to make you pay for what you've done.*

Dragnus's smile was anything but inviting. "I assume you've found the tower room suitable? It was once my mother's room, you know. She lived up there for years until she decided to take the quick way down for dinner one evening. Quite a surprise for everyone. My father was so amused he laughed about it for weeks every time he thought of her flapping her arms like a bird on the way down."

Dragnus flapped his arms wildly and laughed. He seemed indifferent that neither Amicus or Aria laughed with him.

Every gesture Dragnus made and each word that came from his mouth oozed with pride and authority and dripped with lust, but in his eyes, she saw the truth: he feared her. *What is it about me that men fear?*

Dragnus eyed Aria's chest another moment and then returned to his chair behind the desk. "Now, down to business," he said, his firm tone forced. Amicus and Aria turned and faced him.

Dragnus removed his glasses and laid them on the desk. "A man named Lord Rosai will be here tomorrow to see you, Aria." He stared not quite at Aria, but through her. "Lord Rosai's a very important man. You'll do everything he asks of you, no matter what the request may be. If I hear a single word about you refusing to cooperate in any way, you'll find yourself back in the dungeons. Am I clear on that?"

Dragnus continued without waiting for any sort of acknowledgment. "Good. I assure you, your full cooperation will be to your benefit."

My benefit? Aria fumed. *None of this is to my benefit!*

Hatred burned in Aria's heart toward Dragnus. *Smug, little man.* She wanted to rip his throat out with her teeth. Her hands balled into fists at her sides, and she had to force them open to release the energy before she exploded.

If this Lord Rosai lays a finger on me, I'll kill the both of you.

Amicus rested his hand on her bare shoulder and gave it a squeeze. His touch—that single gesture—melted away the anger and tension in her muscles like heat to butter. She loved him like an older brother.

Amicus piped up, "Sire, I request that I be present during this visit with Lord Rosai. I'll make sure Aria's fully compliant."

"Fine, if he allows it." Dragnus grabbed his glasses from the desk and placed them back on his face. "Now, off with the both of you. I've got work to do."

Aria and Amicus turned in unison and started toward the door. Dragnus stopped them with his words. "Oh, one more thing, Amicus."

They turned around and Dragnus looked directly at Aria. A smug, dirty grin curled his lips.

"If Lord Rosai demands a private session with her you'd better make sure no one disturbs them."

Aria's eyes narrowed. *I hope he does. It'll be his final demand.*

"A private session, sire?" asked Amicus.

"Oh, I think you're both fully aware of the meaning." Dragnus smacked his fist in his other palm. "Men of power have needs to fill. Be useful, Aria."

Amicus clenched his jaw. "Sire."

Aria glared at Dragnus. *You're dead!*

Amicus grabbed the back of Aria's arm, turned them around, and pulled her through the doorway before she had a chance to act on her thoughts.

† † †

"I know what you're thinking." Amicus followed Aria up the tower stairs. "I won't let anything happen to you tomorrow. You have my word."

Aria's silence frustrated him. He understood that she'd been through a lot, but he wished she'd open up and talk to him. In the short time they'd known each other, he'd only heard her voice once, and that was while she slept. After he'd rescued her from the dungeon, she'd fallen asleep in his arms and muttered a name.

"Alderan."

Aria spun on her heels and stared at him, wide-eyed.

"What does that name mean to you?" Amicus searched her eyes. "Who is Alderan?"

Tears formed in the corners of Aria's eyes as she continued to stare at him. Her lower lip quivered.

"It's okay, Caterpillar." Amicus took her hands in his. "I didn't mean to upset you. He obviously means a great deal to you."

Aria withdrew her hands from his. He searched her eyes further. *How can I get you to let me in?*

Aria turned and ascended the rest of the stairs without a backward glance. He caught up with her, unlocked the door to her room, and let her inside. He started to follow her into the room, but she put her arm across the doorframe and blocked him from entering.

"Okay, Caterpillar. I understand. You want to be left alone. Can I at least come in and light the fire for you?"

Aria shook her head.

"Well then, I'll see you in the morning." Amicus turned around and pulled the door shut behind him. The door shook in its frame a little bit and he knew she'd slid to the floor and leaned against it.

Through the door he said, "I'm here for you when you're ready to talk."

He engaged the lock, removed the key, and then took the stairs down, two at a time. The night settled in, and his family awaited his return. Vonah's bright smile lit his memories and he chuckled. *I'll be home soon, little one.*

† † †

Aria sat on the floor, cold and alone, and stared out the window at the slivered moon. Tears streaked down her face and she did nothing to stop them. She missed Alderan so much, and she missed home. *Why am I here, 2ätūr? What do they want with me? I'm no one.*

Flashes of her village burning raced through her mind. Screams of terror and anguish from the villagers—people she'd known her entire life—echoed in her head. Not a single soul spared, except her. The attackers dragged the people who tried to escape down from behind and ripped them apart like paper dolls.

None of it made sense. *If all they wanted was me, then why did they kill everyone else? What was the point?* She needed answers and her silence bought her nothing. *I must talk to Amicus tomorrow.*

She pulled herself up from the floor and prepared a fire in the fireplace. With the fire lit and blazing hot, she stripped out of her clothes and curled up in front of the fireplace. Her eyelids grew so heavy that she couldn't keep them open.

As she drifted near sleep, her mind turned to the man named Lord Rosai. *Who are you, and what do you want with me?*

Tomorrow. Tomorrow held answers she needed desperately, and she resolved herself to seek them no matter the cost. *But will I survive?*

Chapter Nineteen

Alderan's mind raced as a frenzied panic set in. Stranded on top of a hill in the middle of nowhere, Rayah lay in his arms, wounded and near death. To compound matters, the coldest part of the night settled in. How could he keep them warm without a fire? Helplessness suffocated him.

He tilted his head toward the sky and screamed, "Ɂäṭūr! Take me, not her!"

He pulled Rayah tight against himself and whispered in her ear, "This is all my fault, Rayah." Guilt twisted his stomach and churned a sea of vomit. "I never should've left you alone. I'm sorry—so sorry. Don't leave me! I love you, Rayah. I love you so much. Please..."

His vision blurred with tears, and it felt like a large stone had lodged itself in his throat. He could barely breathe through the pain of knowing he caused it all. *How could I be so selfish?*

A crazy thought formulated in his head: *If I remove the arrow shaft from her shoulder she'll be able to heal herself.*

Stupid! How could she do that?

With her mezhik.

An overwhelming need to remove the arrow shaft filled his mind and begged him to remove it. Rayah stopped breathing and it pushed him to be decisive. *The arrow shaft must come out!*

Alderan's hands trembled. "Ɂäṭūr, I'm begging You, let this work!"

Alderan laid Rayah face-down in his lap, placed his left hand on her back around the arrow shaft, and wrapped his right hand around the portion of the arrow shaft that he could grasp. He took a deep breath, said one last prayer to Ꙃäṭūr, and yanked the arrow shaft out of her shoulder. Fresh blood pooled around the wound and gleamed in the moonlight.

He gently turned Rayah back over. Even in the pale moonlight he saw that her lips were blue. Her chest didn't move. He placed two fingers on her neck to try and find a pulse, but found none. He lifted her left eyelid open, but her pupil didn't react to the light.

He scooped her back into his arms and rocked himself with her. "Bring her back, Ꙃäṭūr, I beg of You." His heart was an empty hole in his chest without her and the pain overwhelmed him. The loss of Aria had nearly killed him, but Rayah was his soul mate, his true love.

He sat on top of a hill in the middle of a forest, but it felt more akin to Ef Demd Dhä. He'd descended into a self-made hell, damned to be alone.

Let me die, Ꙃäṭūr. I can't live with a broken heart. I can't live without her. I can't live knowing my arrow killed her. Take me, not her. Please!

"Come back to me," he whispered. "Heal yourself, Rayah! I believe in you."

Her sticky blood clung to his hands as it continually oozed from the hole in her shoulder blade. He placed his right hand over the wound and begged it to stop—willed it to stop. He thought about all of the extraordinary things he'd witnessed Rayah do with her mezhik.

You're capable of anything, Rayah. Heal yourself! Don't give up. Don't leave me.

Alderan leaned over and kissed Rayah's forehead. "Give me your pain, Rayah. Let me take your wound. I'm strong. I can handle it. Come back to me!"

A faint tingling sensation tickled his right hand, just like what he'd felt when he'd touched Rayah's scarf in the snow. *Mezhik!* The sensation grew stronger and pumped new life into his aching heart. It crept up his arm and worked its way into his shoulder.

From his chest and straight through his body to his shoulder blade, he burned with fire. His skin pulled itself apart in the exact same location as Rayah's wound. It hurt worse than anything he'd ever felt in his life and he welcomed it. *Give me all of your pain, Rayah!*

Rayah stirred in Alderan's arms. Her eyelids fluttered, and she sprung to life with a loud gasp. A thread of joy twisted through his excruciating pain and he wanted to shout it to the world. *She's alive!*

"Rayah," he said through gritted teeth, trying to hold on to his consciousness. A hot white light blurred his vision, and then his mind finally succumbed to the pain.

†††

Rayah sat in a daze, lost in thought. By all rights, she should be dead. Again, she saw the arrow glance off one of the gnolls' arms and pierce her chest, the pain still fresh and vivid in her mind.

She fingered the hole in her dress made by the arrow; the bloodstain down the front of her proved she hadn't imagined the event. *But the wound? My wound?* She couldn't wrap her mind around the fact that no entry wound existed. *Ɂäţūr, I don't understand.*

The last thing she remembered prior to waking up in Alderan's lap was being tossed at Alderan's feet by that hideous beast. Seeing the gnoll lying there with an arrow lodged between its clouded eyes gave her a small feeling of victory, but the sight of Krag's headless body saddened her endlessly.

I'm so sorry, Krag. He'd saved her, and she'd be eternally grateful for it. *You didn't deserve to die.* If Alderan hadn't shown up when he did she would've been dead too.

Alderan! The thought of him snapped her out of her daze.

Rayah knelt next to Alderan and pulled his bloodied hair away from his face. He breathed heavily and wheezed with every inhalation. Sweat dampened his brow despite the cold temperature. She gently stroked his cheek, hoping to bring him out of his slumber. She pulled her hand back as he stirred.

Alderan sat up, grabbed the right side of his chest, and screamed. Rayah jumped back.

"Alderan?" she said, adding enough volume to top his screaming. "What's wrong?" Her heart raced with fear.

"Get it out of me! It hurts so bad! Get it out!" Alderan fell back against the hard rock. He still clutched his chest and whimpered like a scolded child. He shook from head to toe.

"Let me see what's wrong."

Rayah took Alderan's hand in hers and moved it away from his chest. He didn't resist her. Fresh blood stained his shirt where his hand had lain. She reached up and pulled his shirt down over his shoulder so she could get a good look at his chest.

"Alderan, I need to wipe the blood away. I'll try to be gentle, but it might really hurt." She thought he nodded just a little.

She tore a strip of fabric from the bottom of her dress and wiped away the blood on his chest. Alderan's whole body went rigid, but he didn't try to stop her or cry out.

"Your whole chest is sticky with blood," she said. "I need to get it wet so I can clean it better."

She got up and searched for an undisturbed patch of snow. A minute later, she returned with a handful of fresh snow.

"I'm sorry." She dumped the snow on his chest.

Alderan winced, but he stayed conscious. Everywhere she saw it, his skin turned to gooseflesh. She swirled the snow around with her makeshift rag until it melted, and then she wiped the blood from his chest. Underneath all the blood, she discovered a hole in his chest the size of an arrow shaft.

"Alderan, did you get shot by an arrow?" Confusion stunned her.

"Pull it out," he whimpered. "Just pull it out."

"There's nothing there but a hole. It looks like it went all the way through." Rayah sat back on her heels. "I need to go back for my pack. Krag rushed us out of our camp so quickly that I didn't have time to grab any of my things."

"Don't leave," he begged. "Rakzar may still be out th—"

"I have no choice. I can't just let you lie there and die! I'm in—" She barely stopped herself from blurting out that she was in love with him.

Maybe I should just tell him.

No, Rayah! You promised yourself you'd never let him know.

"I need to pack your wound and get it covered before it becomes infected, and I can't do that if I don't have my stuff."

She saw in his eyes that he wanted to argue with her further, but he didn't have the strength to do so. She pushed his matted hair away from his face. His heated skin against her frozen fingers alarmed her. *Żäṭūr, I cannot lose him!*

Rayah leaned over Alderan and kissed him on the forehead, twice. She really wanted to kiss his lips.

"I promise I'll be careful." She jumped up before she did something she'd regret and walked over to the narrow trail that led down the side of the hill.

"Be back before you know it." She quickly traversed the trail before he said anything to change her mind.

† † †

A few minutes after Rayah left, Alderan fell into a deep sleep, filled with nightmares.

Alderan made haste through the dead forest. His only thought was getting to the obsidian palace before dawn. In the distance, the palace walls rose above the forest, and its ramparts stretched into the darkened sky. Hundreds of large torches, burning like bonfires, lined the outer walls and cast shadows in every direction. The smell of tar and of death hung thick in the air and stung his eyes.

200 yards from the outer wall, where the dead forest ended, he stopped. The torches screamed, alive. They were made of humans and other races, covered in pitch and set ablaze. Wild dogs circled the area and feasted on the scraps of flesh that fell from the bodies. Hundreds of tall poles lined the road that led into the palace, and each sported a severed head.

High above the ground, walkways spanned between each of the five ramparts and formed a pentagram. At the center of the palace, in stark contrast to everything surrounding it, a white tower stretched into infinity. He stood there, his feet anchored to the ground, and watched the battle unfold between the ramparts and the white tower.

His body mimicked each blow the white tower sustained, thrashing him and knocking him to his knees. As if infected with a sickness, the white tower grayed.

Pain in the left side of his chest drew his attention. His gaze penetrated his clothing and his skin and burrowed deep into his flesh, where his heart sat. He gasped as it turned black and shriveled.

His gaze returned to the once-white tower and watched as it faded from grey to black. With the transformation complete, the tower crumbled and crashed to the ground. Despair overwhelmed him and threw him to the ground.

Dawn arrived, and, with it, all hope in the world ceased to exist.

Alderan woke to the sound of his own screams. Sickness swirled in the pit of his stomach and begged for release. The smell of burning flesh still clung to the hairs in his nose no matter how hard he tried to wipe it away. Never in his life had his dreams felt so real—almost like a memory.

What's happening to me?

His heart knocked in his chest and desperation poured from his brow. The thought of the world cast into darkness and all hope extinguished lifted the fog in his mind. He sat up, overcome with purpose.

I'm nothing, Ɛäţūr, but You can make something of me. Take hold of me. Use me for Your purpose. I won't allow the world to fall into darkness. Not without a fight.

Heal me, Ɛäţūr. Heal me.

The wound in his chest tingled and itched, and, within a few minutes, the urge to scratch it overwhelmed him. He tore at his shirt with his nails and gave no thought to opening the wound afresh. Relief came quickly, but its effect only lasted as long as he scratched. He peeled his shirt up to see what caused the itchiness.

Speechless, he watched the skin around his wound slowly knit itself back together. The pain in his chest and shoulder blade faded until nothing remained of it other than a slight annoyance.

"Thank You, Ɛäţūr." He let his shirt drop back down.

† † †

Rayah crested the hill, nearly breathless.

"Alderan, you're awake!" She floated towards him. "What has Ɛäţūr done?"

Alderan lifted his shirt, but she couldn't see what he pointed at. The sun still hung just above the horizon, and the morning haze distorted her view. She settled next to him and bent down to get a better view.

Rayah's eyes widened. "Your wound—Alderan? It's gone! How did that happen? What did you do? How is that possible? When I—"

Alderan pressed his fingers against Rayah's lips. Without thinking, she kissed them, and then quickly turned away as her cheeks flushed with embarrassment. Alderan laughed like he'd done the night she met him, and it made her happier than she'd been in a long time.

I've missed that laugh so much!

Alderan's hand wrapped around her arm and lightly tugged at it until she finally gave in and turned back toward him.

She furrowed her brow and tried to sound cross. "What do you want?" Her smile betrayed her and the snort at the end sent her into a full-on belly laugh.

"Rayah," he said firmly, "we need to talk."

"I know we do. There are so many things I want to tell you. I feel like we haven't talked in forever. How long has it been since we've really been together? Last night didn't really count since we were preoccupied with the fight and the killing and the wounds and all of that." So many emotions raced through her head. "I've had so much time to..."

Alderan stared at her with his mouth agape.

Get a grip, Rayah. Let him talk.

Her brain insisted that her mouth stop moving, but words spewed out anyway. "I'm sorry, Alderan. I've just got so much pent up inside my head that needs to get out."

Shut up, Rayah!

She took a deep breath and then let it out slowly. *Control yourself.*

Rayah tugged on one of her curls. "What did you want to talk about, Alderan?"

Alderan pushed his hair behind his ears. "There are so many things on my mind as well. I have so many questions, and I just had a nightmare so vivid that I thought I was awake. I've never had a dream or nightmare like it before. When I awoke from it, I couldn't get the smell of death out of my nostrils. It was even more disturbing than the images you shared with me of my village being attacked."

Images? Rayah frowned. "What do you mean by 'images'?"

"When we were at your house. While you recounted the story, I felt like I was there, seeing everything through your eyes and feeling your emotions as though they were my own."

Rayah gasped. *Can it be?*

"What is it?" Alderan straightened and then leaned toward her.

She leaned back on her hands, desperate for some breathing room. She searched his deep green eyes. *Ɛäțūr, is he really the one?*

She looked down at the rocky ground and watched her finger trace imaginary letters, a nervous habit she couldn't control. "Oh—nothing."

What am I doing? I want so bad to tell you everything, Alderan. My heart's on fire with love for you. Her cheeks warmed.

The moment he told her he'd seen and felt everything through her, she knew she'd never love another. Once a dryte made an intimate connection with another being like what Alderan had described, there would never be another. It explained her deep love for him.

I'm bound to him for life.

Growing up without a mother to guide her, she hadn't realized what'd happened the first day they'd met. Now, the sun rising in the morning seemed less obvious than the bond she shared with him.

But I can't ever tell him.

"I know you're holding something back, Rayah." Alderan leaned forward a little more and placed his hand over hers. "You can tell me anything, Rayah. You're my best friend."

Best friend? Those two words weighed her heart down like an anchor. She wanted so much more than to be his "best friend." *Why are boys so thick, Ɛäțūr?*

Rayah shrugged. "Really, it's nothing. I just hadn't realized that it had happened when I'd talked to you."

She desperately wanted to pull her hand away from his. Energy flowed between their hands, seeped into her skin, and electrified every atom in her entire body. The intimacy of it drove her mad. She feared what she might do if he continued touching her, but she didn't want him to think she didn't like his touch either.

Please, Alderan, move your hand away.

Alderan's eyebrows raised. "Oh. I thought you did it on purpose. Does your mezhik always work that way? Does it just flow out of you?"

"No. I've never had that happen before. I can usually feel it when I'm using mezhik. It sucks away my energy when I do. I must've been so caught up in the story that I didn't notice it."

"How do you cast spells? Do you do it verbally, or just think it?"

Rayah giggled and used the opportunity to withdraw her hand from underneath his. *Thank You, Zäṭūr.*

"I'm no wizard, Alderan. I can't cast spells." She giggled again.

Alderan sat back, his brow furrowed, and his lips pursed.

"What is it?" she asked.

"I guess I don't understand mezhik. If you can't cast spells, then how did you do what you did with your scarf?"

"My scarf?" Her face mirrored his. "What in Centauria does my scarf have to do with mezhik?"

"The morning after the blizzard I woke up in a pit of snow. I thought you were dead when I saw the end of your pink scarf sticking out of the snow. When I grabbed it I felt a tingling sensation race up my arm and into my head. After that happened everything changed.

"I was suddenly looking up at the giant, and he was smiling at me. But when I saw the reflection of you in his eyes I knew I was seeing through your eyes again. When I let go of the scarf everything went back to normal. I touched the scarf again, but nothing happened."

Rayah sat there, her eyes wide with disbelief. "That wasn't me, Alderan."

"How could it not be? It certainly wasn't me!" Alderan ran his hands through his tangled and matted hair. "Okay then, what about the shield of light that you protected us with when Rakzar tried to attack us? Or when you transferred your wounds to me? Or when you healed my wounds? What about all of those things? Are you saying that you didn't do those things either?"

Rayah's heart raced in her chest, and her lungs burned. She gasped for air when she finally realized that she'd stopped breathing. *Zäṭūr, my God—Alderan's a wizard!* She opened her mouth to speak, but words failed her.

"If you didn't do those things, Rayah, then who did? Are you saying that Zäṭūr did them? Did He save us?"

"Alderan," she said, her volume barely more than a whisper, "it had to have been you."

"That's not possible, Rayah. I've never done mezhik. I didn't even know what it was until I met you."

"How old are you?"

"Sixteen. I turned sixteen the day of the…" His brow furrowed.

"The day of the what, Alderan? The blizzard?"

"Yes, but what does that have to do with anything?"

"Everything!" she shouted. "You're a wizard, Alderan. A wizard!"

"How would I suddenly become a wizard? Wouldn't my father have to be a wizard?"

"Or your mother could've been one." She could hardly contain the excitement building inside of her.

"No, no, no! My parents were ordinary people. They had ordinary lives. There's no way they had mezhik."

"Are you sure they were your parents?"

"Are you mad? Of course they were my parents! They loved me, and I loved them!" Alderan stood and groaned as he clutched his head.

Rayah stood, too. Getting up off the hard rock surface was a relief. How could she make him understand that no other explanation existed for the things that happened? *He's so hard-headed, though. Yet another reason I love him.*

"A wizard gets their mezhik on their sixteenth name day, Alderan. It's not a coincidence. You're a wizard, whether you believe it or not."

Alderan held out his left arm, wrist up. "Is that why I have this mark on my—huh?"

Rayah looked at the three grey symbols on the inside of his wrist. "When did you get those?"

Alderan rubbed the symbols with his thumb. "I don't know. I only had one mark yesterday. What's happening to me?"

She bounced in the air with excitement. "I don't know what the symbols mean, but it explains so much, Alderan. This must be why the gnolls have been after you."

I can't believe he's a wizard! No wonder Master Savric sent me to watch over him.

Alderan frowned. "How would they know I'm a wizard if I didn't even know it myself?"

Rayah grabbed his hands and shook them. "Think about it, Alderan. The gnolls mentioned someone named Dragnus. If we find this Dragnus fellow, then maybe we can get some answers. He must know who you really are."

"Who I really am…" Alderan sighed and pulled his hands away from hers. "Fine, but first I need to go home. I need to see my village with my own eyes. Maybe I can find something there that will help explain some of this. Maybe my father left something behind… something hidden away. How could they have kept this from me? Why would they?"

"I don't know, but I'm sure they had their reasons. Maybe it was to protect you. Now, let's get out of here before these corpses begin rotting."

Alderan smiled. "Best idea all morning, Rayah." He hugged her, and she leaned into him as close as she could get.

She'd do anything for him, and keeping the full truth from him made her feel heartless and wicked. *It's for your own good. And mine.*

One day I'll tell you everything. I promise.

CHAPTER TWENTY

I'm all alone now.

"*No, you're not,*" replied a voice inside Nardus's head.

It wasn't his own.

Nardus reeled from the voice he swore originated in his head. The darkness, paired with his increasing deterioration of sound mind, drove him beyond the point of sanity, and he feared there might be no way back from it.

Vitara. Shardan. Shanara. Savannah. I'm so lost right now. I'm trying to fight this madness, I swear it!

"Who dares enter my temple?" A deep voice reverberated around the room and shook the temple walls.

The sound ripped Nardus from within his mind and hurled him back into the darkness. Fear squeezed his stomach like a vise, and his stomach groaned.

He had no idea where the voice had originated and the thought of finding out to whom or what it belonged terrified him; not knowing its source terrified him more. His hands trembled as he reached into the pack Gnaud gave him. He pulled out a torch and two pieces of flint rock from the pack. He hoped he'd get the torch lit before whatever had spoken came upon him.

"Mmm. Smells human," boomed the voice as it drew closer.

Nardus slid the flint rocks against each other once, twice, got a spark, but the torch didn't light. His sweaty hands shook so bad that he dropped one of the rocks. He cringed at the sound of it bouncing and rolling off somewhere to his left.

Damn! Now what?

The air around him sizzled with life as a deep, guttural laugh filled the room. His heart climbed into his throat as he peered into the darkness. Deep within it, he swore he saw two white orbs floating at his eye level. His heartbeat thundered in his ears, crashing time and again with little delay. The orbs disappeared and then reappeared again, closer.

No time to find the rock he'd dropped. He bent down and struck the remaining flint rock against the stone floor over and over, trying to get enough of a spark to ignite the pitch on the torch. *Light, damn you!*

Laughter erupted again, much closer and with deafening volume. The voice taunted, "I can light that for you."

Finally, a spark ignited the pitch and the torch roared to life, casting a dim circle of light about twenty feet in diameter around him. He peered into the darkness where the orbs hung in the air, but the light didn't penetrate it far enough to see anything. The white orbs drew closer, just outside the perimeter of the light's reach.

Nardus took a small step toward the white orbs and then froze in his tracks.

My God!

From the shadows emerged a large head covered in iridescent scales. Razor-sharp teeth lined the thin lips of its elongated snout. Three bony spikes shaped like a beard sprouted from its chin. A raised ridge of bone split its large, oval-shaped nostrils and ran the length of its snout.

Blade-like, bony plates lined the sides of its jaw. Its ridged brow extended over its slitted, deep-set, white eyes, and two long horns extended backward from the top of its forehead. Large, pointed ears grew back along either side of its horns.

He wished he could blow out the torch, unsee what he saw, and just let it rip his soul from his body. *Vitara, I'm sorry I've failed you again. Forgive me, my children. I love you all, truly.*

Nardus's legs gave out under him. His knees cracked against the stone floor when he fell, sending a wave of pain all the way up his spine and into his neck. The torch fell from his hand as he doubled over and gasped for air from the pain. Shadows raced to and fro as the torch rocked back and forth on the stone floor.

"Glad to see you're showing me the respect I deserve," said the creature.

"I'll turn up the lights so we can become better acquainted."

The creature opened his mouth and spewed a column of fire against the temple wall, fifteen feet above Nardus's head. The fire burned so bright and hot that Nardus would've turned into a pile of ash if he'd been any closer to it.

Nardus watched with amazement as lines of fire raced along the wall in opposite directions and up the wall to the ceiling seventy feet in the air, lighting torches all along the walls and igniting large chandeliers hanging from the ceiling. As the light spread, he saw that the room stretched thousands of feet in either direction and more than a mile in front of him, easily more than a square mile in all. The size and elegance of the hall stole what little of Nardus's breath remained.

Laughter brought his focus back to the floating head that was now attached to an enormous body. He'd heard a few tales of dragons over the years, but never gave any credence to them since he'd never encountered one himself. The creature that stood before him left no doubt in his mind as to the truth of their existence. It was indeed a dragon, both terrifying and beautiful all wrapped into one.

Iridescent scales covered its muscular, elongated body, and razor-sharp claws protruded from the splayed, six-digit knuckled toes and fingers on each of its two hands and feet. Large, arm-like wings protruded from the tops of its shoulders to the middle of its back, and the webbing of its wings stretched from the middle of its back to its hips.

Four elongated "fingers" stretched the length of each wing, and each finger ended in a claw. A thumb-like appendage with a sharp claw extended from the "wrist" of each wing as well. Its wings, when fully extended, spanned nearly fifty feet. Bony spikes, set a foot apart, ran the length of its spine and part of its tail. From the tip of its snout to the spade of its tail measured more than forty-five feet.

Nardus sensed a strange presence enter his mind as it had before, and the feeling of it probing his thoughts unsettled him.

"Ah," said the dragon. "You've come for *Ɇʈōn Dhef Dädh*. You're not the first to seek the stone, and you'll most certainly not be the last."

Nardus squeezed his head between his hands. "Get out of my head!" He felt violated in a way he couldn't even begin to describe.

"A strange darkness enshrouds your mind like a mist and blocks you from knowing your true self. Is this self-inflicted, or from another? Does it drive you mad?"

"I said *get out!*"

"Very well." The dragon withdrew himself from Nardus's mind. "We'll do this the hard way."

"What do you know of madness? Let me inside your head and I'll show you what madness really looks like!" Nardus shot back.

"The line between madness and brilliance is a fine one. I believe you naturally fall toward the latter than the former. The darkness within your mind has set you off balance. I can help you with that—for a price."

Nardus rose to his feet. "The only help I need from you is to point me in the direction of the stone. I've no desire to face my demons or share them with the likes of you."

"So be it. How would you like to die, then? By fire? Or would you prefer I eat you whole and vomit out your bones?" The dragon's laughter shook the very foundation of the temple.

"I'd prefer *not* dying." Nardus kept squeezing his head.

"Since you're the first visitor I've had in a long time, I'm willing to delay your death for a short while," replied the dragon.

"May I know your name?" asked Nardus. "It's only fair that I know the name of the one who's threatening to kill me."

"Interesting." The dragon tapped one of his claws against his chin. "I would've sworn you knew me."

"I've never seen a dragon in my life, let alone you. Until this very encounter I was of the mind that your kind didn't exist."

"Very well, I'll play at your game, son of Ƨätūr. I'm called Tharos the Cunning." He raised his chin and stood tall. "You'll find my name a fitting one."

"Well, Tharos, how do I keep you from killing me? Surely you, being as cunning as you claim, can think of some sort of agreement we can broker to satisfy the both of us."

"How about a game of riddles?" The dragon's thin lips curled into a deadly smile. "Answer three riddles correctly and I'll let you live—for a fee, of course. We dragons love riddles, but it's treasure that we covet most."

"If you truly are cunning, as you say, how can I trust that you're not deceiving me now? Even if I answer your riddles and somehow come up with an item of value, how am I to know you'll keep your word?"

"Call me devious, sly, crafty, tricky, cunning, or anything else along those lines and you'll be justified. Call me a liar or dishonorable, and you'll be dead!" Smoke bellowed from Tharos's nostrils as they flared.

Nardus could think of nothing to get out of his situation and saw no way out of the massive hall. *I'd be praying to You right now, Ɛäţūr, if I thought You'd lift a finger to help. I know better than that though. I'm alone in this as always.*

"Fine," said Nardus. "I agree to your terms. Three riddles and an item of value."

"Agreed, then," said Tharos. "But the item must be of my choosing."

"As you say, dragon." Nardus shook his head. *I'm sure I'm gonna regret this.*

"Excellent! Let's begin then. We'll start with an easy riddle and then get progressively harder."

"Wait." Nardus's eyes narrowed. "What is the item you want?"

Tharos snorted smoke and lowered his head to meet Nardus's gaze. "There's no need for that discussion unless you answer the riddles correctly."

Nardus raised his hands and stepped back. "As you wish. So how long do I have to answer each riddle?"

"Time here's of no consequence. You may take all that you need," said Tharos. "But no longer. I'll give you a clue before we start. The answer to each riddle is something you struggle with daily."

"Well that *certainly* narrows it down," Nardus scoffed. "Let me have the first one, then."

"Very well," said Tharos. "Answer this: *'I'm without beginning or end, but I'm not a ring. Some consider me a friend, but all will call me king.'*"

"I'm not a ring," Nardus repeated to himself.

His mind immediately ran to his furry, little safety blanket, Gnaud. *I'm sure you'd be excellent at this. Surrounded by all those books, you seem to have an answer for everything. But where are you when I need you?*

"That's it!" He snapped his fingers as a rush of relief washed over him. "Ɛäţūr! The answer is Ɛäţūr." *Thank you, Gnaud! You're with me even when you're not, unlike Ꞓäṭūr. He may be King, but I won't be bowing to Him.*

"Very good, Nardus," said Tharos. "As I said, the first would be easy. Now, answer this: *'We hurt from within, fester like thorns in your sides. We get under your skin, bearing both truth and lies.'*"

Nardus scratched his head, contemplating each part of the riddle. He arched his back and then stretched his legs. His knees felt swollen and bruised from falling on them earlier. He paced in circles and led himself further from an answer with each lap.

Think, Nardus. Your family hangs in the balance.

"Can I have a clue?" he asked, unable to pull an answer from his mind.

"I'm feeling generous today," said Tharos. "I'll give you one clue. Ask for a second, and I'll pick my teeth with your bones."

"Fine," said Nardus. "So, what's the clue?"

"We start and end wars, weapons in our own right." Tharos blew smoke from his nostrils.

"Of course." Nardus thrust his hands in the air. "The answer is *words*."

"Precisely. Words are the truth of all those things."

Nardus swung his fist through the air. "Yes! And the last riddle?"

"Yes, the last riddle. Answer this: *'Gods, we're not, but can resurrect the dead. With just one thought, we'll live in your head. Smiles and tears, we're responsible for. Hate and love, your fears, and so much more.'*"

"Ah." Nardus grinned. "A curse and a blessing all wrapped in one. What you speak of is something I long to rid myself of: *memories*."

"You, son of Ꞓäṭūr, are cleverer than I anticipated." Tharos blew smoke from his nostrils. "Never mind that. You still owe me a debt of treasure."

Nardus had a feeling in the pit of his stomach that something was amiss. The three riddles were far too easy. *What is your agenda, Tharos? What am I missing?*

"Well, I suppose I may have something in my pack that you'll find of value."

"Oh, my friend," said Tharos, "that won't be necessary *or* acceptable. The treasure I require of you exists in this very temple." He smiled and then laughed deviously. "You only need to fetch it for me."

Damn! I knew he couldn't be trusted. Nardus sank to the ground, defeat dragging him down like an anchor.

Nothing in this quest had been easy. He realized more and more that he got the short end of the deal he'd made with Pravus. Bringing his family back from the dead seemed like child's play compared to what he'd endured since entering the tunnels beneath Mortuus Terra.

We'll have words when I'm done with this wretched quest. He took a deep breath.

"So be it." He had little choice but to do as the dragon requested. "What do I have to fetch for you?" He closed his eyes and cringed with anticipation.

"There are catacombs below us. Because of my size, I'm unable to go down there. In one of the tombs is an amulet. Retrieve it for me and your debt will be considered paid."

"Retrieve an amulet? That's it? Seems simple enough. What are you not telling me, dragon?"

"Oh, nothing really. No one's been down there in centuries. No one living, that is. There are some spiders, as you can imagine."

Spiders? The thought crawled across his skin with its eight prickly legs. *I hate spiders!* One of his worst memories was entangled with spider webs, in a literal sense. His whole body shuddered.

"If I do this for you, you'll have to do something for me in return," said Nardus.

"Are you trying to change our agreement?" Tharos stamped his foot on the ground.

"You've already altered the original agreement!" exclaimed Nardus. "It's only fair you allow a modification on my side as well."

"You filthy humans are all the same! I should roast you right now and be done with you."

"Do it, then. It certainly won't get you your precious amulet, though." Nardus stood, completely agitated with the beast. He felt inclined to force a conflict and get his miserable existence over with.

As if on cue, images of his family flooded his mind. *You're right. I must go on. I love you all so much.*

He glowered at the dragon. "Do we have a new agreement or not?"

Tharos moved his head just inches from Nardus's and eyed him with his left eye. "What is it you want in return, son of Ʒäƫūr?" His breath reeked of sulfur.

"I need to know where the stone is located in this godforsaken place," said Nardus with a cough.

Tharos raised his head to full height. "Very well. We have a new agreement. Retrieve the amulet and I'll tell you how to locate *ʒt̄ōn Dhef Dädh*. However, you're on your own in getting it."

"Agreed. Now where will I find this amulet of yours?"

"Buried deep within the catacombs, you'll find a marble sarcophagus marked with *ʒäəll Dhef ʒäfn Dhä*. Break it open and retrieve the amulet from the body contained within."

"How will I know this seal?"

"You don't know it? No, of course not. The seal's unmistakable: a golden iris surrounding a vibrant-blue heptagram, and at its center will be a yellow bolt of lightning."

"Heptagram?" asked Nardus.

"A heptagram is a seven-pointed star. Are you taught nothing where you come from?"

Nardus wanted to fire something back at the dragon, but thought better of it. "Let's just get this over with. Where in the catacombs am I going to find this sarcophagus?"

"There are four levels to the catacombs, and you'll find the sarcophagus at the lowest level in the farthest reaches of the tunnels. If you stick to the main passageways on each level, they'll lead you to the stairs descending farther down. If you veer from the main passageway, you'll likely get lost."

"I'll manage," said Nardus, certain he'd add to the number of dead buried in the catacombs. "Lead the way."

With a puff of smoke, Tharos turned and walked a few paces farther into the great hall. He slammed his fist into the floor and triggered a small section to open up, revealing a straight and narrow stairwell that led down into the catacombs.

Nardus walked over to the stairwell and peered into it. *Totally dark. Could've guessed that.*

Tharos turned toward the temple doors and picked up the torch Nardus had dropped earlier. It looked like a toothpick in his large hand. With a small puff of fire, he ignited the torch.

"You'll probably want this," he said, handing the torch to Nardus. "Might keep some of the spiders away." His laughter filled the room.

"Thanks." With a long exhale, Nardus descended the stairs into what felt like a living nightmare.

† † †

The catacombs were dank, but Nardus burned with fever. Paranoia crawled under his skin like spiders. Every few paces he swept the torch in a circle just to verify that nothing moved to crawl into one of his trouser legs.

"Get a grip, Nardus," he said to himself. "Tharos mentioned spiders just to get under my skin. I suppose it worked."

Every twenty feet or so hung a sconce and Nardus lit each one as he moved farther into the catacombs. He began to understand why they'd called it Ţämbəll Dhef Däd Dhä. *The Temple of the Dead.* Burial niches lined the rock walls in six-foot intervals, each containing a fallen soldier from the Great War.

A slab of rock sealed each niche, inscribed with the name of the person buried and the date they died; many of them were inscribed with "*Ännōn*" as the name, and each had the same date: 12.17.Y23.Carac. Hundreds of thousands occupied the catacombs.

Unknown. Nardus stopped. "How did I know *ännōn* meant unknown?"

Nardus felt Tharos's presence enter his mind. "Get out of my head!"

He slammed his fist into the wall. *Wretched dragon!*

"*When you take the amulet, I suggest you exit as fast as you can,*" said Tharos in Nardus's head. A deep laughter followed his words, and then his presence left Nardus again.

Nardus made his way down to the fourth level of the catacombs without incident, but phantom spiders crawled on his skin and drove him mad. His dislike of Tharos grew with every step. *Mezhik and dragons—can't stand the likes of either.* He spat on the floor.

A large white and grey marble sarcophagus sat at the end of the tunnel ahead. His heart raced in his chest as he approached it. Engraved on the lid of the sarcophagus was Ɂäəll Dhef Ɂäfn Dhä, just as Tharos had described it. Also engraved into it was the name of the person entombed within in it and his date of death: Magus Carac, Kinzh dhä Drezhn - 12.17.Y23.Carac.

"Magus Carac." He tried to remember what Gnaud had said about the

Great War. His chest seized up when he finally recalled Gnaud's words regarding Carac: *"The most terrifying king to ever have lived."*

"Kinzh dhä Drezhn," Nardus whispered. "The Dragon King."

Magus Carac started the Great War. He ruled the Ancient Realm for more than two decades and nearly destroyed the entire world. His army of dragons and dragon riders were like nothing the world had ever seen. Their strength and brutality were unmatched. Without Ūrdär Dhef ƨäfn Dhä, the Ancient Realm would've been lost to darkness forever.

Nardus wrestled with his thoughts. *How can I do this? Moreover, what is this going to do?*

But what choice do I have? If I don't do this, I'm dead. If I don't do this, I'll never see my family again.

If I do this, I may still never see my family. Vitara, my love. What should I do? I'm so weak. Please give me your strength!

Nardus steeled his mind and his heart, determined to complete the task no matter the consequence. He'd complete the quest or die trying. *For my family.* He set the torch on the ground, away from the sarcophagus.

He gathered all the strength within him, used the memory of his family as a booster, and shoved the lid of the sarcophagus with everything he had. Blood rushed to his head and pulsed through every capillary as he strained against the weight of the lid. His pounding heart boomed in his ears, and his vision blackened around the edges.

Finally, the seal on the lid gave way, and the lid slid about a foot to one side. Nardus sucked in air and collapsed against the side of the sarcophagus, out of breath. The smell of embalming fluids hit his nostrils and lungs and nearly choked him. He pulled his shirt over his nose and mouth to try to filter out the smell.

After finally regaining his breath and with his vision back to normal, he pulled himself up to his feet. He grabbed the torch from the ground and used it to light up the inside of the sarcophagus.

And now I've seen my future.

Within the sarcophagus laid a withered body, bound in linen. Around its neck hung a golden chain adorned with a magnificent amulet, the likes of which Nardus had never seen. The teardrop-shaped amulet glowed like molten lava, and wings of black onyx extended from its left and right sides.

Nardus reached into the sarcophagus with his left hand and took hold of the amulet and chain. Searing pain ratcheted up the length of his arm, into his neck, and then his head. He tried to release his grasp on the amulet, but it controlled him. Like a bolt of lightning, his vision exploded with a pure, blinding-white light. He closed his eyes, but it made no difference.

A vision filled his head, almost like a memory.

He lay on his back and looked up at a mountain of a man that bent over him. The man wore the amulet around his neck. Magus.

"You're a dead man, Cyrus," said Magus. Spittle rained down on Nardus with each word.

"No!" screamed Nardus.

Nardus crashed to the floor as the amulet's hold on him gave out. He shook violently, still unable to control his body. His left temple tingled with mezhik, and then something burrowed its way into his skull like a rat and ate its way into his brain. Like a phantom finger, it ripped away what remained of his vision of Magus and then retreated, leaving him paralyzed with fear.

Tears streamed from his eyes as he trembled. *Get a grip, Nardus. It's over now.* He checked his trousers and a wave of relief washed over him. *Not soiled.*

Time slipped by as he turned what remained of the vision again and again in his mind, unable to grasp what'd happened. The vision, so vivid, had felt like a memory.

It can't be a memory. I'm a madman. Nothing else can explain it.

He felt around his temple where the object had entered, but he found no hole. *Why would there be a hole? It's all mezhik. Wretched mezhik!* He turned his head and spat on the floor.

With his pain and fear ebbing, he pulled himself to his feet. The fact that he'd managed to keep the burning torch in his hand throughout the ordeal left him bewildered.

His attention drew back to the amulet as it glistened in the torch light and taunted him. *Damn you. I won't let you win. Vitara, my love. Give me strength.*

He reached into the sarcophagus and wrapped his fingers around the amulet and chain. He drew in a breath and then yanked the chain. The chain pulled through the neck of the corpse and severed the head. A bright light flashed, and the sound of thunder rolled through the catacombs.

Ɂäəll Dhef Ɂäfn Dhä pulsated on the lid of the sarcophagus. His heartbeat quickened as thousands of tiny spiders poured out of the body of Magus Carac and filled the sarcophagus. He dropped the torch on them and ran for his life.

Bones and broken tombs littered the floor of the tunnel and he hurdled over the larger pieces. *Must've been where the sound of thunder came from.*

Spiders flowed from the niches like a sea of legs and eyes. They squished under his boots as he flew through the tunnels.

By the time he made it to the upper level of the catacombs, he waded through layers of spiders up to his knees. They crawled all over him, climbed under his clothes, and skittered toward his nose and mouth.

The stairs lie just ahead, but now the spiders came up to his waist, and he could barely move.

"Tharos!" he screamed. He fell to his knees and the spiders overran him. Their bites stung like wasps and his skin swelled.

Tharos entered his mind, and for once it relieved him. *"Place the amulet around your neck."*

He struggled against the spiders as they smothered him. He felt them crawl inside his mouth, their legs sharp against his tongue. Down the back of his throat they traversed. He coughed and swallowed several of them. He finally raised his arms over his head, slid the chain around his neck, and yelled to Tharos in his mind.

A blinding light flashed through the tunnel and swept over his body like a rush of water. Tiny screams filled his ears as the spiders were incinerated. The tremendous weight of the spiders evaporated, and he pulled himself up.

He stared into the stream of fire flowing through the tunnel. The flames licked at him, swirled all around him, but they didn't touch him; nor did he feel their heat.

"Get out of there!" yelled Tharos.

Nardus clambered up the narrow stairs and rolled to the side when he reached the opening at the top to avoid running into Tharos. As soon as Nardus cleared the opening, Tharos slammed his fist into the floor, and triggered the entrance to the catacombs to shut.

"Damn you!" Nardus gasped and quickly stripped down to his undergarments and swatted at the remaining spiders.

Tharos's laughter filled the room. "Now wasn't that a great adventure?"

"I'm going to have nightmares about that forever!" Nardus shuddered.

"Be glad it was spiders you were thinking about. Otherwise it could've been far worse."

"How could anything be worse than that?" Nardus glared at him.

"The spell on that sarcophagus you triggered would've created anything you feared. That's why I put the thought of spiders in your head. At least they weren't *giant* spiders." Smoke bellowed from his nostrils and he let out another laugh.

"I hate you, dragon."

"The feeling's mutual," he said with his ferocious dragon grin.

"So, this amulet protects from dragon's fire?" Nardus gripped it in his hand.

"Oh, something like that," said Tharos. "Now, hand it over and I'll tell you where to find *Ꝫ̧ōn Dhef Dädh*."

"Hold on. When I touched the amulet the first time I got a vision from it."

"Interesting." Tharos's serpentine eyes narrowed. "And what did you see?"

"I can't seem to remember anymore, but I know it felt like I was there, or had been there."

"And what do you make of this vision?"

"What do *I* make of it? No, dragon. *You* tell me what it means."

"Why would I have any idea as to what it means? Besides, you said you didn't want my help. Now, hand over the amulet."

Nardus knew Tharos wasn't being upfront with him, but he didn't want to push the dragon any further. "Not yet. You tell me where to find the stone and then I'll give you this amulet. Not a second sooner."

Tharos growled, "I'm beginning to like you, son of Ꝫä̧ṭūr."

"The feeling's *not* reciprocal."

"In time, you'll change your mind."

"Enough of this! Where do I find the stone?"

"I'll open the entrance to the upper level of the temple. Follow your heart and you'll reach the labyrinth. Find your way out of there and you'll find the stone. Getting to the stone is the easy part. Keeping it and surviving won't be."

Nardus dressed himself and picked up all his things, and then he and Tharos walked to the center of the room. On the floor were six holes splayed like Tharos's fingers. Tharos stuck his claws into the holes and turned the whole section of floor ninety degrees counter-clockwise. At the far end of the room the wall scraped against the floor as it slid apart ten feet, revealing a hidden stairway.

"The amulet, Nardus," said Tharos, holding out his hand.

Reluctantly, Nardus removed the chain and amulet and hung it on one of Tharos's claws. Without a word, Nardus walked toward the stairway.

"Hurry," said Tharos. "That door won't stay open for long, and I won't open it for you again."

Nardus quickened his pace, glad to put distance between himself and Tharos the Cunning.

The doorway ahead vibrated the floor as it closed. Nardus ran as fast as he could, but the distance felt immeasurable. The light from the stairway faded as the gap in the wall narrowed.

Two paces away, Nardus couldn't imagine fitting through the gap—but he had no choice. He turned his shoulders and dove.

CHAPTER TWENTY-ONE

The coals in the fire still smoldered when Aria woke up. From her window, she saw the beautiful morning sky, painted in hues of pink and purple as the sun slowly climbed up the northwestern side of the Procerus Mountains. The air chilled her naked body and swept away the cobwebs of sleep that still lingered. She yawned and stretched her arms and legs.

She stood in front of the full-length mirror and examined every inch of her body with a critical eye. A battered, young woman stared back at her, nearly unrecognizable from the girl she'd been a few months prior.

She'd suffered so much pain, a lot of it physically manifested in the numerous scars spread across her body, but some of it deeply rooted in her heart and soul. The loss of her entire family weighed heavy on her. She longed to join them.

Take me from this world, Zäţūr! Take me home to You and my family.

Disgusted with her broken-toothed smile, she turned away from the mirror and began readying herself for the day. The man named Lord Rosai sat at the forefront of her mind all morning and drove her mad with questions.

Who is he? Where is he from? What does he want from me? How does he even know who I am? What if he finds me repulsive? Or attractive?

I'll kill him.

A knock at the door pulled her from her thoughts and back into the reality of her situation. She quickly pulled her yellow dress over her head and ran her arms through the sleeves. She pulled the dress down, situated her breasts, cinched the tie around her waist, and then smoothed out the rough fabric.

With the lock disengaged, the door swung open. Amicus stood in the doorway with a smile as wide as the heavens and as bright as the sun. Him standing there and not someone else lifted her spirits.

Thank You for sending him, Ʒäṭūr.

"Hello, Caterpillar. You're looking beautiful today. As you always do, of course."

She wanted to respond to him with more than a simple nod and a smile, but the words couldn't find their way to her lips. She hadn't spoken in so long she feared that she might've forgotten how.

Ʒäṭūr, I beg of You, loosen my tongue.

A young girl pushed passed Amicus and into the room and walked over to Aria. Her beautiful, black curls were pulled into braids at the sides of her head. She wore a big smile on her dark-skinned face, crooked teeth and all.

"I'm Vonah." She held her hands behind her back and swayed as she talked. "Papa says you don't talk. Why not? I like to talk. I've had four name days. How many name days have you had? Do you like to play house? I do. I like cats too, but they make me feel bad. But it's okay. I still play with them. Your dress is pretty. Did you make it yourself? Can you play with me? I like dress up and dolls. What do you like?"

Laughter built in Aria's gut, but only produced a smile for the beautiful girl.

Amicus laughed. "Alright, Vonah. Take a breath. You don't want to wear Aria out on your first visit."

Aria reached down and stroked Vonah's cheek.

Vonah stepped back and rubbed her cheek with her shoulder. "Your hands are rough, like Papa's."

She's so adorable. Ʒäṭūr, unhinge my jaw and loosen my tongue.

Amicus stepped into the room with his hands pulled behind his back. He hid something from her. "Turn around and close your eyes. Both of you. I've got a surprise."

Vonah bounced up and down. "I like surprises. One time, Papa came home with a puppy, but Momma made us give it away because it chewed on everything."

Reluctantly, Aria turned around. She tried sneaking a peek at what Amicus held behind his back through the mirror's reflection, but she didn't have the right angle.

"Caterpillar, close those beautiful, green eyes of yours. It won't be a surprise otherwise."

Through the mirror, she gave him a soft smile and then closed her eyes.

What can it be?

Her curiosity heightened with the sound of rustling paper. Then a wonderful smell filled her nostrils and made her mouth water with anticipation. The aroma smelled so familiar, but she couldn't quite put her finger on it. The suspense nearly killed her.

Aria felt a tug on her dress and looked down. Vonah twisted a fist-full of dress in her left hand and held on to it as though her life depended on it. Vonah sucked on her right thumb.

"Okay." Amicus chuckled. "You can turn around now."

Vonah turned around so quickly that she nearly knocked the package out of Amicus's hand. Aria turned around. What Amicus held in his hand made her forget all about her broken-toothed grin.

Chocolate! How could I have forgotten the smell of it?

"Go ahead and take a piece." Amicus extended the package toward them.

Vonah grabbed a piece and shoved it into her mouth. She giggled and twirled around and let herself fall against Aria's bed.

Aria broke off a piece of the chocolate and held it up to her nose. Rich, dark, delectable. She almost tasted the smell. She placed it on her tongue and let it sit there until it started to melt. Not just chocolate—a little piece of heaven in her mouth. She closed her eyes with delight.

Memories from her childhood bubbled to the surface.

She was no more than two years old, barely old enough to walk. Her father came home early that day with a small package wrapped in pink paper. The package mesmerized her, and, when he opened it, the smell it produced brought her joy.

She could barely contain her excitement, and she danced in place as she waited for him to break off a piece. He knelt, but she was too focused on the chocolate to even pay attention to him.

"Give Papa a hug and kiss first," he'd said.

She quickly wrapped her arms around his neck and kissed him on the cheek. His beard tickled her lips and she giggled. He smiled at her with his warm, brown eyes. He handed her a piece of the chocolate and told her to savor it because it might be the last piece she ever received.

She stuck it on her tongue and let it melt into nothing. He was the best papa she could've asked for.

Aria pulled herself back from the memory, confused. Parts of the memory were off. The man that gave her the chocolate wasn't the father she grew up knowing and loving; the man felt so much like her father, but he didn't look anything like him. Her heart pulsed in her ears, faster and louder.

How is it possible to have such detailed memories of my papa and yet the man not be him?

Panic overwhelmed her. Her heart raced out of control and she couldn't draw in enough oxygen. Her head swam, and she felt like she might pass out. She searched her memories for any others that didn't seem to fit.

Sandcastles!

The same man had been there on the beach that day when she and Alderan built sandcastles. He sat next to a beautiful woman she didn't know.

"Are you okay?" asked Amicus.

Amicus said something else, but the sound of his voice faded with her vision.

† † †

Aria awoke lying face up on her bed, drenched in sweat. Amicus sat on the bed next to her and held a cool rag to her head. Vonah lay beside her and held her hand.

She's so precious.

Amicus sighed. "You gave me quite a scare, Caterpillar. I barely caught you before you hit the floor. I hope it wasn't the chocolate that did this to you."

Vonah released Aria's hand, sat up, and crawled to the foot of the bed. "Is she gonna be alright, Papa? I like her."

Aria sat up, pushed herself to the top of the bed, and leaned against the wooden headboard. Her head swam. She tried to force words from her mouth, but her throat was so dry that she went into a coughing fit instead.

Amicus retrieved a cup of water from the table next to the window and handed it to Aria. She gulped it down as fast as she could swallow.

"Easy, Caterpillar. You don't want to make your coughing worse by choking on the water."

Satisfied that her throat was sufficiently hydrated, she handed the cup back to Amicus. Her voice cracked as she said, "Thank you."

Amicus dropped the wooden cup on the floor.

Vonah bounced on the bed. "Papa! Papa! She talked!"

"Yes, she did." Amicus sat back down on the edge of the bed. His smile couldn't have widened farther. "I wasn't sure I'd ever hear you speak."

His excitement made Aria smile. Her voice frail, she said, "I wasn't sure you would either."

Amicus grinned. "I've been waiting so long to hear your voice. I've imagined it sounding so many ways, but I never thought it would be so lovely. You have the voice of an angel."

Vonah giggled. "Papa tells me that, too!"

Aria heard footsteps approaching in the hallway and turned her head toward the door. A few seconds later, a bearded guardsman poked his head inside the room.

"Lord Rosai has arrived," said the guardsman. His deep voice raked Aria's nerves. "Bring the girl down to the library. Immediately." The man turned and walked away without waiting for a reply.

Lord Rosai.

Aria felt sick to her stomach. Despite all she'd endured, she'd never entertained the idea of suicide, but for an instant she thought about throwing herself from the window like Dragnus's mother had.

You know I never would, Ƨäțūr. I beg of You—save me.

Amicus took hold of Aria's arm. "Everything will be okay, Caterpillar. I promise."

"I know." She put her other hand over his. "You're a true friend, Amicus. I would've been dead if you hadn't rescued me. What would I do without you?"

"I hope you never have to find out." Amicus stood and held his hand out. "Guess we'd better get a move on."

She would've given anything to have stayed right there, but she knew better. She put her hand in his, and he pulled her to her feet.

"Promise me you won't leave me alone with him," she whispered.

"I promise, Caterpillar. They'd have to drag me out, and I guarantee I'd put up a good fight." He smiled and jabbed at the air with his fists.

My ebony knight.

Vonah giggled and jumped off the bed. "Papa's silly."

Aria smiled at Vonah. "He most certainly is."

Amicus smacked his hands together. "Alright you two. Let's go before we're all in trouble."

Vonah looked up at Amicus. "Why would I be in trouble, Papa?"

Amicus rubbed the top of Vonah's head. "It's just an expression, angel. You're not going to be in trouble. When we get downstairs, you're gonna go play with Brently."

Vonah whined, "But I want to stay with Aria. Can't I play with her?"

Amicus grabbed Vonah's hand. "Another day, angel."

Aria bent down to Vonah's level. "You're welcome to visit me anytime."

Vonah beamed. "Tomorrow?"

Aria looked up at Amicus. "Your papa will have to make that decision."

Amicus winked. "We'll just have to see, angel."

Aria giggled as they headed out the door and down the stairs. She willed herself to be positive and open-minded about this man named Lord Rosai. Master Dragnus seemed to bear disdain for the man, so how bad could he really be?

† † †

Lord Rosai leaned against the rickety, wooden bookcase and cleaned under his fingernails with a small knife. Dragnus sat opposite Lord Rosai on a tattered and worn couch. Dragnus's brow dripped with sweat as he rubbed his hands together.

Which smells worse? Dragnus or the couch he soils? A toss-up, I'm sure. Pathetic old fool.

"I see you've spared no expense for my visit." Lord Rosai's hollow voice dripped with sarcasm. "The welcome party was exhilarating."

"I'm sorry, my lord," said Dragnus. "Good help is hard to come by."

"Present company included." Lord Rosai closed the knife and slid it into one of the pockets hidden within the folds of his black and gold pinstriped robes. He stared daggers at Dragnus. "Any word on the boy?"

Dragnus looked away. "The matter is... complicated."

"Either the boy's dead, or he isn't. There's nothing *complicated* about it."

"Well, my associates have informed me that unforeseen circumstances have arisen—"

"We're talking about a sixteen-year-old boy!" Anger boiled in his veins.

"You never mentioned anything about him having *mezhik*," Dragnus fired back.

"If you'd taken care of it *before* he turned sixteen none of this would've been an issue. Now get it done, or I'll find someone else who will!" He slammed his fist against the side of the bookcase, and a shelf full of books crashed to the floor.

"Just leave them. I'll have it cleaned up later," said Dragnus.

Lord Rosai glared at Dragnus. "Trust me when I say I'd never stoop to pick up anything for the likes of you."

The double doors swung open with a squeal, and Dragnus rose from the couch. A tall, thin, dark-skinned man entered the room, followed by a young, fair-skinned girl.

Thank the gods they've arrived.

The man bowed to Dragnus and then to Lord Rosai. "Sire," he said, and then, "My lord."

"I'll handle things from here, Dragnus." Lord Rosai ushered him out of the room. "Make sure the other business is taken care of."

Lord Rosai closed the door and walked over to Aria and the ebony man. "Aria—" He took her hand in his and lifted it to his lips. "—it's a pleasure to finally meet you. I am Lord Rosai, Lord of Atrum Moenia." He turned to the ebony man. "And you are?"

"Amicus, my lord." He bowed, but his gaze never broke from Lord Rosai's. "I am a humble servant of Ɛäţūr. And, so we're absolutely clear, I've given Aria my word to protect her, no matter the cost."

"Excellent. Then I can count on your full cooperation?" asked Lord Rosai.

"It all depends on your intentions, my lord."

"I assure you, my intentions are pure and faultless. I come here in pursuit of Aria's best interest."

"If what you say is true, then we will become fierce allies."

"As you say." Lord Rosai turned his attention to Aria and looked her over. "I've been waiting a long time to meet you, my dear. You've haunted my dreams for years. I cannot tell you how excited I am to finally be in your presence."

Lord Rosai mastered reading people. He could peer into someone's eyes and know exactly what they felt, what they feared, and what they longed for. However, when he peered into Aria's haunting, green eyes he lost himself in them.

You're an exquisite young woman, Aria.

He found no fear in her eyes, but the pain in them delved deeper than any he had ever seen, save one man. She certainly bore physical pain, but her deep-seeded, emotional pain fueled his newfound obsession with her. She longed for death—to be reunited with her family—and it heightened his excitement toward her.

I'll give you everything your heart desires.

Lord Rosai smiled at Aria. "You're the first female I've met who didn't cower in my presence. I like that about you."

"My lord, what exactly are your intentions with her?" asked Amicus.

Lord Rosai looked at Amicus. "You're here to observe. Don't open your mouth again unless I ask a question of you. Are we clear?"

"My lord," said Amicus with a curt nod.

"Aria, I understand some wretched men abused you when you first arrived here. I'm so sorry you had to endure that. As you may know, I'm a *healer* of sorts."

Her blank stare told him otherwise.

"I see. I would've assumed that *Master* Dragnus would've told you about me, but never mind that."

"I'm here to heal you, Aria. Physically first, and hopefully mentally as well, given time. Now please remove that beautiful dress and any undergarments so I can see what I'm dealing with."

"You can't expect her to—"

"*Silence*, Amicus. I warned you once. Keep quiet, or I will silence you."

"*No.*" Amicus stepped between Aria and Lord Rosai.

"Have it your way, then." Lord Rosai waved his hand. "*Inţū ęţōn.*"

Amicus's eyes bulged from his head and his mouth opened. He reached for Lord Rosai slowly, then his entire body halted its motion, went rigid, and turned to stone.

"No!" screamed Aria. Tears formed in her eyes.

"It's okay." Lord Rosai held up his hands. "No harm will come to him. I'll remove the spell when we're finished here. Now, please remove your clothes so I can see what I'm dealing with."

The anger in Aria's eyes delighted him. She ripped off her dress and undergarments and threw them in a pile in the center of the room. She still fumed at him as he circled her like a vulture eying its prey.

Exquisite.

Lord Rosai pointed to the couch against the far wall. "Now be a good girl, and go lie down, face-up."

She stormed over to the couch, her hands balled into fists, and plopped down on it. A cloud of dust rose into the air and she sneezed. She lay back on the couch, her fists still clenched.

Lord Rosai walked over to the couch and knelt next to it. Aria met his smile with a scowl. He laughed lightly, knowing he intrigued her more than she let on.

"What I'm about to do for you is going to be extremely painful. If you'd prefer, I can put you to sleep."

She glared at him and crossed her arms over her abdomen. Her movement drew his gaze to her breasts, and he let his eyes linger on them momentarily. *In time.* He pushed a few strands of her blonde hair from her face. The left side of her mouth and nose rose into a snarl, but she said nothing.

"Ah, right. You enjoy the pain, don't you? So be it. It's important that you lie completely still for what I'm about to do. I'm going to cast a paralyzing spell on you so you won't be able to move. You'll still be able to talk, if you wish."

Lord Rosai swept his arm over Aria's body. *"Bäräəllíz."*

Aria grew still and Lord Rosai cracked his knuckles. "Now, let's begin."

†††

Aria felt drawn to Lord Rosai. He seemed her equal when no other man ever had. Most men feared her, as if Diząfär had marked her for himself. *As if that could be true. I'm a daughter of Ząţūr.*

Lord Rosai took her hands and moved her arms to her sides. She felt his touch, but had no control over her body. He placed his hands on her ribcage, just below her breasts. If she'd been able to move, she would've flinched.

"Several of your ribs were broken and didn't heal correctly. I'll re-break them and then stitch them back together properly. This will be excruciating."

A sizzling sensation seared her skin and penetrated the bones of her ribcage. Never had she experienced anything so strange.

So this is what mezhik feels like?

The more mezhik he poured into her, the closer she felt to him. The mezhik intoxicated her, and she wanted more. She breathed in and bit her lip.

He's such a handsome man. Does he think I'm pretty? If I don't smile.

"Diąinţäzhräíţ," he said.

Aria's chest bordered on exploding and she whimpered as she fought against the pain. Three of her ribs cracked loudly as they broke apart. Pain sliced through her mind like shards of broken glass and brought back memories of her ribs being broken before. For a moment she slumped there again, slammed up against the rock wall she'd just thrown Pigman over.

A tear slid down the side of her face. She bit down on her lower lip harder and drew blood. Lord Rosai wiped the blood from her lip with his thumb and licked it off—or did he?

This pain's making me crazy!

She closed her eyes as tight as she could and held back a scream.

Once her bones completely separated, he said, "Beąll ţäzhädhär."

Upon his command, she felt her bones pull straight and grow back together.

Several more times he went through the same process, breaking and resetting bones in her body that hadn't healed correctly. Her head spun like a top from the pain.

I'm not sure I can take much more of this.

"There we go," he said with a smile. "That wasn't so bad, was it?"

Slowly, the pain ebbed until numbness spread over her again.

Immediately, she felt a withdrawal as his mezhik faded.

I need more. Touch me again.

"Please." Her panting voice startled her.

Lord Rosai's eyebrows rose. "Please, what?"

She would've sank into the dank and dusty couch if she could've. "Nothing."

Her cheeks burned when he smiled at her. *I think he knows. He must think me a fool.*

"Now, to remove some of these scars," he said.

"*No.*" Her head snapped up, but she couldn't move the rest of her body.

"You wish to live with these scars?" His eyes narrowed, his lip curled on one side, and his nose wrinkled.

"They're my scars to bear," she said in little more than a whisper. "Please don't take them away. They're part of who I am." A tear slid down the side of her face.

"Very well. I shall leave them. Now, let me fix those teeth of yours. We can't let you go about known as the young woman who never smiles."

She couldn't understand why this man, whom she'd never met before, did this for her. *He's a wizard and the lord of a castle. I'm nothing.*

Why, Ȝäțūr? Why is this man being so kind? Is this Your doing?

He placed the palm of his hand between her top lip and her nose. The smell of his skin stole her breath. She fought against an overwhelming desire to kiss his hand.

What's wrong with me? I've never felt this way about any man. It must be his mezhik.

"This will feel strange, but there should be no pain," he said.

Her lips and tongue tingled as mezhik flowed from his hand and into her once more. Instantly she was intoxicated again, driven mad by his mezhik touch. She heard herself moan and thought she'd die right there on the couch.

Death by embarrassment. Ȝäțūr, please help me control myself!

"*Frʊm nʊdhinzh,*" he said.

Her broken teeth grew and reshaped themselves. The nerve pain she'd grown accustomed to waned and then ceased to exist. She ran her tongue across her perfect teeth and giggled.

"Ah." Lord Rosai smiled down at her. "Much better. Your youthful beauty has been restored."

His mezhik faded and left her wanting more—wanting him. It made her feel dirty, but she liked it nonetheless. She liked *him*.

He swept his arm over her entire body. "*Enämät*."

She curled her hands and toes and rolled her shoulders. "Thank you." Tears filled her eyes.

Lord Rosai stood. "You're most welcome, my dear. Feel free to dress yourself now."

"That's all?" she asked and then covered her mouth with her hand.

"Do you require something more of me?" he asked.

"No, my lord." Her cheeks burned.

You're a fool, Aria. This man heals you and all you can think of is your lust for him? Why would a man like him want anything to do with someone like you? He's a lord and you're nothing.

He wouldn't.

She rose from the couch and walked over to the pile of clothes. She grabbed her undergarments and pulled them on. Then, as she worked herself back into her yellow dress, she said, "I don't know how I'll repay you for what you've done."

"Ah," said Lord Rosai. "The answer's quite simple. You'll become my queen and live with me in my castle. Together, we'll rule the Ancient Realm."

She faced him and laughed loudly. "I'm serious."

"As am I." His deep, golden eyes sparkled, and she lost herself in them.

Me a queen?

Chapter Twenty-Two

Alderan's heart sank into the pit of his stomach as the remains of Viscus D'Silva came into view. Blackened skeletons reached up through the piled snow and into the bleak winter sky, shells of the houses and buildings they once were. Of the nearly 200 structures that comprised the village, not even one still stood.

468 souls lost. Alderan's blood boiled in his veins. *I will avenge you all.*

Hot tears streaked his face and hung on his chin. His jaw ached with tension, but he ground his teeth harder still. "Dragnus will pay for this."

Rayah stood next to him, a sobbing mess. "I can see it happening again."

Alderan wiped his face with his hands. "So can I. It makes me sick."

Rayah slipped her small hand into his; its warmth contrasted his cold, dead heart. "Show me which house was yours."

Alderan pointed north. "It's on the far end of the village. Actually, just beyond the village. It backs up to the northern part of the Veridis Forest."

His stomach lurched. *Can I face it? Can I face you, Father?* Would it bring him closure?

His hand trembled and Rayah gently squeezed it. He looked down at their joined hands, and then at her. Her hazel eyes, moist with tears, reached into his soul and comforted him. From the night they met in the woods, she'd stood by his side and willingly followed him into what felt like the bowels of Ef Demd Dhä. He would've died on numerous occasions had she not been there to rescue him.

He intertwined his fingers with hers and gently squeezed. *I love you, Rayah.* Life without her was unthinkable, but the timing of telling her didn't feel right. Besides, what if she didn't feel the same way about him? Or, if Aria still lives, what would she think of him being with a dryte?

Does any of it matter?

No. When this is over, I'll tell you how I feel, Rayah. I promise.

Alderan released Rayah's hand and walked along what used to be the main road of the village. Every step, every memory, crushed him. *So many friends lost. And for what?*

Human remains littered the ground in various states of decomposition. The freezing cold temperatures and the blanket of snow undoubtedly slowed the process, but many of the bodies had been picked clean by birds, wolves, and other carnivorous creatures. The scene horrified him, but not nearly as deeply as his recurring nightmares.

Alderan stopped partway along the road. "We should bury them, Rayah. It's not right to leave them like this. They all deserve a proper burial."

Rayah came up next to him. "I understand what you're saying, but how do you propose we do that? The ground's frozen solid. It would take us months to bury them all."

Rayah was right, but it didn't settle his mind. "Fine. We *will* bury my father though. I won't leave without doing at least that much."

"Of course, Alderan." Her eyes brightened. "Maybe if we build a fire hot enough it'll warm up the ground to the point where I can manipulate the dirt."

Alderan pulled his hair back. "It's worth a shot, and might be our only option."

"Then it's settled." Rayah looked around. "What were these places?"

He pointed to a burned-out structure to the west. "That was Nevet's Tavern. He was an old friend of my father's. Next to it was Shaya's Meats. She always had the best smoked rabbit and boar."

Despite their dire surroundings, his mouth watered. When had they last eaten? He couldn't recall, and it explained some of his weakness.

They made their way north, and Alderan pointed out several more houses and shops of the people he'd known. The devastation tore at his heart. Only pure evil could cause so much pain and death. Those beasts were heartless, soulless creatures. Rakzar and his cohorts proved as much.

"When we're done here, we'll hunt down Rakzar and get the answers we need. He'll lead us to Dragnus one way or another. And, when we finish with him, he dies."

Rayah tightened the pink scarf around her neck and cradled herself. "It scares me to go after him, but you'll get no argument from me. I wish he was already dead."

They reached the northern edge of the village and Alderan stopped in the middle of the road. He stared 200 yards ahead at the thatched-roof cottage—untouched by fire. His legs buckled, and he dropped to his knees. Tears streamed down his cheeks and fell from his chin.

Father?

Rayah knelt next to him and put her arm over his shoulder. "I'm so sorry, Alderan. You won't find your father alive in there. As I said, only your sister survived the attack."

"I know that." His voice cracked. "But why is my house still standing? I expected to find it burned out like everything else. I don't understand."

"A protection spell saved it from the fire. If your father and your sister had just stayed inside they'd still be alive. Your father knew about the spell, but couldn't just stand by and watch the whole village be destroyed while he did nothing. When he left the house, your sister followed. That's when they grabbed her.

"They put her in chains and put a silver collar around her neck. Your father took a dagger to the spine. They did it on purpose to keep him alive long enough to watch his village be decimated."

Alderan looked at Rayah in horror. "How do you know all of this? How do you know my father? You told me before that you didn't know my sister, so how do you know him? How could you possibly know all of this unless you were in on it too?" He shrugged her arm away and moved away from her.

How could she do this to me? He glared at her.

Rayah hugged herself and looked at the ground. "It's not like that at all, Alderan. You know me. I'd never do something like that to you."

Alderan closed his eyes and ran his fingers through his hair.

Calm down, Alderan. This is Rayah, the one you love. Remember the last time you fought with her? You nearly lost her forever. Just hear her out. She must have a good explanation.

Alderan opened his hands and released his anger before he spoke.

"Explain yourself. Tell me everything you know, and leave *nothing* out. Our relationship hinges on this, Rayah. I don't want to lose you, but I can't be around you if you're keeping secrets from me."

Rayah collapsed on the ground and sobbed uncontrollably. Alderan moved back over to her and sat in front of her with his legs crossed. It reminded him of the time they'd sat on the dirt floor in her house and talked. This time they sat in snow.

"Well?" asked Alderan.

Rayah sat up, pulled out a handkerchief from her jacket pocket, and blew her nose in it. She wiped her eyes with her hand and then returned his gaze. Her eyes were red and swollen from crying. Even in her current state, he still found her beautiful.

I don't wanna lose you. He hated seeing her so distraught, but he needed answers. *I'm tired of being kept in the dark on everything.*

He took her hand. "Please, Rayah. I must know."

She twirled one of her chestnut curls around her finger. "I was sent to keep an eye on you, Alderan. I've watched you from a distance for several years and wanted to make contact with you, but I knew that if I didn't stay in the shadows your life would be in danger."

Alderan couldn't believe what he heard. "You've been watching me? Why? Who sent you?"

She tossed the strand of hair over her shoulder and took his other hand. She searched his eyes. "You're one of the most important people in all of the Ancient Realm. You and your sister. Many prophecies were written about the two of you. A darkness is coming, Alderan—an evil so vile that it will corrupt anything in its path. You and your sister were our only hopes of surviving. Now it's just you. If you die, Alderan, all hope will be lost."

Pain stabbed his stomach and his head pulsed. "Me? Important? You expect me to believe that? I'm no one."

She shook his hands. "That's one of the reasons why you're the perfect person. You're humble."

How can this be? Ɂäṭūr?

Alderan pulled his hands away from hers and ran them through his hair. "What do the prophecies say will happen?"

Rayah shrugged. "I don't know any specifics of the prophecies. I wish I did."

Alderan closed his eyes and rubbed his forehead. "Who sent you?"

"A great wizard named Savric sent me and my friend Leilana. I told you about her when we first met. I was assigned to watch over you, and she was assigned to watch over Aria. Leilana died protecting her, just like I'd do for you."

Alderan looked at her. "But why? You've seen me, Rayah. I'm no savior of the world. I cower every time I see a shadow that looks like a gnoll."

"You're no coward, Alderan. You've faced certain death with a bravery I've never seen the likes of before. You can be fearful of something or someone, but that doesn't make you a coward. I'm the coward. I hid in the shadows and didn't lift a finger as I watched those beasts slaughter all these people."

"You and I both know that's not true, Rayah. One against a hundred. You stood no chance against them. Besides, what could you have possibly done differently?"

Rayah thrust her hands in the air and then let her arms drop. "I don't know, but I've lied to you, and I'm ashamed of it." Tears rolled down her cheeks again. "I feel as though I've lost favor with you and Ɂäʈūr."

Alderan reached over and wiped her tears with his hands. "Just promise you'll never lie to me again."

Rayah sniffed. "I promise."

"Then I forgive you, Rayah." Her smile warmed him. *And I love you.*

Tiny flakes of fresh snow drifted about as the sun melted into the graying sky. "I think we'd better seek shelter before we're lost in another snowstorm."

"Okay," she said. "Can you help me up? I think my legs have fallen asleep."

Alderan pulled himself up from the ground and then helped Rayah to her feet. The flakes came down harder and the temperature with them.

Alderan stared at the lone cottage. "I don't know where else to go other than my house."

"We'll be safer in there than out here in the cold."

He shuddered, but not from the cold. "Maybe, but I'm afraid of what we might find in there."

Rayah frowned. "What exactly are you expecting to find in there?"

Alderan's stomach twisted in knots. "I don't know. I just have a bad feeling."

Rayah took his hand. "I'll be with you, Alderan. I'll protect you. It's my job."

She couldn't protect him, but the sentiment made him smile.

Alderan sighed deeply. "Let's hurry, then."

They ran toward the house together.

† † †

Rayah sat on the floor in front of the fire and warmed her hands and feet. She'd determined to tell Alderan everything before they left the village. He deserved the whole truth, and she couldn't stand to keep it from him any longer.

I'm in love with you, Alderan. It doesn't even matter if you love me back. I am yours, forever.

Alderan sat in the rocking chair next to her, deep in his own thoughts. He clutched a brown and yellow blanket his mother had made for him. He looked so lost. She wanted so desperately to make him feel better, but only time would ease his pain.

She placed her hand on his leg. "Alderan, we need to finish our conversation. There's more I need to tell you."

He didn't respond, so she gave him a little nudge. He blinked a few times then turned toward her.

"Did you say something?" he asked.

"I wasn't done telling you everything."

He sat up in his chair and his brow furrowed. "What more could you possibly have to tell me?"

"I communicate regularly with Master Savric. Or rather I did until yesterday."

"Communicate?" The lines in his brow deepened. "How do you communicate with him? What do you tell him when you do?"

She shrugged. "I tell him everything that happens. That's my job. I had a small book with me that I used to talk with him."

Alderan pushed his hair behind his ears. "What do you mean you *had* one? What happened to it?"

"When the gnolls came after Krag and me, all my things got left behind because he didn't give me a chance to grab anything. When you were passed out on top of the hill, I went back to get my stuff so I could bind your wounds. I searched everywhere, but couldn't find my book."

"Rayah, I don't understand all of this, but I'm trying to trust that your intentions are sincere. When I tracked your giant friend, I found your campsite. As I was about to continue tracking you I saw something gleaming out of the corner of my eye. When I got closer to it I saw it was a book. I grabbed it and put it in my pack. I'd forgotten that I had it until you mentioned it."

She jumped up and kissed him on the lips. She ran to get the book and got halfway to it before she realized what she'd done. Embarrassed by it, she decided she'd pretend it hadn't happened. She retrieved the book from his pack and returned to the fire and sat down again.

Alderan had slipped back into a daze and held his fingers to his lips.

She smiled to herself, said, "*In alldheft Hiz*," and then opened the book.

"What does that mean?" asked Alderan.

"In His light," said Rayah. "This book was created by *Ūrdär Dhef 2äfn Dhä*—The Order of the Seven—to communicate secretly. The enemy never understood how they did it. The symbol on the cover is *2äall Dhef 2äfn Dhä*—The Seal of the Seven. To those that follow the darkness, it appears to be nothing more than an ordinary book."

"Ah." He still thumbed his lips. "How does it work?"

"This book is one-half of a pair. When I write in this one, my words are transferred to the other, and vise-versa. Once the message is received, it is removed. If you look at its pages, you will find nothing on them. The symbol on the front of the book will glow when there's a pending message. Now, I need to send a message to Savric and let him know that we're still alive."

Alderan leaned on the arm of the chair. "What exactly will you tell him?"

"Where we're at now and what happened yesterday." She looked up at him, but he stared vacantly into the distance again. "Is there something wrong with your lips?"

"I'd never been kissed before. I've always wondered what it would be like, but I never expected it to be quite like that."

She frowned. "What do you mean?"

"My lips tingled. They're still tingling." He looked down at her, his features as soft as she'd ever seen them. "Does it always feel like that?"

"There's one way to find out!" Embarrassment warmed her cheeks.

Alderan kept his eyes trained on hers.

"I'm sorry, Alderan. I shouldn't have kissed you. I was just so excited that you had my book. I wasn't thinking."

"Rayah, I..."

"You what?" She hoped beyond hope that he loved her and wanted to tell her.

Please, 2ăṭūr—let him love me?

"I... I'm just tired and need to go to bed. That's all." Alderan got up and quickly walked into the small bedroom, not once looking back at her.

She buried her face in her hands and cried. *I shouldn't have kissed him. Nothing's going according to plan.* Nothing ever did for her.

† † †

The cold night air burned his lungs and the wind stung his eyes, but even they held less bitterness than Rakzar did. He sat outside the thatched-roof cottage and waited for an opening to exact his revenge. The smell of them— their wretched blood—filled his nostrils and fueled his hatred.

The White Knight's blood will spill tonight, or I'll die trying.

All day, he'd stalked them like the prey they were. Not once had they doubled back to see if they were being followed.

Amateurs... but he's bested me twice.

Rakzar beat the sides of his head with his fists.

There's nothing special about him. He's just a boy. Right?

Yes.

Then why did they send me to kill him?

He dug his claws into his head and ripped out his doubts about the White Knight, or so he wished. He grabbed a handful of snow and squeezed it until it turned to water. His claws dug into his flesh and drew blood. He squeezed his paw-like hand and watched the droplets of blood fall into the snow.

Soon the snow will be red with your blood, White Knight.

A few hours after all went quiet and the lights extinguished he'd draw them out. His mouth salivated at the thought of sinking his teeth into the worthless boy.

But first I'll tear out your little girlfriend's throat and make you watch her bleed to death.

✝ ✝ ✝

The necromancer stood atop the wall of the obsidian palace and commanded the dead to rise from their graves—an army of the dead. Alderan stared into the cold, black eyes of the necromancer and saw death itself contained within them. Darkness poured out from the necromancer's mouth and filled Alderan's lungs with the taste of death and left his heart cold.

✝ ✝ ✝

Alderan jerked straight up in bed. His heart raced tirelessly. The cold house lay in darkness, save the minimal light that came through the lone window next to the front door. Through that window, eyes watched him. Perhaps only in his mind, but he lifted the covers to his neck anyway.

Coward! What good would the covers do anyway?

Rayah!

He pulled himself out of bed and quietly made his way into the room around the corner where Rayah lay sleeping.

"Rayah," he whispered into the darkness.

She didn't answer, and panic swirled in his chest.

"Rayah?" he said, more firmly.

Still no answer. He felt around on the bed, but she wasn't in it. From what he could tell, the bed hadn't even been used. He ran back into the living area to see if she remained by the fire, but she was nowhere to be found.

Just beyond the window—peering through the glass—hovered two hateful yellow eyes, glowing defiantly. Alderan's throat tightened and his stomach lurched.

Rakzar.

CHAPTER TWENTY-THREE

Nardus's skin crawled with phantom spiders even as he reached the top of the stairway. Three hallways, carved from the earth, branched out from the landing, one to the left, one to the right, and one straight ahead. The hallways to the left and right mirrored each other, but the one straight ahead sat half as wide and its ceiling hung low.

A child's laughter drifted down the hallway to his left. A small figure stood at the far end, partially obscured by the shadows. Something about the figure felt familiar to him.

"Come play with me, Papa?" asked the male child's voice with excitement.

Nardus recognized the voice as that of his eldest, Shardan. He fought back an avalanche of tears. *You're not real. I buried you, my precious son.*

"No, Papa. Come play with me," squealed a female child's voice from the right.

Shanara. Joy and sorrow shook Nardus and brought him to his knees.

"Papa play?" called a third female child's voice, directly in front of him.

Savannah, my precious angel.

Rational thought gave way to the desire to hold them again. Nardus held his arms out to his sides and swept his head from left to right. "Come to Papa."

Savannah ran toward him with her precious, waddling gait, a smile beaming across her face. From his left and right, Shardan and Shanara raced toward him and leapt into his arms. He pulled them tight as Savannah reached up and put her arms around his neck.

Nardus kissed their foreheads as tears flowed down his cheeks. A happiness he hadn't felt in ages washed over him like cleansing water.

"My precious children," he repeated, again and again.

He knew they weren't real, but he didn't care. The loss of them kept him in a constant torment. He blamed himself daily for his failure to protect them and keep them safe. With them in his arms—real or not—he wanted so desperately to stay in that moment with them, forever.

Don't take this away from me. Don't You take this away. You owe me this, Ɂäṭūr. Don't take my children away again.

Their wonderful smell intoxicated him. He hadn't realized how much he'd missed it until that instant. He breathed in deep and savored the moment. And their laughter—their wonderful laughter—soothed his soul. Joy overwhelmed him and spun his head like a top.

As one, his children pulled away from him and moved just out of reach. He desperately grasped at the air.

"Children, come closer," he pleaded. "Come back into my arms!"

All three stepped farther back.

A deep, guttural laughter filled the hallways and set Nardus on edge. A deep, guttural voice boomed, "Choose one."

"Choose one," repeated the children in unison.

"I choose them all!" shouted Nardus. "I choose them all!"

"One or none," said the voice and the children.

"You cannot ask this of me! You cannot ask me to choose one of my children over the others. They're all precious and special in their own way."

He watched in horror as Savannah dropped to her knees.

"Papa?" She reached out for him. A trickle of blood streamed down her forehead, between her eyes, and down the side of her nose. She fell face-first onto the floor. An arrow shaft protruded from the back of her skull.

"No!" he screamed. He lunged forward in his mind, but his body refused to move.

Savannah twitched. Nardus tore at his hair as he watched her die again. He doubled over, dry-heaving, wanting to rid himself of the images and pain. He pulled and ripped his shirt down the front as agony twisted and stabbed his heart.

His vision blurred with tears and the hallway in front of him darkened.

Shadows raced toward Savannah and then pulled her into the darkness. He reached out for her, but his knuckles slammed into a wall that wasn't previously there. He beat his chest like a wild animal, felt a pop when one of his ribs cracked, and he roared with fury and pain.

"Ɂäṭūr!" he screamed. "Why must You torture me so?" *I hate You!* He clutched his side and sat back on his feet, defeated.

"Choose!" The voice shook the ground.

"What difference does it make?" Nardus cupped his head in his hands. "They're already dead."

"Don't leave me, Papa," pleaded Shanara, her arms outstretched.

"Don't let me die," Shardan begged.

"But I already have," he said. "I already have."

"I'm scared," they cried.

"So am I," said Nardus. "I'm afraid of what I've become. I've driven myself mad with rage. I no longer see the man you called Papa. He died with you. I'm dead inside."

"Choose!" boomed the voice.

Nardus pulled himself to his feet. "Leave me. I'm done playing games."

Nardus turned to go back down the stairs he'd come up, but in their place, he found another wall. *Perfect.* He slammed his fist into the wall and pain shot up his arm and into his neck. *Drat! I hate mezhik!*

"You *must* make a choice," said the voice.

Nardus massaged his knuckles. "What you're asking of me is impossible. How could I possibly choose one child over another? They're equally precious to me. Ask me to chop off one of my arms and I could easily decide."

"If they're dead, as you claim them to be, then where's the harm in making a choice between them? They'll never know your decision."

Nardus held a finger up. "But I will. I'll have to live with the decision for the rest of my life, just as I did the day I chose to seek vengeance instead of protecting them."

"So be it," said the voice.

The screams of his children filled the hallway and he covered his ears. He closed his eyes, unwilling to witness their bloodied and tattered bodies again. He leaned against the wall and let his body sink to the floor. *I'm so sorry. Forgive me, children. Forgive me!*

"You had your chance to die peacefully with one of your children in your arms," boomed the voice. "You've chosen to forgo that. Now prepare to face your death alone."

Nardus opened his eyes. Four walls of clay and dirt surrounded him. No signs of his children remained. He sighed with relief.

"I'm ready to die. Now show yourself."

The wall he leaned against crumbled under his weight, and he sprawled flat on his back. The other walls and ceiling shook violently and then turned into dust. He covered his eyes with his arm as the dust rained down on top of him.

He pushed his way out of the blanket of dirt and sat up. Well beyond the fallen walls stood the temple's walls; they stretched unnaturally into the red sky, seemingly without end.

The loose dirt that surrounded Nardus vibrated and pulled together and formed a large mound of earth. The ground trembled as the mound rose up and transformed into some kind of giant beast. Moments later, Nardus found himself staring into the silver eyes of a great beast made of clay and dirt.

The beast stood across from Nardus. Its massive arms reached all the way to the ground and dwarfed its small waist and legs. The beast had no nose or ears on its squat, narrow head, and its mouth had no lips, teeth, or tongue.

The beast pounded its large, block fists into the ground repeatedly and caused the ground beneath Nardus to tremble with seizures. The beast roared so fiercely that it blew back Nardus's hair.

"Stand up and face me!" cried the beast. Dirt flew from its crude mouth with each word.

Nardus rose to his feet and calculated his next move. Brinzhär Dädh sang as it slid from its scabbard, and its tingling mezhik bled into Nardus's palm.

"Ah." The beast's laughter rumbled through the air like thunder. "You think a sword will work against me?"

Nardus held the blade above his head. "This is no ordinary sword."

Nardus winced as pain pulsed in his chest where he'd cracked his ribs. He focused his thoughts and energy into the sword and let the sword's presence slither into his mind and push away his pain. He stood tall, poised for an attack.

"And I'm no ordinary earth golem!" It launched toward him.

Nardus twisted and ducked, and the golem's sledgehammer fist missed the side of his head. With his momentum, Nardus pulled the blade into an upward arc and sliced through the golem's arm at what he assumed to be its elbow. Its forearm and hand crumbled as they hit the ground.

Nardus retreated a few steps and eyed his handiwork. A smile worked its way across his face. He twirled the blade in his hands. "I'm just getting warmed up."

The golem laughed at him. "So am I!"

The golem raised its arms to the sky, puffed up its chest, and roared at the sky. The ground trembled again.

Nardus watched in awe as the ground pulled toward the golem and climbed up its legs. With every passing moment, the golem grew larger and larger until it towered over Nardus at twice its original size. Its arm grew back too, now the size of a large tree trunk. The golem stood more than fourteen feet tall.

The golem pounded its fists into the ground, split the earth, and sent Nardus tumbling out of its way. The ground caved in all around them—all the way back to the surrounding walls of the temple—and left them stranded on an island of dirt no more than twenty-five yards in diameter.

Nardus signaled the golem forward with a wave and then clutched the sword with both hands. The golem came at him, swinging its sledgehammer fists back and forth like pendulums. Nardus ran full speed at the golem and used its swinging arms to launch himself into the air.

In mid-flight, Nardus flipped, just clearing the golem's left shoulder. From behind, he drove the sword into the golem's back, burying the blade all the way to the hilt. He tried to pull the sword back out, but it wouldn't budge.

The golem staggered as it twisted its arms and legs backward. With its massive hands, it twisted its own head 180 degrees to face Nardus. A twisted grin spread across its deformed face.

Nardus released the sword and fell to the ground, flat on his back. The jolt made him bite through his lower lip and sent pain spidering through his whole body. He barely had time to roll out of the way as the golem pounded the ground with its fists where he'd lain.

Nardus scrambled to his feet and moved to the opposite end of the island. Blood ran from his pierced lip and down his chin. He wiped it away with the back of his hand.

The golem ripped the sword from its chest and tossed it to the side. "You're pathetic. I'll rip your head and spine from your body!"

"I'd like to see you try." Nardus spat blood on the ground and eyed the sword.

The golem charged him again. Nardus stood there, waiting. The energy of the sword still pulsed in his veins. He was ready.

The golem cut the distance between them in the blink of an eye. In one constant, fluid motion, Nardus slid between the golem's legs, somersaulted toward his sword, picked it up, and jumped back to his feet.

The ground shook as Nardus turned back toward the golem. The golem knelt, just inches from the edge of the island. Nardus ran toward the golem, launched himself at it, and twirled in the air as he brought the sword around. The sword slid through the golem's stout neck like it was made of butter. The golem's head rolled off its massive shoulders and fell over the edge of the island and disappeared into the darkness below.

The golem planted its fists on the ground and pushed itself to its feet. Nardus jumped back. The ground trembled as more dirt pulled toward the golem again.

"Oh, no you don't!" yelled Nardus.

Nardus lunged at the golem with his sword held high, but the golem twisted its arms backward and swiped at the air. The wild swing glanced Nardus's right shoulder and sent him tumbling to the ground, writhing in pain. He pushed himself away from the golem with his feet.

Nardus forced himself to sit up. His right arm hung limp at his side, his shoulder clearly out of its socket. A new head formed on top of the golem's shoulders.

Damn!

Nardus reached over and grabbed the sword with his left hand. He moved it to his side as he sucked in air; each breath pierced his chest like a dagger.

The golem turned its newly formed head around and faced Nardus. Its laughter roared through the air and echoed off the walls and through the surrounding chasm.

"As I said, you're pathetic."

Nardus clutched the sword in his left hand and drew energy from its touch. *Vitara, my love, give me strength one last time.* He stumbled as he pulled himself to his feet and used the sword as a cane. He willed the pain to be gone one last time. He wrapped both hands around the hilt of the sword, leapt into the air, and drove the sword into the ground.

The golem laughed at him. "Was that supposed to do something?"

Nardus pulled back on the hilt of the sword. A fissure jutted out from either side of the sword, spread to the edges of the island, and separated him from the golem. The part of the island the golem stood on slid backward and at a downward angle, toward the chasm.

The golem leapt toward Nardus, but, against the momentum of the ground that slid in the opposite direction, it slipped to its knees instead. It clawed at the ground and roared as it, and the part of the island it clung to, plummeted into the chasm of lava below.

Nardus fell backward, the sword still clutched in his hands. He wheezed with every labored breath. Every muscle in his body burned with fire. The pain in his right shoulder brought him to the brink of passing out, and the edges of his vision grew dark, but he refused to succumb to it.

I'm so sick of darkness. I'll surely go mad if I have to endure it one more time.

The red sky above him swirled in circles. The circles darkened at first and then became a dull white as they drew toward him. He blinked a few times and then realized he stared at the ceiling of a hallway. He sat up and pulled himself over to the wall.

At the end of the narrow hallway, a bright blue door with a silver knob beckoned him. He let out a long sigh, totally worn out from everything he'd endured.

Two more trials. Two more trials, and then I'll get my family back. I won't fail you this time.

CHAPTER TWENTY-FOUR

*M**e a queen?*

Aria staggered over to the couch and sat. She couldn't breathe and pulled at the top of her dress, even though it hung nowhere near her neck. The cloud of dust provided by the couch didn't help either. Her thoughts swirled like leaves caught up in the wind and dizzied her.

"But I'm nothing. No one." She looked at the floor, but found no solace there. "I'm unworthy of being your queen."

I want to be, though. Unless I'm just hypnotized by your mezhik. Is that possible?

Lord Rosai walked over to the couch and sat next to her. "There's never been one worthier of me than you. As I said earlier, you've haunted my dreams for years. I cannot imagine my life void of you."

She peered into his eyes. Everything about him seemed perfect. "Did your mezhik do something to me?"

He cocked his head and squinted at her. "Besides healing you?"

She ran her fingers through her hair and twirled the ends around her fingers. She studied his features like one would study a piece of fine art, looking for flaws, but finding none. *You must've been sent by Zätūr. I cannot stop thinking about you.*

"Never mind," she said. "It's nothing. So, what would I be the queen of, exactly? I thought King Zaridus was the ruler of the realm."

"He may be king for now, but an uprising is coming."

Aria's eyes widened. "Uprising? You mean like a war?"

Lord Rosai chuckled. "Power is a funny thing. Most who hold it don't deserve to. My father was a true king. I will rule one day soon, just as he did."

The pride in his voice reminded her of her father and made her feel good. *He cares about family, too.*

"Why did you choose me? How did you even know of my existence?"

His eyes twinkled. "The answer's simple, my dear: *prophecy.* I've studied it my entire life. The bulk of the prophecies have surrounded certain bloodlines for millennia. Mine is one of them, and yours is another. I found you because it was prophesied that I would. We're destined for each other, Aria. I think you felt it when our eyes first met."

Destined?

Aria's brow furrowed. "But I believe in free will. How's it possible for something to be written that hasn't happened? What if I decide to stay here?"

"I don't believe you will. However, there are always multiple paths to prophecy. We all make choices that influence the paths of prophecy that come to pass."

I don't even know this man. How could I be his queen?

The bleakness of the room surrounded her and closed in on her. *If this is my only alternative how could I possibly refuse his offer?* The more she thought about it, the more she realized she had no choice to make.

Destiny. Prophecy.

Excitement drove Aria to her feet. "I can't believe that someone wrote about my family." She paced in circles and chewed her lower lip. "Will you show me these books?"

"Of course. If you come with me, that is." Lord Rosai rose from the couch.

Yes. No. How can I refuse him? I do want to be with him. But is it him or his mezhik?

Lord Rosai placed his hand on her shoulder and stilled her nerves. "When we return to my castle, I'll show you everything."

Even if it's his mezhik I'm attracted to, does it matter? I've nothing to lose.

She closed her eyes. *Ʒätür, first You sent me Amicus. Now You've sent me Lord Rosai. Thank You.*

But her mind contained so many questions she needed answered. Those answers would mold her response to him. *Why was my village attacked? Why did they kill my father? Why was I taken here? Why am I forced to wear this collar? Is Alderan still alive? If he is, why do I not feel his presence?*

No, no, no. I can't stay bound to the past anymore. None of it matters. They're all dead, and I'm no longer that girl.

Today marked the happiest moment she'd experienced since they'd dragged her from her village. "My life will never be what it once was. I must move forward." She opened her eyes and peered into his; they melted her cold heart and kindled her passion. "I'll do it. I'll become your queen."

"Excellent. Now, let's get out of this horrific place. My castle's a great distance from here, more than a two-week journey." Lord Rosai turned toward the door to leave.

"Wait!" She grabbed the sleeve of his robes and pointed to Amicus when he turned around. "You can't leave Amicus like this. He's my friend."

"Very well." Lord Rosai waved his hand. "*From ɛţōn.*"

Amicus reanimated with a deep gasp. He coughed and doubled over.

Aria wrapped her arms around Amicus and kissed his cheek. She whispered in his ear, "Everything's okay." Then, with excitement, "I'm going to be a queen!"

She pulled away from Amicus and looked at him. He just stood there, hunched over and a blank stare on his face, obviously unable to process her words.

"We must go," said Lord Rosai. "He's welcome to come along if he so chooses."

"He can't come with us," she said with disappointment. "His family's here. Can you give us a few minutes alone, please? I need to say goodbye."

Lord Rosai dipped his head. "As you wish. I'll wait outside, but don't take too long. We must leave before sunset."

As soon as the door closed behind Lord Rosai, Aria started talking. She wanted to get everything out before Amicus had a chance to speak.

She grabbed his hand. "I know what you must be thinking, Amicus. I'm just a foolish girl being swept off my feet by a rich and handsome, older man. Part of that may be true, but you know I have nothing else. I'm a captive here, Amicus.

"I know you're my friend and you've done everything you can to keep me safe, but the fact is you can't. You're not always around, and you have your own family to worry about and take care of. Lord Rosai seems like a decent man.

"I really appreciate everything you've done for me. I'll never forget you, Amicus. You're my friend forever, and I'll miss you dearly."

Tears streamed down Aria's face. "Once I'm settled in I can send for you and your family if you want me to. I'm sure there are plenty of jobs you could do there. And besides, Dragnus is a terrible man. You shouldn't have to work for him."

Amicus just stood there, eyes wide and mouth agape.

She took a deep breath, wiped away her tears, and then continued, "Please understand, Amicus. Please be happy for me. Look what he did for me!" She smiled wide and showed off her beautiful, new teeth.

Amicus smiled, and her fear melted away.

"Caterpillar," he said in his soft, smooth tone. He reached down and pushed her hair behind her ear. "Indeed, you've emerged from your cocoon a beautiful butterfly, just as I knew you would. I won't try to stop you from leaving, but be careful of this man. You know nothing about him or what he's truly like. I'll be praying constantly that Zäțūr keeps you safe."

"Thank you, Amicus." She wiped a rogue tear from her eye and wrapped her arms around his scrawny neck. "Take care of yourself."

"And you as well, Butterfly. I will miss you terribly. As will Vonah. You changed our worlds for the better."

Aria pulled the bracelet off her wrist and placed it in Amicus's hand. "Keep this to remember me by."

Amicus frowned and shook his head. "This bracelet's the only possession you had when I found you. I can't possibly take it from you."

"I insist." She stood on her tiptoes and kissed his cheek. "You may return it to me when we meet again. No sooner."

"I'm honored." He pushed the bracelet over his right hand and it dangled on his wrist. "I'll cherish this just as I do our friendship." He hugged her again, lifted her off the floor, and then sat her back down.

Aria pulled away from Amicus. Her heart hammered with excitement. She let herself out of the room, elated at her newfound prospect in life.

My life's in Your hands, Zäțūr.

✝ ✝ ✝

Aria stared out the window of the horse-drawn carriage as it bumped along the dirt road, pulled by six of the largest, pure-black horses she'd ever seen. The minute they pulled away from Castle Portador Tempestade she started second guessing her rash decision to marry Lord Rosai.

What am I doing? How am I going to be a queen when I hardly even know how to be a woman? Ɂäţūr, what have I done? A lone tear drifted down her cheek, and she quickly wiped it away, lest Lord Rosai see.

Lord Rosai sat across from her, leaning against the side of the carriage, fast asleep. The dim moonlight barely penetrated the carriage windows, and the shadows it cast on Lord Rosai's face turned his pleasant features into those of a waking nightmare. The shadows deepened his eye sockets and morphed them into black holes. She imagined him to be Diƶäfär, incarnate.

She shivered from head to toe from the idea of it.

The coldness of the night crept into the carriage and bit at her bare arms and legs. She drew her legs up on the seat and pulled her blanket around her shoulders and legs as tight as she could. Her life had changed so much in the last few months and it was about to change again. *For the better.*

I'm ready to start a new life. She *needed* a new life. In a single day, everyone she knew and loved was ripped away from her. Knowing she'd never see her father again brought sorrow to her heart, but the loss of her brother tore it to pieces. Even apart, they were always near each other.

They shared a bond like most twins, but theirs went far deeper than any others. They could always find each other no matter the distance between them. When those beasts attacked her village, captured her, and killed Alderan, a part of herself died—their bond severed.

I'll never forget you, brother. I miss you so much.

A warrior at heart, she and Lord Rosai mirrored each other so well. He answered a prayer she'd never had the courage to pray. *As prophesied!*

Prophecies were something new to her expanding world. The idea of someone ages ago dreaming and writing about her and her family filled her head with so many questions that it made her head hurt.

Was the attack prophesied? Could all of it have been avoided if we'd known? How detailed are prophecies? Was there a path where I could've had children?

Children.

She pulled the blanket over her head as the tears rolled down her cheeks. *Does he know I can't have children? Will he still want me as his wife and queen if he finds out I'm unable to have his children? Oh Ɂäţūr, what am I going to do?* The thought of him rejecting her and casting her aside tore her heart with razor-sharp claws.

You know me, Ɂäţūr, and I know You. Your hands created all that we see, hear, feel, touch, and smell. You tell the flowers when to bloom and the rain where to fall. You control the wind. Please, Ɂäţūr, hear me now. Hear your servant.

I'm not asking You to move mountains; I'm begging You to heal me. Give me back the ability to bear children again. I have faith, Ɂäţūr. A mustard seed is all You require, but I'm putting all my faith in You. Everything I have, everything I am, I give to You. So, please, heal me.

A sense of relief washed over her entire body. She felt no different, but her mind rested with confidence that Ɂäţūr would do as she had asked of Him. She couldn't help but smile at the thought of having children. She wiped the tears away with the blanket and unburied her head.

From across the carriage, Lord Rosai stared at her with his golden-brown eyes.

She jumped. "I didn't realize you were awake."

"Just so." His perfect teeth glowed in the dark carriage as he smiled at her. "Have you slept at all?"

"No." She straightened in her seat. "I can't seem to turn my mind off. I have so many questions."

"I'll answer a few questions for you if you'll allow me to cast a sleeping spell on you afterward. We have such a long journey, and I'm afraid you'll never get any sleep otherwise."

Sleeping spell?

Her stomach gurgled. "How does that work? Will I feel rested afterward? Will I be able to awaken on my own, or will I sleep until you remove the spell?"

Lord Rosai laughed. "The spell will put you into a deep sleep, but you'll wake up on your own. When you do, you'll feel more refreshed than you've ever felt before."

Aria yawned. "Okay, I'll try it your way. I haven't slept well in quite some time."

"Excellent." He smoothed his robes. "What can I answer for you?"

"Why am I being forced to wear this collar? What does it do?"

He leaned forward in his seat and closed the distance between them. He stared into her eyes, into her soul. A rush of blood warmed her cheeks and she thanked Ʒäţür they sat in near darkness. He reached out and took her right hand in his left.

She wanted to pull away or at least look away, but she could do neither. Her heart raced as she sat there, held captive by his stare.

What is he going to do next?

"The collar protects you—" Lord Rosai paused and squeezed her hand gently. "—from yourself."

She pulled her hand back and crossed her arms, confused and insulted by his answer. Her voice sharp, she asked, "What do you mean by that?"

"I'll explain more about it when we get to the castle, but let's just say your body went through changes when you turned sixteen."

She pushed her feet off the edge of the seat and her feet hit the floor with a soft *thud*. She leaned forward and glared at him. "Oh, you know me so well now? My blood flows started when I was twelve, not sixteen. I assure you I've learned to *control* them." She smacked the seat with an open palm.

Lord Rosai leaned back and laughed heartily. "I'm not speaking of your womanhood, Aria. You're more woman than most I've met who were twice your age. No, I'm speaking of changes that require some learning on your part to deal with them. Once you're inside the walls of the castle and have learned to control your changed body, I'll remove the collar."

Aria smacked the seat again, this time with both hands. "You haven't explained anything. What *changes* have I gone through? I feel no different now than I ever have."

"The collar you're wearing blocks mezhik," he said.

"That makes no sense. I wore it when you performed mezhik on me. How did I heal then?"

Lord Rosai leaned forward again and she withdrew. "It doesn't block others from using mezhik on you, Aria. It blocks you from using your own mezhik."

She laughed. "That's ridiculous. I have no mezhik."

Lord Rosai's white teeth gleamed when he smiled, and his smile cooled her anger. "You're the first female mage to be born in more than 1200 years. You're one of the most significant people in this world."

Mage? She'd never heard the word before. "What is a mage?"

"A mage is akin to a wizard, but their grasp and use of mezhik exceeds the most well-trained and knowledgeable wizards."

"So, you're a mage then?"

Pravus's features darkened for the briefest of moments, but his tone remained soft. "I'm only a wizard. I'd sacrifice everything to become a mage, if it were possible. A wizard can only master a single type of mezhik—the one they're born with. However, a mage can master them all, given the proper knowledge and training.

"I will always be by your side to guide you and nurture your potential. The prophecies foretold of your great power so long ago. You were born with a destiny, Aria. A great purpose. Together, we will fulfill that destiny."

Aria couldn't wrap her mind around his words. How could she possibly be the one from prophecies? *I'm just a girl from Viscus D'Silva.*

"I..." Words escaped her.

"A mage, such as yourself, must be born of two wizard parents."

Her heart raced with the implications of his words. She studied him hard, but found no answers in his eyes or his smile. She knew the truth, didn't she? Her parents were good people and wouldn't have kept something so significant from her, would they?

Doubt brought her to the edge of her seat and she pushed her blanket aside. "But... that's not possible. How could I be a mage? My parents couldn't have been wizards. My father would've fought back. He wouldn't have let them kill him the way he did. It can't be."

Lord Rosai took her hand in his again. "You must trust me on this, Aria. I wouldn't lie to you. You're a mage. And, until you've learned how to control your mezhik, you must wear that collar. Except when training, of course."

She glared at him and her cheeks warmed. "Why does it matter if I don't even know how to use these *supposed* powers?"

"Mezhik can be used without even knowing how to control it. As a young wizard or mage, your mezhik will be driven and heightened by your emotional state. Until you learn to control it, you'll be a danger to everyone around you.

Therefore, we sought you out and collared you before you turned sixteen. Your mezhik was buried deep within yourself, lying dormant until your sixteenth name day."

His words gutted her. "Are you saying that *you* did this to me? Are you telling me that *you* had my family and my whole village destroyed to *protect* them from me? Is that what I'm hearing?" She yanked her hand from his and pushed herself into the corner of the seat, as far from him as she could get. Her collar glowed and lit the inside of the carriage.

"Aria," he said, in his soft, smooth tone. "You must believe me when I tell you that I had little to do with what happened in your village. I asked Dragnus to find you and have the collar placed around your neck. I never dreamt he'd set those bloodthirsty beasts loose to do his bidding. It was never supposed to be like that. No one was supposed to be harmed. You must believe me."

Rage pulsed through Aria's body. The man sitting across from her may not have been Diзäfär, but perhaps one of his minions. Her blood boiled as she fought to restrain herself from ripping his throat out with her teeth. She pummeled the seat with her fists.

What have You done to me, зäţūr? I thought You were saving me, but You've led me straight to the monster who took my life from me! Why have You forsaken me?

"I'm sorry." A tear rolled down Lord Rosai's cheek. "I shouldn't have trusted Dragnus to do anything right. I assure you, he'll pay for what he did to your village and for what he allowed them to do to you."

Lord Rosai moved from his seat and knelt next to hers. He slid his hand under her blanket and caressed the top of her foot. She started to pull her foot away, but his mezhik flowed into her and calmed her rage. She relaxed further as it flowed deep within her.

Lord Rosai withdrew his hand. "By tomorrow night, Dragnus will be dead. They'll all be dead. I promise."

Aria glared at him and gritted her teeth. "I swear in the name of зäţūr that if anything happens to Amicus, I'll kill you. Do you understand me?"

He eyed her glowing collar and smiled. "No harm will come to him. I give you my word. He and his family will be brought to the castle."

Aria buried her face in her blanket and cried. *Why am I such an emotional disaster?* Still angry with him, she longed for his touch again.

She unburied her head and fingered her collar. "Why is this thing glowing? It never has before."

"It's absorbing the mezhik you're trying to use."

"I'm not *trying* to do anything," she snapped.

Lord Rosai's hand found its way under her blanket again, and he slid it underneath her dress and up to her knees. She froze, and her breath caught. Her pulse quickened.

What should I do? Endless scenarios pummeled her mind. Did he want her? If he did, would she allow him to take her? Did she have a choice? Did he own her like property?

I've agreed to marry him. Am I not his already?

He squeezed her right knee. "I know. That's precisely why you're wearing it."

Her mind reeled. Had she asked him a question? She searched her mind as to what he referred to.

The collar!

"Your rage is fueling your mezhik. Without having control of it you could easily destroy more than just a village."

Aria's eyes widened with his words, and amazement and terror fought for dominance within her mind. *Zätür, what's happening to me? I'm so lost. I need You. I need Your strength.*

Sorrow filled his eyes. "I hope you can find it in your heart to forgive me, Aria. I swear to you that none of what transpired was ever in the plan. I only wanted the collar put on you. I would've done it myself if I could've. Now I must live with the burden of all those deaths weighing on my conscience. Don't make me live with the thought of you hating me as well."

She wanted to hate him forever, but the regret in his eyes and the sincerity in his voice pulled at her heart. He was everything she'd ever wanted in a man and more. She felt connected to him, not like the way she was with Alderan, but in a deeper, more carnal way.

"You need rest, Aria. Let me help you sleep, and I'm sure you'll wake up with a clear head." His hand slid over the tops of her knees and rested on her right thigh.

She wanted to refuse his suggestion, but his hand on her bare flesh sent chills through her entire body. Her thoughts coalesced into a raging storm of chaos. She felt her lips part as a soft moan rose from her throat. His touch fueled her lust. In her mind, she urged and begged him to fill her with his mezhik as she pressed her leg hard against his hand.

"I submit," she said, nearly out of breath.

His mezhik flowed into her thigh and spread through her body. *"Ɂəlläb."*

She reached for his hand, and then she slumped against the back of the seat.

† † †

Lord Rosai sat back against the carriage seat and watched Aria sleep. Her chest rose and fell, and her nostrils flared subtly. He traced the contours of her silhouette with his eyes and reflected on the day's prior events. She'd been delivered to him broken, but his godly hands had repaired her.

Such a magnificent creature. Even more so now.

Lord Rosai smiled, proud of his own accomplishments. *The perfect plan.*

He pulled a diary out of his leather satchel and flipped it open to the first page, a blank one. From within a hidden pocket inside his robes, he withdrew a fountain pen. He pressed the pen's tip against the blank page and sparks flew up and fizzled out like miniature fireworks.

He pressed down hard and wrote the following words: *'Kill Dragnus and burn Castle Portador Tempestade to its foundation. Leave no witnesses. You have one day. -Lord Rosai'*

Lord Rosai lifted the pen from the page and the inky words soaked into it and then disappeared. A few minutes later, the page sizzled and words wrote themselves onto it: *'We're already in position. Dragnus and every other living soul will be dead before the sun rises. -Murtag'*

"Excellent." Lord Rosai tapped the page with the pen's tip and the words disappeared.

He flipped to the second page in the book—blank as well—and wrote further: *'The girl is with me. Prepare for our arrival. Make sure she feels at home when we arrive, or you'll be praying I kill you quickly. -Lord Rosai'*

Again, the words soaked into the page and faded. Moments later, more words appeared: *'As you wish, my lord. We'll begin immediately. -Credan'*

Lord Rosai tapped the page with the pen and then tucked the pen back into the hidden pocket in his robes. He closed the diary and placed it back in his satchel. He sat back again and smiled to himself as he focused on Aria once more.

With you by my side we'll rule this world.

With his mind, he reached into the darkness beyond the carriage and spoke into the minds of the band of gnolls that escorted them. *"Keep your distance,"* he ordered them. *"If the girl finds out you're here everything will be ruined."*

He knelt in the middle of the carriage floor and gently lay Aria back on her seat. He lifted her legs onto the seat and then pulled the blanket over them. He leaned over her and kissed her forehead and then returned to his seat.

You and I will be unstoppable, my queen.

He smiled and lay back on his seat, closed his eyes, and dreamt of darkness.

CHAPTER TWENTY-FIVE

Alderan stood frozen by the window, petrified by Rakzar's yellow eyes. Rakzar made a throat-slitting gesture and smiled with his wicked, yellow teeth. Rakzar howled into the night, and several other howls returned his call. *Close.*

They had the cottage surrounded, and Alderan couldn't find Rayah.

He panicked. "Rayah!" he screamed at the top of his lungs. His heart thundered in his ears. A few seconds later, Rayah emerged from his room. She stretched her arms and yawned.

"Why are you yelling?" She rubbed the sleep from her eyes.

He pointed at the window. "Rakzar's outside, and he brought a lot of friends with him."

The color drained from Rayah's face and panic settled in her eyes. "What are we going to do? How did they find us so quickly?"

"I don't know. He can't do anything to us while we're in here, right?"

"Come out and face me, you coward!" growled Rakzar.

Alderan drew the curtains over the window, unable to even think while Rakzar waited outside and watched them with his hateful glare.

Smack.

The front door shook in its frame. Alderan and Rayah both jumped back, and Rayah squealed.

Alderan swallowed hard. "I hope the protection spell holds."

"We can't—"

Smack.

Again, the door shook in its frame.

"I'll find a way in," roared Rakzar. "And then you're both dead!"

Alderan walked in circles and tried to formulate a plan, but his mind wouldn't cooperate. He pulled at his hair.

Rayah fluttered back and forth, pacing in the air. "There must be something here that we can use to our advantage."

"Do you have to do that?" snapped Alderan.

Without a word, Rayah settled to the ground and walked over to the fireplace hearth.

Alderan sighed. *Why am I always snapping at her? None of this is her fault.*

He walked over to Rayah and put his hand on her shoulder. "I'm sorry. I just don't know what to do next. Nothing good will come of us facing Rakzar. He and his friends would tear us apart as soon as we step outside."

"I know. I'm just as frustrated as you." She slipped her arm around his back and pulled herself against him.

"Rayah…" Alderan looked down at her, and she looked up at him and smiled. *You're so beautiful!* He kissed her forehead, unable to find the right words to explain what he intended to do.

"Tell me what's going through that big head of yours." Concern laced her voice. "After watching you for so many years, I know you better than you think. You're about to do something stupid, aren't you?"

"No," He couldn't suppress a sheepish grin.

She shook her head. "Whatever it is, I do *not* approve."

His heart raced in his chest as he searched for courage. *She needs to know before you die. Just spit it out.* "I… I love you Rayah."

Rayah gasped and dropped to the floor.

Embarrassed, he quickly added, "I mean, you're my best friend."

"I know." The smile on her face brightened the whole room. "You're my best friend, too."

He stared into her beautiful hazel eyes and then backpedaled further, "What I mean is I really like you and I enjoy spending time with you."

Rayah's smile faded and her head lowered. "I feel the same."

Ugh! I don't just love you, Rayah. I'm in love with you. Why can't I just tell you?

"I wouldn't be able to live with myself if something happened to you." He turned and took a few steps toward the front door. "That's why I need to go out there alone and draw them away from here."

"No!" She flew around him with a fury of beating wings. She floated up to his eye-level, her beautiful face reddened. "I'm not going to let you sacrifice yourself for me. You can't."

"It's me they're after, not you."

"I don't care what they want. I won't let you do it!"

But I must save you.

"There's no other way, Rayah," he said with disappointment.

Her face brightened. "Maybe the ground is warm enough underneath the house. If we can find a way to pry up a few of the floor planks I could check."

Alderan sighed deeply. "There's no point. My great-grandfather built this cottage to last. Before he set the floor and raised the walls, he hauled in wagonloads of sea rocks and laid a foundation with them, just below the dirt surface."

"There still has to be another way."

"There's not!" Alderan slammed his fist against the top of the mantle, and something clicked.

The mantle flipped forward ninety degrees and spilled its contents on the floor with a *crash*. Rayah leapt into the air as shards of glass from a shattered picture frame flew about. He stood there and stared at the hole behind the mantle, his mouth wide open and lost for words.

Rayah clapped and drew close to the mantle to get a peek. "What's in there?"

He thought he saw something deep inside the hole, but his hand didn't fit into the narrow opening. Rayah tried wiggling her hand into the opening too, but hers also proved too big.

Alderan pulled his knife from the sheath on his belt and stuck the blade into the hole, but the short blade didn't quite reach the back of the hole. He looked around. "Help me find something long and narrow to stick in there."

Rayah grabbed the poker nestled in the corner next to the fireplace and handed it to him. "Try this."

Both the handle and hook sides of the poker were too large to fit into the hole. Frustrated, he threw it to the floor. "That's not going to work."

Rayah picked it back up and examined it. "The size of this square shaft seems to be the exact same size as the hole. I think this'll work if we can get the handle off."

He held out his hand. "Let me see it again."

Rayah handed the poker back to him. Alderan held the shaft in one hand and torqued the handle with his other, but it wouldn't turn.

"Hold the poker while I try to unscrew the handle from it," he said.

They worked together at it for about ten minutes, but the handle still wouldn't budge. He smacked the handle of the poker against the rock face of the fireplace. Nothing. He placed the hooked end against the floor, stepped on it, and then cranked on the handle with everything he had. Still nothing.

He torqued on it one last time, and the handle finally turned. A minute later, he had the handle removed from the shaft.

He shoved the poker shaft into the hole about two feet, and it knocked against something with a *clank*. He pushed a little harder and felt it slide into a slot another two inches. He then slid the shaft along the narrow opening of the hole, first to the left and then the right, and then brought it back to the center.

Nothing.

He yanked on the shaft and heard a loud *click*.

He and Rayah both stepped back as the entire fireplace swung into the room and away from the wall about two feet. Chills crept down his back and arms. He grabbed Rayah and hugged her.

"Thank you," he whispered in her ear. "What would I ever do without you?"

She squeezed him tight. "Hopefully, you'll never get an answer to that."

Rayah grabbed his hand and pulled him around the side of the fireplace. A sixteen-inch, square hole opened in the floor where the fireplace had sat; a wooden ladder clung to the side of the hole and faded into the darkness.

Mother? Father? What else did you keep from us? Who were you?

Rayah squeezed his hand with excitement. "This may be our way out!"

Alderan untangled his hand from Rayah's and went into the kitchen and grabbed a candle from the table. When he returned to the hole, Rayah had already descended halfway down the ladder. A few seconds later, she completely vanished into the perfect darkness below.

Alderan swallowed hard. *Braver than me.* "Rayah? Can you see anything?"

"Not until you bring a candle down, silly!" Her voice echoed as though she stood inside a large cavern. "Are you coming or not?"

With Rakzar and his friends the alternative, what choice did he have? *Down the ladder, it is.*

Excitement and dread filled his head as he carefully made his way down the ladder. Twenty rungs later, he stood nearly at the center of a massive room. Rows of bookshelves ran in every direction. At the room's center, several candle-holders sat atop a large wooden desk.

He walked over to the desk and lit the candles with the one he'd brought down with him. The room filled with light, and the shadows scurried into the deep recesses between the tall bookshelves.

He set the candle on the desk. Perspiration wet his brow and dampened his palms. "What is this place?"

He walked over to one of the closest bookshelves and ran his finger across the spines of several books. His finger left a clean streak through the layers of dust and a lint ball where he'd stopped.

"Did my parents know about this?"

They must've.

His pulse quickened. *Did Aria?*

No. There's no way she would've known. She would've told me if she had.

Why would they have kept this a secret from us? Why didn't they tell me I was a wizard?

What about Aria? Is she a wizard too?

Can females be wizards?

Was my father a wizard? Or my mother? Or both?

Questions swirled in his head and left him dizzy and overwhelmed.

"Over here." Rayah's voice pulled him from his thoughts and he turned his attention in her direction. She stood on the far side of the room, a silhouette inside the frame of an open door.

Another room?

"You need to see this."

The light poured forth from the room behind her and nearly drowned out her dark form. He wiped his sweaty palms on his trousers and walked toward her. The nape of his neck prickled.

What's my problem? Is it her, or is it this place that's making me feel so anxious? That's a stupid question. Why would it be her?

Alderan stopped in front of Rayah. "Am I going to regret this?"

Rayah's translucent wings glimmered in the light. "No, but nothing I can say will prepare you for what's inside this room."

His heart knocked against his ribcage and his throat grew dry. Rayah grabbed his hand and pulled him into the room. The source of the room's light took his breath away. A three-foot-wide and seven-foot-tall mirror stood in the center of the room. He'd never seen a mirror like it before. Stones of all shapes and colors framed the mirror's glass and shone like the stars in the sky.

He stood in awe of it—transfixed by its beauty—and held onto Rayah's hand as though it were his lifeline between this world and the next.

"Have you ever seen anything so beautiful?" she asked.

"No," he said. "Why would they have kept something so magnificent locked down here?"

"It's not just a mirror, Alderan. It's a gateway."

"A gateway," he said with wonder. "To where?"

"I don't know, but we need to be careful. Anything or anyone could be waiting on the other side of it."

"How do you even know what it is?"

"I've read about them. They're called *Zhäítfäíz Dhä*. The Gateways. Powerful wizards created them to be able to move great distances very quickly. They can only be used by those with mezhik. If one without mezhik were to try and use the gateway, they'd be driven mad by it."

He held onto Rayah's hand and circled the mirror, pulling her with him. The other side of the mirror paralleled its counterpart with a beauty all its own. He lifted his free hand toward the mirror, but Rayah quickly pulled him out of reach.

"Have you not been listening to what I've been saying?" She glared at him. "Dangerous doesn't even describe it."

"I wasn't going to touch it," he said. "I swear! I was just wondering how it works."

"If you touch its surface, it will open a portal to the other side. Once it's opened, you can see through it like a window—from both sides. If someone stood on the other side, they'd be able to see us, too."

"Wow…" Many questions floated through his head, but one kept coming back to the forefront of his mind.

"How do you know where it leads? Can you control it?" he asked.

"I'm sure there's a way, but I have no idea what it is."

The mirror scared him. *What if I'm not a wizard?* Could he risk the chance of going mad?

"Now what? We're stuck?"

"No, Alderan. We must go through the mirror. If we try to leave any other way, we'll be killed."

"You just said it's really dangerous and not to touch it because you don't know where it goes and you don't know how to control it. Now you want to go through it?"

Rayah groaned. "I wish you knew how to use your mezhik. Those gnolls would be no match for you if you did."

Alderan plopped to the floor and pulled Rayah down with him. He lifted the back of her hand to his lips and kissed it. "I'm sorry. I wish I knew, too."

"Well, we can't just sit here." Rayah pulled herself to her feet. "We need to get our things from the house and figure out where this gateway leads. The sooner we can distance ourselves from Rakzar and his friends, the better."

Alderan stood. "I'll go get our things. You should look at the books in the other room. See if there's anything that might help me with my mezhik."

"Okay," she said with a smile.

Alderan made his way back to the ladder and climbed back up into the house.

†††

Rakzar rounded the thatched-roof cottage and sniffed at the ground and air, trying to find a hint as to the location of Alderan and Rayah. He howled into the cold morning air and summoned the others to him. From the shadows all around, seven more gnolls joined him.

Rakzar circled each of them and peered into their eyes, looking for a hint of fear. "Have any of you seen or heard anything?" Spittle flew with each word.

"None of us have moved from our posts," said Borsha with a half snarl. "Perhaps *you* let them slip by, Rakzar."

"Say that again, and I'll make both sides of your face match." Rakzar glared at him.

"Wouldn't be the first time, would it boss?" said Brux.

"Or the second, huh Brux?" Creeb piped in. The seven of them howled with laughter.

"Enough!" Rakzar paced back and forth, brooding.

What are you up to, White Knight?

"Hey Brux, maybe they melted into the ground again?"

"Good one, Creeb!" said Brux. They all howled with laughter again.

"I didn't bring you here to listen to your banter!" roared Rakzar. "Find a way in, or you're all dead!"

Why am I always surrounded by fools?

"We'll find a way in, boss," said Creeb. Then, to the others he whispered, "No need to lose your head, like Farqel." They all chuckled under their breath.

Rakzar glared at Creeb. "If you fools find a way in, keep the boy alive and bring him to me. Do what you want with the dryte."

"What happens if the boy is *accidentally* killed during his capture?" Creeb chuckled.

Rakzar whirled toward Creeb, grabbed him by the throat, and lifted him off his feet. "I'll hunt you down and rip your beating heart from your chest!"

Creeb swallowed hard, and fear flashed in his eyes. Rakzar wanted to end him right there and make an example of the young gnoll. Instead, he threw Creeb to the ground like a rejected toy.

Rakzar growled, "Now find a way in."

Brux extended his paw-like hand toward Creeb. Creeb grabbed it and pulled Brux to the ground with him. The two of them rolled around, laughing. Rakzar shook his head. *I ask for warriors and this is what I get? A bunch of snot-snouted pups.*

Creeb sat up. "I think I have an idea, boss."

Rakzar stood over Creeb with his arms crossed. *Well this ought to be good.*

"Give Brux and me a boost onto the roof. Maybe they forgot to protect it when they cast the spell."

Rakzar scoffed, "Do you really—" His brain finished processing Creeb's words. *Actually, that's a brilliant idea. Maybe the pup's half-useful after all.*

Rakzar bent his knees and locked his fingers together. "Well, don't just lie there."

Creeb and Brux scrambled to their feet and Rakzar boosted each of them up to the roof.

Rakzar growled, "If either of you find a way in, come get me. And, whatever you do, don't engage the boy by yourselves. He's a lot more dangerous than he looks."

Brux winked at Rakzar. "Don't you worry, boss. They won't escape us."

Brux and Creeb disappeared from Rakzar's view, and he leaned against the wall of the house. He had a sinking feeling in the pit of his stomach. Nothing ever worked in his favor concerning the White Knight.

Maybe the boy is special. Rakzar scoffed at the thought. *And maybe wizards fly.*

† † †

Rayah searched through the shelves of books, but most of them were in a language she couldn't understand, and it frustrated her. *Zäţūr, please help me find something useful.*

Rayah thought she heard a noise come from the room with the mirror and turned toward it. Quietly, she flew toward the room, her pulse rising. Through the doorway, she saw nothing amiss.

She moved toward the center of the room, next to the mirror. Turning in circles, she saw nothing that would've made a sound. The mirror—still a mirror and not a portal to somewhere else—reflected her and the doorway behind her.

But the mirror had a blemish or crack in it. It hadn't before, had it? She moved within an inch of it, and when she looked closer, the crack moved a little.

She gasped and backed away. She turned around again and looked for anything that could explain the phenomenon, but found nothing. Looking back in the mirror, she couldn't find the crack again. *Odd.*

The hairs on the nape of her neck rose. *Am I not alone?*

She thought she heard Alderan coming back down the ladder and turned toward the doorway.

"I'm in here," she called out.

From out of nothing, a lizard-like man appeared before her. He lashed his scaly hands out for her, wrapped her up, covered her mouth, and held a blade to her throat—all before she had the chance to scream.

"Make a sound—" The lizard man's words slithered from his mouth like the hiss of a snake. "—and I'll slit your throat."

Alderan!

The lizard man whipped around her and pulled her into the mirror.

CHAPTER TWENTY-SIX

N ardus wrapped his hand around the silver doorknob, turned it, and then hesitated. *Am I ready to face another trial?* Physically his body healed quickly, yet the mental pain lingered and tormented his soul.

No, but I'll be damned if I ever let my family down again.

The *click* of the latch as it disengaged from the strike plate on the door's frame quickened his pulse. He let go of the knob and the blue door slowly swung outward, revealing a terrifyingly beautiful scene below.

Translucent, pale-blue stones made of pure celestine hung in the air like stairs. Each misshapen stone, roughly three to four feet in diameter, looked as if they were cut right from the sulfur deposits of a volcano; no two matched.

The stones spiraled their way down more than a hundred feet and ended in the middle of what he could only describe as a labyrinth. From his vantage point, the white labyrinth walls bent and arced as though the whole maze were built on the outer surface of a massive sphere. Nardus swallowed hard, but the lump in his throat held fast.

He looked down at the first stone and the four-foot gap between it and the doorway he stood behind. Not just a good distance away, the stone hovered about two feet lower than where he stood. The knot in his stomach tightened as he tried talking himself into making the jump.

Nardus repeated the names of his family again and again in his head and drew courage and strength from their memories. He wiped his sweaty palms on his trousers and positioned his feet at the edge of the threshold. He took a deep breath, muttered a few choice words under his breath, and then jumped toward the first stone.

His feet landed square in the middle of the stone, but he nearly lost his balance as the stone dipped and swayed under his weight. He held his arms out to his sides to gain balance. His vision swam with the motion, and the motion stirred his stomach and brought him to the brink of vomiting. He wanted to close his eyes, but the thought of it made him even dizzier.

I'd surely plunge to my death.

A faint crackling noise drew his attention to the stone under his feet. Panic wrenched his heart as the stone splintered under his weight like an ice cube plunged into warm water. Pieces of the stone broke away along its edges.

The stone shifted under his feet as a large crack raced its way through the middle of the stone. The back portion of the stone fell away and left his heels unsupported. Unbalanced, he swayed backward, and the stone tilted with him.

Nardus bent his legs and leaned forward, desperate to gain back his balance and bring the stone back level. The stone tilted forward, and he used its motion to launch himself toward the next stone. The added momentum carried him farther than he'd anticipated, and he nearly overshot the second stone, landing just shy of its jagged front edge.

The stone plunged a few feet under his weight and tilted forward so much that he lost his footing and balance. He fell backward as his feet came out from under him and smacked his tailbone against the edge of the stone.

Crack!

The edge of the stone broke away under the force of the collision. For a brief moment, he felt as though he were suspended in mid-air. Memories, both good and bad, flashed through his mind. *I'm about to die.*

Whoosh.

A rush of air pushed past his ears and blew his hair in his face as he fell. The blue door pulled farther and farther away from him, and he wished he hadn't leapt from its threshold.

Smack.

Every bone in his back jarred when he landed flat against another of the stones. His head and legs arced backward unnaturally, having nothing to support them or stop their motion. The air rushed from his lungs and he swore his ribcage had collapsed into his spine. He gasped for air and he fought against the piercing pain.

Crackle.

The stone under him fractured and turned to dust. He closed his eyes and prayed to the god he so desperately hated. *Don't let me live and be paralyzed. I'd rather be dead.*

Whoosh.

He plummeted again and did everything he could to relax. He closed his eyes and focused on Vitara and her vibrant violet eyes.

My love, my life, my anchor. In his mind, he drew her into his arms and held her close. *Every day without you is an eternity in this hellish world. I cannot die. I'll make this right. I'll be with you again, my love.* So wrapped up in his thoughts, he barely even noticed colliding with two more stones.

Splash.

He plunged into a pool of water and sank to the bottom, still lost within himself. In his mind, he ran his fingers through Vitara's auburn hair; it felt wet against his fingers. Her wet hair pulled his thoughts to the day she died. Blood oozed from her fresh wounds. Sorrow poured into his lungs, and he couldn't breathe.

His eyes fluttered and then opened as he forced himself back from the depths of his memories. Disoriented, he was unsure of where he even was. Above him, white walls swayed back and forth, a shimmering image in the water above.

His body quaked, deprived of oxygen for way too long. He gasped for air, but a salty liquid filled his mouth and choked him as it poured into his lungs. The water's surface rippled above him as a piece of translucent blue stone broke through and floated down next to him.

He flailed at the bottom of the pool like a fish on a hook, struggling to pull himself up from his watery grave. He struggled just to sit up as his vision darkened around the edges. Everything went black for a moment. He had precious little time before death pulled him into its clutches.

Something pinned his left ankle. He reached down and found large pieces of stone piled up around his ankle, trapping it. *Damn!*

He flapped his arms and his right leg in the water, trying to create enough pull to free his foot. His vision shrank to a pinhole of light as he struggled to stay conscious. Harder and harder he pumped his arms and legs until he finally broke free of the stones and shot upward.

He broke through the water's surface and coughed violently as he struggled to push the water out of his lungs and get air into them simultaneously. He swam to the edge of the pool and pulled himself out of the water.

He lay on his stomach with his head to one side and spat up the water from his lungs. He sucked in the air as fast as he could and coughed violently between breaths. He rolled onto his back and lay there with his eyes closed. His throat and lungs burned from the saltwater.

"Never again," he said, still out of breath. "Never again."

Nardus checked himself over as he lay on the labyrinth floor. He found nothing broken or out of place. *Damned lucky.* He sat up and rubbed his swollen lower back; intense heat radiated through his shirt. *I'm too old for all this abuse.*

He pulled himself to his feet and stumbled over to one of the labyrinth walls. He leaned against the wall and fought an overwhelming urge to vomit as his head spun out of control. His vision darkened as the blood drained from his head. Lightheaded, he closed his eyes. Pain pulsed through his body with every heartbeat.

He pulled at his hair and raked his knuckles over the top of his head, but the pain only intensified. *Surely Ef Demd Dhä would be like a walk in a sunny meadow compared to this wretched place.*

His thoughts swam in a cesspool of madness and bombarded him with feelings of hate, guilt, sorrow, anger, and loss all at once.

Nardus peered into the darkness above. "You did this to me!"

"I hate You, Ɂäʈūr! Why did You create me just to let me suffer?" Tears welled in his eyes. "I beg of You, unmake me. Let me suffer no longer!"

If You won't kill me, then please take my heart and leave me without feeling. Take my memories. Damn me no more!

In the far reaches of his mind, nearly undetectable in his current state, a small spark of light blinked on and off like a beacon.

What's that?

The more he focused on the beacon the brighter it pulsed. Faster and faster it blinked until the light became constant.

Warmth radiated from the light like sunshine. The darkness of his thoughts—the madness that consumed him—faded. A distant voice called to him, and he strained to hear their words. He closed his eyes and focused on the voice. He pushed away the buzzing static of all his thoughts until the words became clear.

"You have a purpose," said the voice.

A man's voice. So familiar.

His eyes snapped open as realization settled in. *It's my voice.*

"You have a purpose," he said again, this time with determination.

Family.

The pain in his head and his body fell away like skin shed from a serpent. He felt like a new man—refreshed and ready to take on the world.

"Mezhik be damned! I won't let you win!" His words echoed off the walls and floor in every direction.

Nardus stood tall, his eyes open wide for the first time in a while, and took in his surroundings. The labyrinth's glassy, silver-white walls and floors gave off a warm glow and lit the entire area. The floors were a sheet of ice beneath his feet; water gathered inside their concave pockmarks and made them even slicker.

He turned and faced the wall he'd been leaning against and ran his fingers along its surface. The natural, conchoidal fracturing of the chert rock felt cold and smooth to the touch. He placed his palms against the wall and welcomed the coldness that penetrated his skin. He put his forehead against the wall and leaned into its comforting touch.

"Where've you been all my life?" He laughed.

Focus, Nardus.

He stepped back from the wall and nearly turned away before noticing the dark spots where his hands and forehead had rested. Upon closer inspection, he realized the spots were actually letters. He rubbed the wall with the sleeve of his shirt, but it didn't produce more words.

Think, Nardus. Think!

"What do my hands and forehead have in common?"

Skin.

He looked at the wall again. The letters where his forehead had been were dark and legible. Where his hands had been, the letters were lighter and a bit fuzzy.

"Why would my forehead make the letters darker than my hands?" He put his hand on his forehead and the answer became obvious: *heat.*

"My forehead's much hotter than my hands."

Having no other source for heat, Nardus blew hot air on the wall with his mouth. After about fifteen minutes of huffing and puffing, he finally warmed the wall up enough to reveal the hidden message.

The foreign words swam in his blurred vision. He stepped back several feet and wiped his eyes, but the words still swam. He sunk to his knees. "How am I supposed to get through this when I can't even read the instructions?"

He blinked several times and then stared at the wall, determined to decipher the scribblings. He fought against the voices in his head that told him to give up. *I'm doing this for my family. I will not quit. Vitara, my love, give me wisdom.*

It started with just one of the scribbles, "need." Then, several more of them solidified into words he recognized. His pulse quickened as the whole message came into focus. *Thank you, my love.*

The message read as follows:

One little game of hide-and-seek

Is all you need to play

The clues below are just a peek

To get you on your way

At the bottom of the pool you'll find me

But I will not be easily found

To get just a glimpse of me

You'll have to seek higher ground

In this puzzle there are several pieces

My brothers and I make three

Keep us apart and nothing ceases

But together we're the key

Once I've been drawn into the light

You'll know what you need to do

To finish this game will take mind over might

The answer's right in front of you

The means to the end will become clear

Once you have found us all

Be driven by courage and not by fear

And never heed the whims of the wall

Once you engage us just give us a turn

But make sure you've countered the clock

Veer from these steps and you will learn

The door will never unlock

- Pharius, Ef Ƨäfn Dhä -

"Higher ground," he muttered. "Wish I'd read that before I fell all the way down here."

The only places higher than where he stood were the walls of the labyrinth. He raised his arms and reached above his head as far as he could. The wall towered over him, more than ten feet in height. He ran his fingers through his hair and walked in circles, trying to figure out how he'd get on top of the wall.

I'm too short to pull myself up. I need to find another way up.

"Bottom of the pool..."

He walked around the pool over and over, looking for anything of significance. The pieces of stone sitting at its bottom, the ones that had fallen with him, were now a hindrance, blocking his view of more than half of the pool's floor. *Might as well pull them out of the water.*

He dove into the pool and made quick work of removing every stone from it. He pulled himself from the water and then eyed the mess he'd created; pieces of stone littered the deck around the whole pool.

"They really should warn swimmers of the danger of falling rocks. And men." He laughed at his own joke.

The piles of stone lying around gave him a brilliant idea: stack them against the wall and create a makeshift stairway. Within a few minutes, he'd created stacks of stones tall enough for him to reach the top of the wall.

He carefully climbed up the stones and pulled himself on top of the labyrinth wall. The wall was more than a foot thick and just as slick as the floor had been. He sat there for a moment with his legs dangling in the air, amazed he hadn't fallen and cracked his skull open.

He craned his neck and peered into the pool below, but still saw nothing at its bottom. *Guess I'm gonna have to stand up on this damned thing.*

He rolled onto his stomach and swung his legs onto the wall. He pushed himself onto his knees and then lifted himself onto his feet. His legs trembled, and he thought he might lose his balance.

Get a grip, you old fool.

His heart pounded as he took a few steps along the wall to try to get a better view of the pool. The pool's surface rippled and made it impossible to see the bottom. The sound of stone scraping stone filled the air. He watched, mouth agape, as sections of the labyrinth twisted and turned and reconfigured themselves.

Perfect. Just perfect.

"I *hate* mezhik." He spat at the ground below.

Nardus's section—four walls and a pool at its center—didn't connect with the rest of the labyrinth. A twenty-foot-wide void surrounded it and soured his mood further. A prisoner in mezhik hell unless the labyrinth reconfigured itself again with a path that connected to his section.

After a few minutes, the labyrinth walls stopped moving and the vibrations ceased. The pool's surface calmed and its bottom became clear once again, yet nothing came into view. Nardus tried everything he could think of, from squinting to closing one eye and then the other.

Every passing moment ratcheted up his agitation level. Madness crept into his mind again and fragmented his thoughts.

A fool's errand is what you've gotten yourself into. You can't bring your family back. No one can. Just give up. You'd be in no worse position than you already are. Throw yourself from the wall and end your pathetic existence. You're a madman, Nardus.

Am I? The question stuck in his mind like a thorn. *Am I mad?* He wanted so desperately to tell himself no, but all signs pointed to yes. *I'm a fool.* For so long, desperation drove him to seek righting all the wrong choices he'd made. *My family's dead because of me. How will I ever find forgiveness for what I've done?*

You won't. You don't deserve it.

He closed his eyes to try and drown out the noise of his twisted, calloused mind. The moment he did so, his vision became clear as day. One small portion at the bottom left corner of the pool—a rectangle about three inches long and an inch wide—glowed through his eyelids. His mood soared once again as the madness crawled back into the shadows of his mind.

A moment later, the glowing rectangle faded until nothing existed of it but a memory. He opened his eyes and dove off the wall and into the pool.

He quickly swam to the corner and felt around for something laying there, but he found nothing. He pressed his fingers into the bottom of the pool where he remembered it glowing. Part of the pool's bottom depressed a few centimeters. He lifted his fingers away and a small stone shard rose about an inch. He grabbed the shard and swam toward the surface with it.

Nardus broke through the water's surface with the stone shard clutched firmly in his fist, and the ground trembled violently. *Did I cause that?*

He grabbed the pool's edge with his free hand and held on as best he could. The water sloshed back and forth, spilled over the top of the pool's lip, and ran across the floor. The stone shard glowed with a translucent green hue and his hand tingled where it touched his skin.

He groaned. *Mezhik.*

He placed the shard on the pool deck and pulled himself out of the water. Directly in front of him, a large section of the wall descended into the void below. Stone by stone, a bridge formed in its place and spanned the void.

Nardus picked up the shard and turned it over in his hands. Two edges of the flat, inch-thick shard were slightly jagged and formed a perfect, 120-degree angle. Its other edges formed what looked like three points of a star.

He slipped the shard into his pocket and walked over to the wall where he'd discovered the words. Unsurprisingly, the words had vanished and no amount of heat brought them back.

"Drat! I hate this place!"

He took in a deep breath and then slowly let it out. *Keep your head on your shoulders. Things could be worse.* He recalled the gist of the words, but another look at them would've made him feel a lot better. *Suppose I have a bridge to cross.*

The shaking subsided as the bridge finished forming all the way across the expanse. The distance to the other side seemed miles away and grew farther with every passing moment. He walked over to the front edge of the bridge and stared down at the translucent, blue stones that formed it.

Nardus spat on the ground once more. "I know what you are, and you'll not better me again."

His legs trembled, and his hands dripped with sweat and fear. *Be my anchor, my love. Steady my nerves. Guide my heart and my mind.*

His heart hammered, and he set his gaze on the other side of the bridge. "Death may find me, but I will not fail out of fear!" His words echoed into the distant reaches of the labyrinth and returned to him in waves of whispers.

He took a couple of steps back, pushed the air from his lungs with a quick burst, and sprinted across the bridge as fast as his legs would carry him. Each step gave in under his weight and the sound of cracking ice filled the air.

Nardus held his head high and refused to acknowledge the fissures that sprinted ahead of him. Each step became softer and softer until he ran on air. Or at least it felt that way.

Three yards from the far end of the bridge he lunged forward, head-first. His heart knocked in his chest as the last of the bridge shattered and fell into the void. His momentum slowed, and the sensation of falling left his stomach twitching.

I must make it!

With a *thud*, Nardus crashed onto the floor on the other side of the void, slid another ten feet, and then came to a stop. He rolled onto his back and gasped for air. His heart hammered so hard he thought it might break free from his chest.

Nardus shook his fist in the air. "I win!"

He pulled himself to his feet, turned in a circle, and took in his new surroundings. He stood in the middle of a half-circle area. Four paths led away like wagon wheel spokes, and each one faded into the distance. He pulled at his hair. *What did those words say?*

"The answer's in front of you..." he said to himself.

He reached into his pocket. Mezhik tingled the tips of his fingers as they brushed against the shard. He wrapped his fingers around it and withdrew it from his pocket. He opened his hand and the shard rose a few inches above his palm. The hairs on his neck stood on end.

"I'll be..."

The shard pulsated with green light like a heartbeat, slow and steady. It settled back down on his palm and continued to pulse; chills raced up his arm with each beat.

With his eyes locked on the shard, he walked over to the path on his far left. The shard still pulsated, but its glow grew faint. He stepped over to the second path and the light brightened. At the third path the pulsing quickened. Before the fourth path—his far right—the shard hummed as it vibrated in his hand.

Is this thing leading me to the other pieces, or to certain death? Guess there's only one way to find out.

"The fourth it is." Nardus closed his hand, placed the shard back in his pocket, and started down the fourth path. A little more than 200 paces in, the path made a 90-degree turn to the left. He rounded the corner and walked into a dead-end.

Damned shard! Guess that's what I get for relying on a glowing piece of stone.

He stared at the wall in front of him. Something looked off about it, but he couldn't grasp what it was. The shard still hummed in his pocket.

Maybe this is the right path. I'm obviously missing something.

Nardus closed his eyes, hoping to glimpse something like he'd done with the pool, but he only saw the darkness of the insides of his eyelids. Anger and frustration welled in him again and he punched the wall. The solid surface jarred his bones and granted him no favors.

He leaned back, chest swollen and arms raised in the air, and roared. The outburst felt so good that he did it again.

He shook his fist at the wall. "Don't tempt this madman. I'll find a way to tear you down, stone by stone." He laughed at himself, amused by his maniacal mood.

He turned to leave, but something glinted in the corner of his eye. He turned his head back toward the wall, but saw nothing. He slowly turned his head away again and stopped when part of the wall faded in and out of view; one moment he saw the wall and the next he saw what looked to be a square hole of some sort.

He kept the wall locked in his peripheral view and crab-walked toward it. A foot away and eying it indirectly, he reached out to touch the wall where the hole continually phased in and out of view. He paused, his fingers just millimeters away from its surface, afraid of what might happen.

Will the hole suddenly transform back into wall and sever my hand? The hole morphed into a gaping mouth with rows of sharpened teeth and snapped at his fingers. He shrugged away the image.

He took a deep breath and forced himself to extend his arm farther. His fingers tingled as they pushed through the point where the wall should've been and into the space beyond. He felt around in the small space until the tips of his fingers swept across something at the very back of the hole. He leaned into the wall and stretched his arm as far as it would go, straining to get enough reach to grasp the object he'd felt.

Just a little more.

The coldness of the wall seeped into his cheek as he pressed ever closer to it, trying to gain another inch. Finally, he gained enough length to grasp the object and pull it from the hole.

Another shard!

Nardus stepped back from the wall and held the shard up to examine it in the light. Like the first shard, this one had the same 120-degree angled sides, but it only had two star-like points as opposed to the three of the first one.

He withdrew the first shard from his pocket and compared it to the second, turning them both over in his hands. They were of equal size and weight and made of the same green stone. Both pulsated with green light.

The shards vibrated and spewed green sparks. A magnetic force formed between the two and increased until he could barely keep them apart. He released his grip on them and they flew together, connecting perfectly along one of their straight, but jagged edges. They fused together and then stopped glowing.

"Magnificent." He inspected the enlarged shard. Had he not just put the two together, he would've sworn they were always a single piece. There were now five points to the star, and one last piece to be found.

Where to go now?

On cue, the walls and floor vibrated, and the wall next to him slid open, revealing a new passage. From every direction, he heard stone scraping against stone as the labyrinth reconfigured itself once more.

What kind of wretched fools conjured this damned place?

He stepped through the opened wall and the passage stretched to his left and right. Deciding to stick to the right, as he had from the start, he moved forward. At every fork and intersection, he kept to the right-most path, determined it held a significance.

A few times he had to double back when the path led to a dead-end. He weaved his way in and out of passages for hours, pausing each time the labyrinth reconfigured itself, and then continuing. Completely lost, he could've gone through the same part of the labyrinth again and again.

Damned mezhik.

Only two sounds existed in the labyrinth: the ones he made as he shuffled along and the ones it made each time it reconfigured itself. Every time he stopped to try and figure out which direction he should go he felt as though he'd gone deaf. *Alone in my head. Not the best place to be.* He laughed at the thought.

Again, the labyrinth reconfigured itself. A wall slid in front of him and cut off his current path. He turned in a circle and found himself surrounded by four walls. Panic ate at his nerves as the walls on either side of him closed in. The air thickened like gel, and he labored to fill his lungs with it.

Is this really happening, or is this just my twisted mind? As of late, his mind felt so unreliable.

Scrape.

The walls moved in a few inches. "*That* wasn't my mind!" He leaned against one wall and put his feet up against the far wall, and braced himself to try and stop them from closing further.

Scrape.

Sweat poured from his brow and thoughts of defeat slithered into his mind as his knees buckled under the building pressure. He knew time was running out, but what could he do?

Scrape.

He forced everything from his mind but one image: the wall with words. The words scattered across the wall were nothing but dark splotches in his mind. Pain radiated from his knees and reached a point nearly unbearable. He closed his eyes—ready to give up the fight—when three words formed on the wall in his mind: "mind over might."

Scrape.

His might clearly wouldn't stop the walls from closing in, and the thought of relying on his mind to pull him from his current situation bordered absurdity. At that point, he did the only thing he knew he could: turn to his one constant—his true north.

Vitara, I need you, just as I always do. Be my strength and my guide.

Scrape.

In his mind, he saw her beautiful smile as she peered down at him from the top of the wall. She beckoned him to climb up to her.

Of course! Thank you, my sweet angel.

Scrape.

He opened his eyes and set his mind to the task of climbing up the narrowing walls. He dropped back to the floor and then used both walls to shimmy toward the top.

Scrape.

More than once, he slid back to the bottom. *One more try before I'm squished like a bug in here.*

Scrape.

The gap between the walls narrowed to the point that he barely had enough room to climb between them. Relief swept over him as he grabbed hold of the top of one wall.

Scrape.

The two walls squeezed against his chest as he struggled to pull himself out of the gap. He quickly pulled the sword from its scabbard and set it on top of the wall, but it didn't give him any additional room to pull himself out. He pushed every ounce of air from his lungs and lifted himself out of the gap just before it narrowed enough to trap him.

Thud.

The two walls crashed together. Nardus slipped on the slick surface and slid right over the edge of the wall. He reached back as he fell, but his fingers found nothing to grasp. He fell flat on his back and it knocked the wind out of him. The back of his head cracked against the floor.

Well, that went better than expected.

Having suffered so much of it, the pain started to become like an addiction to him. *Progress through pain. I am mad.*

Brinzhär Dädh teetered on the edge of the wall. Nardus's eyes widened as it fell, blade first. He had no chance to move. Cold steel slid in between his thighs and sliced through his trouser legs. The sword stood on end, hilt up and blade embedded in the floor a few inches.

Nardus sat up, his heart pounding. Relief washed over him when he found no blood between his legs. His vision blurred, and he felt the back of his head. *Fresh blood and a wicked knot. No worse for wear, I suppose.*

He pushed away from the sword and spun around on the slick floor to see what terrors lurked behind him. *Nothing, of course.* More paths and walls led in just about every direction.

He stared at the small smear of blood on the floor left from the wound on the back of his head. He pushed his finger through the blood and swirled it into the puddle of water next to it. The blood separated itself from the water and rose to the top of the puddle.

"Curious..."

He leaned over and stared at the blood and then at his reflection in the water. The image of himself sickened him; he was a shadow of his former self. Wrinkled skin drooped from his sunken face. In his eyes, he saw not a man, but a wild animal, driven by rage and madness.

How did I get to this point? How low I've sunk.

A lone tear fell from his cheek and rippled the puddle's surface as it plunged into the water. In the reflection, his cheek glowed where the tear had run its course. He wiped his face, but the glow persisted. He lifted his hand to his face, and the glow moved to his hand.

The puddle of water looked no more than half an inch deep. He stuck his hand into it, but felt no bottom. He pulled his hand back out and leaned all the way to the ground, placing his face an inch above the puddle's surface. Something at the bottom definitely glowed.

Against his better judgment, he stuck his face in the water. A moment later, he jerked his head up. He spewed water from his mouth and smoothed back his wet hair. He pulled himself closer to the puddle and plunged his hand into it, and then his arm, all the way up to his shoulder before getting his fingers around an object.

Excitement raced through his body as he clutched the object. He jerked his arm out of the water and let out a cry of victory when he saw that he held the third shard. It was identical to the last shard he'd found. He let the shard lay in his left hand, prepared for it to leap from his palm and join its two brothers once he brought it close enough to them.

He carefully pulled the two melded shards from his pocket, made sure his fingers were nowhere near where the third shard would attach itself to them, and watched as the third shard flew from his hand and melded to them. Again, he detected no seams between any of the pieces. Together, the three shards formed a flat, inch-thick heptagram.

Immediately upon joining, the shard faded from green to a deep black. Then, at the center of the heptagram, the shard turned a bright yellow and eventually formed a lightning bolt. From there, the outer edges of the star points turned bright-blue.

Ꝛäǝll Dhef Ꝛäfn Dhä.

Thunder rumbled through the labyrinth, and the ground quaked. Nardus watched as section after section of walls opened up and formed a single path. The line of walls stretched beyond the horizon in both directions.

Now what? He looked at the shard in his hand, but the thing gave no indication as to what he should do.

Once the shaking ceased, he pulled himself to his feet. *Left, or right?* Neither direction gave him a clue as to which way to proceed. *Guess I'll just go right.*

He placed the shard in his pocket and walked down the path. The enormity of the labyrinth blew his mind. *How does this all exist within the temple? Or is this all in my head?* Everything he'd suffered since entering Zhäíţfäí Fäíţ₂ was surreal.

Am I really here, or am I passed out somewhere? Maybe I'm already dead and I'm just too stupid to have figured it out yet.

Every trial he'd faced so far brought with it new challenges and fresh wounds, but somehow, his body healed itself. He welcomed the healing, but only mezhik explained the phenomenon.

Healing or not, mezhik be damned! He spat on the ground.

Time had become nearly immaterial to him since he'd started the journey; whether it'd been hours or days or weeks made little difference. Now, he felt as though he'd been walking along the path for days.

His surroundings never varied no matter how many steps he took, and it irritated him. *How do I know I'm not walking in a big circle and going nowhere? Maybe I should've gone the other direction.*

He stopped walking. His legs swayed under him as though he'd been out at sea, and his head swam atop his shoulders. *Is this labyrinth moving?* His stomach turned like his head, and bile rose in his throat and gagged him. He spat, but the vile taste lingered.

He reached out to brace himself against the wall and fell right through it instead, landing on the floor on the other side of it. His left shoulder took the brunt of the blow and pain flared from it. He massaged his shoulder with his right hand until the pain faded into a dull throb.

Nardus glared at the wall that wasn't. "Quit messing with my head!" To his relief, the wall didn't respond. He'd half-expected it to.

Madness.

Nardus rolled onto his back, sat up, and faced away from the wall he'd just fallen through. Dense fog distorted his vision and rivulets of water formed on his skin and soaked his clothes. The sound of moving water lapped at his ears and prickled his skin. His pulse raced, and his heart hammered.

What lurks in the fog?

Death.

Nardus drew Brinzhär Dädh and plunged into the fog.

A hundred paces ahead, steam rolled over the edges of a six-sided fountain made of silvered marble. He slowly circled the fountain, his sword held out and ready to defend against an attack.

Life-sized statues of robe-clad men and women, one positioned on each side of the fountain, stood like sentries guarding their king. Each statue demonstrated true craftsmanship with its painstaking details carved from the same marble as the fountain. Crystal-clear, blue water arced from each of their open mouths.

At the fountain's center stood a six-foot-tall hexagonal platform. Each of the platform's sides measured roughly four feet wide. A robe-clad man stood atop the platform, his stone gaze cold as ice.

Nardus paused and choked the hilt a bit harder.

Come to life and fight me, you bastard!

Nardus gazed at the water, and, the longer he gazed at the water, the drier his mouth became. He'd sucked the waterskin around his neck dry some time ago, and the thought of being thirsty hadn't even registered until that moment. He wanted to scoop up some of the water and suck it down but thought better of it.

Probably poisoned with mezhik.

The dense fog thinned to a mist and then dissipated completely. Paths led in all six directions from the fountain, including the direction he'd come from. *Surely a distraction.*

He circled the fountain repeatedly, mesmerized by the lifelike detail.

Handiwork or mezhik?

That's a stupid question. Everything here is woven by mezhik. He spat.

The statue atop the platform turned as he walked and continually faced him. *I'm being watched!* The feeling fed on his nerves. *Are you alive? I've been tricked before.*

Something about the statue—about the man depicted by it—seemed familiar. Maybe it was the light, or maybe just in his head, but the man looked a lot like him. *A relative, perhaps? More likely just my twisted mind playing tricks. This place feeds off my thoughts. I hate meƷhik!*

Deep within his pocket, the shard hummed and vibrated, and he startled. He reached in his pocket and pulled it out. The yellow bolt of lightning at its center flashed continually.

Are you trying to tell me something? He flipped it over in his hand. *Maybe this thing goes somewhere.*

He sheathed Brinzhär Dädh and searched around the fountain's front edge and inside its rim for a place to insert the heptagram shard. Finding nothing, he searched the six lower statues.

Nothing. He scratched his head. *What am I missing?*

He rounded the fountain again and focused on each side of the platform at its center. Each side of the platform bore Ɂäəll Dhef Ɂäfn Dhä, centered both horizontally and vertically and beautifully colored. Each of them looked to be an overlay as they protruded from the platform about half an inch.

Do they all? Or am I just assuming?

Again, he circled the fountain, but this time he looked at the seals indirectly. Five of them stayed true from an angle, but the sixth disappeared.

His heart leapt. "Yes!"

Nardus hurdled the short fountain wall and splashed through the foot-high water. He held the shard up to the concave heptagram on the platform's side, and the shard slid into the hole. The shard ceased humming, and its lightning bolt stopped flashing.

He stepped back, expecting something to happen, but nothing did. He stepped back farther and sat down on the edge of the fountain wall. The warm water soothed his aching calves, but did nothing for his mind. He raked his fingers through his hair, trying to remember the words from the wall.

"Think, Nardus. You're so close now." He beat the palm of his hand on his forehead, hoping to jar the memory loose. "Something about a key..."

He closed his eyes and pulled at his hair with frustration.

Your family depends on you. You swore you'd never let them down again. How hard is remembering a few words? Remember, Nardus.

Like the hands of a clock spun backward, he traced his steps back through the labyrinth and returned to the wall. An image of the wall formed in his head.

My hands were against the wall. And my forehead. Heat. The heat gave life to the words.

At first the wall in his mind stayed blank, but then letters here and there popped onto its surface like kernels of corn erupting over a fire.

"Give us a turn." The sound of his own voice surprised him. "I thought I was thinking that." He chuckled.

He stood and walked back to the platform. He placed his hand on the shard and started to turn it to the right, but then hesitated. *I'm forgetting something.*

Clock. There was something about a clock.

He strained to remember the words again, but nothing came to mind. He pictured a clock in his mind and focused on it. Time ticked away, second after second. Then something peculiar happened. The clock stopped, hesitated a few beats, and then ticked backward.

Counter the clock.

Sure of himself, he turned the heptagram counter-clockwise a full turn-and-a-half before it stopped. He let go of the shard and something clicked, and then the shard sank into the platform two inches.

He stepped back as the water drained from the fountain. The entire side of the platform slid down into the ground and revealed a tight, spiraling passage. He stepped forward and peered into the opening.

Darkness, of course. Where've you been, my friend?

He took a deep breath and squeezed into the passage. The platform's side slid back in place and encased him in darkness. *My sarcophagus.* Heart pounding and palms damp, he spiraled his way down into the unknown.

Please don't let there be spiders.

Chapter Twenty-Seven

Aria stared out the window of the carriage. The morning sun crept over the tops of the rolling hills, slid its way into the carriage, pushed the darkness into the corners, and brought with it a welcomed warmth. She yawned and stretched her arms and legs out like a cat after a nap. She rubbed her eyes with balled fists, and then pulled the sleep from them with her middle fingers.

She turned and gasped. Lord Rosai watched her from the other side of the carriage. He wore a crooked smile, and her face flushed with embarrassment.

"You startled me," she said with little more than a whisper. Her throat felt like gravel, and her mouth tasted like dead fish. She quickly hid the lower half of her face under her blanket, afraid he might get a whiff of her odorous breath.

I can only imagine how bad I look. He must find me repulsive. And where does he get off looking so good in the morning? Ugh!

"Good morning, my queen." Lord Rosai still smiled. "I trust you slept well?"

"Well enough, I suppose." Aria sat up and kept the blanket pulled over her mouth. Her stomach rumbled with hunger and deepened her embarrassment.

"All that sleep must've built up quite an appetite." He chuckled.

The nerve! She glared at him.

His eyebrows rose high like two stretching cats. "Touchy in the morning. Duly noted."

THE DRAGON'S STONE   261

Her chin sank to her chest and buried her face farther. "I'm sorry," she said from under the blanket. Her voice quivered, and she fought back a torrent of tears. "I'm not upset with you. You've shown me nothing but kindness. I get a bit touchy and testy when I'm hungry. Please excuse my rudeness." She raised her head out of her blanket fort. A lone tear crawled its way down her cheek.

Lord Rosai leaned across the carriage and wiped the tear from her cheek with his thumb. "You have nothing to apologize for. It is I who should apologize." He pushed her hair behind her ear with his hand and cupped her chin in his palm. "It's been so long since I've had a woman in my life that I've forgotten my manners."

Woman? I've never been called a woman before. Woman.

Ridiculous.

Then again, what else would I be?

Not a girl I suppose. But a woman?

Women have children and responsibilities. I have neither of those.

Lord Rosai smiled at her. "What I wouldn't give to understand what's going through that pretty little head of yours."

"Food," she blurted. Her stomach growled with agreement. "I think I may pass out if I don't get some food in me soon."

Lord Rosai nodded with agreement. "Ah, yes. Food it is."

"And fresh air. I feel like I've been cooped up in here for days. I haven't been able to walk about on my own since..." Memories of the attack on her village flooded her mind and left her without words. Her lower lip trembled, and she bit down on it to keep it still.

"We'll stop for a short time. It'll be good to stretch out the old legs." He reached up to the ceiling. "You might want to brace yourself."

Brace for what?

Lord Rosai knocked twice on the ceiling and the carriage dipped forward as it came to a sliding halt. The abrupt stop nearly dumped her from her seat and onto the floor. He rose from his seat, opened the carriage door, climbed down the two steps, and hopped down to the ground. She followed his lead and took his hand as she descended the steps.

She took in a deep breath, savoring the moment and enjoying the fresh air. She raised her hands above her head, closed her eyes, and twirled around in the morning sunlight. The taste of freedom overwhelmed her with joy. She giggled and twirled.

She lifted her head to the sky and opened her eyes. The beautiful blue sky circled her. She dropped to her knees and then sat on the ground as the world spun around her.

"Thank you!" she exclaimed, barely able to get the words out through fits of giggles.

"No, my queen, thank *you*. You've brought happiness back into my cold, dark heart. You've stirred feelings in me buried so deep that I'd forgotten their existence. Honestly, I'm certain they hadn't existed before yesterday."

Lord Rosai sat down next to her and pulled a large, paper-wrapped package from inside his robes. The oversized package couldn't have fit inside his robes without creating a bulge, yet it had.

Mezhik? Of course.

Suspense punished her as he slowly unfolded the outer wrapping of the package. *Hurry up, already!* She wanted to snatch it from his hands and tear into it.

Hidden underneath the last fold of paper were pieces of dried fish and small chunks of cheese. Her mouth watered with anticipation and her stomach rumbled.

Lord Rosai lifted the package to his nose and breathed in the aroma. "Ah, it smells so good." He looked at her with a mischievous grin. "What are you having?"

She scowled at him. "Don't make me take that away from you. I'll chew your hand off if I have to."

Lord Rosai laughed. He pushed the package toward her. "By all means, you can have it. As tasty as it may be, it's not worth losing a hand over."

She reached out and snatched a piece of fish off the paper. He set the package on her lap and stood.

"Aren't you going to eat?" She stuffed the whole piece of fish in her mouth.

"That's all for you, my queen. I rarely eat in the morning. It clouds my head."

"Suit yourself," she said between chewing. "You're not getting this back, you know."

He smiled down at her. "There's plenty more where that came from."

"I hoped you'd say that." Aria smiled, stuffed two pieces of cheese in her mouth, and lay back in the luscious grass, savoring the flavor of the cheese and the perfectness of the moment.

Thank You for this, Ɂäṭūr.

She propped herself up on her elbows and took in the glory of her surroundings. The luscious landscape of green grass and rolling hills transcended any beauty she'd seen before. The hills stretched for miles to the north and south. To the east and west, forests of yellow aspens rose more than twenty feet in the air and donned small, beautiful, orange and red leaves.

Is this what Kinzhdm ef Häfn is like, Ɂäṭūr? I can't imagine anything more spectacular.

"Where are we, Lord Rosai?" She looked up at him.

"We're in the northern part of the Daltura Hills," He shielded his eyes with a hand and looked across the hills.

"It's so peaceful here. I'd love to just build a house here and grow old with you."

"This place may seem serene on the surface, but it's anything but that. Below ground are networks of tunnels and large caverns where the *zheballin* dwell. They're nasty, ruthless creatures."

"I've never heard of the *zheballin*," She wrinkled her nose.

Lord Rosai looked down at her. His golden eyes sparkled in the light. "They're mostly night-dwellers, but some do come out during the daylight. They'll sneak around and steal everything you have while you're asleep. When they're particularly bold, they'll attack you in large numbers and take everything you possess, even the clothes off your back. They've also been known to eat small children and enslave others to do their bidding."

Aria sat up and cocked her head. "How do you know so much about them? Are there books about these creatures? Have you seen them before?"

Lord Rosai's eyes moved past her, behind where she laid. "I'm staring at the back of one now," he said in a quiet, but serious tone. He put his finger to his lips and signaled her to keep quiet.

She began to sit up, but Lord Rosai raised his palm and she stopped. Her heart raced in her chest. Flashes of the beasts that attacked her village flew through her mind. She would've never believed in their existence had she not seen them with her own eyes.

Please, Ӡӓţūr, she prayed. *I can't believe You'd drag me all the way out here just to let me be eaten alive. Save us!*

"Don't move," he whispered. He lowered into a crouch. "Where there's one, there will be many."

She could scarcely breathe. Her heartbeat drummed in her ears and boomed like thunder. *Quiet, heart! You'll give us away.*

Lord Rosai stretched his right arm out in front of himself, palm up. "*Fírbūall*," he whispered. A ball of orange and blue flames grew and hovered over his outstretched hand.

Aria stared at the flames, mesmerized by their sensual dancing as they pulsated and twisted around each other. Thoughts of the zhebəllin faded and her fear ebbed. *This man will soon be my husband. What do I have to fear with him by my side?*

Lord Rosai drew his left arm back, keeping his elbow tight against his side. With his wrist bent up and palm forward, he thrust his left arm forward and propelled the fireball from his right hand like an arrow from a bow.

Without thinking, she twisted around on the ground and watched the fireball streak through the air and explode against the side of the face of a hideous, humanoid creature. The creature let out a brief cry like a wounded animal, dropped to its knees, and then fell flat on the ground, dead.

She turned back around and saw Lord Rosai had conjured another fireball. The world around her slowed to a crawl. Lord Rosai's lips move, yelled something to her, but the sound had yet to reach her ears. She strained to hear his words, willed them to slide down her ear canals and come to life against her eardrums.

Finally, the sound of his voice reached her, "Get... in... the... carriage!"

She jumped to her feet as three more fireballs streaked through the air and met their targets. Her beautiful world descended into chaos. She sprinted toward the carriage and then slid to a stop as a zhebəllin stepped between her and it.

Her heart dashed against her ribcage like a boat on the rocks. *Now what?*

The little man-beast stared up at her and grinned a mouth-full of small, sharp, yellowed fangs. His flattened face drew back from his broad nose and stretched into a long forehead. His red eyes were deep-set under thick brows, and his elongated and pointed ears were pinned back against his skull.

His dark, orange-colored skin resembled nothing she'd ever seen before. He stood about three-and-a-half-feet tall and wore dark leathers on his lower extremities. A necklace of small bones hung on his thick neck, and he wore spiked gauntlets on his forearms. In his right hand, he clutched what looked to be a crude short sword.

She gagged as a repulsive smell filled her nostrils. He reminded her of Pigman in a way, and the memory of that worthless pig brought with it an overwhelming rage. Every fiber of her being wanted to rip him apart.

Fury roared from her open mouth and she charged forward. Her boldness stunned the zhebəllin and left him rigid as a stone statue. She leapt into the air and planted the heel of her foot straight into his nose. The crack of bone reverberated through her foot and up her leg. The zhebəllin grunted, fell backward, and dropped his sword.

Aria somersaulted across the ground and sprung back to her feet. She wheeled around, grabbed the zhebəllin's fallen sword, and thrust it into his neck. His eyes bulged, and his throat gurgled as he reached for the blade. She twisted it in his neck and his arms fell limp. She ran to the carriage, climbed into it, and slammed the door behind her.

Lord Rosai!

She looked out the carriage window and gasped when she saw Lord Rosai surrounded by a hoard of zhebəllin. He turned and looked directly at her, grimacing. His lips moved, but she couldn't read what he'd said.

I can't leave him to die!

† † †

From his vantage, Lord Rosai saw Aria's terror-stricken face through the window of the carriage. Her safety brought with it a sense of relief that spread through him like wildfire.

Lord Rosai yelled, *"Brätäkt ṭūō."* The protection spell rippled the air as it sped toward the carriage. The spell rocked the carriage, encapsulated it, and sealed it inside an invisible barrier. He shot a quick look and nod to the driver, and the carriage sped away. Aria beat her fists against the window, her face contorted with terror.

I'm sorry, my queen, but it's for your own protection.

The carriage dropped into the valley between the hills and out of sight. He turned his attention back on the hoard of zhebəllin that surrounded him.

"Enough!" he yelled in the zhebəllin native tongue. "Bring me the one you call Lord."

From amongst the ranks, one zhebəllin pushed his way through the crowd. He stood a head taller than the others.

"I am he!" said the zhebəllin in his own language. He beat his fist against his bare chest. "Kaja."

"Kaja, I am Lord Rosai. You may not know me, but I'm sure you knew my father, Pugnus Rosai."

Kaja held his ground, but his eyes had flashed with fear when Lord Rosai spoke the name. "Don't care. You trespass, you die."

"You and your little friends hold little value for life, and that's why I'm here. A war is coming, and I want you fighting on my side."

"Bah." Kaja crossed his arms. "You humans war all you like. We care little of your affairs. We take no side."

"The coming war will change the world for us all. If you're not with us, then we'll have no choice but to eradicate you."

"Our shaman has foretold of this coming war. When it ends, we will be the only race left standing, and we will rule the Ancient Realm. We will no longer hide underground and in the shadows."

"Join me and you'll have the same freedom. When the time comes, I only ask that you fight for me. We will not lose."

"Joining you wasn't foretold." Kaja stomped.

Lord Rosai scowled at Kaja. "Bring your shaman forward. Let's see what he has to say now."

"Joora!" bellowed Kaja. Moments later, the shaman squeezed through the crowd and stood at Kaja's side.

"Joora, at the end of the coming war will you be standing by your Lord's side?" asked Lord Rosai.

"Forever!" cried Joora.

"Liar." Lord Rosai turned to Kaja. "How can you believe the lies of this creature?"

"What he says will come to pass," said Kaja with finality.

Lord Rosai pointed a finger at Joora. "*Ţōírn inţū eɛzh.*" The shaman's flesh turned black as night and then he dropped into a pile of ash, clothes and all.

"As I said—" Lord Rosai smiled deviously. "—he's a liar. Now, kneel before me and swear your loyalty, or you'll all die this day."

"Joora was one, as are you. We are many. You can't possibly take us all on at once."

"And what makes you think I'm alone?" Lord Rosai reached out with his mind to the band of gnolls that hid amongst the hills and trees. *"Show yourselves."*

From every direction, the gnolls appeared, poised and ready for a slaughter. Kaja dropped to his knees at the sight of them. In a wave of movement, the other zhebəllin followed his lead.

"Our lives are yours, Lord Rosai," said Kaja, his voice laced with disgust. Fear filled his red eyes.

Lord Rosai pulled a small knife from within a pocket of his robes. "Hold out your hand."

Reluctantly, Kaja complied.

Lord Rosai bent down and slit Kaja's palm with the knife and then slit his own. He locked hands with Kaja. "*Būfnd bəllʊd.* Our arrangement is now bound by blood. Even in death this arrangement cannot be broken. If you attempt to back out of this arrangement or try to kill me, you will die."

"So be it." Kaja rose to his feet. "Now rid yourself from my land and take your filthy dogs with you."

"With pleasure." Lord Rosai reached out to the gnolls with his mind again. *"Move out. We still have a long journey ahead."*

As one, the gnolls retreated into the shadows.

Lord Rosai turned from Kaja and took a few steps. Then, from over his shoulder, he said, "You'd better be ready when I call on you."

Kaja puffed up his chest. "We are always ready."

Lord Rosai smiled, excited by the prospect of war.

"*Diɛäbir.*" He stepped forward and vanished.

CHAPTER TWENTY-EIGHT

*C*rash. *Thump. Thump.*

Alderan froze. His foot rested on the top rung of the ladder. *What was that?* The sounds had come from one of the bedrooms. The clicking of claws on the wood floor set him in motion again. He flew down the ladder.

"Rayah! We must go, now. They've found a way in." She didn't answer. He reached the bottom of the ladder, but didn't see her in the room.

His heart raced as he ran into the far room with the mirror. The mirror no longer held a reflection of the room, but an image of Rayah being dragged through a burning hallway with a blade to her throat. Flames leapt from the walls and ceiling and the fire roared.

No!

"Rayah!" he screamed. The image of her faded into his own, horrific reflection. Worse, he wasn't alone. He turned around and faced the two gnolls.

"Going somewhere?" snarled one of them.

"He's just a boy, Creeb. No need to wait for Rakzar," said the other.

"I think you're right, Brux."

Creeb and Brux stepped into the mirror room. Alderan stepped back and put his hand against the surface of the mirror; it tingled with mezhik. Creeb and Brux froze.

"How did you do that?" asked Brux.

Alderan started to turn around.

"Don't even think about it." Saliva hung from Creeb's chin.

The roar of the fire returned. Alderan pushed against the surface of the mirror with his hand; cold and wet, it gave little resistance as he pushed his hand through it. He no longer felt his hand. He pulled his hand back through the opening and the feeling returned.

"Grab him!" shouted Brux. Creeb and Brux lunged toward Alderan.

Alderan fell backward through the mirror and landed on his back in the burning hallway. The two gnolls burst through the mirror as well, but turned into ash before they landed on top of him.

Guess gnolls don't have mezhik.

Through the mirror, Rakzar glared at him. Rakzar reached behind his back and withdrew his double-edged battle-axe. He cocked his arm back and swung his axe at the mirror. Alderan cringed, but Rakzar faded and the burning hallway reflected in the mirror. A piece of metal—the tip of Rakzar's axe—fell to the floor.

The roar of the fire deafened him, and he couldn't see anything through the thick smoke. He flipped over and lay flat on his stomach where the smoke was much thinner. He glimpsed Rayah and her captor at the far end of the hallway just before they rounded the corner.

His pulse accelerated. "I'm coming!"

He jumped to his feet and ran down the burning hallway after them.

† † †

Rakzar tore through the Veridis Forest, still furious about the man-child called Alderan, but driven by the excitement of smoke in the air. He lived for destruction, and nothing more destructive than fire existed in nature. He moved fast on all fours, but today, with the wind at his back, his speed was exceptional.

Hope I get there before it's over.

Rakzar's mind drifted back to Alderan as he ran. *The White Knight.* The boy had burrowed under his skin like a thorn and wounded his pride. *What is it about him that's so special?* No prey had ever escaped him before. *How could a mere boy best me three times?*

He's not just a boy.

In his mind, the odds of that happening transcended the realm of possible, yet it stood as fact. *This whole thing's Dragnus's fault. If he'd told me the boy wielded mezhik, I would've approached the whole situation differently. And that sneaky, worthless little dryte. Dragnus never said anything about her either.*

He's not just a boy.

His hate for Dragnus surpassed that of the White Knight. His reputation hung in the balance, and his being made to look the fool grew tiresome. *I'm a fierce warrior. These mind games are for the weaker races.* He wondered, though, if giving the boy the title of White Knight had empowered him somehow.

That pathetic boy holds no power over me, does he? Absurd! Yet there's something different about him. But what?

He's not just a boy.

Rakzar loved war, and chaos befriended him, too. Mindless destruction: he never questioned any order having to do with it. But the boy changed things. *He's a different matter.*

The boy. Why is he such a threat? Why is it so important that this one boy die? Grown men demanding—no begging—that he be killed. Perhaps I should find out why. He liked the idea. *I'm a servant to none! I'll still kill the boy, but on my own terms, when I'm ready. Dragnus be damned.*

He's not just a boy.

The smoky scent increased significantly as the trees thinned out near the southwestern edge of the forest. Adrenaline pumped through his veins and pushed him even faster. He felt possessed as he flew through the trees and scrub brush like a wind spirit. His even breathing impressed him. *Not bad at all. Probably in better shape than pups half my age.*

He slid to a stop at the edge of the forest. Smoke filled the valley below and impeded his view, but he knew what it hid. Along the valley coast—under the veil of smoke—lay the port town of Solasportus.

Humans. Waste of flesh.

Castle Portador Tempestade sat less than ten miles out, situated on the edge of a cliff on the south side of the valley. It overlooked the Discidium Sea.

Dragnus. Slippery little worm of a man.

His hackles rose as the wind shifted his direction. He lifted his snout and sniffed the air, confirming his suspicion: *orcs.* Their unmistakable stench sickened him. *Where there are orcs, there's Murtag.* He growled deep in his throat.

"Worthless brute." He snorted with disgust. Things were growing overly complicated and he didn't like it. He had too many things going on to be dealing with Murtag as well.

He first met Murtag when he was still a pup. That day was forever ingrained in his head; Murtag had thrown him to the ground, jumped on his back, and then tried to ride him like a mindless ferzh, completely humiliating him in front of his whole pack. Had it been the only run-in with Murtag, he might've let it slide, but the day Murtag slaughtered his young siblings drove him mad with vengeance.

Don't think I've forgotten, varlet.

Orcs or otherwise, he couldn't pass up the opportunity to see what kind of destruction befell the valley. He raced down the hill and into the smoke-filled valley, cutting through the dead grass and snow. If not for the snow, the whole valley would've been ablaze. As it was, Solasportus amounted to little more than smoldering ash, and the sight of it left him brimming with excitement.

He continued to the other side of the valley and made the ascent toward Castle Portador Tempestade. As he neared the top of the hill, the wind shifted direction again. With the smoke cleared, he got a good view of the castle. Flames engulfed it from top to bottom.

He howled with excitement. *Now that's more like it!*

Rakzar quickened his pace up the latter part of the hill and stopped at its crest to get a better look at the situation. From his vantage point, he saw the whole eastern side of the castle and a small portion of the northern side. Most of the northern side of the castle sat along the cliff-edge and faced the sea.

At the top of the eastern wall—suspended by his neck—hung the unmistakable form of Dragnus. Clearly still alive, Dragnus struggled to hold his weight with his flabby arms.

Murtag's sadistic. I'll give him that.

As Rakzar saw it, three clear paths led to Dragnus's imminent death: his arms could give out and he'd choke, the fire could burn its way through the rope and he'd plunge eighty feet, or the wall could topple over and crush him.

Little worm on a hook. I hope the rope burns.

Rakzar stood and jogged toward the castle. The orcs already headed south, their job done.

If it were me and my brothers, we'd stay until the last stone fell.

Murtag stood in the distance, alone and with his back to Rakzar. His long, wiry red hair hung down to the small of his back in twisted braids, and nearly blended in with the fox hides draped around his neck. His sledgehammer fist gripped the five-bladed mace that hung at his side.

Rakzar imagined tearing Murtag's throat out and could almost taste the blood. *That'd make for a perfect day.*

Murtag turned and faced Rakzar, his pure-blue eyes ablaze. "Ah, the prodigal dog makes his appearance."

Just the sound of Murtag's harsh, slurred voice enraged Rakzar.

Rakzar stopped a few feet in front of Murtag. He towered over the orc by nearly a foot. "You best watch your tongue you freak of nature. I'm not a pup anymore."

"Still living in the past, are we? A pity." A string of snot hung from Murtag's porcine nose, and he wiped it with the back of his hand. He lifted his hand toward the burning castle. "As you can see, we've done your job. As usual."

"This wasn't my job." Rakzar reigned in his raging anger.

"Oh, that's right. You're supposed to be killing a human boy half your size. How's that working out?"

He's not just a boy.

Rakzar set his jaw and gritted his teeth. "Give me one reason why I shouldn't kill you right now."

"Other than you are too weak to do so?" Murtag covered one nostril and blew snot from the other. "How about the blood pact Lord Rosai forced you and I to make? We're bound together. Trust me, I hate it just as much as you."

"I'll find a way to break that pact."

"I'm sure you'll try. I've really enjoyed this chat of ours, but I've got other business to attend to." Murtag turned and headed in the same direction the other orcs had.

"Good riddance," said Rakzar with a growl.

"Enjoy the rest of the show, *friend.*"

Friend. A foreign concept.

Rakzar had no friends, and he needed none. The only thing he needed—no craved—hung at the top of a wall. *Which death will Dragnus succumb to?*

The roar of the fire and the crackling cedar and pine sung in his ears like a lullaby. He yearned to go inside the castle and get closer to the destruction. *Just a peek. In and out in a few minutes.*

He decided he'd be content watching, right up until he heard screams coming from inside the castle. *Someone's still alive in there?* He turned toward the source, focused on it, and filtered everything else out. *Come on. Scream again.*

Finally, another scream sounded from the castle. His heart raced as his brain slowly translated the scream into a single word. *It can't be. Must be wishful thinking.* A moment later, he heard that single word again, but this time it was unmistakable—

"Rayah!"

The White Knight. This day just keeps getting better.

He dropped on all fours and bolted toward the castle.

He's not just a boy.

CHAPTER TWENTY-NINE

E very breath was like inhaling an inferno. Alderan wished he had some water to pour on the piece of cloth he held over his mouth and nose. His eyes burned too, and the moisture they produced only made it worse. He kept wiping them just to see.

Anger fueled him as he staggered from room to room in search of Rayah. The thought of losing her again tore at his heart, and the guilt ate him alive. *Three times. Three times you've let her down. Never again will I leave her side.*

Even though he knew the smoke slowly killed him, he screamed out Rayah's name when he entered each room. He hoped and prayed he wouldn't find her because she'd made it out of the castle already. Every room he encountered pulsed with smoke and flames, some filled with burning bodies.

Given the excessive amount of smoke, the overpowering smell of burning flesh surprised him. He cringed every time he encountered a burning body, prayed it wasn't Rayah, and then breathed a sigh of relief when he confirmed it wasn't. Some were beyond recognition, but Rayah wouldn't be among them.

Not yet, but I might be soon.

A minute into the castle and sweat soaked him from head to toe. His body had run out of moisture long ago, and the heat flared worse than anything he'd experienced before. Every time he opened his mouth and screamed for Rayah he swallowed daggers—not literally, but he guessed the feeling similar—and, with the added element of smoke, his lungs shuddered as though on the verge of collapse.

Every moment within the castle walls he ventured closer to death. But how could he give up on Rayah? She needed him, and he needed to rescue her, but dying without finding her wouldn't save her.

I've got to find a way out.

Crack.

He dove out of the way just as the ceiling crashed down behind him.

Save me, Ẕäṭūr! I don't think I'm going to make it out on my own.

Soon the entire castle would collapse on itself. Smoke and chaos surrounded him and left him disoriented. *Am I even heading in the right direction?* On top of that, he'd lost his breathing cloth to the fire when he dove to the floor. He did his best to pull his shirt up over his mouth, but it wouldn't go high enough to cover his nose as well.

Crack.

Another part of the ceiling crashed down in the room to his left, and brought more smoke and flames with it. The thick smoke blinded him, even at floor-level. He pulled himself back up and stumbled forward with his arms outstretched, desperate to find a way out.

Wham!

Something hit him so hard it took him off his feet, through the burned-out wall he stood next to, and slammed him into the floor in the next room. Pain exploded in his head and ripped through his body. He hurt so bad, he couldn't even manage to open his eyes. Was he beginning to black out?

Crack.

The floor supporting him gave out and he fell, and his stomach leapt into his throat. He quickly put his arms over his head and curled into a ball, hoping to curb the impending impact with the floor below.

Smash.

A human boulder, he crashed through the burned-out floor below. He fell two more levels, crashed through some debris, and thudded against the hard, rock floor. His head spun as he tried to get up from the floor, but he stumbled and fell back down.

Boom.

The ground shook as part of the castle fell in on itself. *Please, Ẕäṭūr, just save Rayah.* His back burned with fire. His mind demanded his body to roll around and put out the fire, but his body just wouldn't cooperate. *What in*

Centauria hit me up there?

Boom.

Another portion of the castle fell in on itself. He coughed and brought up what he knew to be blood even though he couldn't see it. *Rayah, I love you!* The thought of her gave him a needed burst of strength. He managed to roll over on his back and squirm around until the heat dissipated. He rolled back on his stomach and crawled on his hands and knees, but he still had no idea which direction to head.

Bam!

A large, burning beam slammed into the floor just inches from his head. He couldn't risk standing up again, so he crawled over the beam as fast as he could. His left knee rested on the beam a moment too long, and fire burned through his trousers and into many layers of his skin. Somehow, he managed to suppress a scream.

Ꝛäṭūr, protect Rayah. Let her know I did everything I could to find her.

Boom.

The castle wall directly behind him crashed down and lifted his entire body off the floor. The anticipation of being crushed pumped more adrenaline into his system and accelerated his pulse. To his left—through the smoke and flames—something rushed toward him. A moment later, something lifted him off the floor by his throat and then slammed him back down.

"Hello, White Knight," said an all-too-familiar voice.

In that moment, he knew he'd breathed his last breath. *I'm sorry, Rayah. I'm sorry.*

Rakzar's fist slammed into the side of his head, and everything went black.

† † †

Amicus stood at the southwestern edge of the Veridis Forest. Across the valley, Castle Portador Tempestade burned. Though elated to see it burn, the thought of all those who probably perished within its walls left tears in his eyes.

He'd been scheduled to work the dungeons last night, but Master

Dragnus sent him out to check the forest traps at the last moment. Had he not done so, he would've been counted among the dead as well.

He lifted his head and raised his arms to the sky. *Thank You, Ʒäţūr, for keeping me safe.* He turned the bracelet he wore around his left wrist in a circle and thought of Aria. *My butterfly. Thank You for keeping her from harm's way, too.*

He settled his eyes on the valley below—a sea of smoke. His stomach sank at the thought of his family down there, and of all the other people in Solasportus, too.

I pray you're all safe.

With the castle burning, he could only imagine how scared and devastated they must be feeling. He covered his mouth and nose with his shirt and sprinted down the hill and into the thick smoke.

Had the smoke not stung his eyes, he could've imagined it to be a thick fog that had rolled into the valley, as it so often did. Now, how could anyone stand to be down in the valley? A lump caught in his throat as images of his wife, Vorene, and his little girl, Vonah, flashed through his mind.

Ʒäţūr, my God, tell me I'm wrong. Tell me they're okay.

Tears burned in his eyes as he forced his legs to pump harder. By the time he made it down to the floor of the valley and to the edge of the village, he trembled from head to toe. Grief ripped through his heart and ate at his soul as he ran passed the burned-out structures.

I should've been here. I should've been here!

His legs gave out just before he reached his house, and he fell on his knees and then face-first onto the ground. *Please don't be here. Please, please, please. Ʒäţūr, tell me they got away.*

His legs refused to function, so he dragged himself through the snow and ashes and clawed his way into what remained of his single-room house. Through wisps of smoke, his eyes caught sight of his wife and daughter. Little more than ash and bone, they embraced each other unto death. Sorrow and guilt twisted his heart and shattered his mind.

No, Ʒäţūr! No, no, no!

"Why!" he screamed at the sky.

He beat the ground with his fists and ripped his shirt in half. He lifted his head and screamed with everything he had. His chest heaved, his heart stuttered, and he turned his head to the side and vomited.

"Why, Ɂäṭūr?" he cried, barely able to get the words out of his mouth. "How could You allow something like this to happen? Why did You take my little girl from me? She was so innocent. She didn't deserve to die this way. It should've been me."

Snot hung from his nose and lips, and tears streamed from his eyes, endlessly. He felt completely lost and abandoned. *What am I to do? How can I go on? I should've been here for them. Somehow, I should've known what was coming.*

"How was this Your plan, Ɂäṭūr? How could You just stand aside and let this happen? Help me understand. Please, Ɂäṭūr, bring them back! Take me in their place."

He wanted to keep shaking his fists at the sky and blaming Ɂäṭūr, but he knew Ɂäṭūr wasn't the one responsible. The answer was much simpler than that: *Dragnus.* The wicked little man had surely brought ruin on them all. Deep down, he surmised that Lord Rosai had something to do with it as well.

Like the flipping of a coin, his sorrow turned into resolve. He sat up straight, his mind transformed into an iron fortress against what he knew had to be done. He wiped the snot from his nose and mouth with the back of his hand and rose to his feet.

This will not defeat me. Ɂäṭūr, strengthen me.

He pulled a blanket out of his pack and gathered the remains of his family in it, and then he carried them back up the hill and to the edge of the Veridis Forest. He dug a small, shallow grave with his dagger and hands and placed their bones and ashes into it. He prayed over the grave and then covered it with dirt.

He turned back toward the valley, his personal shadow of death. "Never again will I fear evil! I swear, in the name of Ɂäṭūr, that I will make a stand and fight for the fallen! I will find those responsible and bring them to justice!"

† † †

Rayah sat in a dungeon cell, bound in chains and tethered to the wall. Across the cell, the lizard man leaned against the wall with his left foot propped back against it. His grey-eyed, reptilian gaze bored holes into her skull.

On the floor between them lay a pile of bones picked clean by the rats. *Human bones.* She desired to be anywhere else in the world than right there.

Her eyes were itchy and sore from crying and the smoke, and the dungeon stench kept her gagging and dry heaving with almost every breath. On top of everything else, she worried herself sick over Alderan. The last time she'd seen him, he'd flown through the mirror in the castle. Every moment since, she'd spent praying for his safety.

Just let him be alive. Please, ʒäṭūr, he's the one the prophets spoke of, our savior. Take me in his place if You need someone.

Silence hung in the air and gnawed at her nerves. She'd grown accustomed to Alderan's sparse words, but she always filled in the silence with dialogue of her own. Something about the lizard-man made her want to hold her tongue, but she couldn't place her finger on it.

I'm never gonna get out of here by doing nothing. Ugh! Just say something, Rayah.

The lizard man spoke first. "When we're all done here, you and I'll have to get to *know* each other a little better, if you catch my meaning."

His words wriggled across her skin like maggots, and crawled into her ears and ate away any thoughts she had of befriending him. "As if I'd ever want to *know* you. You and your clammy, scaly skin are repulsive."

He placed the back of his hand on his sloped forehead and let out a whimper. "Your words are so hurtful. How will I ever recover from their devastation? Maybe I should just let you go so I can sulk in my own sorrow, my heart rent by the likes of a filthy dryte."

"When Alderan finds us, you'll wish you'd been nicer to me."

"Ah, yes. Alderan. Isn't that what the boy calls himself? The bastard son doesn't even know his true name."

The slithering of his slurred words penetrated her skin and irritated her like a rash.

Rayah leaned forward and pulled her chains taut. "You don't even know what you're talking about."

"Sure. Let's just live in your perfect, little fantasy world, content pretending everything is just as you see it," His foot slid down the wall. "After all, you're the queen of your world and know all there is to know of it. Nothing escapes your perfect perception."

"He's the prophesied savior of the world. You'll see."

"And what exactly is he *saving* the world from? Is there some sort of hidden agenda that only *you* are aware of? Are we all doomed? Please, enlighten me, great faerie of the soil."

Faerie! Why does everyone call me a faerie? Rayah wanted to scream. "Do you know nothing of the prophecy? Can't you feel the impending darkness coming?"

"The prophets have indeed written about the world transformed into darkness. Its meaning is nothing more than a matter of perception, I suppose. Those such as I thrive in the darkness; we welcome it. It's nothing to be *saved* from, but something to *embrace*. The light does nothing but expose our shortcomings. Who would want to live that way? The darkness covers our blemishes, and in it we will thrive."

"And what of Ɛätūr and His everlasting light? Do you deny it as well?"

"Ɛätūr—" He sneered and stepped toward her. "—a false god made up by those too weak and afraid to face the harshness of this world. There's nothing beyond this life. Of that, you can be assured."

"Aren't you afraid of death, then?"

"Death is meaningless. We're all made from chaos, and in the end, we'll return to it. I'll embrace my death when it comes."

"If nothing holds meaning for you—even death—then why are you holding me captive? What are you seeking to gain from this?"

"Nothing more than the assurance that the darkness will prevail. If there is no *savior*, then there is no way to stop the darkness."

"And you think the darkness will choke out the light? You actually believe that?"

"The darkness grows, even as we speak."

"Have you ever noticed that the darkness cowers in the light? Light a torch and the darkness scatters, seeking refuge in the shadows. The darkness cannot win, and neither will you."

"Ah, but the light can be extinguished." The lizard man sneered at her again. "When that happens, the darkness comes rushing back in, even stronger than before the light appeared."

"If the darkness is so strong, why do you feel the need to intervene?"

"My intervention only ensures its arrival more quickly."

"I know Alderan, and he's driven by three of the greatest forces in this world."

He whipped the floor with his tail. "And what forces are those?"

"Faith, hope, and love. He has faith in Ɂäṭūr, a hope for this world unparalleled by any other, and love great enough to bring back those on the cusp of death."

The lizard man laughed. "I've brought weapons and might to the fight, and what have you brought? Faith, hope, and love. I promise you I'll make a quick battle of it."

"Everyone underestimates Alderan. That's his advantage. You'll follow the same pattern and fate as the others."

The lizard man flicked the air with his tongue. "We'll see about that soon enough. Someone's coming." He pulled the hood of his cloak over his bald head, cinched the belt at his waist, and faded into the surroundings.

Rayah gasped. "That's not fair!"

From thin air, the lizard man's hand grabbed her jaw and forced her mouth open. His other hand appeared and stuffed the rag it held into her open mouth. Then, he wrapped another rag around her head to hold the first one in her mouth. The rag tasted like a rancid apple; she gagged and swallowed back bile.

The lizard man's hands disappeared once again. "Fair has nothing to do with it." His voice slithered back into the cell from beyond the cell door.

Please, Ɂäṭūr, watch over Alderan and protect him. I love him so much.

CHAPTER THIRTY

A four-foot-tall crystal pedestal stood at the center of the dark room, glowing with a yellow light. A small reddish-black stone, smaller than Nardus's balled fist, sat atop its flat surface.

Nardus stood at the edge of the room, paralyzed by the voice in his head. *'Come closer,'* it said. *'Touch me and I'll end your pain. You've suffered long enough. I'll comfort you.'*

Nardus's hands trembled at his sides. "Who are you?" he whispered.

The light faded from the pedestal and cast the room into darkness. Nardus reached back to brace himself against the wall, but his hand found nothing.

Maniacal laughter broke through the silence and swirled around him like a tornado. Nardus recognized the laughter as his own, but it hadn't come from him. He turned in a circle, weary of what he might find lurking in the darkness.

"Face me," came a voice from behind him.

Nardus swiveled around, confused. The voice was his own.

Six paces away, a circle of light pierced the darkness and silhouetted a cloaked man. The man held something in his left hand and tossed it toward Nardus's feet. It thumped as it bounced along the floor and rolled to a stop just in front of Nardus.

Nardus's heart pounded and jerked the veins in his neck. Beads of sweat trickled down his brow and stung his eyes. He slowly bent down to pick up the object, but in his heart, he already knew its form.

The tangled hair slid through Nardus's fingers as he reached down and picked up the severed head by its scalp. He lifted it up and into the light. Nardus stared at the familiar face—his face—and gasped.

This can't be happening.

Nardus staggered backward and released the head from his grasp. It fell and hit the floor with a *thud*. His legs trembled and barely held his weight.

Nardus eyed the cloaked man. "What is this madness?"

The cloaked man laughed at Nardus. "Your future."

The cloaked man raised his arms over his head and fire shot from his hands. Five torches hung from a metal chandelier and roared to life as the fire reached them. The light chased away the darkness.

Vitara, my love, I need you again. Give me your strength.

Nardus's legs ceased to shake and he stood tall, renewed. "Show me your face," he growled.

The cloaked man reached up and pulled the hood back from his head.

Nardus fell to his knees. "It can't be—"

The man that stood before Nardus mirrored him, right down to his weathered face and brown eyes. Even the scar on the man's left cheek matched his own.

The other Nardus shrugged the cloak from his shoulders. "Stand up and face me, impostor." He drew Brinzhär Dädh from its scabbard on his back.

The sound of steel against steel rang in Nardus's ears. Panicked, Nardus reached over his right shoulder with his left hand, but only grasped air. His breath caught in his lungs.

How did he get my sword?

"*Your* sword?" The other Nardus spat on the ground. "Gnaud gave this sword to me to fight off the *Dämnz Fallíinzh*."

Nardus's head spun. "Gnaud gave *me* that sword, not you!"

The other Nardus scoffed at him. "You? Impossible." He pointed at Nardus. "Look at yourself. Those arrows tore through your flesh just as they did your family's—one through the head, one through the throat, and one through your heart. You died with them that day."

Nardus closed his eyes. The scene of that fateful day was as clear in his mind as if it'd happened just minutes before.

Part of me did die that day.

"Not just part of you. *All* of you. When you died, I was born." The other

Nardus held his sword above his head. "Now it's time to sever the link between us. Both of us can't survive this, and you're too pathetic to do what needs to be done."

Nardus stood, fists balled and muscles tensed. "This place and its *mezhik* has conjured you from my mind." He spat on the floor. "You're not even real."

The other Nardus stepped forward. "Not real? Have you noticed anything different in your mind? Do you feel as though you've lost something?"

"I don't feel any diff—" Nardus crossed his arms and grimaced. "You think I'm a fool? I know what you're trying to do to me. It's exactly what I'd be doing to you. It won't work."

The other Nardus grinned. "If you take the stone for yourself we'll be put to death."

Nardus spat on the floor again. "You're a liar. There is no 'we.'"

"Me? A liar? And what would I gain by lying to you?" The other Nardus lowered the sword and pointed it at Nardus. "Touch the blade and I'll show you your fate. *Our* fate."

Nardus stepped back. "This is madness. If I touch the sword, you'll run me through with it."

"I swear on our Vitara's soul. I will not harm you while showing you our fate."

Nardus sighed deeply. "This is gonna be one more thing on my long list of regrets." He reached out and touched the tip of the sword.

A flash of light filled the room and blinded Nardus. He closed his eyes and an image of the room—burned into the backside of his eyelids—floated across his vision like a ghost. A rush of wind blew through his hair as he felt himself being pulled. Faster and faster he flew. His cheeks pulled back by the pressure and left his lips parted in a grin.

Madness.

Nardus opened his eyes, but the light and the wind burned them as with fire, so he shut them again. Tears leaked from the corners of his eyes and blew across the sides of his face and into his hair. The flying sensation exhilarated and nauseated him all at once. Never before had he ever wanted to laugh and vomit simultaneously.

In the back of his mind, Nardus thought he heard a hammer slamming against wood, repeatedly. He strained to hear over the roaring wind in his ears and willed himself to filter out the noise.

Like a whisper at first, and then growing in volume, a male voice cried out, "I will have order in front of this council!"

Nardus's eyes snapped open as the flying sensation came to an abrupt halt. He stood before two massive wooden doors. Guards flanked him, armored for war.

What's happening? Am I going further mad? Is that even possible?

The doors parted on their own. Beyond the doors, many familiar faces stared at him from either side of a center aisle. A long, tall platform sat at the front of the room, and a long table stretched across it.

Six people, three men and three women, sat behind the table. They all wore white robes and donned the same symbol on their left breasts: *Ƨäall Dhef Ƨäfn Dhä.*

Another man stood behind the table, between the other six. He wore dark blue robes with the same symbol on his left breast. He beat a gavel against its sound block with an angered urgency.

A lump in Nardus's throat grew like a bubble filling with air and labored his breath further. *Where am I? What is this? Why am I being treated like a criminal?*

"Silence!" yelled the man in blue. His voice boomed like thunder. He slammed his wooden gavel into the sound block repeatedly.

Nardus recognized the man in blue. *From where?* Then it hit him: *He's the man atop the platform in the fountain!* The others, three to either side of the man in blue, were those from the other statues in the fountain too.

The veins in Nardus's neck throbbed and threatened to burst from beneath his skin. *Just calm down. You don't even know what this is.*

He did know, though: the culmination of a manhunt for him.

The crowd quieted and took their seats on the long, wooden benches; some of them still eyed him with hate. The two guards pushed him through the doors, down the center aisle, and to the front of the room. His heart thumped in his chest as he peered into the flashing yellow eyes of the man in blue.

Something about the man in blue troubled him, but he couldn't put his finger on its source. It hid in the shadows of his memories and nipped at recollection, but failed to make itself known to him. Did something—or even someone—hold the memory at bay?

Absurd. My madness strikes again. It shall be the death of me.

The man in blue sat down. His gaze bore holes through Nardus's skull. "State your name for the council."

"Nardus," he croaked.

The man in blue glared at him. "Your *full* name, sir."

"Nardus Remison." He swallowed, but his parched mouth gave little relief to his raw throat.

The man in blue cocked his head. "Nardus Remison? You're certain?"

"I am," said Nardus.

Am I? Is that who I really am? Or did that man die in the forest with his family? Am I just an animal? A savage with no soul? Is the other Nardus right? Am I lost?

"Nardus Remison." The man in blue pushed his glasses up his nose. "Please keep your thoughts to a minimum. You're disrupting this council."

Nardus's jaw dropped. "You're reading my thoughts?"

The man in blue lifted a paper from the table. "No need. You're projecting them."

Projecting? Impossible!

"Silence!" The man in blue's eyes flashed and his voice thundered. He read from the paper he held. "You stand in front of this council accused of murder, torture, lying, adultery, abandonment, and thievery."

Each accusation punched Nardus's gut and left him breathless.

This isn't right!

The man in blue laid the piece of paper on the table and peered down at Nardus. "How do you plead?"

Nardus coughed and swallowed hard. Dryness clung to his tongue like an arid desert, and his lips felt as though they would crack and burst with blood if he pulled them apart. His voice cowered in his gut.

I'm not guilty! he screamed in his mind. *Not guilty!*

"Liar!" The man in blue pointed his finger at Nardus. "Have you no shame? Do these men to your left not look familiar?" He swept his hand to his right.

Nardus looked over his left shoulder at the three men sitting on the front row. The men turned toward him, eyeless and heartless—blood seeped from their gaping holes. He knew they were all castrated as well. Anger raged in his heart just as it had the day he'd ripped them apart.

You all got what you deserved!

"Even now, you seethe at the sight of these men and curse them further. You murdered each of them."

Nardus returned his gaze to the man in blue. The accusation breathed life into his voice. "You know—"

"Silence. You'll refrain from speaking unless we request it of you." The man in blue glared at him, and Nardus glared right back.

Nardus clenched his fists and set his jaw. *Murder? I've never had a desire to murder anyone as much as I have right now.* How much more could he take before bursting a vein?

"You'd best keep your thoughts in check, Mr. Remison. Now, your murdering of those men directly resulted in the death of your twins, correct? You abandoned them for revenge. Did that work in your favor? I think not."

Nardus spun around and searched the courtroom for his precious children. *Shardan? Shanara? Where are you?*

"You won't find them here, Mr. Remison. Now focus."

Nardus's heart sank. *I miss you so much, my precious children.* Tears welled in his eyes.

The man in blue cleared his throat. "Now, have you ever *known* a woman other than your wife? Or even looked upon another woman with lust in your eyes?"

"No," growled Nardus. He turned around and stared at the man in blue. "Never."

The man in blue slammed his fist against the table. "Again, you stand there, lying to our faces." He removed his glasses and set them down on the table. "The woman to your right has been *known* by you, has she not?"

Nardus peered over his right shoulder. The filthy demon known as Akuji sat in the front row. She wore Vitara's skin once again. She ran her tongue around her lips and winked at him.

"This is asinine!" screamed Nardus as he faced the man in blue once more. His head pounded. "You know very well—"

"Silence!" roared the man in blue. "One more outburst and you'll be bound and gagged."

Nardus shook from head to toe with rage. *Madness! This is all madness! This cannot be happening!*

The man in blue returned his glasses back to his face. "I assure you, Mr. Remison, this is indeed happening. Every action you take yields consequences befitting the action."

The other Nardus is right. I've no chance here.

The man in blue cleared his throat. "Last, but certainly not least, we have the matter of thievery."

Nardus thrust his hands in the air. "I'm no thief!"

"No?" The man in blue shook his head and let out an exaggerated sigh. "Guards, empty his pockets."

I've nothing to hide.

The guards turned out all his pockets and found nothing in them.

The man in blue smiled a wicked grin. "Check the inner left pocket of his jacket."

The guard on Nardus's right reached into Nardus's jacket pocket and pulled out a small reddish-black stone.

Nardus gasped.

"Ah, yes." The man in blue rubbed his hands together. "*Ɛʈōn Dhef Dädh.* I don't suppose that just fell into your pocket by accident, did it?" His hearty laughter filled the room.

"That wasn't there before," said Nardus. "You're setting me up!"

"I'm merely presenting the facts, Mr. Remison." To the six men and women sitting on either side of him, the man in blue asked, "Do any of you require further proof of this man's guilt in any of the charges brought upon him?"

"No," they said in unison.

"Perfect," said the man in blue.

The guards flanking Nardus grabbed him by the arms.

"I hereby sentence you, Nardus Remison, to death," said the man in blue.

The word "death" hung around Nardus's neck like a noose and hindered his breathing. The other Nardus had spoken the truth.

Nardus had no words. He'd courted death on many occasions, but the finality of knowing he'd now face it head-on left him frail and vulnerable. He couldn't bear its weight. His legs faltered, and he fell forward, but the guards held onto his arms and kept him upright. His heart thrummed in his ears like a funeral dirge.

Death? What was this all for? What about my family?

The man in blue continued as Nardus silently hung between the guards, "You'll be taken to the temple's entrance where your soul will be fed to *Dūrz Dhef Zōallz Demd*. Your body will be left for Tharos the Cunning."

The man in blue raised the gavel for a final swing.

No, no, no!

"Wait!" exclaimed Nardus. The gavel slammed down on the sound block with a final *whack* and expelled what remained of his hope. The room and the council drifted from his vision and the room with the other Nardus came rushing back in its place.

The other Nardus laughed. "As you saw, there's no point in you continuing. Be at peace with yourself and know that you died with our family."

Nardus held his head, dizzy. "It's not that simple."

The other Nardus withdrew the sword and rested it on his own shoulder. "But it can be. I'll take the burden of Bradwr's betrayal and of his death. I'll take the pain of knowing that our twins died because of us. I'll bear it all and you can die blameless."

Vitara, what should I do? Can I trust myself? Can I trust this other Nardus?

The burden of Nardus's past weighed him down like an anchor in the sand, a constant reminder of all his shortcomings. The idea that it could be erased from his memory filled him with hope. He imagined peering into Savannah's beautiful violet eyes and hearing her precious laughter again.

I don't deserve happiness. I forsook everything. I'm damned, aren't I?

The other Nardus chuckled. "That's the beauty of my plan. Let me take your place and all wrongs *will* be righted. Zäțūr *will* welcome you into *Kinzhdm ef Häfn* where you can spend eternity with Vitara and our children."

Is it really possible? Can it be so simple?

The other Nardus lowered his sword and rested the tip of its blade on the floor. "Not everything has to be difficult. All you must do is drop to your knees and allow me to finish this."

Nardus closed his eyes as all the deaths played in his mind. His heart rent as he watched Vitara and Savannah fall from Rydar's back. A dagger twisted his gut as he pulled back the black scarf worn by Bradwr. Tears slid down his cheeks as he crawled over to the remains of Shardan and Shanara.

So much blood. So much pain. Let it be done, Ӟäțūr. Let it be done.

Nardus dropped to his knees. His pulse quickened. He opened his eyes and stared up at the other Nardus—his mirrored self. "Make it quick."

I'm coming, children. I'll see you soon, my love.

The other Nardus screamed with rage and lunged forward, his sword held high. He spun around and swung the sword low.

This isn't right. This isn't me. This is madness!

Nardus dropped to the floor and rolled to the side, narrowly escaping the wrath of the other Nardus's blade.

I must fight for my family, not give up!

Nardus rolled again and the blade sliced into the floor where his head had just been, sending splinters of wood flying.

This isn't right!

"Stay still!" screamed the other Nardus. He thrust the sword down, through the side of Nardus's thigh, and into the floor, pinning Nardus down.

Nardus screamed as pain shot up his leg and into his side. "I've changed my mind. I don't want to die. Stop this madness!"

The other Nardus yanked on the hilt of the sword, but it was lodged deep in the floor. He spat on the floor. "Your fate's sealed. Death approaches." He stepped on Nardus's pinned leg and yanked on the sword again. Nardus screamed.

Ӟäțūr, my God. I'm so sorry. Save me!

Nardus's vision blurred and he wiped away the tears. He fought against the pain and reached for the knife at his belt. His hands trembled violently and made the simple task nearly impossible.

The other Nardus worked frantically to free the sword and paid Nardus no attention. He grunted and tilted the sword from side to side. "Why won't you come out?"

Every movement of the sword in Nardus's thigh was brutally painful. Nardus grimaced and ground his teeth to counter the pain. His eyes crossed, but he kept his fingers working on freeing his knife.

Come on! Just free it, already.

"I'm working on it," barked the other Nardus.

Nardus pulled the knife free. He sat up and yanked the knife across the other Nardus's groin and severed his artery. Blood spewed from the wound and the other Nardus screamed in agony. The other Nardus collapsed to the floor and clutched his groin.

"What have you done?" whimpered the other Nardus. Blood pooled around him.

"What's right. The past cannot be undone. Those memories are mine to bear. Every single day I wonder if Shardan and Shanara would still be alive had I stayed with them. Had my reaction to the first arrow been faster, would Vitara and Savannah still live? Could I have warned them in time?" Nardus spat on the floor. "I'll never know those answers. I may never see my family again, but I'll be damned if I ever stop trying."

Nardus took a deep breath and placed the hilt of his knife between his teeth. He twisted and yanked his leg away from the blade of the sword until it cut its way through. He spat out the knife and gritted his teeth. "Damn!"

Nardus's heart hammered and his fear drove him. He tore off part of his shirt, pushed the flap of flesh hanging from his thigh back together, and wrapped it tight with the piece of his shirt.

"Let me live. Let me live."

I must finish this. I'm so close. I can feel it.

He pulled himself up and leaned against the sword.

The other Nardus lay there, whimpering and bleeding out. "You'll never bring them back. They're dead. And you will be too."

Nardus grabbed the hilt of the sword. Its mezhik flowed into him. "Maybe. Maybe not. But one thing's certain—you're dead!"

Nardus yanked the sword free, limped over to the other Nardus, and cut off his head.

The five torches in the chandelier dimmed and then fizzled out, leaving him in darkness.

Nardus spat. "Mezhik be damned."

Yellow light emanated from the crystal pedestal and lit the room. Nardus looked at the floor, where the other Nardus had lain. The other Nardus and the pool of blood were gone.

Nardus stood right in front of the pedestal, close enough to touch it. The small reddish-black stone, ʔțōn Dhef Dädh, sat twelve inches from his outstretched fingers. He didn't remember putting his hand out.

For my family.

The stone shot from the pedestal and into Nardus's hand. He closed his fingers around it. It beat in his hand like a heart. He shivered.

The heart of darkness.

CHAPTER THIRTY-ONE

Aria teeter-tottered between anger and fear, sadness and longing, and every other emotion imaginable. The way Lord Rosai had locked her in the carriage and sent it speeding through the Daltura Hills boiled her blood. He gave no thought to her abilities and skills; she could've helped him escape as well. The fear of Lord Rosai never returning, having been killed or captured, paralyzed her.

I'm nothing without him. I'm a hollow shell, void of everything, without him. Ɂäʈūr, bring him back to me. Maybe injured just a bit, but not a lot, though. Or maybe just damage his pride.

Ugh. That's selfish of me. I know he was only trying to protect me. Ɂäʈūr, please bring him back safe and in one piece.

The past few hours dragged like days as the carriage continued its journey south and forced her along for the ride. No matter the tactic she used to get the driver's attention, he paid her none.

She plopped down on the seat, having exhausted all her ideas and herself in the process. She decided her time would be better spent daydreaming about her new life and coming up with a list of questions she felt pertained to her future role as queen.

I wonder what it feels like to use mezhik. Does it feel the same as it does when it's being used on me? Her arms and legs prickled with gooseflesh as she thought about the first time Lord Rosai touched her with his mezhik. Heat warmed her face as the desire for him rose inside her.

If that's how using mezhik feels, why would anyone ever stop using it? She giggled as an image of people walking around and using mezhik on themselves popped into her head. *It'd be a much happier world.*

She had no idea what it felt like to be with a man who hadn't forced himself on her, and, until she met Lord Rosai, she hadn't cared to know. *He's so kind and gentle with me. Not a worthless pig like the others. Oh, I want to make him happy. Ƨäţūr, please heal me and let me bear him children. I know he'd make a great father.*

Does he already have children? Aria sat up straight as a sense of alarm rose within her. *If he does, is he already married? Did she die? How did she die? He didn't tire of her and put her down like a lame horse, did he?* Her heart raced in her chest with so many questions and images of all the ways he could've killed his wife.

She balled her fists. "Enough!" Her chest heaved like she'd ran a great distance. "Why am I driving myself mad with conjecture?"

She slumped onto her side and then drew her knees to her chest. *I'm a bit unhinged. How will I ever be queen when I can't even settle my mind? I'll be no more than a shadow at his side, or maybe something he uses to distract the men he deals with. I should just tell him I've changed my mind, that I don't care for him, and that I find his presence repulsive.*

But how could I look him in the face and tell him those lies? I do care for him, and he's the most handsome man I've ever met. Ugh. Ƨäţūr, what should I do? Why is everything always so hard?

Then there's the issue of mezhik. If I left, how would I ever learn to use my mezhik? He'd probably force me to wear this stupid collar for the rest of my life.

Aria's eyes bulged, and her chest tightened. *If he's dead, how will I ever get this thing off? Is he the only one who can take it off? Are there others like us? Do all mezhik people have the same powers, or do different people have different powers? There are so many questions I need answers to. Where is he?*

Tears filled her eyes as worry over Lord Rosai settled in again. She reached down and pulled the blanket up from the floor and stretched it over herself. *Ƨäţūr, I trust You and Your plan. I just wish I knew what it was.*

† † †

Lord Rosai walked into existence just outside the northern town gates of Daltura. A portly boy stumbled and fell to the ground—his eyes stricken with disbelief. Lord Rosai offered him a hand, but the boy shrank away.

Lord Rosai stared down at the boy. "What's your name, boy?"

"C-Calen," said the boy.

Lord Rosai looked around. They were alone. "And what is it you're doing out here?"

Calen stood and dusted off his trousers. "Nothing, sir. Sometimes I come out here to be alone. No one ever bothers me out here."

Lord Rosai chuckled. "Yet here I stand, more bothersome than most."

"No sir, you've not bothered me one bit."

Lord Rosai reached into his leather satchel and withdrew his diary.

Calen's eyes filled with wonder. "Is that like your field guide? Do you keep track of everyone you meet in there? Or do you go on quests and draw plants and animals and creatures that you encounter? Sometimes I draw things I see. I'm not very good at drawing though. No one ever seems to guess what it is that I've drawn."

Lord Rosai shook his head. "This book is certainly none of those. It's rarer than you could possibly imagine."

"May I touch it?"

"No," snapped Lord Rosai. "Hold on a minute, Calen. I must check on something."

"I can go." Calen turned to leave. "I—"

"We've not finished our conversation. Would it not be rude of you to up and leave? Give me a minute."

Calen turned back around and kicked at the ground. "Yes, sir."

Lord Rosai flipped the diary open to the first page. He pulled his fountain pen from its hiding place within the folds of his robes and tapped the blank page with its tip. A moment later, words bled onto the page in thick, black ink.

'All you commanded has been completed. -Murtag'

Lord Rosai tapped the page again with the tip of the pen and the words disappeared. *Aria will surely be pleased with the news.* He closed the book, placed it back in his satchel, and slid the pen back into his pocket.

Soon everything will be in place. My father's fallen kingdom will finally rise again.

Had he been alone and a man of lesser constitution, he would've danced around and expunged the excitement bundled up inside. Instead, he allowed himself a smile.

Lord Rosai eyed Calen. "Do you have a father?"

Calen pushed a small rock around with his foot. "No—well yes. Sort of I guess. I don't ever see him. He's in prison."

Lord Rosai hadn't thought about his father, Pugnus, in a long time. The people had called the man the Iron Fist because of his barbaric and sadistic ruling methods.

Can't say I miss you, Father. I do envy the power and control you possessed, though. But it will soon be mine anyway.

Amidst one of his military campaigns, Pugnus raped and impregnated Lord Rosai's mother and left her for dead on the side of the road. Lord Rosai harbored no ill will toward him for it. His mother, Dedre, was a weak and feeble-minded woman. Had he been in his father's position, he would've killed her when he'd finished with her.

Lord Rosai crossed his arms. "Never be ashamed of where you come from, Calen. I never even knew my father. Do you live with your mother then?"

Calen rubbed his eyes and sniffed. "No sir. She died when I was little. I live with my aunt."

"Be thankful you have someone who takes care of you. I knew my mother, but she certainly had no love for me. Sounds a bit like your father."

Dedre's passing a few years back held no significance to Lord Rosai either, seeing as how she'd sent him away to a group of religious zealots known as Fekᴇzhn dhä Räd just weeks after giving birth to him. *Brain-washed bleeders are what they are.*

In Lord Rosai's early teens, Dedre came crawling back, seeking a relationship with her precious son. *Pathetic.* He acquiesced to her request only to learn the truth of his roots.

With the aid of a memory spell, she finally revealed his father's identity. From that moment forward, he took on his father's last name, Rosai. He'd never had the opportunity to meet the man face-to-face, since Pugnus had been killed in battle long before Lord Rosai knew of his biological connection.

I will not waste my seed as you did, Father. As my wife and queen, Aria will bear me many children.

Aria.

The thought of being with her again, of sitting across from her in the carriage, fueled his desire for her. He willed the horses pulling the carriage to run faster, begging them to bring her to him as quickly as possible. He loathed the idea of growing fond of anyone, especially a woman, but something about her left him powerless in her presence.

I will take the world and give it to you, my queen.

The thundering of hooves clopped in the air, pulled Lord Rosai from his thoughts, and sent his heart into a frenzy. He smiled at Calen, rubbed his thumb across his fingers, and produced four copper coins where there'd been none before.

Calen's eyes widened.

"Well, Calen, forget everything you've seen and heard here, and these copper coins are yours." He smiled at Calen and extended his coin-filled hand forward.

"I can't take your money, sir." Calen stepped backward. "Don't worry, though. I won't say anything. I don't have any friends, and no one would believe me if I told them what I saw anyway."

"I have a way of reading people, Calen. I trust you're true to your word. And don't be bothered by those around you. They may ignore you now, but one day, I believe, they will look to you in the time of their greatest need." His words had no backing, but the look of wonder on Calen's face was worth the white lie.

Lord Rosai grabbed Calen's wrist with his free hand and dropped the coins into Calen's hand. He pushed Calen's fingers closed over the coins and stopped him from saying anything else.

"I insist. Now, off with you before someone sees us together." He shooed Calen away with his hand.

Calen stuffed the coins into his right trouser pocket. "Yes, sir." He ran through the tall, wooden gates and disappeared into the hustle-bustle of the town.

A few minutes later, the carriage rounded the top of the last hill, still in the distance. Lord Rosai walked thirty paces toward the speeding carriage before he realized he'd moved at all.

Just the thought of that woman makes a fool of me.

The carriage approached him and slowed. Its wheels threw globs of mud about as they dug into the deep-rutted road and slid to a halt. The horses' nostrils flared, and plumes of vapor rose into the crisp winter air. The driver sprang from his seat atop the carriage and hustled to open the door as Lord Rosai marched over to it.

Aria leapt from the carriage seat and pushed through the door, nearly knocking the driver over. She jumped into Lord Rosai's open arms, wrapped hers tightly around his neck, and planted a kiss on his lips. Before he even had a chance to secure her in his arms, she pulled away. She smacked him across the face with an open palm. He gawked at her.

"How dare you lock me in that godforsaken carriage and send it racing off when you're surrounded by a bunch of well-armed *zheballin*!" Her cheeks flushed. "I thought you might be dead! How could you do that to me?"

He wanted to inject a response into her ranting, but she continued, "You think that just because I'm a woman that I have no place fighting at your side? I'll have you know that I've fought many worse things than those creepy little *zheballin* and survived. I don't need or appreciate you trying to protect me. I'm not a helpless young girl. I can take care of myself.

"And, furthermore, don't just stand there with a smirk on your face while I stand here making a scene. You're lucky there's no one else around besides your worthless driver. And, speaking of him, he didn't stop once to make sure I was okay. How rude can he possibly be? I'm a woman. I won't be silenced and locked away again." She punched him in the chest, but softly. By the end of her tirade she panted like the horses.

Lord Rosai broke into laughter. "I've never been put in my place like that, not even by a man. You truly are my missing half, woman. I was so empty inside while we were separated, my heart an open chasm without a bottom."

"If that's supposed to be some sort of apology, you'll have to try harder." Her voice was stern, but she couldn't hold back the beginnings of a smile. In her eyes, he saw the truth behind her shallow words: a longing to be with him. A longing that mirrored his own.

He took her hand, bent down on one knee, and kissed the back of her hand. He lingered a while with his lips pressed against her soft, cold skin.

He looked up at her radiant green eyes. "My queen, please accept my sincerest apology for placing my needs above yours. I am truly sorry for locking you in the carriage and sending you on your way. I promise it will not happen again. I believe a lavish lunch is in your near future, if you'll forgive my folly and accept the invitation to dine with me this fine day."

She smiled down at him. "Food isn't the way to a woman's heart, but it's a good start." She pulled on his hand and he rose to his feet. She wrapped her arms around his waist and drew in a deep breath as she squeezed him. "How do you always smell so good?"

"Some secrets can never be revealed." He put his arms around her, lifted her off her feet, and twirled around. "That one will follow me to my grave."

"Fine," she said. "But you must agree to answer some questions for me before we travel any farther."

"Oh?" His eyebrows rose in feigned surprise. He set her back down, stepped backward, and wrapped his chin in the palm of his hand. "And what might those questions be?"

"Have you ever been married before, or are you still married?"

"No to the first, and that makes the answer to the second obvious."

"Good. Do you have any children?"

"Not yet," he said with a smile and a wink.

Her half-smile response left him uneasy. *Doesn't she want children? Surely it can't be me.* He'd mastered the art of reading people, but somehow, she was even more skillful at hiding her true self. *I'll find a way to get inside that beautiful head of yours.*

"How did you escape from the *zheballin*, and how did you get here before I did? How is that even possible?"

"There are many types of mezhik, and many ways it can be used. For example, a wizard may have been born with *mezhik äällämäntall*, that is, elemental mezhik. Such a wizard would be able to manipulate an element like water. There is also *mezhik mäntall*, or mental mezhik. Those born with this type of mezhik can manipulate space and move things with their mind."

"Manipulate space? How do you mean?"

"Like teleportation. This ability allows the wielder to move between locations in an instant, never occupying the space between the two points. I have this ability, and that's how I got here before you. Once I knew you were safely inside the carriage, I teleported here and waited for your arrival."

Aria's eyes narrowed. "Why didn't you just teleport into the carriage? Better yet, why are we even using the carriage? Can't you just teleport us to your castle?"

He smiled at her. *Perceptive girl.* "Well, you can't teleport into a moving target; bad things would come of that. And as far as teleporting the two of us to the castle... well that's not possible. One can easily teleport while carrying inanimate objects, but not with another living being."

Aria frowned. "Well, that seems a bit limited."

"Oh, I'm not saying that it's impossible. However, every time a wizard uses their mezhik, it depletes their energy. The amount of energy that it would take to teleport just two people would most likely kill a wizard."

"I see. So how do you know when you need to stop using mezhik? And how do you recover from it?"

"Think of it like a physical ability. When you run, your body expends energy and you grow weak. To recover, you need food and rest. It's the same with mezhik. You'll feel it draining you. Most wizards wind up passing out before they get to the point of killing themselves."

"Huh. I guess that makes sense. So, what kind of mage do you think I am? Can you tell just by looking at me?"

"Of course."

Aria's eyes widened.

"The combination of your hair and eye color, along with your aura, determines the type of wizard you are." He circled her, taking in every revealing curve of her body. *Magnificent creature.*

"Well?" she asked, her hands firmly on her hips. "What am I?"

Lord Rosai laughed. "You're a beautiful woman."

"Ugh." She crossed her arms and turned her back to him. "I should know better than to believe you."

"I wish it were that simple. Mages have the capacity to master most types of mezhik, but they usually concentrate on two or three main types. We won't know what your naturalistic abilities are until we begin your training. That's why it's so dangerous for new wizards to roam about without proper training. Even more so for mages. That's why the collar you're wearing was created—to prevent potential catastrophes."

"I don't care anymore," she said with a huff. "What are we eating for lunch? I'm starved."

"For you, my queen, the sky's the limit. Maybe a bowl of oxtail soup and a nice roasted boar sandwich to go along with it. Oh, and a nice glass of ale to wash it all down."

Aria's face turned a few shades whiter. "I'm sure whatever you decide will be perfect."

He placed his hand on her shoulder and lightly squeezed. "Is everything okay, Aria?"

She turned and rested her head on his chest. "I just feel so out of place at times. I've never had any of those things, and it embarrasses me. How will I make a good queen when I know so little of the world?"

He placed his hand on the back of her head and held her tight. "You're an exquisite woman and will come into your own soon enough. In time, there will be none the world has seen such as you." He kissed the top of her head.

"Food, then?"

"Certainly. Let me just change out of these dingy robes." He spun in a circle and his robes were replaced with slacks, a white, collared shirt, and a black overcoat lined with fur. He donned a black, wide-brimmed hat on his head too.

"I can't wait until I can do that."

He squeezed the brim of the hat between his thumb and pointer finger and pulled the hat down slightly. "Soon enough, my queen."

He grabbed Aria's hand in his, twined his fingers with hers, and led her through the town gates. In his mind, everything at that moment was a picture of perfection. The woman at his side was more beautiful than any other in the world.

Aria halted at the corner of two roads, and brought Lord Rosai to a stop as well. She turned to him. "I have one last question."

He looked down at her. *My world's already yours.* "Anything for you."

Aria squinted in the bright sunlight. "If we're to be married, shouldn't I know your first name? Or am I to always call you Lord Rosai?"

He chuckled. "To the world, I am Lord Rosai. You may call me Pravus."

CHAPTER THIRTY-TWO

Rakzar grabbed the White Knight by his feet and dragged his limp body through the ground level of Castle Portador Tempestade. Smoke and flames surrounded them, and the castle crashed down around them, but Rakzar ignored the danger. In fact, he relished it.

What else did he have to look forward to? Once he dealt with the White Knight, his life would be meaningless. The truth of it struck a nerve and set him on edge.

Over the last few days, a single thought buzzed around in his head like a swarm of wasps and stung his resolve: *He's not just a boy.* He swatted the thought away several times, but each time it flew right back into his mind and stung him again.

Nestled into the northwestern corner of the castle, a small courtyard overlooked the edge of the cliff. From the courtyard, a set of stairs led down along the face of the cliff and into the dungeons below the castle. He'd escorted many prisoners down to the dungeons over the years, but the thought of taking the White Knight down there set his heart racing.

The fates are shining down on me today. First the fire, and now this.

Just ahead of them, daylight shone through the smoke and highlighted the archway that led into the courtyard; it looked like a portal to another world. The first time he'd walked through it he'd smacked his head against the solid rock surface and had earned himself a horrendous headache that lingered for hours after. This time, he ducked under the four-foot deep archway and dragged the White Knight's body behind him.

At the center of the courtyard, a large pile of ash had replaced the enormous frilac bush that once stood there; it still smoldered. Rakzar inhaled deeply, happy to be outside again and mostly free from the toxic smoke; the smell of the sea refreshed him.

Rakzar looked down at the White Knight. *Still out cold. He really is just a boy.* Rakzar just couldn't wrap his head around how this boy struck such fear in men—powerful men, at that.

Rakzar picked up the White Knight like a sack of potatoes and threw him over his shoulder. He walked across the courtyard—to its northern end—and made his way down the steep and narrow stairs. At the bottom of the stairs, the door that led into the dungeons hung wide open.

The smells of mold, urine, feces, and death mixed in with the salty smell of the sea and the smoke created an interesting concoction as it wafted from the open doorway; the stench both repulsed and stimulated him all at once.

He ducked through the doorway and made his way along the dark passage to one of the first cells. He pulled on the door. *Locked.* He peered through the slit in the door, but saw nothing. Every other cell seemed to be locked and unoccupied as well, save for one on the right—nearly at the end of the fourth block of cells. The cell door stood wide open.

His hackles rose. *Something's not right.*

He stopped in the middle of the passage and laid the White Knight on the floor. He grabbed the battle-axes from his back and twirled them in his paw-like hands. He sniffed the air, but couldn't get a read on what stalked them.

Rakzar turned in a circle. "Show yourself." His ears twisted forward and backward as he listened for the faintest of sounds.

Click.

Rakzar spun around but found nothing behind him. "I'm not fond of games, my friend." He growled deep in his throat, frustrated. "You're taking away from my perfect day. You don't wanna be doing that."

Scratch.

The sound—a blade scraped across a whetstone—came from his left. He twisted and swung his axes wide, but connected with nothing. "I assure you, you're toying with the wrong beast. Show yourself, and I'll consider not killing you."

"Drop your weapons," hissed a voice.

Rakzar couldn't pinpoint its location. *Where are you hiding?*

Rakzar gritted his teeth. "And why would I do that?"

"Perhaps you need some incentive."

The White Knight's limp body lifted from the floor and a blade slid under his neck.

"Show yourself," growled Rakzar, fed up with the game of cat and mouse. *You're dead, plain and simple.*

From nothing, the creature materialized as it pulled a brown hood from its bald head. "This cloak is a wonder, is it not?"

"Saurian." Rakzar snorted. "How did I not smell your wretched presence?"

"It hides not only sight, but also most sounds and smells, even from ones with heightened senses such as yourself."

Rakzar stepped forward. "What's your name, saurian? And why are you here?"

"I am called Sardis. My master sent me here many months ago to wait for this boy. I didn't know when to wait, but I knew where."

"Well, *Sardis*," he said, mocking the lizard's hissing voice. "Kill him now, or I'll kill him later. It makes no difference to me. He's my enemy. But if you do kill him, I *will* kill you."

He took another step toward Sardis and the White Knight. *I need a distraction.*

"Back off, or I'll kill all three of you."

Rakzar sniffed the air. *The dryte.*

"Three, you say?" Rakzar knew full well whom the saurian meant by it.

"Never mind that. Drop your weapons, or the boy dies. Now!"

Rakzar bent down and gently laid his axes on the ground. "Satisfied?"

"Good choice. Now step back."

"Perhaps we can come to some sort of arrangement." Rakzar turned his back to Sardis and walked a few paces down the passage, showing the saurian that he had no fear of him. "You give me the boy, and you can do whatever you like with the girl."

"I never said anything about a girl," he hissed.

Rakzar turned back to Sardis. "You didn't need to. I can smell her."

"I have a better plan. I'll take them both and you walk out of here alive."

Rakzar thought he saw the White Knight's eyes flutter under his eyelids.

He drew closer to Sardis to confirm it. *Just the distraction I need.* He took two more slow steps toward Sardis, closing the gap to a mere three feet.

"One more step and he's—"

The White Knight moaned. Sardis looked down for the briefest of moments and gave Rakzar the opening he needed. Rakzar lunged, grabbed Sardis's face in his paw-like hand, and slammed him to the floor. He dug his claws into Sardis's slippery, ugly face, and Sardis screamed.

Sardis relinquished his hold on the White Knight, and the White Knight rolled to the floor. Sardis stabbed at Rakzar's arm with his blade, but the blade failed to penetrate Rakzar's thick fur and skin.

Sardis stood no chance against Rakzar's strength; Rakzar lifted Sardis's head up and slammed it into the floor, repeatedly. Sardis squealed and whipped his tail around and struck Rakzar's face with it.

Rakzar roared and rose to his feet. He still held Sardis's head in his paw-like hand, and hurled Sardis against the wall. He wrapped his massive arm around Sardis's torso and twisted Sardis's head until his neck snapped. Sardis's body slackened, and Rakzar let him fall to the floor in a heap. Blood oozed from his punctured face.

Words are meaningless if you can't back them up.

The White Knight leaned against the wall and clutched his throat—blood ran between his fingers. Rakzar grabbed the White Knight by the back of his shirt and dragged him down the passageway to the cell with the open door.

In the cell, he shackled the White Knight and chained him to the wall—opposite the dryte.

Rakzar ripped the cloth off Rayah's head. "I'll be back in a little while."

Rakzar exited the cell and slammed the door shut behind him.

He's not just a boy.

✝ ✝ ✝

With a final gag, Rayah spat the rancid rag from her mouth. "Alderan!" His condition broke her heart, but the fact that he still lived overjoyed her.

Thank You for keeping him alive, Żäṭūr!

"Rayah?" Alderan coughed, his voice barely a whisper.

Rayah leaned forward and the chains that bound her rattled. "Are you okay?"

"I think so, but I can't see anything. My eyes feel as though they're on fire. How about you?"

"I'm okay now that I know you're alive!"

Alderan slumped against his restraints. "I just don't understand."

"Understand what?"

"Why *am* I still alive? How is it possible?"

"Rakzar brought you down here. How did he find you?"

"I don't know, Rayah. I think he saved my life, though."

"What? He's hunted you for months and now you think he saved your life? Why would he do that?"

"I don't know. Maybe killing me that way wasn't satisfying enough for him."

She worried for him; he'd obviously endured a great ordeal and talked nonsense. *Maybe he hit his head really hard, and his memories are all mixed up.*

"Are you sure you're okay?"

"I came through the mirror after you and got lost in all the smoke and fire. I was nearly dead when Rakzar showed up. I thought he'd finish the job right there, but instead he knocked me out, and then I woke up here with you."

Rayah's world spun upside down. *What's Rakzar's plan for us? Why didn't he kill us already? What's he waiting for?* None of it made sense. Unease stirred her stomach.

"Where are we?" he asked. "It smells terrible."

"In a dungeon cell below the castle."

"How did you wind up down here?"

"That lizard man brought me down here. He was waiting for you to show up so he could kill you."

"What happened to him? Is he still here?"

"I can't be sure, but I think Rakzar killed him."

"But why? Why would he kill him? He wanted the same thing. They both wanted me dead. What's changed?"

It all confused Rayah; less than a day ago Rakzar stood outside Alderan's house, ready to kill them both. *Ʒäţūr, I hope this is all part of Your plan.*

Outside the cell, claws clicked on the floor.

"I think he's coming back," she whispered.

The clicking grew louder.

Tears trickled down Alderan's blackened face and left streaks in the layer of soot. "I'm sorry I let you down again, Rayah. You deserve someone far greater than me."

"I'm sorry, too."

The cell door swung open; Rakzar stood there with a strange look on his face. He turned around, picked up two buckets that sat on the floor behind him, and brought them into the cell.

What in Centauria's going on? Is he going to drown us?

† † †

Rakzar set the buckets down. "One's for washing, and one's for drinking."

Rayah stared at him, her mouth agape.

Rakzar looking straight at Rayah. "I'm going to release you from your restraints. If you try anything other than cleaning yourselves up and drinking some of the water, I won't hesitate to kill you. If you try to remove his restraints, I'll kill you both. Understood?"

Rayah nodded, her eyes wide and her mouth clamped shut.

Good. You'd better stay scared.

Rakzar removed her restraints and then walked out into the passageway. He shut the door behind him and slumped against the wall, exhausted and confused.

What am I doing? His mind swirled with so many questions. *Have I come to kill them or to help them? Why would I even want to help them? He's a worthless human, and she's a filthy dryte! They mean nothing to me.*

He's not just a boy.

Nothing in his life had ever been confusing before receiving this task. Everything had always been so simple: follow orders and you'll be rewarded. *Why do I feel compelled to break away from my orders now? How did this boy get under my skin?* He slammed his fist into the stone floor.

He's not just a boy.

Rakzar stared down the dimly lit passage and at the body of the saurian.

Why didn't I just let you kill them both? He'd killed so many times before that it was like second nature. Men, women, and children of all races and breeds—he never discriminated. On a few occasions, he'd even killed some of his own kind.

The. White. Knight. I've breathed life into this fantasy and now I can't seem to bring myself to kill him. Had he not just killed the saurian, he would've questioned his warrior's resolve. As it was, he felt very off.

Maybe I need to go run this off, see what came of Dragnus. That prideful fool's the one who brought this on me in the first place. Some fresh air might clear my head, give me the resolve to finish the job.

He's not just a boy.

He pulled himself up and unstrapped the pack from his back. He removed all his other personal effects and armor as well, save the brown sash around his waist. Already, he felt freer than he had in a long time.

He dropped on all fours and bolted through the passageways. When he reached the stairs that led out of the dungeons, he took them three at a time. From the courtyard, only the archway that led into the castle remained of the western wall. Most of the northern wall had fallen over the cliff and into the sea below.

Rakzar navigated the smoldering rubble and headed toward the part of the eastern wall that still stood. *Figures the single portion of wall still standing would be the part where Dragnus hanged from.*

He made his way around the wall—to the eastern facing side of it. Dragnus still hung from the end of the rope and clung to life. Rakzar growled. *Climb up there. Cut him down and watch him fall.*

I'd probably die along with him.

Would that be so bad? What do I have to live for anyway?

Rakzar shook his head, but the chaos in his mind remained.

But think of the rush! Maybe the wall would fall if you were to climb up there. You could ride it all the way to the ground.

"No. Dragnus will die either way." He grabbed his head in his hands. "I just need some fresh air."

He raced down the hill and into the valley, and followed the Solas River upstream into the western section of the Reis Duron Grasslands. He ran as hard as he could for about an hour before he collapsed into the snow-laden grass.

The crisp air invigorated him, and the sweet smell of the winter silverbuds that grew along the river bank intoxicated him. He rolled around in the snow like he had as a pup. He'd forgotten the feeling of being free, how good it felt.

He lay on his back and stared up at the blue sky and the thin, wind-blown clouds. *How can I go back? Better yet, why should I go back? I have no allegiances. Why should I have to answer to anyone?*

The White Knight. Alderan. He's not just a boy.

It became more and more obvious that he had no chance of killing the boy. However, he knew with certainty that he needed closure with the boy-who-would-be-knight. If the boy didn't have the answers he sought, he knew of someone who just might.

From the time he was a young pup, he knew he was nothing more than a ruthless killing machine. He was born and bred for it; killing pumped through his veins just as much as blood did.

Yet something new grew inside of him, a yearning to be more than what he was bred for. His cunning and ruthlessness had brought him to this exact moment, but he knew they wouldn't be his driving force going forward.

He stood with a renewed sense of self-worth. Though still uncertain of his purpose, he knew he'd just have to find it. At present, he had some unfinished business to attend to. *Wouldn't be surprised to find the boy and his girlfriend long gone by the time I get back.*

He smiled, a genuine smile. *Life's full of surprises. They won't be prepared for me.* He dropped on all fours, shook the snow from his fur, and headed back downstream.

He's not just a boy.

Then what is he? Did he even want an answer?

✝ ✝ ✝

Amicus crawled through the rubble of the castle, distraught by the loss of his family and everyone he knew, but he'd resolved to fight back. He had no hope of finding anyone alive, but a voice in the back of his mind urged him to search for survivors.

If there are survivors, guide my hands. Make me Your instrument, Zäṭūr.

The rubble was piled so high and the stones so large that he knew in his heart that no one could've survived, even if they'd survived the attack. *I'll still search.* Amicus called out several times as he moved from one section to the next, but he never received a response. He'd all but given up when a thought popped into his head: *the dungeons.*

The dungeons sprawled deep beneath the castle, and the two didn't actually connect directly. Centuries before, the lord of the castle at the time contracted the derros to scale the cliffs and carve the dungeons out of them. The massive job took decades to complete, but the effort paid for itself. The most ruthless men, women, and beasts in the Ancient Realm called the dungeon's rock walls home, and not one of them had ever escaped.

Amicus made his way to the northwest corner of the castle and descended the narrow stairs. At the bottom, he slipped inside the open door and then set his pack on the floor. The dungeons were his life for so long, so he anticipated the horrendous stench, but all the crying and smoke left him so stuffy that he smelled nothing.

Ɂäṭūr, guide me. If it's Your will, keep me safe.

A few of the torches in the passageway still burned. He pulled the closest one from its sconce. Three main passageways branched from where he stood. The ones to his left and right led down to the lower sections of the dungeons, and the one straight ahead led to many offshoots and more than a thousand cells. Because of laziness and ease of access, the main level housed all the prisoners. In his many years of service, Amicus knew of no exceptions.

If someone were hiding, they'd most likely go down to one of the lower levels. Less chance of being discovered. Much smaller areas to search as well.

He closed his eyes and slowed his breathing. He drew a map of the dungeons in his mind, tracing every nook and cranny he could remember. He recalled that to the left, a floor below, a narrow opening sat at the far end of the passageway. Without having direct knowledge of its existence, most anyone would miss it. To the right, two floors below, he could think of no place one could hide other than in the cells.

The left it is.

He opened his eyes, turned to the left, and made his way along the narrow passageway and down the crudely formed stairs that led to the floor below. No windows existed in the dungeons. A few vent holes snaked up through the layers of rock, but their distance from the surface kept the natural light out. And, because of the scarcity of prisoners at this level, they never kept the torches lit. Without his torch, Amicus would've ventured into complete darkness.

The clicking of his boots on the hard, rock floor echoed through the passageway as he crept from cell to cell. Fear prickled his skin, and his pulse raced as he peered through each of the narrow slits on the cell doors. Large rats startled him a few times, but nothing else moved.

Amicus stopped just past the last cell. A few feet ahead, the passageway ended—unless you knew of the narrow opening like he did. He waved the torch in front of him, but saw nothing.

Something leapt onto his back. He cried out and dropped the torch. He reached behind his head with both hands and tried to pry the thing off his back, but the thing held on with surprising strength and worked its hands around his neck.

Amicus backed into the wall repeatedly before the thing finally released its grip on him. He whirled around quickly, but only got a glimpse of the thing's naked, smooth-skinned, stark-white backside before it darted beyond the reaches of the torchlight.

"Wait!" Amicus said. "I won't hurt you."

During the scuffle, his torch had rolled across the floor and over to the entrance of the narrow opening. He bent down to pick it up, but the stash of items piled inside the small space stopped him short. Every kind of item imaginable filled the space from front to back and top to bottom: brushes, mirrors, rings, bracelets, pendants, goblets, wooden cups, old paintings, knives, daggers, and many other things.

How long has that thing been down here?

Amicus picked up the torch and squeezed into the narrow opening to get a better view.

"Mine!" cried the thing.

Amicus turned and waved the torch around to try and get a better idea of where the thing stood. About ten paces away, just beyond the reach of the light, two lime-green eyes glared at him, glowing like those of a cat. Amicus stepped out of the narrow space and a silhouette of a small person or child came into view.

Amicus held up his hand. "I'm not here to take your things."

"Mine." It beat its fists against its chest.

The thing was humanoid in shape, but definitely not human. *What are you? And where did you come from?* Amicus hadn't been down in this part of the dungeons for months and figured none of the other guards must've either.

"Amicus." He placed his hand on his chest. "I am Amicus."

"Eshtak." It beat its chest again.

The thing called Eshtak stepped into the light and Amicus nearly gasped.

Intricate skin art covered its pale white skin from head to toe, and it didn't seem to have a single hair on its entire body. Or clothing. *Definitely male.* Amicus wanted to avert his eyes, but where else could he look? He felt awkward no matter where he placed his focus.

Eshtak's bulbous nose protruded from his otherwise normal face and nearly consumed his thin, upper lip. His black lips cracked and peeled, and his non-existent chin sloped right into his neck. His ears were little more than holes on the sides of his head.

Amicus knelt. "Where did you come from, Eshtak?"

Eshtak bounced from one foot to the other. "Eshtak lives in castle. Eshtak uses hidden passage to stay out of view. Humans dislike Eshtak."

"Do you not wear clothing?"

Eshtak grinned at him with a mouthful of stained teeth. "Eshtak's clothes burn in fire. Eshtak free now!" He danced in a circle.

"I see. I think I may have a scarf you can wrap around yourself until we can find some proper clothes for you. I left it in my pack upstairs."

Eshtak clapped his hands together. "Eshtak find already!" He turned and disappeared into the darkness only to return moments later with Amicus's pack. He pulled the green scarf out of the pack and wrapped it around his neck several times.

Amicus laughed. "I was thinking you might want to wrap that around yourself a bit lower."

Eshtak shook his head violently. "Eshtak wear scarf on neck."

Can't argue with the logic, I suppose.

Amicus amazed himself at how quickly he'd grown fond of the little guy.

An hour ago, he thought he'd never laugh again. The pain of losing his family still gripped his heart and made him want to lay on the floor in a fetal position and cry, but knowing himself still capable of joy raised his spirits a little.

"Are there others down here, or just you?"

Eshtak's lower lip quivered. "Eshtak see dead. Eshtak cry for them. Eshtak see boy and girl. Eshtak see bad things too. Eshtak sorry."

A boy and a girl. Thank You for Your guidance, 2äṭūr.

Amicus took his pack and slung it over his shoulder. "Are they still here?"

Eshtak's face brightened. "Eshtak will show!" He lifted his four-fingered hand toward Amicus and waited for him to take it.

Amicus pulled himself back to his feet and took the little guy's hand. He nearly lost his footing and thought his arm might come out of its socket as Eshtak pulled him along the passageway and up the stairs. They started making their way along the main passageway when Amicus tripped over something and fell to his knees, bringing Eshtak down with him. Amicus looked back.

"Not sure what I tripped over," he said.

Eshtak stared at him with a puzzled look on his face.

"What?"

"Eshtak see dead. Amicus not see dead?"

Now he was the one puzzled. "What are you talking about?"

Eshtak let go of his hand and maneuvered around and behind him. Eshtak pointed at the ground, "Eshtak see dead lizard man."

Amicus still saw nothing but the floor. "There's nothing there, Eshtak."

I think there's something wrong with this little guy.

Eshtak nodded vigorously. He reached down, grabbed at the air, and then pretended to lift something up. "Here."

"There's—"

Amicus jumped back as a grey, scaly head materialized in the air. A moment later, the entire body became visible. Eshtak let go of the hood he held, and the lizard man's head fell back to the floor. *How did he see that?*

"Eshtak not lie." He grinned.

"Indeed, you haven't." *How could Eshtak see it when he couldn't?*

† † †

The last torch at their end of the passageway fizzled out and cast Alderan and Rayah in darkness. The deep shadows conjured images in Alderan's mind of his first encounter with Rakzar and the other gnolls. Yellow eyes surrounded him, and he shivered.

Rakzar left them alone hours before, but something had changed in him. *To what end? He's still gonna kill me, right?*

Rayah sat on the floor next to Alderan and rested her head on his shoulder. She squeezed his hand. "I never—"

"Shh!" said Alderan. "I think I heard voices." He held his breath and strained his ears.

"You're right," whispered Rayah. "Two distinct voices, but I can't make out what either of them are saying. Neither one of them is Rakzar though."

"I think you're right. Can you see anything through the slit in the door?"

"I doubt it, but I'll check."

Rayah flew over to the door and hovered in the air as she tried to see through the slit. The faint light silhouetted her.

"Well?" asked Alderan.

"I don't see anyone, but I think the light in the passageway might be getting brighter."

He pulled against his restraints and reaffirmed they hadn't wondrously come undone. The clanging chains shattered the silence.

"I thought you said to be quiet?" whispered Rayah from across the cell.

"I didn't know they'd make so much noise."

I really need to figure this mezhik thing out. We wouldn't even be here if I knew how to use it. The idea of having the potential for greatness yet being weak and powerless frustrated Alderan to no end.

"We can hear you," came a man's voice from farther down the passageway. "We're coming your way."

Rayah zipped back over to Alderan and settled down next to him. She wrapped her arm around his and squeezed it tight.

"I promise I won't let anything bad happen to you, Rayah. I swear it."

Rayah giggled. "My white knight in shining chains."

Alderan sighed. "You know what I mean."

"I do, but it's not me that I'm worried about. It's you. Losing you again isn't an option. We live together, we fight together, and we die together."

I love you.

He leaned over and kissed what he thought to be her right temple.

She giggled and shuddered. "That was my earlobe. I think I like that."

A small beam of light poured through the slit in the door and through the space under it. "You okay in there?" The man held a torch up to the slit in the door.

He knows we're in here. I suppose there's no point in pretending we're not. He might be able to help us.

"I think so," said Alderan. His voice cracked.

"Good," said the man. "My name's Amicus. I used to work in this dungeon. I'm going to unlock the door and come in. I'm here to help you, but I need you to stay where you are. Please don't make any sudden moves. I don't want anyone getting hurt. My friend Eshtak will hold the torch."

"Eshtak hold torch," said another voice. "Eshtak likes fire."

Alderan heard a key slide into the lock. Rayah squeezed his arm a little tighter. *Please, ẑäṭūr, let this man be a friend. If not, help me protect Rayah.*

A clicking sound reverberated as the key turned and disengaged the door's locking mechanism. The door swung outward, and the silhouette of a man stood in its frame, backlit by a torch. Alderan swallowed hard, unsure of what might happen next. The man stepped into the cell, followed by a smaller figure who wore nothing but a scarf around his neck and held the torch.

Rayah trembled next to Alderan, and he thought she was crying until she snorted and burst into a fit of laughter. Her laughter spread rapidly, and everyone in the cell succumbed to it within seconds. Eshtak danced around the cell, twirling the torch and laughing. After the last few days, Alderan needed a good laugh.

Amicus cleared his throat. "Eshtak, please settle down so we can talk to these people."

"Eshtak is happy! Eshtak likes girl and boy." He stopped twirling the torch around but continued bouncing from one foot to the other.

"How did the two of you wind up in this cell?" asked Amicus.

Alderan looked at Rayah, wondering if she would talk first. *I wish I could talk to her without speaking.* He hoped she could read his face; she was usually good at it.

Rayah began, "I was kidnapped by some lizard creature and brought down here as bait."

Perfect. Not too much information, but enough. He smiled at Rayah.

"My name's Rayah. I live in the Veridis Forest." She squeezed Alderan's arm.

Rayah! Ugh! Why did she tell him that? He wished she could take back her words.

"Ah, very good." Amicus turned his gaze on Alderan.

"And you are?" asked Amicus.

Alderan just stared at him.

"Eshtak, bring the torch over here," said Amicus.

Amicus stepped closer to Alderan and knelt. Eshtak bobbled his way over and handed Amicus the torch with a smile. Amicus lifted his hand toward Alderan's face, and Alderan instinctively jerked his head backward and smacked it against the wall.

Ouch! He wanted to rub his head but couldn't with his hands chained to the wall.

"It's hard to be sure in this poor light, but you remind me of a friend." Amicus turned the bracelet on his wrist around and around.

Alderan stared at Amicus's wrist and the bracelet wrapped around it. The square knot bracelet, woven with yellow and green cords and faded with age, taunted him. Heat rose in his face and rage pumped through his veins.

"Where did you get that bracelet?" Alderan lunged forward, but his constraints held him back.

Amicus jumped back and dropped the torch.

Alderan pointed at the bracelet. "That doesn't belong to you!"

"It was given to me by a friend."

"You killed my sister!" Blind with rage, Alderan fought against his restraints.

"Aria's your sister?" asked Amicus, retreating a little farther.

"You killed her! I'm going to kill you!" His restraints turned red.

"No, Alderan!" Rayah shrank into the corner.

Amicus backed all the way against the opposite wall, clearly terror stricken.

Eshtak ran from the cell with his hands in the air, screaming.

Alderan's restraints liquefied from the extreme heat and he sprung to his feet. The fire from the torch leapt into Alderan's hands as he willed it to obey him. Every ounce of his energy poured into the ball of fire and it grew and lit the cell like a sunny day.

Rayah flew to his side and tried grabbing his arm, but he shoved her into the wall without even a glance.

"You'll burn for what you did!" Alderan stalked closer to Amicus.

"I swear to you," pleaded Amicus. "I didn't kill your sister. She's still alive."

Rage consumed Alderan, and he only heard the voice in his head. *He killed your sister. He's responsible. He deserves to die. Killing him will feel good.*

Do it!

† † †

Rakzar loped through the passageway and toward the cell with the open door. A strange little man ran toward him, screaming, arms flailing, and wearing nothing but a scarf. Rakzar growled as they passed each other, and the little man screamed louder.

Had he not known better, Rakzar would've sworn the cell door led outside with the amount of light that poured into the passageway. He slid to a stop when he reached the door, unsure of what he should do.

"Die!" yelled the White Knight. He pulled his arms back, ready to release the massive ball of fire that hovered over his hand.

Stay out of it. This isn't your fight. Just turn around and walk away. The White Knight will survive this.

Rakzar was very familiar with killing someone out of rage, and he knew that it never solved anything. He also knew that killing his own kind was even worse for some reason. He likened it to killing a small part of himself. *Makes you numb inside.*

He's not just a boy.

Rakzar felt as though he moved outside of his body and watched from above as he lunged at the White Knight.

The White Knight's arms moved forward.

Rakzar flew back into his body and crashed into the White Knight's side just before the ball of fire left his hands.

The impact twisted them around ninety degrees and sent the ball of fire screaming through the open door and into the wall opposite the cell.

The blowback from the blast slammed the cell door shut and shook the ground. Rakzar landed on his back with the White Knight wrapped tightly in his arms, and they slid against the far wall.

"No!" yelled the White Knight, fighting to free himself from Rakzar's grip.

"Stop before you kill us all!" screamed Rayah.

Amicus scrambled to his feet and tried to open the cell door, but it'd locked itself when it slammed shut by the blast. "We're trapped in here!"

Rakzar tightened his hold on the White Knight. "Stop struggling, or I'll knock you out again."

"He has to die," said the White Knight, crying and struggling to fight back.

Amicus beat his fists on the door. "Eshtak!"

"Alderan—" Rayah sniffed. "—I don't think he killed your sister."

"I didn't, you crazy fool!" said Amicus. "You almost killed us all!"

"Then why do you have her bracelet?" asked Alderan, coughing. "She would've never parted with it."

"She asked me to return it to her the next time I saw her. I swear it."

"Why did I even come back?" Rakzar asked himself. He shoved the White Knight away and onto the floor.

Amicus pulled the bracelet off his wrist. "If you can see my hand, take the bracelet."

Rakzar, the only one in the cell who could see in the dark, snatched the bracelet from Amicus and threw it at the White Knight. The bracelet hit the White Knight in the face.

"You're all pathetic," growled Rakzar.

† † †

Alderan took the bracelet in his hand and closed his eyes as a tingling sensation raced up his arm, across his shoulder, and up the back of his neck. In his mind, Amicus smiled down at him. He handed Amicus the bracelet, but it wasn't his hand. It wasn't even him.

I'm Aria.

"Aria's alive? Aria's alive!"

Chapter Thirty-Three

Nardus stood at the crystal pedestal, lost in the memories of his family. How close he drew to seeing them again. His heart swelled with joy. A red door appeared just ahead of him and drew his attention.

I'll be happy to rid myself of all this mezhik.

Nardus looked down at his hand. He no longer held the stone. He placed his hand over his jacket pocket and felt a lump within it. Relieved, he stepped around the pedestal and over to the red door.

His pulse quickened as he reached for the doorknob. With it in his grasp, Nardus turned it and pushed the door open. Through the red door came destiny. *Family.* Tharos stood in the great hall and awaited his entrance.

The great dragon's presence entered his mind. *"By all means, step on through."*

Nardus walked through the door and into the great hall; the door behind him vanished, along with the room from which it led him. Nardus bowed slightly. "Greetings, Tharos."

"I never thought I'd see the day when the stone's prophecy would be fulfilled," said Tharos. "This day marks the beginning of a new era. Once you step outside of this temple, the Ancient Realm will never be the same again."

Nardus rubbed his left bicep. "After everything I've endured, I sure hope that's true."

Tharos snaked his head down to Nardus's level. "Be careful of your wishes, my friend. The stone you carry holds great power—terribly great power. Its presence alone will bring the world to the brink of darkness. Be certain in what you do with it."

Nardus frowned. "What do you mean?"

Tharos stomped the ground. "You think that stone was placed in this hellish world without reason? *Ūrdär Dhef 2äfn Dhä* sacrificed everything to create this place to contain it and its power."

Nardus shrugged. "If I'm fulfilling prophecy by bringing it out of this place, isn't that a good thing?"

"Depends on the prophecy and which branch of it you fulfill. Any one of the multitude of futures could spring from this; everything lies within your hands now."

Nardus's stomach twisted as he contemplated what he was doing for the very first time. From the moment he started the journey, his focus had been locked on getting his family back; he'd cared about nothing else, the world be damned. Now, at the pinnacle of his journey, doubt arose.

What am I doing? I don't even know what this stone does, but I can't live without my family. Can I?

"How do I know if I'm doing the right thing?" asked Nardus.

"What's the right thing? A matter of perspective to those on both sides of the issue. You can do nothing but trust your instincts. Your heart will deceive you in matters such as these."

Nardus took the stone out of his jacket pocket and rubbed it between his fingers. "What exactly does this stone do?"

"It's said that the stone can resurrect the dead, but in the wrong hands..." Tharos spoke further on the subject, but Nardus withdrew into his own mind.

Resurrect the dead? That's how Pravus plans to bring my family back. I must get back as soon as possible. It won't be much longer now, my love.

"How exactly do I get back?" he interrupted Tharos.

"Patience, my friend. We're not quite done here." Tharos held out the amulet and chain that Nardus had retrieved from the temple's catacombs. "I insist you take this. I have a feeling you'll need it soon."

Nardus returned the stone to his jacket pocket. "Do you see the future, dragon? Is that why you sent me after the amulet?"

Tharos blew smoke from his nostrils. "Call it premonition. Now, take it."

Reluctantly, Nardus took the amulet from Tharos. "So... I have need of it. I'm not going to like this, am I?"

Tharos grinned wickedly. "It's a covetous treasure, and those who know of it might take your life to get it. Show it to no one, son of Ƨäʈūr. When the time's right, you'll know its purpose."

Nardus lifted the chain over his head and placed it around his neck. He tucked the amulet underneath his shirt. He scratched at his chest as the tingle of mezhik spread across his skin like a rash.

"Thank you, Tharos. And thank you for not killing me when you had the opportunity."

"Speak of it no more," said Tharos. "Now, step through *Dūrz Dhef Ƨōallz Demd* and be off."

The temple doors swung open and revealed the all-too-familiar courtyard. A chill swept across Nardus's body as he peered through them.

He turned toward Tharos and scowled. "You're certain that's the way out of here?"

Tharos shepherded him up to the doors' threshold. "As I said, just step through."

"Well then, I guess I should get going."

Nardus took a deep breath and then stepped through the temple's double-doors. As he crossed the threshold he felt a brief, but distinct, resistance, and then it gave way like a bubble bursting. A shock wave, like a ripple in a calm body of water, pushed the air in every direction and boomed like thunder. The temple walls shook for a moment and showered them with dust.

A golden vortex opened and swirled in front of Nardus. He stepped back, stunned by its molten waves.

Nardus turned to Tharos, eyebrows raised. "You expect me to go in there?"

The great hall echoed Tharos's laughter. "It's the only way you'll leave this place. Do you wish to stay here forever?"

Nardus turned back to the vortex. Golden eyes formed at its center and he gasped. A woman's face emerged from the swirling liquid, bathed in gold. Strands of golden hair, twisted into braids, encircled her head like a crown. The rest of her hair hung low, pulled behind her pointed ears.

Nardus felt Tharos's clawed knuckle at his back. "Take her hand, son of Ƨäʈūr."

Nardus blinked. The woman, covered from head to toe in gold, stood before him. Transfixed by her beauty, he hadn't noticed she'd stepped out of the vortex.

Nardus looked down at his arm as it extended toward hers. His hand opened to receive hers. He commanded his hand to halt, but it wouldn't obey. Their fingers met, and her smoldering touch ignited his skin.

My soul's on fire.

He stepped forward, embraced her, and closed his eyes as the vortex sucked them into its molten chaos.

"Breathe me in." The presence in his mind wasn't Tharos, but it felt familiar. Did he know her? How could he?

Nardus relaxed and inhaled the liquid gold. It soothed as it slid down his throat and quenched the fire in his lungs.

Who are you? And what are you?

"I am Sarai and I am ţrenɜbūrţ, a transport. I provide travel between worlds, master."

Nardus opened his eyes. Through the liquid gold shone a pinpoint of light, far in the distance. The light rapidly approached.

Tharos's presence entered Nardus's mind. *"We're nearly there, son of ɜäţūr."*

We? You've come as well, Tharos?

"Naturally. I was bound to Ţämbɜll Dhef Däd Dhä by the stone, but you've released me from that bondage. I can finally return home. Thank you."

Will there still be a home for you to go back to?

"We dragons live thousands of years. I'm certain my brothers and sisters await my return."

"We are here," said Sarai.

Nardus burst through the surface of the vortex, gasped for air, and landed on his hands and knees with a grunt. He coughed, but only produced air. He rolled over and lay on his back just as a shadow passed over him.

Tharos's wings beat fiercely—the sound like ship sails catching wind. He climbed high in the sky and glided just below the clouds, headed west.

In Nardus's head, the great dragon spoke one last time. *"Farewell, my friend. Until we meet again."* With that, Tharos disappeared into the clouds.

Farewell, indeed... friend.

Sarai and the golden vortex disappeared, and the ruins of Mortuus Terra surrounded Nardus—the place where his journey began. He gazed at the sky above him, awestruck by its beautiful, dark-blue hue; it felt like ages since he'd seen a blue sky. The crisp, clean air tasted sweet on his tongue—like honey. Clear-headed, he felt better than he had in a long time.

I can't believe I'm back. I made it, my love! Soon, we'll be together again. His excitement swelled.

Just another minute and I'll get up.

The muscles in his chest seized up and hampered his ability to breathe. He grabbed at his throat, but felt no flesh underneath his fingers—the muscles and tissues were hardened stone. His lungs ignited with fire and his chest swelled.

Pain raced through every inch of his body and he convulsed. His back and midsection arched above the ground, leaving only his head and feet touching it. Trapped in his mind, he had no control of his body.

What in the name of Ẑäṭūr is happening?

Tears streamed down the sides of his face like miniature rivers as terror screamed inside his head. *Make it stop! Make it stop!*

His mouth opened, and he screamed, but no sound came forth. The fire in his lungs raced up his esophagus, into his throat, and out of his mouth and burst into the air like a shooting star. High in the sky it raced, a pillar of fire from his mouth to the clouds above. The sound of thunder rumbled in the air as the sky burst into flames and formed a ring of fire.

Nardus collapsed to the ground as the last of the fire left his body. He swallowed shards of glass, and the coppery taste of blood filled his mouth. Completely drained of energy, the thought of moving pained him. Even if it hadn't, the sky held his attention.

The ring of fire expanded outward and left a blood-red sky in its wake. Fear paralyzed him, and his mind wrapped around a single thought. Four simple words strung together, and the fate of the world hung from them.

What have I done?

TO BE CONTINUED ...

The story continues in *Reborn*, Book #2 of *The Dark Heart Chronicles*.

Visit **danielkuhnley.com** for details.

Tell Others What You Thought

Reviews are important for indie authors like me. I appreciate you leaving a review of *The Dragon's Stone* on Amazon, Goodreads, and BookBub. Also, remember to tell your friends about the book through social media to help spread the word. This will help me write more books.

Get Exclusive Content for *The Dragon's Stone*

danielkuhnley.com/become-a-conqueror

READ *SCOURGE* FOR FREE

Curious about Eshtak's tattoos?

danielkuhnley.com/become-a-conqueror

Sign up and read *Scourge*, A World Of Centauria Novella, and also get **EXCLUSIVE** access to additional *The Dark Heart Chronicles* series content. Be the **FIRST** to get sneak peeks at my upcoming novels and the chance to win **FREE** stuff, like signed books.

Thank you for reading!

To save her son she must destroy a civilization.

Emorith used her persuasion magic on the wrong man, and he's controlled her ever since. Now, she must find a test subject for his spell, Scourge. She knows Magus, the powerful wizard who rules the southern realm, will use the spell to obliterate anyone without magic. But she can't live without her son, and Magus will kill him if she fails...

To defeat Magus's ominous plot, Emorith must betray him and trust a friend with her young son. However, her smooth talking and determination may not be enough to prevent an apocalypse.

Scourge takes place in the World of Centauria 1200 years prior to the events in *The Dark Heart Chronicles* epic fantasy series. If you like thrilling adventures and heroic characters, then you'll love Daniel Kuhnley's dark and creative novella.

ABOUT THE AUTHOR

I'm Daniel Kuhnley, an American author of dark fantasy and mystery thrillers. My novels include *The Dragon's Stone*, *Reborn*, *Rended Souls*, and *The Braille Killer*. I enjoy watching movies, reading novels, and programming. I live in Albuquerque, NM with my wife.

CONNECT WITH DANIEL

danielkuhnley.com
www.facebook.com/DanielKuhnley
goodreads.com/DanielKuhnley
amazon.com/author/danielkuhnley
bookbub.com/authors/daniel-kuhnley